Book I of the Stone War Chronicles

A.J. Norfield

Cover art © 2015 A.J. Norfield
Edited by Amanda J. Spedding

ISBN: 978-90-824945-2-5 (kindle)
ISBN: 978-90-824945-0-1 (epub)
ISBN: 978-90-824945-1-8 (sc)

For my two greatest—and most wonderful—distractions in the world
and she who takes care of them.

BY A.J. NORFIELD

Stone War Chronicles
Windcatcher
Wavebreaker – Trickle
Wavebreaker – Flood (coming soon)

Other
Revolt of Blood and Stone
(A Stone War Chronicles Novella, Sebastian #1)

ACKNOWLEDGEMENTS

Many thanks to my friends and family for their support. Especially, Josh and Jeltje; for feedback and grammar checking in the early stages of writing.

My love and thanks to my amazing wife, Desirée, and our wonderful children, Emily and Tobias. You all brighten my life beyond measure.

And last—but not least—thank you, the reader, for getting this book and supporting my dream of being an author.

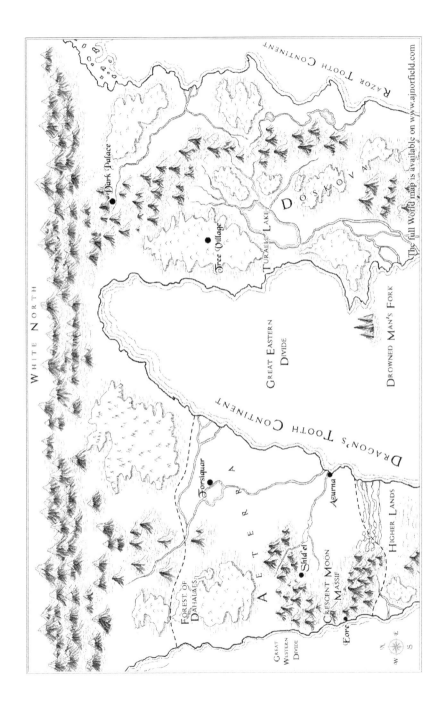

RAZOR TOOTH CONTINENT

The full World map is available on www.ajnorfield.com

DOSSOV

WHITE NORTH

Dark Palace

Tree Village

Turael Lake

GREAT EASTERN DIVIDE

DROWNED MAN'S FORK

DRAGON'S TOOTH CONTINENT

FOREST OF DRHALAES

GREAT WESTERN DIVIDE

Torsiquar

AETER

Sild'et

Azuma

CRESCENT MOON MASSIF

HIGHER LANDS

Fore

N
W   E
S

PROLOGUE

THE MORNING DAWNED crisp and cold. Its chill plagued Lai'Ping Wén's aching bones. Then again, he always had trouble feeling warm nowadays. His joints were old, held together by old muscles. The soft morning wind stroked his cleanly-shaved head. His lengthy, thin beard of pure white not enough to keep his face warm. Carefully, he straightened his back, trying to ignore the small muscle between his ribs that heavily objected. He exhaled slowly. Long ago he had accepted his life now moved at a much slower pace than those of the younger men in the monastery.

Looking out into the garden from his seat of meditation, he calmly drew in his breath again. It had a certain magical feel to it this early in the day. The sun's first light just crept over the garden wall. Small drops of last night's rain sparkled in the light as they lingered on the bamboo leaves at the far side of the courtyard.

Beyond the low, white wall, the snowy peaks of an impressive mountain range bathed in the early autumn rays as they sluggishly crawled down the tree-covered slopes. Lai'Ping expected most of the mountain-side inhabitants were already up as well. A redwing sang to greet the morning, while all kinds of scurrying animals were doubtlessly preparing for the winter to come.

Before long, the black-tiled roofs of the monastery, which curled upward, would be covered in snow, hiding the small swirls and globes that even Lai'Ping—at times—found too much decoration. In his long life, he had learned to keep things simple, without too much distraction.

'There is beauty in the simple things' his old master used to say. It left the focus on the things in life that were more important… like family. His mind wandered to what his only granddaughter might be doing. The faintest of smiles curled his lips before he gently pushed the thought out and emptied his mind again, like the masters before him had so often instructed. Of course, now *he* was the master.

Never too old to learn, he thought.

Being located on the top of a high mountain slope, the rear of the monastery had no need for high walls as the ground disappeared in a sheer drop. The original builders had used the location to their advantage and designed the back courtyards and gardens in such a way that they were almost one with the panoramic view of the Wutao Mountains. It provided a deep, calm and near infinite feeling inside the garden; one of the main reasons Lai'Ping so often enjoyed his morning meditation here.

The largest part of the monastery's central building consisted of the great hall, in which the monks would normally gather to meditate. Lai'Ping often found it too cramped, preferring the openness of the garden. Wooden statues and images of grand dragons decorated the walls and pillars of the hall's meditation area. Sometimes just the head or the claw of one of these magnificent creatures; at other times, an entire dragon curled around a pillar, carved in full detail with scales, legs and wings.

It seemed excessive and distracting to Lai'Ping, but it was their connection to the past. These mythical creatures had once shared their wisdom with the monks, and he often meditated on the question of what had happened to make them disappear over two centuries ago. Enlightenment had unfortunately never been provided; the question remained unanswered after all these years.

Behind the great hall were buildings only the Shikktu—high monks of the inner circle—were allowed. The Inner Sanctum housed the Empire's most sacred item—the relic the monastery had the honor of protecting these past centuries.

Lai'Ping considered the thick, wooden double door that blocked the entrance to this holy place. Each door was so large and heavy it required four men to open it. Carved with a magnificent depiction of two dragons that mirrored each other, their front claws and noses touched where the doors met. Despite the majestic feel, Lai'Ping always thought the dragons seemed to be joined together in an awkward, human-like courtship dance.

Behind those doors was the long Path of Scales—a hallway with a floor completely covered in the scales of dragons of old, one for each dragon said to have helped make the monastery a reality. The path always had guards stationed in its hallways; and while it was a great honor, Lai'Ping knew from his younger years it was quite a boring duty.

He smiled at all the memories the monastery had given him. How quiet and busy it could be at the same time.

The main courtyard at the entrance of the monastery easily held well over a thousand monks. Often they all trained there in the arts of the Dragon's Claw. In comparison to the low walls surrounding Lai'Ping's private meditation garden, this main courtyard was enclosed by massive walls, each many times taller than a man. They held the main gate to the monastery, whose height rivaled the size of the walls themselves.

Lai'Ping grabbed his numb leg to unfold himself, and slid to the side of his meditation cushion. It had been a long time since he actively participated in the morning exercises. Cautiously, he stood, making sure his legs would not give way under him. He heard the vague shouts and clatters of the monks training in the main courtyard and shuffled slowly toward his private chambers, pleased that at least his hearing had not failed him yet.

Approaching the steps to his own quarters, he noticed one of the senior monks waiting for him. The man sat quietly on his knees next to the thin sliding wall-panel.

Ah, To'Pal, he'll make a fine Shikktu one day, he thought as he carefully moved up the steps toward the wooden walkway where the senior monk was seated. The man bowed deeply to show his respect, then slowly rose to his feet.

"To'Pal, how are you this morning?"

"I'm fine, Grand Master Wén. There will be much to do today," said the monk, as he produced a small scroll from his sleeve. "Preparations for the royal visit are now fully underway."

"Good, the monastery has to be in perfect shape before the Emperor walks through those gates," said Lai'Ping.

Every year the Emperor—accompanied by his wife, both sons and his daughter—attended the sacred ceremony led by Lai'Ping. It was a long ceremony, filled with many specific rituals during which the Emperor prayed in the Inner Sanctum. There, he asked the sacred item for its blessing and for its continued protection of the Tiankong Empire, as it had done for almost two hundred years now.

"Did they start on the new sleeping quarters for our guests yet?"

Thousands of people traveled to the monastery to attend the festivities. The pilgrims brought rice and dried fruit from the year's harvest as small offerings for the monks, prayed for a plentiful harvest season the following year, and shared their abundance with deceased relatives and friends to honor them.

"Not yet, Grand Master," said To'Pal, bowing his head in apology. "We're waiting for the last supplies to come in tomorrow. The details are all in here." Respectfully, the monk handed over the scroll.

The Emperor's visit was a little less than a month away now, planned in the middle of the season of colors. It gave the royal convoy enough time to return to the capital before the expected first snow. Lai'Ping looked at the small scroll in his hands, no doubt filled with the challenges of today that needed to be solved. But, as his fingers fiddled to open it, a loud crash and a rumble shook the monastery.

Both men looked up in the direction of the main courtyard. Smoke circled skyward from behind the roof of his private chambers. Judging from the distance, it seemed to be near the main gate.

Shouts filled the air, and Lai'Ping heard the hollow thumps of people running across the walkways between the buildings. Worried, he looked at To'Pal.

"By the Emperor's grace, I hope no one is seriously wounded," he said, then frowned when he heard heavy hoofbeats, nervous neighing horses and shouted war cries coming from the other side of the building.

"This is no accident, Master Wén," said To'Pal, shocked. "We're under attack!"

"The relic!"

Moving as fast as his old legs could carry him, Lai'Ping made his way through the corridors toward the main hall. He *had* to get to the Inner Sanctum. Smoke filled the tight hallways. His eyes tried to take in everything at once. The walls were built of a thin, paper-like material; which of course meant any fire would spread swiftly. Lai'Ping kept his sleeve to his mouth and took a left turn with To'Pal hot on his heels. A heavy crash behind them drew their attention; one of the younger monks flew through a wall-panel. A massive black horse followed directly in the man's wake, ridden by a black-armored figure holding a thick spear. It happened in the blink of an eye; the horse crashed at full speed through the walls, like they were nothing but air.

As they continued their way, Lai'Ping heard more shouts coming from the main courtyard. Monks ran past with buckets of water, while others carried bladed staffs.

"Let us take the left corridor," suggested Lai'Ping, trying to determine the safest route to The Sanctum.

As they made the turn, a man wearing black armor burst backward around the corner ahead. He parried a bladed staff thrust at his face—completely oblivious of the Grand Master and To'Pal behind him. With a powerful shout and swing, a younger monk jumped around the corner, knocking the soldier's sword from his hand. The monk rushed forward, staff aimed at his enemy's throat. His opponent leaped to the side as he grabbed the dagger from his belt. Dodging the incoming staff, he rapidly stabbed the monk twice in his stomach, but a third stab was intercepted.

Abandoning his staff, the monk twisted the dagger from his foe's hand and drove it into the man's neck. The soldier dropped to the floor, dead, while the monk sagged next to him. To'Pal ran over to pull the monk upright. Blood gushed from the young man's stomach.

"Easy, easy," said To'Pal when a cough in pain sent blood flying from the monk's mouth.

Lai'Ping solemnly approached them. "You fought with honor, brave Samané," he said loud enough for the young man to hear. "You've done your family proud."

The monk slumped sideways without uttering a word.

Lai'Ping gently touched To'Pal's back. "We must hurry to The Sanctum," he said, feeling terribly ashamed for not giving more time to honor the fallen monk.

Together they set off again. Several corridors later, Lai'Ping and To'Pal, both panting heavily, burst into the main hall but faltered at the view. The smoke was less dense here, mainly thanks to the high ceiling. What the clear air revealed was devastation. A massacre. Dozens of monks lay dead, spread across the hall. Some were pinned against the wall, pierced by spears, while others just lay—heads unnaturally twisted—on the floor in pools of blood. The illustrations on the walls were blood spattered, and several dragon statues were overturned, their pieces scattered across the ground.

Lai'Ping carefully stepped around one of the main support pillars to get to the sanctum doors. As he did, a tall soldier in black armor came into view. The man stood silently in front of the sanctum doors, deep in thought.

These soldiers were clearly not from the Empire—their faces were too long; their eyes set differently; their skin so pale it looked like they had never seen the sun in this lifetime. So Lai'Ping spoke in the only foreign language that he knew, that of the mid-kingdom laying to the east.

"What is the meaning of this?"

The soldier slowly turned and regarded the two monks in silence. Lai'Ping met the soldier's eyes as they calmly scrutinized him. The outsider sauntered toward them.

"What are you doing here? Outsiders are not allowed to enter our Empire, let alone these sacred grounds. You must leave at once!" said Lai'Ping sternly, but the man in front of them acted as if he heard nothing.

The soldier's eyes remained locked on the old monk as he approached. The man's armor looked to be mostly leather, with some metal pieces stained black. A cross of four diamond-shaped icons were displayed on his left chest piece. Lai'Ping found himself focusing on the man's dark, smooth cape billowing gently from his shoulders as he came toward them.

"Please step back, Master Wén," said To'Pal, politely, as he shifted in front of Lai'Ping and used his body to shield the Grand Master from this unknown threat.

Lai'Ping put his hand on To'Pal's shoulder and gently shook his head as their eyes met. "No, the monastery is my responsibility…"

Lai'Ping had no intention of letting anyone else speak for him. The monks were under his protection—even the more experienced senior monks. He tried to get a feel for the soldier coming their way; although many lay dead around them, he did not feel any murderous intent coming from this particular individual.

The soldier, now only a few feet away, still had not uttered a word.

Lai'Ping tried one more time. "Why have you come here?"

The soldier stopped two steps short of them. "My good sir! Why… we've come for your most sacred treasure," said the man, grinning.

It was not the completely unnerving friendliness of the soldier's tone that surprised Lai'Ping, but the fact that the words were spoken in their own language.

Lai'Ping looked into the cold, blue eyes of the soldier, slightly confused by his mother tongue spoken with such a thick foreign accent—a language no foreigner should have been able to learn. Teaching Tiankonese to outsiders was forbidden.

An unexpected, sharp pain ripped into his belly. Perplexed, he looked down; the hilt of a knife stuck out of his side. He had not even seen the soldier move.

*When did he take a knife in hand? He wondered as h*e looked at his fingers, coated red with his blood. With a shout, To'Pal jumped forward and lunged at the soldier's throat with a high-speed thrust.

Lai'Ping knew the movement well, it was one of the more dangerous Dragon's Claw techniques, designed to hit and grab an enemy's throat and tear out the larynx with one quick motion. But the outsider reacted with lightning speed. He deflected the monk's attack to the side, and followed through with a full swing. An armored backhand crashed into To'Pal's temple with such force, the monk slammed sideways against the pillar. The young monk would never get up.

The soldier pulled the knife from Lai'Ping's side and returned to the sanctum doors.

Lai'Ping felt the strength drain from his legs. Slumping to his knees, he held one hand to his wound trying to stem the bleeding. His other hand desperately sought to support his body and prevent himself from collapsing any further.

The sacred relic… it must be secured! The doors will delay them. It should be enough time for them to get away. They have to get away… the safety of the Empire relies on it!

Lai'Ping felt colder than he had ever felt. No longer having the strength to support his body, he slowly lay upon the floor, staring at the Sanctum doors and imploring them to remain closed.

The soldier turned suddenly and gave a shrill whistle toward the main courtyard.

As the cold seeped deeper into his bones, Lai'Ping's body grew heavier. His heart rate slowed. His vision blurred, but he refused to let the Inner Sanctum doors out of his sight. His heartbeat grew louder, the sound so heavy, he swore the floor vibrated with each thump. Every beat grew louder than the last, making the ground shake harder.

As the light slowly faded from Lai'Ping's eyes, two shadowy figures, twice the size of a man, stomped past him toward the Sanctum doors. Their heavy steps shook the floor in unison with his own heartbeat.

The image of the outsider pointing toward the heavy doors, and those colossal shadows following his command, faded into darkness.

What kind of inhuman abominations are those things? The words lingered in his mind.

His bones felt so very heavy and his muscles felt so very tired. The image of a girl's face floated into his mind. The warmth of love rushed through his cold body.

I wonder how she's doing… I hope she's happy… A tear ran from his eye. May she forgive me.

His hearing was the last of his senses to go. That same sense that had delighted him with the monastery's sounds that very morning. But these new sounds were the unwelcome, deafening cracks of thick wood splitting apart. They forced their way into his head as his life slipped away. And as his heart gave its final beat and the world disappeared into nothingness, Master Wén realized—to his horror—the Sanctum doors had not merely been opened… they had simply been shattered.

CHAPTER ONE

Wait

Raylan felt his legs cramping up. How long had they been waiting in the dark? His breath plumed in front of him as he forced his jaw to stay still. He peered around the rock that hid him in its shadow. Nearby, the dark leather armor of his squad mates shimmered wet from the rain. They had blackened their blades with soot, but errant raindrops had begun to wash it away, so whenever the moonlight broke through the clouds, everyone kept their swords and knives close. They could not lose the element of surprise; their success depended on it. Raylan's sword was held loosely in his hand, ready for the time to act.

His fingers fell into the familiar grooves of the sword's hilt, its leather worn down by hours and hours of training. The blade was thick and straight, wide near the hilt, it narrowed slightly into an otherwise still-broad tip. It was on the short side, but was forged sturdy and well-balanced. Designed to be handled with speed, the weight of the blade gave it extra impact.

Back home, his father had forged some amazing swords over the years with sparkling stones and intricate engravings, none of which you would find on Raylan's. It was not a display piece, nor a work of art; just a very effective tool, efficiently designed and made for its intended purpose—to cut and to kill.

Although very familiar with the sword, Raylan disliked using it. He preferred to avoid confrontation rather than seek it out. In fact, he would rather not be here at all, in the rain and the cold. Unfortunately, he had been one of the best sword fighters during training, which made him of interest to the High Commander, and earned him a spot on this special reconnaissance squad—a group under command of his older brother, Gavin, to make matters worse.

14

His heart raced as he shifted his weight nervously. It would be his first real combat experience, something he did not look forward to. Of course, it was exciting in a way; it was not that he was scared, he told himself, and he loved to travel, to see the world… but why did they have to drag him to this cold and dark land?

He sighed and located Gavin crouched on higher ground about ninety feet from Raylan's position. His brother had chosen his position wisely. The high spot allowed him an excellent view of the enemy camp, and the squad as they waited for his order to advance.

Raylan stretched his fingers and wondered what Gavin was waiting for. The cold night air numbed his fingers; he had to make sure they would not lose their grip on his sword when it was needed most. His fur coat would have been a welcomed layer of warmth against the bitter night; but the coat was too bulky for combat, so he had been ordered to leave it behind. The only clothes trying to keep him warm now was a thin tunic beneath his armor.

As Raylan considered his older brother, he felt a mixture of annoyance and pride. Growing up, with only three years between them, they had not always seen eye to eye; but Gavin was an exceptional squad leader, making well-weighted decisions in the field and avoiding unnecessary risks. His big brother had joined the armed forces at the age of sixteen, years before Raylan. It had been a career choice for Gavin to serve, who had aimed to join the royal guards of the king. That was eight years ago, but circumstances were slightly different now and it seemed to him that his brother was stuck within the normal command structure instead of working his way into the honored king's guard.

Raylan traced the lines of a scar that twisted from his wrist up and around to his elbow, passing back and forth under his armor. A memento of days better spent. Of the merchant ship he had sailed on, enjoying the freedom of the open sea. An immense storm had rolled in, unexpected and turning the ocean into a rough landscape of mountains that rose and fell by the will of the wind. Halfway through the second day of it, he had tried to secure a line. Completely exhausted, it had wrapped itself around his lower arm when the ship slammed into an oncoming wave. The impact yanked the line from his hands, burning across his skin. He had been lucky not to lose the arm completely.

The burn mark had never properly healed and left a scar that flowed around his arm like a snaking whirlwind. It had been his constant reminder to respect, and never underestimate, the power of the wind—such a fierce but unseen force of nature.

Raylan was convinced the crew had only survived because of the wits and experience of their captain. The man had steered the ship like a mad pirate. Instead of fighting the waves, he rode them like a dancer moves through a room. For three and a half days they battled the winds and sea before the first rays of sun finally lightened their hearts and gave them their well-deserved rest. They smiled, and then laughed, glad all of the crew had survived. And although most of their precious cargo had been lost, the captain did not hesitate to open an extra bottle of rum, or two, to celebrate their victory over death.

He let out a small sigh. Those times seemed a lifetime ago.

Wiping his forehead, he glanced to his left and spotted Xi'Lao, the only woman in their party, preparing herself for the attack. Despite being the reason they were all here, he knew very little about her. She had arrived at Aeterra's court a few months back, as an official emissary of the Tiankong Empire. Meriting the request she had brought from her emperor, their king had granted aid in retrieving a stolen item of great importance. It had been the beginning of their months-long journey through these cold northern lands.

But with a little luck, it will all be over soon. Raylan tried to cheer himself up.

Xi'Lao quickly scanned the many small knives on her belt, assuring none would easily drop out or get stuck when needed. Her brown, close-set eyes suited her well; slightly narrowed, they were sharp and alert. Her hair, normally long, black and straight, had a blue shine in the moonlight and was tightly tied up in a top-knot for the occasion.

She flashed him a look, but barely acknowledged him before continuing her check.

She was small, compared to him, and of a slender build. During their traveling, he had noticed multiple times how her movements were much more reserved than the others of their group—never making any large gestures when telling stories or doing chores. She truly had a foreign way about her.

He wondered how the Tiankong Empire expected such a refined woman to undergo the long journey between their two nations alone, and fight beside them during such a dangerous mission. Yet, she looked not the least bit worried about the upcoming attack; and the movement of her hands bespoke a very different story. She had displayed great skill handling her knives as they rode north into the wilderness. Whether preparing the catch of the day, hunting a rabbit from afar, or helping others with a needed chore, she was quick and efficient. With little experience in dueling with women during his training, Raylan was curious to see how it all would translate into combat.

I guess I'll know soon enough.

He had attempted to talk to her during their hastened journey, trying to discover what this mysterious item was they were chasing. But she had provided little information; her answers always polite but short. She mainly spoke to Gavin, as he was in command; and even then, only about their pursuit.

Richard, their second-in-command, sat beside Xi'Lao. He leaned forward out of the shadow and gave Raylan a quick nod, a serious look in his eyes. Raylan responded in kind; he was ready and waiting.

Ready and waiting, but not at all comfortable, he thought bleakly. Raindrops stung his eyes and his own dark brown hair stuck annoyingly to his head. He clamped his teeth together again for fear of giving away their position. He firmly believed there was no piece of dry clothing left on his body. The rain had been falling for weeks, ever since they crossed Aeterra's northern border and exchanged the welcome lands of their kingdom for the unknown northern wilds. The clouds only gave way to a tempered sun every couple of days which, according to Regis—one of the more timid and younger members of their group who excelled with the sword, much like Raylan—was not unusual this far north.

Regis, Richard and Raylan. If he did not feel so miserable, he might have laughed. What was the chance of having such similar names in such a small squad? *And of course, Rohan*—one of their archers.

Kevhin, the squad's second archer—and Rohan's friend—had wasted no time in calling them the four Rs, after the famous play by Ethan Tomas. 'Rowdy Rest & Rigid Relaxation' was enjoyed across all of Aeterra by young and old, and being so far from home the references had given them quite a few laughs. Until, after the tenth time, Richard's look had made the archer wisely decide to leave the joke be for the remainder of the trip.

Raylan shifted his weight and, once again, wiped the water from his eyes. A chuckle escaped him, despite his dreary state. *I thought it was funny.*

Movement from his brother's direction drew his attention. He caught Gavin's eyes as he did a quick check around the group to see if everyone was ready.

Finally, it seemed the wait was over.

Raylan did not look forward to what was to come, but somehow the waiting was worse. Apparently satisfied by what he saw, his brother gave the signal to begin their attack. Raylan's heart rate increased, his nerves giving way to the adrenaline that started to pump through his veins.

Following the plan, he waited five counts, during which the world seemed to slow for his senses.

Then, he began to move.

"One-one-hundred, two-one-hundred," Raylan counted under his breath. From the corner of his eye, Kevhin and Rohan rose, positioned heavy crossbows to their shoulders, and pulled their triggers. He heard the faint *thwap* of both strings releasing, almost immediately followed by the thuds of the thick bolts hitting their targets. The first projectile disappeared into a guard's left eye, while the other pierced a second guard's heart, straight through his armor.

Raylan was already moving before both bodies hit the ground. He burst out from behind the cover of the rock to see Gavin—who had snuck up behind the third lookout—cover the guard's mouth and slit the man's throat.

A knot twisted in Raylan's stomach. It was disconcerting to see the person you grew up with take another man's life so easily.

Sound seemed to phase out of the world, his own heavy breathing all he could hear. His legs were wobbly and weak; but with each step, he felt them regain their strength as he ran straight for his designated spot.

A shadow flitted on his left. Raylan glanced up to see Xi'Lao choose a path over the rocks, instead of around. Her face held nothing of the normal gentleness, instead owning angry determination as she took one leap after another, moving swiftly across the boulders. She was as surefooted as one of the mountain cats Raylan had once seen on his travels, jumping across gaps with ease. Suddenly, she dropped silently out of sight on the far end of a rock; she had found her first mark.

The enemy soldiers had managed to find enough dry wood to build three campfires in the shelter of the boulders. As he heard the clash of Xi'Lao's knives from behind the rocks, Raylan sprinted toward the nearest campfire where a group of soldiers rested. He tightened his grip on his sword and burst into the circle of light cast by the fire. By chance, an enemy soldier entered the circle of sleeping men from the other side. As Raylan emerged from the darkness, sword at the ready, a look of surprise crossed the man's face. The soldier's hand moved to his own weapon but, before he could raise alarm, or fully draw his blade, Raylan lunged. Striking on the left side of the man's unprotected neck, Raylan felt the sudden resistance of human flesh. He pulled back his sword, creating a large gash all the way down to the collarbone.

Blood gushed from the wound. The soldier grimaced in pain as he grasped his neck, stumbled forward and crashed directly into the campfire. The fire exploded in a cloud of ash and sparks, suddenly plunging the surroundings into darkness. Raylan hesitated… he just killed a man for the very first time. A shudder ran along his spine.

One of the two scouts within their group, Ca'lek, entered the circle of light to his right, cleaving his sword through the neck of a soldier who slept with his back against a stone. The white of Ca'lek's eyes were a strong contrast against his dark skin and frightening to see the flames reflected in them. Raylan swallowed hard at the sight and had to remind himself the scout was on his side.

Raylan's squad mates closed in on the enemy soldiers. Across from him, Galen—a gigantic man with a neck as thick as a log and consequently their heavy hitter—swung his two-handed war hammer straight into the chest of a soldier charging him. Raylan almost felt the shockwave, and the dull *thump* as the force of the impact surely shattered multiple ribs. The soldier went down with a grunted scream. Galen raised his war hammer over his head and in one fluid motion crushed the soldier's skull, cutting the scream short.

The sound of fighting startled their enemy awake, their weapons in hand as they scrambled to their feet. Raylan shifted his stance and struck down the nearest soldier who tried to stab him in his kidneys. As he turned, a whistle passed his ears. A second swish immediately followed, close enough that he could have sworn his hair moved. Following the direction of the sound, he saw two soldiers taken down by the salvo of crossbow bolts.

The full encampment was now to high alert. Raylan noticed a small cave in the center of the camp, just past the second campfire. Those soldiers who had taken shelter in it now poured out, swords swinging in anger. At the far end of the cave's entrance, the soldiers' horses, tied to some low branches, snorted heavily at the fresh smell of blood. With their eyes stretched open in fear, they reared and pulled at their reins. The branch proved no match. Several horses broke loose and charged straight through the camp. Two enemy soldiers were knocked to the ground and violently trampled by the fleeing horses.

Regis turned too late to the thunder of hoofbeat. One horse knocked him down and another galloped over him. He tumbled, and his body slid to a halt, face down in the mud, where he remained awfully still. Their second scout, Stephen, and Harwin—the oldest member of their group and most experienced veteran—immediately fought their way to the fallen lad.

A furious scream from behind spun Raylan around just in time to the charge of an enemy soldier. Diving under the sword swing, Raylan rolled to his feet and brought his own sword around, cutting the back of the soldier's leg. Screaming an unknown curse, the man fell to one knee. Raylan drove the point of his sword into the back of the man's neck then scanned his surrounds to determine the nearest threat.

He spotted Xi'Lao in the middle of a fight. She swirled around a soldier's overstretch lunge and thrust her knife into the man's armpit, severing an artery then jabbed a second knife through the space beneath his helmet and sliced across his neck. It was a clean kill; but, as the enemy's body dropped, a big soldier emerged from the shadows behind her, battle axe already in a full horizontal swing.

"Xi'Lao, watch out!" he screamed as certain doom approached.

But the warning had been unnecessary. Xi'Lao dodged the attack with ease, dropping flat to the ground. As the battle axe passed over her, she rolled forward, reaching for one of the smaller knives on her belt. Rising to her feet, she spun as the soldier hefted his axe above his head, intent on splitting her skull—only to find she was faster. Her knife left her hand with lightning speed, boring itself deep into the throat of the axe wielder. The big man keeled over backward, and Xi'Lao sped off to help Galen, who was surrounded by three soldiers wielding spears.

Another volley of crossbow bolts flew into the entrance of the cave, taking down two soldiers entering the chaos from the dry shelter. The ground, already muddy from the rain, mixed further with the dark red blood of the fallen. It was hard to maintain a good footing on such a treacherous, slippery surface.

Raylan moved into the fray at Ca'lek's flank, taking on a second attacker that had approached the scout from the side. It gave Ca'lek the freedom to focus on the soldier in front of him. Raylan parried a stab to his leg, swiftly conceding ground to his opponent.

As they both shifted back and forth, Raylan noticed the black armor of his adversary was more decorative compared to the other soldiers he had fought. The dark metal was artfully engraved with golden prints on the shoulders, while the armor itself looked of higher quality and was clearly better maintained. An emblem of two small, golden diamonds was displayed on his chest. This man was also more skilled with the sword than the others Raylan had faced. A well-timed horizontal slash had Raylan step back to dodge the attack.

A squad leader or a commander, perhaps?

Another slash from above, followed by a stream of powerful blows from the sides. The wet ground made blocking difficult—each time a hit landed, his foot wanted to slip away from the force of the impact. Another stab tried to get in the opening of his leather armor. Raylan barely parried it to the side. His opponent shifted his balance slightly forward to come back quickly with another forward stab. Raylan sidestepped the attack, grabbing the soldier's wrist, pulled, then brought up the back of his sword and landed a powerful blow to the face. The soldier's nose cracked so loudly, chills ran down Raylan's spine.

Dazed, the soldier grabbed at his broken nose as a steady stream of blood dripped off his chin. Raylan raised his sword to deal the final blow, just as he saw Ca'lek slip in the darkened mud. The scout's opponent jumped at the opening. The slash took Ca'lek on his arm, cutting through the leather armor into his triceps. The scout's sword spun from his grip, landing between the grass and the rocks. Abandoning his own fight, Raylan shot forward, striking Ca'lek's attacker down.

"You okay?" Raylan panted, offering his hand to Ca'lek to help him up.

"Yeah, it didn't cut deep," grunted Ca'lek briskly, pulling himself back to his feet. His pride was more wounded than his arm.

Gavin's voice thundered from behind. "Raylan, watch out!"

Raylan turned to a sword in full motion, slashing down toward him—the bloodied soldier's face grinning behind it in certain victory.

Time slowed.

There's no way I'm going to make this.

His mind fought the sudden panic and mortal fear. He kicked out, attempting to roll away from the descending steel messenger of death. To his horror, his foot slipped in the same mud that had brought down Ca'lek. As his back hit the mire, his instinct told him to look away from the incoming sword, but he found himself mesmerized, unable to drag his eyes from the heavy blade speeding toward him.

As the blade drew closer, time seemed to slow further—all the way to the point where it stopped.

CHAPTER TWO

Counterattack

*T*IME SLOWED… IT STOPPED…

"Come on, Father's gone!" Gavin called out while he beckoned to Raylan.

Raylan looked at his older brother and let his shoulders drop. He didn't really feel like practicing swords today. He felt hot and filthy from moving bags of coal into storage all morning. "Maybe another time, it's too hot."

He looked at the large pillar of sails that towered over their street. It gently turned in the morning's breeze. Perhaps he could ask their father if he could work at the mill during the summer months. He had always liked how they managed to capture the wind and, with at least half of the kingdom's grain coming through the capital, Shid'el's mills were constantly looking for additional help. Besides, he would not mind working up high where the airflow would cool him during the hot summer days.

"Oh come on, just wait until you see what's waiting in the workshop. Father finished it! Or, perhaps… you're afraid you'll lose again." Gavin baited him.

Their father had been working on an impressive sword for weeks. Laid out with rubies and emeralds, it was meant to be used in a special ceremony later in the summer. They knew their father was well regarded for his work, but he rarely received a request from a nobleman for anything as special as this. This was a great opportunity for him to get his work out there.

Conceding to his own piqued curiosity, plus knowing Gavin would keep taunting him until he caved, Raylan reluctantly jogged after his brother to the workshop. They poked their heads around the opening of the door. Nobody around…

Gavin was the first to the worktable; he opened the wooden chest where the sword had been placed. The gem-covered weapon sparkled in the flames of the fire roaring in the hearth.

"Beautiful," said Raylan. "Father really outdid himself this time. How does it feel?"

Gavin stepped back and took a couple of practice swings. "The blade is really singing."

Raylan rolled his eyes at the remark. "Father must have folded and hammered that blade a thousand times. Do the gems put you off when slashing?"

"No, it feels very well balanced."

"Let me have a try."

"No way," countered Gavin. "I have it."

"Come on, don't be such a jerk. I just want to check it out up close, too."

"Forget it. If you want it, you'll have to come and take it."

Gavin spun around taking a defensive stance while shifting away from his little brother, his eyes narrowed in challenge.

Raylan moved in and reached out, barely pulling his hand back in time when Gavin cut the sword through the air. "Hey! Watch it!" Raylan spat.

"You'll have to do better than that, little brother."

Glancing around, Raylan grabbed a plain blade from the sword rack and launched a stab at his brother. They had been practicing with real swords for quite some time now. He knew the reach and amount of thrust he could use to make the attack feel real but not pose any real danger of injury.

Gavin easily parried the attack with the gemmed sword. The metal clash rang through the shop. "Nice try, but you're too slow."

Raylan tried a couple more slashes.

"Nope, still not there, little brother. You'll never beat me," taunted Gavin. "Not fast enough, not strong enough. You'll never touch a sword as fine as this."

Raylan did not know if his brother was pushing his buttons more than usual, or perhaps it was the heat, but something in him snapped. Instead of focusing on his sword, he stepped in, sliding his blade along their father's masterpiece. Pushing it out of the way, he brought up the back of his sword and slammed it into Gavin's face. A big gash opened across his brother's nose and blood rushed out.

"Oof! What the hell, Raylan! We never practiced that!" yelled Gavin, losing his temper in turn.

His brother pushed him back with furious slashes. Shocked that Raylan had finally broken through his defense and landed a blow. Raylan could do nothing but step backward, parrying strike after strike. When his back hit the wall, Gavin came at him with a powerful downward slash. Raylan held up his sword, trying to defend against the attack; but the power of the blow slammed away his sword, nicking his right eyebrow.

Raylan cried out in pain and grabbed his eye. A moment of uncertainty flash across his brother's face, before Gavin quickly stepped back and regathered himself.

"See? It will take more than that to beat me," he said with a smile that was a somewhat hesitant cross between smug and teasing. Both now had blood gushing down their faces. Gavin wiped the blood away that was seeping into the corner of his mouth. "But don't worry... I'll be sure to protect my little brother in real life, when he needs it."

Raylan never liked it when his older brother made him feel like he could not do anything right. He was about to retort, when the workshop door slammed closed, startling them both.

The world around them came rushing back in.

"What on King's earth is going on?" boomed their father. "What happened to your faces and why are you holding swords? GAVIN! Is that the sword I finished this morning?"

Their father grabbed Gavin's arm and yanked the sword from his hands.

Raylan's breath caught in his throat. He stared at his father with wide eyes, as if just realizing what they had done. Too shocked to blink, his eyes began to water from the forge's heat, while the furious smith shouted every curse word of the known kingdoms.

"Your mother would turn in her grave if she saw you both right now! Be gone! You're not allowed in the workshop without me anymore! Go on, skit! Get those cuts cleaned and then start cleaning out the forge furnace, now!"

"But that will take us the entire night!" protested Raylan.

"Precisely. Perhaps that will teach you not to take my hard work and damage it!" roared their father.

They raced from the workshop, their father still cursing as the door closed.

"Guess you can't protect me from everything," said Raylan, looking at his brother.

The baffled look on Gavin's face felt like a small victory...

...The image of Gavin bringing down the gemmed sword toward him, faded away. It took Raylan a moment to realize Gavin was still there, towering besides him. But instead of the gemmed sword coming at him, it was the enemy soldier's sword that hovered no more than two inches from Raylan's face—his brother's sword blocking the incoming attack at the very last moment.

24

Both swords trembled from the power struggle. Gavin released a roar as he used both hands to force his sword up, throwing the broken-nosed attacker onto his back. The enemy soldier hit his head on a large rock protruding from of the ground; the force of the impact could have been fatal, had the man not been wearing his helmet.

Disoriented by the second blow to his head, the soldier scrambled backward—away from Gavin, Raylan and Ca'lek—struggling to get his bearings.

The immediate danger averted; Gavin looked over his shoulder with a big grin. "Seems like I can still protect my little brother when needed. You all right?"

Raylan blinked for the first time in what seemed like ages. His eyes felt as dry as they had done that day in the workshop.

"T-thanks," he stammered, relieved. "That was close." He rose on trembling legs. "Do you intend to let him get away? We need to go after him."

Gavin turned just in time to see the soldier disappear behind a larger rock formation.

"Not too many soldiers are still breathing. I'd like to get some information from this one, if we can take him alive," Gavin explained. "Ca'lek, go check on the others and see where enemies still remain. Raylan and I will pursue our bloody-nosed friend here for questioning."

Ca'lek jogged off in the direction of clashing metal and vanished from the soft light of a smoldering campfire that seemed to be finally losing its fight against the rain.

Raylan followed his brother along the path the soldier had scurried toward. It ran away from the campsite and rounded a corner where multiple wagons of the small enemy convoy came into view. Edging forward, they glanced around, trying to determine where the soldier hid himself.

Approaching the wagons, Raylan heard a soft mumbling. Signaling his brother toward the closest wagon, they both moved to the back of it. The mumbling grew louder, but it was hard to determine from where it came. It was not a language Raylan recognized; a strange, deep tone shifted beneath the words. Signaling three fingers to Raylan, Gavin counted down before grabbing the edge of the cloth and whipping it aside while Raylan braced himself for a possible attack. The wagon was empty bar a stack of dried wood. Not much was left, but it seemed the soldiers had brought firewood to keep them warm in the harsh environment of the White North. Raylan could not imagine how many of these wagons, filled with wood, would be needed to keep a large attack force from freezing in those mountains.

Pebbles rolled from a rock above. Raylan's heart jumped in his chest as he jerked his head around at the sound, but it was Kevhin taking a high-ground position, crossbow at the ready. Raylan rolled his eyes at the archer's apologetic face and snuck toward the next wagon with his brother. The mumbling grew more intense and a deep humming began resonating through their surroundings. As Gavin pulled the cloth of the next wagon aside, Raylan stood sword-ready; but what they found inside was not what they expected.

Once his sight adjusted to the twilight within the wagon's interior, Raylan saw two giant feet pointing toward him. Nearly pure black, they could not belong to a real man and after a more thorough second look, it appeared to be the bottom of a black stone statue.

Why would they be hauling such a thing around? Is this the item Xi'Lao is looking for?

Raylan looked around wondering. *Then what happened to the chest it was supposed to be in?*

The mumbling increased. Peering into the far corner of the wagon, he spotted the soldier with the broken nose. On his knees, clutching a small scroll of parchment, the soldier rocked slowly back and forth, as if in prayer. The deep humming grew louder, and the wagon rattled as it vibrated with the sound.

"Come out of there!" he yelled.

Gavin shifted close, sword at the ready.

The soldier did not react to the command. His mumbling became louder, as he repeated a phrase in a language Raylan had never heard. The man's voice seemed to build with resonating intensity. The vibration painfully burrowed into Raylan's head, like it was splitting his skull. Both brothers covered their ears, trying to block the sound.

More members of their squad ran up.

"Stay back!" shouted Gavin.

The soldier continued to chant as he made a deep cut to his palm with his dagger, and as his bloody hand grabbed the scroll, a faint blue light began to emanate from the parchment. The glow increased to such a bright flare that had Raylan divert his eyes. The squad called out to them, but their words were drowned out by the pulsating hum. The blue light beamed out through the holes in the cloth around the wagon as the drumming vibration seemed to echo all around the rocks.

Pain pierced through Raylan's ears; the sound affected his equilibrium. He saw Gavin wobble as well as his brother tried to stay on his feet. Gavin turned his head further from the light, but Raylan used his hand as a shield against the blinding flare and squinted to keep the enemy soldier in sight.

The sides of the scroll had long, pointed blades at each end, as if the parchment could be rolled out and stuck in the ground, forming a small banner or paper fence. But those sharp tips were not meant to be stuck in the ground.

The soldier raised the scroll high above the chest of the large, dark statue. Jerking his head sideways, the man stared straight at Raylan. His voice thick with a foreign accent Raylan did not recognize, the soldier roared at the top of his lungs, "Long live the Stone King! You won't stop the mountain from crushing you! You'll all be buried under it in darkness!"

With one mighty thrust, the man plunged the pointed scroll directly into the statue's chest. A high-pitched screech blasted out of the soldier, as his head snapped backward, his face staring up to the heavens.

The blue light engulfed the soldier's entire body; it looked liquid—almost alive—swirling around the skin and armor, sometimes sparking like lightning. Blue flames burned the soldier's eyes out of their sockets, while a glow emanated through the stretched cheeks as light seeped from his mouth. The blue aura flowed out of the soldier—toward the scroll—at an increasing speed, feeding into the bright blue flare. Spellbound, Raylan stood rooted to the sport.

"We've got to stop hi—" began Gavin.

The thunderous noise imploded, and Raylan felt the air being sucked into the wagon. The last of the blue light rushed from the soldier, directly through the scroll and into the statue. A shockwave erupted from the statue's chest. Both brothers were blown off their feet, losing their weapons. The others, not being as near to the blast, withstood the sudden wall of wind, turning their heads away for protection. Kevhin was not so lucky; tumbling from his position on the rock.

Rohan quickly disappeared after him, shouting if he was all right.

The silence now, was as deafening as the chanting had been. As Raylan scrambled to his feet, he shook his head, trying to get rid of the painful buzzing. He braved a look inside the wagon. The soldier lay slumped over the large statue. His face looked like it had been dried in the sun for a hundred years. The eye sockets were two gaping black holes with burns around their edges, and his mouth stretched open far more than was natural. Raylan turned away in disgust, but movement caught his eye.

The wagon creaked, struggling under a sudden shift in weight. Hardly believing his eyes, Raylan watched the giant statue tremble. It lifted its head, then its torso. Two glowing blue eyes stared directly at Raylan from the darkness of the wagon. His body turned hot then cold as the inhuman eyes measured him with an icy indifference.

Slowly, the statue looked at the soldier's lifeless husk. It stared at it for a moment, before swatting the corpse through the wooden floorboards of the wagon. With a loud crash, the wagon broke in two, slamming the now-moving statue onto the ground. As it rose, Raylan clearly heard the sound of grinding rocks between the splintering of wood.

"Get back!" Raylan yelled to Gavin, who was still struggling after the sudden blast.

Raylan grabbed his brother's arm and dragged him away as the statue broke free of the wreckage. It straightened, and for the first time Raylan saw the full height of the stone man. The hair on his neck instantly rose. This thing—this non-living, moving thing—was gigantic.

It was at least three heads taller than Galen, the largest in their group. Small chunks of rock broke off from its knees, elbows and other joints as it moved; its once very square body turned more human-like with every crumble. The stone giant looked down at its hands; singular, solid pieces of rock, as if someone had glued its fingers together. Cracks started to form, until the stone slabs abruptly broke into fully functioning hands with five wide-stretched fingers.

The statue took in its surroundings as it flexed its newly-made hands. Its gaze focused on Gavin and Raylan as they backed cautiously away toward Galen, Xi'Lao and Stephen. Raylan had to remind himself to breathe as those eyes stared right into him.

"Here, use these," a voice called out to them. It was, Peadar, the youngest member of their squad. The young bird handler had mostly stayed out of the earlier fight, but now saw a chance to help by retrieving two replacement swords for the brothers.

"Thanks," muttered Raylan, his attention firmly locked on the unfolding horror.

Seemingly satisfied with its hands, the stone giant looked down at them. Taking a step toward them, it stretched its neck forward; its arms trembled in front of it, as a low sound resonated again. Its face had no distinct features: no eyebrows, barely a nose and hollow eye sockets—with the icy blue light deep within. Raylan's grip tightened around the handle of his sword as Peadar hurried to the back of their little group again.

"Are we really going to fight this thing?" Raylan asked his brother somewhat nervously, when he noticed Harwin and Ca'lek circled around to take up flanking positions.

"I don't think we have a choice," replied Gavin, who finally seemed to have regained his focus.

The sound of splitting rock was barely noticeable as a thin crack slowly formed in the place where lips would have been. Its body trembled with effort as the crack grew wider and finally formed a mouth. It released a deep roar that Raylan felt in his bones.

"It doesn't sound very happy," Raylan hissed as he noted a few of their group flinch.

"Well, he doesn't look like it either," Galen added. The heavy hitter appeared to be the only one not entirely stunned by the scene before them.

"Maybe we should get out of h—," Stephen began, when the stone warrior picked up one of the wagon's large wheels and flung it at them. The movement seemed effortless, yet the enormous wheel flew at them with incredible speed.

"Move!" shouted Gavin.

Everyone dove out of the way and the wheel shattered against the rocks behind them.

"Holy Mother, it would take at least three of us to even put that on a wagon," Peadar called with shaking voice from behind a rock. "How strong is this thing?"

The giant launched at an unexpected speed toward Stephen, who had ended up closest to the stone horror. With three big strides, the thing was on top of him. The scout yelled out in surprise as the dark shadow towered above him. The giant slammed its fist down, but Stephen rolled aside at the very last moment. The impact of the stone knuckles shook the ground beneath Raylan's feet.

"Rohan, Kevhin! Bolts!" Gavin shouted, his voice strong and confident.

The archers had climbed back atop the boulders, and Kevhin appeared to show no serious injuries. Both stood paralyzed, gaping at the stone figure until Gavin's command pushed them into action.

Both men had their crossbows ready at the same time the stone warrior raised his fist for a second attack on Stephen. The strings released and the bolts flew toward their target. The first ricocheted off the stone torso as the second hit the giant squarely in the eye. The giant froze, fist poised, slowly turning its head toward the archers. Without any indication of pain, the giant plucked the cross bolt from its eye socket and pulverized it.

Deciding not to stick around, Stephen crawled away as fast as he could. He managed a small distance, before a stone hand grabbed his leg and flung him directly at the archers. Protecting his head, the scout slammed into Rohan and

Kevhin, knocking them down. All three crashed down the boulders; Kevhin cursing heavily as he, once again, smacked onto the unwelcoming ground.

Raylan did not really want to get any closer than necessary, but when Gavin sent Xi'Lao and him forward, he knew he could not let her go at it alone. As they moved in, he tried to determine a weak point on their gigantic enemy. Dodging below its arms, Raylan slashed at its side, but it was literally like hitting rock. Xi'Lao drove her knives into the back of the statue's knees, where they instantly got stuck. The giant turned, as both Raylan and Xi'Lao rolled away. Xi'Lao threw a salvo of knives at it, without effect. As it moved, the knives in its legs bent, dislodged, and dropped to the ground, ruined.

"Stay out of its reach," Gavin yelled.

"It does not feel anything," Xi'Lao shouted back.

"And it's dangerously quick!" added Raylan, backing away from another punch.

"Peadar! Go find some heavy spears… perhaps we can pierce it through the cracks in his chest," Gavin ordered over his shoulder.

The young bird handler ran off as Ca'lek and Harwin charged at the giant from the side and slashed at its stone legs.

"We tried that already," shouted Raylan.

Ca'lek jumped back and forth seeing if his sword could do any damage without being caught by the giant's flailing arms. Harwin circled toward its back, but the giant suddenly twisted around, aiming a full swinging kick toward him.

Since he did not have the speed of the younger men anymore, Harwin often preferred the defense of a shield together with sword. It was a vital part of his survival on the battlefield. Turning into the approaching kick, Harwin brought up his shield, and braced for impact. It was like being hit by a rock slide. The giant's leg did not even slow as it kicked the old veteran off his feet. The iron shield wrapped around the giant's foot upon impact and Raylan heard the air explode from the shield-warrior's lungs. Harwin tumbled across the ground and crashed into the wreckage of the wagon.

Peadar came running with two spears and passed them to Gavin. He immediately tossed one to Galen, who lined it up and threw it with all his might toward the stone giant. It hit the titan in the back of its upper arm, lodging in the crack where the arm attached to the shoulder. As it reached for the spear, Gavin charged in, thrusting full force into the spot where the scroll had pierced the statue. It did little damage, but the spear did get wedged in. As the giant turned toward him, Raylan's brother pushed the spear sideways to widen the crack in its chest.

It was a mistake to linger so close to the stone man. The giant warrior brought its arm around and hit his brother with an outward swing. Gavin flew through the air and smashed into a boulder, his head slamming into the rock before he slumped forward onto the ground.

"Gavin!" Raylan screamed as he ran toward his brother, but the stone abomination cut him off.

Raylan slid to a halt and jumped back, barely able to dodge the giant's interlocked fists that were aimed toward his head. The impact shook the ground beneath Raylan's feet, leaving a crater in the soggy earth.

A pebble hit the back of the giant's head; it turned to find Peadar on top of a small boulder. Vulnerable atop his perch, Peadar looked unsure of what to do next, now that he had diverted the giant's attention. He stood like a startled deer staring at a hunter.

A battle cry broke the silence as their second-in-command, Richard, jumped from higher ground, slashing his sword across the giant's stone neck. The blade sparked from the impact of the attack, but there was no visible damage.

"Where the hell have you been?" shouted Galen.

"Sorry, I got caught up at the other end of camp," Richard called back.

Drawn by Richard's shouting, the stone giant refocused his attack and moved in on Richard and Raylan.

"It's easily distracted," Raylan called out to Richard as they dodged the attacks and retreated around the smashed wagon.

Raylan glanced toward the wreckage and spotted Harwin's legs sticking out from the pile of wood and canvas, but he had no time to see if the veteran was breathing or not. Jumping out of the way of an incoming punch, his eye caught a small glimmer near where Harwin lay. When their enemy's next punch focused on Richard, he rolled forward and moved in on the pile of wood and metal to have a better look. Ignoring Harwin—for now—he grabbed the big iron chain and gave it a strong pull. A few feet of chain slid from under the wreckage, before it got caught on some of the wood.

"Richard, distract it as long as possible," he shouted over his shoulder. "I've got an idea."

"Distract it? I am trying not to get killed here!"

Their second-in-command sounded out of breath, but it could not be that bad if he had the energy to make light of it... still, Raylan figured he had better hurry. Kicking at the wreckage, Raylan worked as fast as possible to free the chain. He grunted as he gave another mighty pull. Behind him, the others tried to help Richard, but it seemed their enemy had learned from his unfocused approach.

Raylan watched over his shoulder as Richard was pushed into a corner. He yanked hard on the chain. "Come on!" he grunted.

The chain unexpectedly sprang free, and he stumbled and fell backward. Jumping to his feet, he ran around the stone giant in a large arc, toward Richard, who had just run out of space to dodge its attacks. Heaving one end of the long and heavy iron chain, Raylan called out, "Catch!"

Even before he caught the chain, Richard seemed to have figured out what Raylan had in mind. Sprinting to opposite sides, Richard went low while Raylan jumped over the chain. They twisted the links around the massive stone legs, crossing back to the front.

Trying to move toward its enemies, and with its legs tangled up by the iron, the stone giant lost its balance and crashed heavily to the mud. Both men dashed back and forth to twist the chains around its stone arms and entangle the giant further.

Raylan looked back and spotted Galen. Relieved, he saw the war hammer was already waiting in his comrade's hands.

"Galen, hurry up! We can't hold him for long!" he yelled as the statue started to move.

The statue's power was too much. The giant rolled onto its back, twisting the chains around its torso even more, but then simply sat up. The chain slipped through Raylan's hands, as his feet dragged ineffectually across the ground.

Galen charged forward, shouting at the top of his lungs, and put all his momentum into a horizontal swing. His timing could not have been better.

With full force, the war hammer hit the stone warrior square in its face, knocking it straight back to the ground. Its head smashed onto the flat rocky surface of a buried boulder. By the sound of the impact, Raylan hoped a crack had formed on the stone skull.

Skidding to a halt, Galen immediately turned, raising his war hammer above his head. As the stone menace tried to lift its head once more, Galen brought his weapon straight down, time and time again, smashing the stone skull between the hammer and the buried boulder. A crack started to show, becoming more visible as Galen struck blow after blow. With the dozenth smash, the crack widened. Galen let out a roar as he brought the hammer down once more. The final blow shattered the emotionless stone face, and it erupted in another outward blast of sound. Blue light sparkled then faded from the crumbling stone. Finally, the giant statue remained motionless.

Out of breath, both Raylan and Richard dropped to the ground and released the chain. Raylan's hands throbbed painfully. Next to him, Galen let go of his hammer and sat back as well, panting heavily. Raylan lifted his head to faint golden light crawling across the land. Sunrise? Had the fight truly taken that long?

Gavin. Raylan's fatigue vanished as he jumped to his feet. He spun to find Xi'Lao crouching next to Gavin, holding him with his back against one of the boulders.

"Is he alive? Is he still breathing?" said Raylan—the words cracking in his dry mouth as he rushed over.

Arriving at his brother's side, he heard a low groan as Gavin grabbed the back of his head. He lifted his face slowly and finally opened his eyes, trying to focus.

"What the hell was that?"

CHAPTER THREE

Egg

GAVIN LEANED AGAINST the rock with a blanket around his bare chest. "Here," said Raylan, passing him the waterskin.

Gavin grimaced in pain as soon as he lifted his arm but slowly tipped his head and took a sip. They had removed his armor and his shirt so Xi'Lao could examine him. Her extensive medical training had already become invaluable in the field.

She slowly followed Gavin's ribs from his chest to his side, applying pressure lightly along the way. Gavin let out a soft groan when she reached the spot where the stone giant had punched him. He did not look happy.

At least the rain stopped. The red morning sun rose above the horizon. It would give his brother some warmth while he rested.

"How bad is it?" asked Raylan, as Gavin struggled to put his clothes and his armor back on.

"I'm fine," said his brother.

Xi'Lao gave Raylan a faint smile. "His head was hit hard, but at least his ribs do not seem to be broken. He will need to take it easy for several days, if that is possible. He might vomit. His bruised ribs will take longer to heal. Breathing will most likely be uncomfortable for some time."

"It's nothing. It was my own fault for not moving quickly enough."

As Gavin got to his feet, he stumbled. Raylan and Xi'Lao shot forward and lowered him to the ground where his brother immediately closed his eyes and let out a sigh.

"Is everyone all right?" Gavin directed his question to Raylan. "Did we lose anyone?"

Raylan took in the squad. "Galen and Richard are fine; they did a great job taking out that thing. Peadar is okay, just a bit shaken. He's been helping the others. Harwin still stands; it seems his shield took most of the impact. There're some cuts from the crash and there was a nail in his leg from the wagon, but that has been taken out and disinfected. He assured us it was nothing serious, just a couple of more scars to brag about during drinking night."

"Sounds like him," remarked Gavin, his eyes still closed. "What else?"

"Kevhin and Rohan are good, only some bruises from that tumble off the boulders. Stephen's leg is in pretty bad shape though. It seems the stone giant broke it when it grabbed him. Peadar is currently making a splint for him."

"And you two?" asked his brother.

"Xi'Lao and I have no serious injuries. Ca'lek only has a superficial cut on his arm. It's been bandaged up already."

For a moment, Raylan hesitated, while Gavin pinched the bridge of his nose.

"Regis?" he asked, his voice a mere whisper.

Raylan shook his head. "He's gone. Stephen and Harwin fought their way to him right after the horses trampled him, but when they pulled him to the side he wasn't breathing. Ca'lek went to double check just now, but his body's already gone cold…"

"How many enemies dead?"

"Thirty-nine… forty, if you include the statue. I still can't believe that thing moved," said Raylan. "What kind of force could do such a thing? I mean, that soldier looked like he had been sucked dry of all life. And that blue light? That surrounded him once he cut his hand. It looked like water and fire at the same time. You saw it too, right?"

Gavin nodded and looked sideways at Xi'Lao. "I think it's safe to say none of us have ever seen anything like that before. Have you?"

She urged Gavin to take another sip from the waterskin before answering. "Nothing like this. But back home, it is a common belief that all living things have energy, a 'force of life' one could call it. It flows through every person, animal, plant and thing. Even rocks have their own energy," she said. "In my language they call this *Chi*. The way you describe this light, it reminds me of it. Chi moves around the body of a person in a certain flow. We are taught this energy pattern is built up out of channels and points, across the entire body. And it is said the grand masters of the temples are able to see, feel and manipulate the current of Chi in a person. It is the source of miraculous stories, about people seeking help from grand masters for incurable diseases or used as an explanation for the abilities of extraordinary fighters." She glanced at the stone giant then back to Gavin. "I, too, have heard many of these mystical stories back home, but none that I remember mentioned anything about making a statue move."

Xi'lao's words piqued Raylan's interest. He had never heard about such a thing, but he soaked in all the details. "Have you ever seen it?" he asked curiously, as he wondered why he was drawn to something so untouchable and vague.

"No, but as warriors, we are taught to memorize the Chi pattern of a human body. Many of the channels and points are vital spots, important to the human body. Focusing an attack there will often cripple your enemy quickly—or worse—even if you do not wound him much."

Gavin had been listening with his eyes closed. It looked like he had a hard time focusing on the conversation. "What about the item your empire is looking for, Xi'Lao? Was it in one of the wagons?"

Xi'Lao's voice instantly lost its softness. "We have not found it yet. Harwin checked the wagons after Peadar helped him, but it was not there. Perhaps Ca'lek did not see it correctly and made a mistake?" she said, looking at where Ca'lek stood.

"I know what I saw," said the scout. "It was precisely as you described—red wood, gold-colored metal frame. It must be here somewhere."

Raylan felt the tension in the air. It was not the first time people had been at odds with each other. His brother had been about to cancel the mission when they finally picked up the enemy's tracks a few days ago. Morale had been at an all-time low after months of traveling through the cold and rainy region. Their provisions were running low and the men had grown restless and angry from the wet and cold, the uncomfortable nights. Quarrels had started on a regular basis as everyone felt the pressure, and some of it still lingered—even though morale had vastly improved.

Thankfully we've got something to focus on again, together. Raylan waited while Gavin processed everything.

"Okay, gather the others," Gavin eventually said. "We can't afford to sit around here for too long. We're too exposed and too far from friendly ground."

Everyone gathered in wearily while Raylan tried to ignore his own muscles' demand for more rest. Once their group was complete, Gavin continued.

"We've been on the road for months. We're far from Aeterra and the safety she offers us. We've crossed the most northern tip of the Great Eastern Divide weeks ago, which means we are now a fair distance into the Dark Continent and likely in enemy territory. We all know it's rumored to be home to many savage tribes of hunters and scavengers, but looking at these troops, I fear we don't know the whole situation.

"Raylan, Xi'Lao, first we have to find the empire's stolen item. You two will check the enemy camp again, including all the places we've already searched. We haven't spotted any soldiers leaving the encampment, so it must still be there. If not in the wagons, then somewhere else.

"Kevhin, Rohan, take care of Regis; balm his body, and handle him with respect. See if you can find a cloth to wrap his body. After that, put him in the wagon with the least wear and tear. We will use it to transport his body—as well as the chest—back home. Make sure he's secured well; those horses stomped on him too much already. I would like his mother to be able to say goodbye to her son while she can still recognize him. After that, go through the camp and salvage any food you can find. We need to restock our rations if we want to make it back home.

"Ca'lek, I want you to take a horse and ride out to the ridge we passed half a day ago. If you ride fast, you should be able to get there and back before the sun reaches its highest point. Use that vantage to scout for a safe route back to the kingdom. With the growing unrest around Forsiquar we'll likely need to travel further west before turning south again. I don't want to be caught in a clash between Aeterra's main army and Forsiquar's city forces."

He looked at Stephen. "How's the leg?"

Showing a slightly embarrassed smile, Stephen gave a small tap on the splints but immediately flinched in pain. "Could be better. Peadar added an extra splint to improve the support, but it's not very comfortable. Horseback riding is out of the question; I can't put any weight on it or push my leg inward."

"All right, maybe we can find you a solid walking stick for support. And you'll have to travel in the wagon for now; hopefully, that will give your leg enough rest to heal while we move. But I'll have to send out someone else in your place."

Gavin surveyed the group for a moment. His gaze stopped on his second-in-command. "Richard, go and scout in the opposite direction from Ca'lek. We need to know what lies ahead of us in case we can't take the road back, or in case we are about to be boxed in. I want to know if this is truly all that remained of their force. The White North can be unforgiving, but more of them might be out there. Ride out for half a morning before turning back. Ride fast and safe… and keep your eyes open for anything suspicious."

Gavin closed his eyes for a moment and took a deep breath, before he continued. "Also, we've seen the footprints of larger predators lately, as well as some kill spots of their prey. So, be aware of your surroundings at all times, especially when alone.

"That goes for you both," he added, looking at Ca'lek.

Ca'lek gave a short nod of acknowledgment. Scouting solo was always a risky business; if anything went wrong, there would be no backup. Unfortunately, they just did not have time to scout the area in pairs to decide the safest route home. If not hostile territory, they were at least in unclaimed lands, which meant an unfriendly stronghold could be around the very next turn, or another enemy force could run into them at any time.

"Harwin and Galen… I want you to secure the horses still in the camp. See if you can catch some of those that escaped, too. It will help us move faster, if we have more horses to rotate through wagon duty."

Raylan frowned as his brother shivered. "Peadar, once we're done here, can you please help Gavin move to a place higher up in the camp?" asked Raylan. "Let's make him a fire for some extra warmth now that the rain has stopped. He needs to rest."

"I told you, I'm fine."

"You're not," said Raylan, this time more firmly. "If you're to lead us out of here, you need to rest."

Gavin looked at him, then Xi'Lao and back. He let out a sigh. "All right, you're right. Maybe it will stop my head from spinning if I take a breather. But before I lie down, I want Peadar to grab one of the birds and help me prepare a report of our encounter. The king and the council will be wondering what has become of us since we sent the last bird several weeks ago. The rest of you go find that chest. I, for one, will be glad to leave this cold, barren land and to get back to the comforts of our home. Now get to it."

Raylan scoured the enemy camp. He and Xi'Lao had double-checked the wagons but like Harwin had said, they could not find the chest amongst them. The enemy would probably have moved it for safekeeping, hiding it amongst the many boulders; or, it could be nearby, perhaps camouflaged. Raylan decided it would be easier if they split up and searched separately. He took the enemy encampment, while Xi'Lao climbed up to higher ground to check if any of the wagonloads were hidden between the boulders.

The battle left a grim scene in the camp. Dead soldiers lay everywhere. He had to give it to his brother, the element of surprise gained through their night attack had worked perfectly in their favor—as expected. Raylan estimated that by the time the camp was on full alert, more than half the group had already been taken out. It would have been a very different story had they tried a direct daylight attack.

Raylan stepped over the dead soldier in the campfire—his first kill. The upper body and face were charred black from the fire. The stench of burned flesh, mixed with the already thick smell of blood and dirt, lay thick on the tongue.

He could see why his brother had reconsidered his earlier decision to rest in the main camp. Gavin had claimed a spot on the other side of the main rock formation that housed the cave. It was upwind, and would soon be in the sunlight as the sun rose higher.

Although the north here seemed very isolated, the dead bodies would attract scavengers soon enough. Raylan waved away flies darting at his face, already irritated by their constant buzzing near his ear. With the tiny nuisances here, decay would soon set in. He expected they would not stay longer than necessary. The smell would only get worse and the flies would bring diseases, which would be especially dangerous for those with open wounds.

Harwin and Galen untied the remaining horses that were secured in the corner of the encampment. The animals had calmed down as soon as the fighting stopped; although they still looked a bit skittish. Neither man had trouble leading the horses out of the camp, but as soon as the horses saw the now motionless stone giant, they started pulling at their reins, bucking and rearing to get away from it. They had no choice but to move the steeds downhill to the foot of the rock formations.

"We'll try again later," Harwin called up toward Raylan. "First go find that chest."

Raylan made his way to the cave where several of the soldiers had been resting before they launched their attack. Many lay dead at the entrance, most of them taken out with cross bolts. Raylan picked up one of the torches that lay nearby and used the smoldering fire to ignite it. Holding it above his head, he stepped inside.

After a few steps, he halted. He could have sworn he heard a sound coming from the cave. He carefully passed the torch to his other hand and drew his sword, inching forward, trying to make out what lay ahead in the dark.

Had anyone bothered to look inside the cave for remaining enemies? Surely the others would not leave such a place unchecked after taking out those in the camp. He tried to remember if anyone had mentioned something about it but came up short. There could still be an enemy waiting in the dark, hoping to ambush an unsuspecting intruder. A small chill went down his spine as a worse thought entered his mind; perhaps another stone giant waited for its chance.

No, we would've heard that strange sound... felt that windblast... seen that strange blue light.

As quietly as possible, he snuck further into the cave, stepping over the simple beds the soldiers had made. Small personal effects were scattered around, probably kicked about when the soldiers had exited the cave, spurred on by the sounds fighting. He held the torch away from his direct line of sight, allowing his eyes to slowly adjust to the low light inside the cave.

"Well, no sign of people or moving statues, yet," he muttered.

Moving further into the dark, the cave tunnel slowly curved away to the left before turning sharply out of sight.

There it was again—a soft thud as if someone knocked on a table or a door. Something was around the corner; he was sure of it. Soft light emanated from around the bend. Edging along the cave wall, he moved toward the corner, his grip tightening around his sword hilt. Shadows danced on the far wall, playing tricks on his eyes. He peeked around the corner, but the shape of the tunnel made it impossible to see everything. Drawing in a deep breath, he stepped around the corner in one fluid motion, sword ready and torch high, casting light as far as possible.

Nothing moved.

Raylan stared at the dead end of the tunnel. On either side, a torch hung from the wall, softly flickering the last of its flames. Soon they would extinguish.

Against the back wall, on the ground, sat the chest. At least he figured it must be the chest they were looking for. The flames made it hard to see colors, but it looked like it was made of red wood with a gold frame. It fit the image Xi'Lao had described and Ca'lek said he had seen.

Raylan started to turn back—he would get Xi'Lao right away to come and confirm the item—when the soft *thud* sounded again. It was much louder now. *It's coming from inside the chest?*

With caution, he headed over to it, sheathing his sword. He crouched, putting his free hand on the lid and letting his fingers follow the curve of the chest. The metal frame and the wood felt strangely warm to the touch. Bringing his torch closer, flickering light danced across strange symbols inscribed in the golden-colored metal. The wood seemed incredibly hard, with only minor superficial scratches from the travels in the wagon.

Thud.

Another unexpected knock vibrated through the chest's wooden frame, startling him.

"You just survived an attack where we were outnumbered three to one—not to mention that stone colossus that tried to smash in your head—and you jump at the sound of a small knock on wood," Raylan mocked with a grin.

He tried to open the chest, only to find a heavy lock hanging from the side that kept the lid securely fastened. Using the hilt of his sword, he hit it a few times.

"That's a tough lock," he grumbled.

Another four hits saw it buckle slightly. He continued his efforts until he was rewarded by the clank of the broken lock dropping to the floor. Raylan pushed open the lid with both hands, freeing the trapped warm air inside. It nearly burned his skin, but he barely noticed. Gazing inside, he shook his head, trying to grasp what he was looking at. The bottom of the chest seemed to be filled with red-hot glowing rocks and embers; and there, atop these layers of stone and smoldering wood, lay the biggest egg he had ever seen.

* * *

At first Ca'lek rode as fast as he could, until he realized what an idiot he was being and depending on what he might find, may need to make a hasty retreat. His father had taught him better.

He and Richard had immediately set off to scout their assigned areas. None of them wanted to be stuck in this dark and cold landscape any longer than necessary. Now, Ca'lek forced himself to spare his steed, but he kept a steady pace to ensure he could complete the round-trip in time.

Approaching the area of the cliff, he slowed his horse to walking pace. Deciding to go the last stretch by foot, Ca'lek dismounted and secured the animal to a tree with a patch of brown grass around it.

"I know it isn't much, Aine," he said as he softly stroked the horse's nose. "But be a good girl and wait for me here. I won't be long."

He wished there was more for the mare to eat. Their mounts had been on a diet of withering grass and dead twigs since they entered the northern region and it was beginning to show. Still, he figured that in this isolated place every little bit helped. Walking toward the cliff, he felt his own stomach's emptiness.

You've known worse, he reminded himself, trying to ignore the feeling.

Ca'lek was born in the south region of Aeterra's continent. Those parts still had much unclaimed land with hot weather and vast deserts, completely different from where they were stuck now. For one thing, there were a lot more trees here—the kind that kept their thin needle-like leaves all throughout the cold of winter.

He moved through the artificial dusk of the forest floor, grateful there was a carpet of fallen needles softening his footfall instead of a slush of snow to trudge through. At times like this, he really missed the warmth he remembered from his younger years. Sure, they had often been hungry, but that warmth... even on Aeterra's plains, the summers rarely hit that sweet spot of high temperature with slow, warm winds. It was as if his dark skin craved the touch of the sun.

Not that the sun here has much of that to offer. He looked up between the branches at the overcast sky that tried to swallow the sun again.

The path they had followed when tracking the enemy group had not been very big as it snaked through the forest; but as Ca'lek approached the cliff's edge, that same path widened into a small clearing before it continued and twisted down the mountainside. He took a quick look around before moving to the edge. There, he crouched near a small natural barrier of bushes that grew along the ledge and let his gaze float over the valley below.

His thoughts drifted briefly to the hunting trips Ca'lek had spent as a youngster with his father and the other men of home. Revered by many, his father had always excelled and survived as a hunter in a region where many dangerous animals lived. Those trips, despite the dangers, had given Ca'lek the needed experience to track prey and scout the land for possible threats. It had served him well in his current role and he often found himself using his skills to try and achieve a similar level of respect among his squad mates. With a quick prayer he thanked his ancestors that he had not just inherited his parents' sun-craving skin, but also his family's exceptional eyesight, for which their bloodline had always been admired.

He let his eyes wander the land, reading it like his father had explained to him so many times. The valley stretched out westward before his feet. To the north, the dark mountains of the White North loomed on the horizon; their black silhouettes covered with frozen white tops. As the barren slopes descended into the valley, the first trees stood as lonely mountaineers trying to scale the dangerous slopes. Below, a thick forest filled the bottom of the valley, while further along a thin silver line twisted through it.

Ca'lek remembered the river well. They had followed it for several days. Its cold melt water flowed southward, going all the way around the mountain range he crouched on. The valley narrowed toward the path that led up to clearing on top of the cliff, but he could only see a small part of it from his current vantage point.

Far past the tops of the southern mountains, Ca'lek saw the dark ocean's shimmers of the Great Eastern Divide on the horizon. The coast was at least a ten-day journey on foot, maybe more, depending on the terrain beyond the southern mountain ridge. From there, it should be several more days to get to the northern most point of the sea, where the coastal area was actually a very small crossing between the oceanic waters and the first slopes of the White North mountains.

Ca'lek scoffed and shook his head in disbelief. The White North, connecting the eastern, middle and western continents together, was said to be almost impossible to cross. And yet it seemed probable that the men they attacked had traveled for months on its border region. It was a grim landscape, with little to sustain life. It was difficult to believe the enemy troops had apparently chosen to cross it. Ca'lek thought it sheer madness.

Pushing the thought aside, he studied the ocean on the horizon to see if he could spot any sails. He knew it was a long shot, but Aeterra's trading ships had not always focused solely on the southern and western seas. Numerous attempts had been made to map the coastline of Doskova, as this region was called. Scouting vessels and pioneer trading ships had tried their luck, hoping to find fame and fortune; but very few actually returned.

Those that did told stories of dark cliffs rising out of the sea, and lands with thick, dark forests full of witches and trolls. It was enough to keep people away. Ca'lek had always thought it was probably the dark forest playing tricks on people's minds, though his father had often warned him, growing up, that those tricks were not always lies.

And it seems you were right, baba, he thought, recollecting their fight with the statue. *I'll tell you all about it when we're back home.*

In any case, it had been years since an official expedition had set out to the east. Doskova had earned its name over two centuries ago. It was the old language—which was all but lost—meaning 'dark hollows', most likely referring to the dark forests that stretched the continent. In the common Terran language, people simply referred to it as The Dark Continent—the part of the world where you did not venture.

Not voluntarily, at least. A wry smile crossed Ca'lek's lips.

As his experienced gaze scanned the valley, his eyes caught movement a fair distance away, down in the valley. It was in a part of the forest near the river. The canopy opened up in some places, like holes in a worn-down roof. It was there he saw shadows move amongst the trees. Crouching lower, he kept an eye on the shadows for some time, focusing on a part of the forest that widened into a small clearing a little further along the path. If he was not mistaken, it was the same path they had followed some days ago, before it actually crossed the river. Holding his hand above his eyes to shield them from the clouded sun, he saw multiple foot soldiers enter the space. In rows of four, a group of twenty figures marched into the clearing, followed by several wagons.

"That's not good," whispered Ca'lek as he continued to count.

At least a hundred and fifty men had crossed the clearing and waded through the river which, although very cold, was not too deep. Ca'lek and the squad had spent time near the river, trying to catch fish. The fish were a strange variety, long and sleek. Their backs were dark, making them hard to spot against the dark soil of the river bottom, while their bellies were painted with all the colors of broken light. Their fishing had been only mildly successful as the creatures were deviously fast and slippery.

He suddenly realized the clearing lay, at most, a half day's ride from the cliff. *But this army moves at a slower pace than we've been riding*, he calmed himself. *There's no doubt they're marching this way. They're coming up this mountain.*

The valley had no other exit from what he could tell.

Tracking the rows of men across the river, Ca'lek became aware of a distant, rapid rumble. He checked around but saw nothing on the cliff responsible for the sound, when he heard multiple shouts spurring on horses coming from below. Dropping flat to his stomach, he scrambled toward the edge. Peering over, he saw four horsemen suddenly burst into view as they sped their horses up the path toward the clearing atop of the cliff. With the riders' backs still toward him he had not been spotted yet, but they would be on him in a matter of moments as they approached the last turn. With no moment to spare, Ca'lek rolled under the bushes, crawling backward out of sight of the rapidly approaching horsemen.

The thunder of hooves rolled closer as the riders steered their horses onto the plateau and into the clearing. The first rider pulled hard on his reins, bringing his horse to a sliding halt. Ca'lek shook his head in disapproval; the maneuver lacked any regard for the animal's safety, as the loose gravel in the clearing could have easily made the horse lose its footing.

The rider laughed loudly as he turned his horse around to regard the others who brought their own mounts to a halt. Boasting another laugh, the rider's deep voice spoke a language Ca'lek was not familiar with. It sounded thick on the tongue; and although he listened intently, Ca'lek could not understand a single word of it. The rider swung his leg forward over the horse and jumped to the ground, grabbing the reins to lead his horse to a nearby tree. These men were large and muscular, but their movements were quick and nimble, especially the rider who had apparently just won a race. The others slowly followed his example, while laughing and talking back to the winner.

The group had to be a scouting party, most likely riding ahead of the main force to explore the path and terrain. Observing them, Ca'lek took in as much of the details as possible. The race winner had a completely shaved head with a rugged, long beard. His dark armor protected vital organs, much like the Aeterran squad's own leather armor. The protection was tied together with thick leather straps, giving a lot of freedom for movement of arms and legs, but leaving exposed parts on the inside of their arms. The only metal present was in the shoulder plates, blackened in the same color as the leather.

One of the men removed his armor and lifted off his shirt, and Ca'lek noticed black drawings, patterns and symbols across the arms and chest. Some of the men even had the black patterns marked on their face, perhaps to impress their foes. What bothered Ca'lek more, was that they were armed to the teeth. However, they were all close-quarter weapons; short sword on the back, a knife on the side of a belt and another strapped to each of their leather boots. Two of the other riders threw down an axe, but it was clear none of them had spears or bows.

Once the horses were secured, two of the men started making a campfire, talking and laughing amongst themselves. Ca'lek inched further back under the bush. The bushes did not have many leaves, and the only reason they had not spotted him was because they had moved away from the ledge to have a break and perhaps to eat. He tried to move back further, but his feet were already dangling over the cliff edge. Turning himself around slowly, and as quietly as possible, he checked over the edge. It was a long, straight drop—a fall that would surely kill him; but he spotted a narrow ledge just below the overhang he was on. Hearing one of the men suddenly raise his voice, he glanced back at the riders in time to see the rowdy winner of the race get up and start walking toward him. Panic sparked in his brain.

Did they spot me?

It did not seem so, as the soldier said something over his shoulder to the small group around the fire; he was not even looking Ca'lek's way.

A second man jumped up and followed his comrade toward the edge of the cliff. Ca'lek had to move quickly or they would spot him for sure. Looking back over the edge, he moved his body sideways over the ledge, his stomach sliding across the ground. If he could reach the ledge, hopefully, the overhang would shield him from sight.

The two soldiers slowly approached the bushes that shielded him. He watched their feet step ever closer, while leaning on his elbows over the edge. Sweat wet his back as his dangling feet searched for the ledge but found no support. Gripping the ledge with both hands, he lowered himself further until his arms stretched all the way. He looked down into the depths below, it was enough to make his head spin. Quickly focusing on the wall in front of him, he tried to see the ledge he had spotted from the top. The change in viewpoint made it tricky; he found himself looking lower than needed, at first. The ledge was actually at knee height for him now; but more toward the actual rock wall, so his feet had overshot the safe haven. Ca'lek pulled his legs up onto the ledge, and having support for his feet, dared to release one hand to find a fingerhold as a handle to pull himself onto the safety of the ledge.

Just as he released his second hand, he heard the two soldiers move through the bushes and come to a stop right above him. Gravel trickled off the cliff past him. He fought the urge to watch the small stones' trajectory for fear of losing his balance. He pressed himself against the mountain wall, turning his knees sideways as much as possible.

The two soldiers quietly shuffled above his head. Right at the point that Ca'lek wondered what they were doing, a thick, steady stream of yellow liquid dropped off the top of the cliff, as one of the soldiers let out a sigh of relief. A second stream soon followed, as he heard one of the men make an incomprehensible comment that had both men laugh.

Finishing up their business, Ca'lek heard them talking to each other. Glancing up, he saw one of the men's arms stretched across the cliff's edge, pointing toward the area where he had seen the larger group of soldiers cross the river. It seemed they were discussing it, but still he could not understand what was said. Ca'lek doubted the language existed at all on the mid-continent. One of the men turned, followed by the sound of him slapping the other man's shoulder, their voices fading as both started to walk back toward the fire.

Ca'lek released a breath he did not know he held, and carefully relaxed his muscles—his legs trembling in objection. As the voices trailed off, he checked around him for a way back up. Part of him wanted to stay on the ledge, safely hidden. He looked down again. *Well, not that safely.* But it could very well be that the scouts would stay here the entire day as the cliff had an excellent viewpoint of the area… or worse, they might decide to push on. His horse was tied up further down the path, out of sight—and hopefully out of hearing range—but if they continued their way, they would surely realize someone was about and probably reach—and discover—the others at the encampment, before he could warn them about the approaching danger.

No, I must get out of here as soon as possible.

Ca'lek squirmed one foot in front of the other, turning his stomach to the rock wall. He inched forward to his right, where he saw the ledge slope up a little. If he could find a foothold, it should not be too difficult to get up on that ledge again. The challenge would be not making any sound. Up there, he should still be behind the cover of the low bushes and out of sight of the men around the campfire. He could feel the rock below his feet through the suppleness of his leather boots as he tested his footing each time before he put weight on it. Gripping a crack with his left hand, he pulled it a couple of times to make sure it would hold. Slowly, he brought his foot high on a small jutting rock. He carefully moved his weight on it and stretched out his hand to grip the top ledge firmly.

Kicking out his leg, Ca'lek peeked over the edge and saw the four men in deep conversation at the campfire. A few sticks of meat were stuck in the earth next to the flames. It suddenly reminded Ca'lek how hungry he was, and his stomach rumbled so loudly he was afraid the men heard it.

When none looked his way, he pulled himself up to the plateau again, rolling onto his back, away from the edge to catch his breath. His heart throbbed in his throat as he listened intensely to any change in the men's conversation. When it continued as normal, he flipped on his stomach to take a look underneath the bushes. One of the men picked up the smoked meat and tore off a piece with his teeth, washing it down with a big gulp from his drinking bag.

Ca'lek turned right and began to crawl along the cliff's edge, keeping his body as low as possible. Slowly, very slowly, the voices of the men became softer, fainter. He moved like a snail, afraid to make any sound.

After a while, several trees and low bushes gave enough cover for him to dare and move into a crouch. He circled the clearing in a large arc, forcing himself to stop every few steps and to make sure the group had not been alerted to his position. Finally, he snuck far enough away that the terrain completely shielded him from their eyes. He jumped to his feet and ran as fast as he could. Reaching his horse out of breath, the animal looked at him with blank wonder, having no idea of the danger nearby. As he untied the mare, he ducked underneath her large head and let his hand glide along her neck.

"Thank you for being so quiet, Aine," he whispered. "But we have to go. Now."

Turning her around, he continued his soothing words and led the horse away from the clearing. He glanced back. *This should be far enough.* He jumped into the saddle and set off in full gallop.

He was riding against time now.

CHAPTER FOUR

Cleanup

Raylan's eyes widened with wonder. He slowly put down his sword and reached for the egg. He hesitated slightly, not because he was afraid, but because he did not want to break it. With a gentle touch, he slid his hand along the shell. It was warm to the touch, but unlike any egg he had ever held. Its surface was not rough and hard, but slightly supple and smooth like tooled leather. He remained baffled at the size of it; it was so big that if he put both arms around it, he would just about be able to grab his own wrist.

It was difficult to make out by the torchlight, but it looked to be a soft yellow color with patches of light brown, making it look like a spotted egg he knew from some of the smaller bird species back home. The shell waved as his fingers moved across it. Lost in thought, he rested his hand on the shell, wondering what kind of bird would be big enough to lay such an egg.

Suddenly, something bumped against his hand. His heart skipped a beat as he yanked his hand away—an involuntary reflex. A vague shadow moved inside the egg. Raylan jumped to his feet; something was definitely alive in there! He put his torch in the standard in the wall and approached the chest again. Heat from the stones and embers radiated on his cheeks. He put his hand on the shell again wondering if the reaction had been a coincidence. After a few moments, he felt a soft bump against his palm. Changing hands, he touched the opposite side of the egg and waited. Within an instant, he saw the shadow move and surely felt the now more familiar bump against his other hand. A warm feeling resonated in his body and he broke into the grin of a child seeing the wonders of the stars for the first time.

"What are you doing? Do not touch it! You are not allowed to touch it!"

Startled, Raylan jerked his hands away, grabbing his sword as he spun to see who had snuck up on him. A furious Xi'Lao stared back at him, breathing heavily, torch in one hand and a knife in the other.

Raylan lowered his sword, his gaze switched between her eyes and the knife in her hand. In their time traveling together as a group, he had never heard Xi'Lao raise her voice, or seen her filled with such raw emotion for that matter.

'A woman's fury should not be taken lightly', his father always used to say.

"I'm sorry, I meant no harm. I didn't know we weren't allowed to touch this… whatever this is. I wasn't even sure if this was the chest we were looking for; and when I heard a noise from inside, I thought perhaps someone, or something, was locked inside."

He quickly continued when Xi'Lao did not utter a single word.

"Then I saw it move and when I touched it…" Raylan broke off as he basked in that moment once more, "the touch of it felt, well, wonderful!"

Xi'Lao's fingers relaxed around the knife, and Raylan saw a moment of doubt flash behind her eyes.

"What do you mean it moved? You cannot be speaking truth."

The initial tension gone, Raylan relaxed as well. "I'm not lying, come and see for yourself," he said. "I don't know why, but the bottom of the chest is covered with hot stones and embers. I think to keep it warm. And the egg really moved."

As she stepped closer, Xi'Lao held her torch higher to increase the light; the red glow from the chest burnishing the frown she now wore. "But it is not supposed to move, it should not, that is all wrong."

Raylan shrugged, giving her some space. "Well, I definitely felt something move in that egg, it seemed to react to my hands when I touched the shell. It felt very strange though, almost like leather," he said, looking at the chest then back at Xi'Lao. "What? What did I say?"

Xi'Lao stared at him with a puzzled expression on her face. "What do you mean reacted to you?" she asked, blinking slowly.

"Well, it seemed to push against my hand when I put it on the shell. It even followed my hand around, I think." Seeing the mixture of horrified confusion that remained on Xi'Lao's face, Raylan suddenly got nervous he had done something unforgivable. "Why? What's so special about this egg? What kind of egg is it?"

Turning back to the chest, Xi'Lao crouched beside the egg. "This relic is one of our Empire's most sacred treasures. It is an artifact of ancient times, kept under strict supervision by the Shikktu, special monks, led by the monastery's master. Very few people have ever seen it outside of the Inner

Sanctum, where it was kept for hundreds of years. Only the Grand Master and the Shikktu have ever been allowed to touch it. The chance of damaging it was too great a risk. I have only seen it once, during a special ceremony for the royal family. It is believed to be one of the guardians of the Tiankong Empire. Some people even say it is part of a prophecy that is centuries old."

Hearing her voice filled with solemnity, Raylan moved closer again, crouching next to her and close to the chest. She looked at the egg, her eyes no longer filled with threat and anger but soft and shining with admiration.

"You obviously seem happy to have found this egg, and I'm sorry if I was out of place by touching it," Raylan spoke carefully. "I never intended to damage it… or hurt what's inside. See, it doesn't look damaged in any way, so why the troubled look?"

"Last time I saw it, it was completely solid, nothing but a stone fossil. It looks like something is happening to it, something I thought would not be possible. I cannot explain it, but it feels like it is of… of great importance." She spoke softly, as she looked at him. "Raylan, what you see here, is a dragon's egg…"

Raylan stared, mouth half open, then laughed and shook his head. "You're kidding, right? A dragon's egg? Ha! Dragons aren't real. People created them for stories of bravery and conquest. Vicious beasts, many times the size of a man, that would attack villages and burn them to the ground. Long necks and tails, and… and wings that could equal the size of a ship's main sail. You mean *that* kind of dragon?"

Xi'Lao smiled gently at his reaction.

Raylan stared back for a moment, then gave an uncertain laugh. "Oh, I see what you did there! You almost had me, with your serious look and tone. But come on, everyone knows dragons never really existed."

"Oh no, I tell no joke. Dragons are certainly not made up and were once very real. They were powerful creatures, living centuries ago. The history of our Empire is filled with stories and references to these magnificent, intelligent and often wise creatures. Not just fiction but official government papers and reports. It is very much a part of our culture, even today."

Xi'Lao's face lit up with enthusiasm as she warmed to the subject. "From what I have read, dragons can indeed be fierce opponents. However, they were not just savage animals. At some point, men and dragons even lived together in a thriving society. Many of our documents describe a very strong bond that could exist between a dragon and a single person." She frowned. "Unfortunately, the flow of time has made many scrolls unreadable; so, beside the fact dragons once lived among us in the Empire, most information available is segmented."

Raylan did not know what to say anymore. He would never have thought it could be real, but the egg in front of him was bigger than anything he had ever seen. He wondered if it could be true. If dragons really did exist in the past… and if one would hatch from this egg…

He was surprised to find he wished it were. *How amazing would it be to see such a magnificent creature?*

Raylan felt the same glowing warmth from before coming over him again as he imagined all the possibilities. He wondered what such a dragon would be like. What would it look like? Would it have wings and be able to fly? Would it be a smart hunter, or even intelligent? All these questions raced through his mind. It felt so much stronger than just curiosity. It was a… *need*. Then it dawned on him. He would do everything he could to ensure this egg hatched successfully.

"If there's really a dragon in there, I know it's alive. We've got to take care of this egg and make sure it survives long enough to hatch. Do you have any knowledge on hatching dragon eggs?"

Xi'Lao shook her head. "No, like I said many scrolls are too damaged or lost, so specific details of that time are scarce. I have no idea what the needs of such an egg are."

Raylan examined the egg and the chest. "Well, looking at the situation, I think we can assume that it likes the heat. Perhaps even needs it," said Raylan. "Just look at all those embers and hot stones. It's probably the same reason they put the chest in the cave away from the cold and the rain and wind." A thought sparked in the back of his mind. "That's it!"

"What is it?" Xi'Lao asked, her brows knotting together. "Did you figure something out?"

"That half empty wagon with dry wood Gavin and I saw earlier when we were looking for the escaped soldier. It's for the egg. At the time, I figured it was used to keep the soldiers warm during their march through the White North, but now… it was for something much more important. Here look, the metal lining on the lower bottom and these stones seem to be the kind that store the heat inside and radiate it outward for a long time. They wanted to keep the egg warm at all times, even with the extreme low temperatures they've traveled through."

Raylan looked around the chest some more. "Perhaps they did something special with the egg, too, but if they did, it's not clear *what*. It could be that the heat was all that was needed to revitalize it."

Xi'Lao nodded slowly. "If that is true, we need to make sure the egg stays warm enough. We should add some more wood to the embers—it looks like they are cooling down quite a bit."

"Good idea. And I think we better close the lid now, too, so the heat stays inside as much as possible."

They closed the lid of the chest together, flipping the clasp closed. Raylan tested how heavy the chest was by grabbing one of the four handles on the side.

"I can barely get it off the ground. It will be too heavy for the both of us to carry alone. Let's go and get two of the others, so they can help us get it toward the wagons. Ca'lek and Richard could be back at any moment, so we need to prepare everything for our departure."

Walking out of the tunnel together, Raylan could not help but glance back into the darkness of the cave. He did not like leaving the chest unprotected, even for a little while. He shook his head. *Best to hurry then;* and broke out into a run.

Raylan searched for Harwin, Kevhin and Galen by himself as Xi'Lao thought it better if she reported their findings to Gavin immediately. With the stolen item located, even in its unusual state, the written report was quickly completed. Gavin chose to leave out the surprising condition of the egg but added some details on their stone warrior encounter. Then, the pigeon was sent off with the news for the king, which in turn would get forwarded from the king's court to the Tiankong Empire via birds Xi'Lao had left at Aeterra's capital.

After moving the chest to the wagons, Raylan restocked the inside with firewood, much to the amusement of Harwin, Kevhin and Galen.

"Do you just want to keep us warm or are you planning to build a stick shelter every night," teased Kevhin, pointing at the load of dry wood in the wagon.

"Some more warmth wouldn't be a half bad idea in this godforsaken country," added Harwin. "Ain't that right, big guy?"

Galen did not bother to answer. Instead, he threw a look in the chest as Raylan finished up with the wood. "Is that a real egg?" asked the heavy hitter, but Peadar's voice coming from the lookout cut their conversation short.

"Richard's back!"

They quickly joined Gavin and the others as their second-in-command rode up and dismounted. His horse, restless from the sudden inactivity, scraped its right leg along the ground. Shaking her head, Richard gave the mare a small pat on her neck, before handing the reins to Peadar and joining the encircled group.

Kevhin threw him a waterskin, which he opened, taking a big gulp of cold water. "What did you find?" Gavin asked.

Even though his brother had stayed seated against the rock, Raylan was glad to see a morning of rest had done Gavin well. His words seemed more focused, and gathering his thoughts before he spoke appeared to be less difficult. His eyes were clearer too, although he kept them closed from time to time when it seemed he was plagued by a sudden headache.

"Nothing dangerous." The words were ushered between gulps of water. He closed the waterskin and passed it back to the archer. "Thanks," said Richard, before continuing. "I rode out toward the east for half the morning. On the edge of this clearing there was a path that looked only lightly traveled, so I followed it through the needle forest as long as I could. Made some good time and rode a fair distance.

"Most of it wasn't very interesting. The path went straight east. I passed several smaller clearings and it stayed level most of the time. I didn't see any people, settlements or even animals and I was debating whether to turn back or not, when I found myself at the top of a large slope providing some oversight of the land. The path runs down into a valley due east, while the mountain ranges to the north form a natural barrier for as far as I could see. It looked as uninviting as ever."

Richard took a deep breath, giving his horse another pat. "It was difficult to spot anything after that. Several hills and valleys rose and fell, obstructing the view. There might have been chimney smoke coming from the second valley, but it was too far to go and check it out and I didn't wish to risk being discovered. Then there was a second path winding south at the bottom of the slope, so the pathway I was on might fork south at some point. It looked even less used but should still be wide enough for a wagon to travel."

"Good," Gavin nodded. "We should be nearly done here. We recovered the chest and item. The wagon is loaded up with all the food we could find in the camp, and we have six extra horses to pull it in turns. They're not in the best condition; they look underfed. I imagine they had as much trouble as we did, finding food for the horses, but the rotation should make it easier to travel."

Peadar cleared his throat. "Ca'lek is coming back too. He looks to be in a hurry."

The entire squad looked up to the lookout, who had returned to his viewing point to keep an eye on their surroundings.

"*Really* in a hurry."

54

With a groan, Gavin rose to his feet. Raylan stepped forward to help, but Xi'Lao beat him to it. She supported him, as he leaned back against the rock while the others shifted positions as Ca'lek raced into the clearing.

Ca'lek ordered his horse to a hard stop and Raylan grabbed the reins as the scout jumped from the saddle, panting heavily. Stretching his legs, he bent forward, hands on his knees. The horse was foaming at the mouth and was completely covered in sweat.

She must have been running full speed for quite some time.

Aine shook her head and gave a small neigh of restlessness, stepping back and forth as Raylan kept her on a short rein.

"We've got a big problem," Ca'lek panted heavily, while pointing to the west. "There's a large force traveling toward the cliff. At least two hundred and fifty men, most likely more. Spear men, sword fighters, and soldiers on horseback. An advance scouting party nearly cornered me on top of the cliff, but I think I got away undetected."

"Are you sure they didn't follow you?" Raylan asked, doubt tingeing his voice as Peadar clambered back up to act as lookout.

With a worried look, Kevhin handed Ca'lek the waterskin.

Ca'lek took a large gulp of water, then nodded. "I'm sure. I've been checking constantly. They were taking a break for midday eating when I snuck away and got back to Aine. The main force won't reach the cliff for another day or so. They were still at least a few leagues out and they'll be moving slowly with those numbers. They'll probably have to set up camp before they start their climb up the cliff. But that scouting party won't take that long to get here."

"Time to go, then," stated Richard. "How much time do we have, you think?"

"A few more hours at most," said Ca'lek. "Unless we're lucky and they return to the main force for the night. At which point we might have until tomorrow morning before they show up here."

"Any way around them?" Gavin looked at Ca'lek with little hope in his eyes to support his question.

"I wouldn't recommend it. The valley and area on top of the cliff aren't very wide, so risk of discovery would be high; besides, we have no idea how stretched out their forces are. We might end up between their main force and the rearguard."

"This could be the main force returning after their diversion attack on the Empire," Xi'Lao interrupted, lightly touching Gavin's arm.

When she looked at Gavin, Raylan could not help but notice Xi'Lao's expression softened. Her touch lingered on Gavin's arm—ever so briefly.

Raylan smiled to himself, perhaps their time on the road together had drawn her closer to Gavin, or maybe it was because he got hurt that morning. Though Raylan doubted if his brother had noticed it, too.

She looked back to the group to include everyone. "Perhaps last night we had the luck of facing only part of the temple attack force. We just assumed most of them died traveling through the harsh region of the White North, but it could just as well be that they split off a smaller group to make haste and secure the sacred item as fast as possible. If that is the case, those soldiers coming up the cliff are only part of the problem we might have to face while traveling back to Aeterra."

"There's no way we can we take on that many soldiers," Harwin added, with a low grumble. "And they might have more of those stone things as well. I don't fancy taking on one of those again. Without my shield, it would've broken me in half with that kick."

"I agree," said Gavin.

He lay his head back against the rock and closed his eyes for a moment.

Raylan frowned. *Another headache?*

It grew darker as the sun disappeared behind a steady layer of gray clouds floating in from the west. Raylan scrutinized the sky. The rain would soon come down again.

"With the wagon, we can't travel very fast," said Gavin, his eyes still closed. "Which means there's little hope we can outrun them, if we are discovered; so, we must stay hidden for as long as possible. We'll go further east and then turn south, away from those valleys Richard mentioned. That way, perhaps we can stay in front of the main force long enough to disappear into the wilderness."

"That makes sense," Richard said. "We're less likely to be discovered in a less confined region."

Raylan preferred to take the shortest road home, but now it was more important to protect the chest and its valuable content than to return to the comfort of civilization as soon as possible. Still, something bothered him.

"What about the encampment?" he said, gesturing around. "Once this is discovered, they'll know something is wrong and send out scouting parties to hunt us down. They have the advantage, with knowledge of the terrain and sheer numbers. It probably won't take them long to find us. I'd prefer we don't get chased as we try and find our way home."

Gavin opened his mouth to respond, but drew in a sharp breath instead and put his hands to the side of his head as he clenched his teeth. Thinking of all these variables likely did not help his headache.

56

Xi'Lao briefly observed their leader, before stepping in. "I agree with you," she said, looking at Raylan. "But what do you suggest we do?"

Raylan took a moment to gather his thoughts before putting forward the plan he felt forming in his head. "Well, since we'll only need one wagon to transport the chest and provisions, we can use the other two wagons to load up the bodies and equipment we don't take. We should check around to see if there's a place to hide everything."

He craned his neck and took a quick look around. "The north is going up the mountain side fairly quickly and the west is no option with those soldiers on their way here. Given the path continues to the east, that way is not very wise to hide something. Which leaves the south. It will probably be the least likely area the enemy force will travel through. If we can clear all the bodies and equipment, get rid of the wagon wreckage and statue, we should be able to leave these surroundings in a state that gives the impression that they traveled on as normal. We can leave some of the old campfires sitting out and put some torches ready at the entrance of the cave."

"We should also throw fresh dirt over the spots with a lot of blood," offered Rohan.

"And hope the rain will wash away the rest before the soldiers arrive," added Kevhin.

Raylan gave a thankful nod at the offered support.

"What about the scout unit I encountered?" asked Ca'lek.

"Like you said, we might get lucky and not see them at all," said Richard nodding to his commander. "But we can put Rohan on watch here in the encampment, while Kevhin takes up position near the forest exit. If we let them enter the rock formation, we can surprise them and take them out before they find a way to retreat. If one or two do get away, Kevhin can take them out while they retreat toward the cliff area to warn their forces."

Gavin let out a slow breath. "I don't look forward to cleaning this place up, but under the circumstances, I believe it's a decent plan. If we can pull it off, it will give us a much-needed head start to find another way home." He looked at each man in turn. "But taking out the scouting unit will raise suspicion, for sure, so we better be quick about this and hope we'll be long gone before any of them get here."

Raylan stood pondering next to the motionless stone giant. Everyone was helping; even Stephen and Gavin hobbled around the encampment. The scout gritted his teeth with every step, and Gavin shuffled from boulder to boulder for support, but neither could be convinced to sit this one out. They focused on gathering small things to be loaded on the wagons, leaving the heavy lifting to the rest of their group.

As suggested, Ca'lek had quickly scouted the area south and returned with some positive news; the wagons would have no problem passing through the forest, and better yet he had discovered a chasm deep enough to be useful. They had already dumped one wagon load into it and another was currently being filled for a second run.

For now, Raylan stood next to Galen, pondering the statue. Galen had brought his hammer so they could break it up into smaller pieces and move them with the wagon. Taking a moment to look at the stone terror, Raylan noticed the amount of detail the giant statue received during its transformation. It made him pause and take a good look at this fearful and unknown opponent.

When he first saw it in the back of the wagon, it was no more than a rugged, squarely-formed man with big blocks for feet and hands, barely containing any definition at all. Looking at the fallen foe now, he noticed it looked remarkably human. There were detailed toes and fingers; he could even see cracks resembling veins running along the stone's surface, here and there. Its chest, arms and legs had all formed into the shape of stone muscles, but the surface itself was very rough. It was as if the statue was cut out of the side of a mountain—no polishing or caretaking, no smoothing by water. Its neck ended in a crumbled stump where Galen had swung his war hammer, time and again. The complete body looked immensely heavy.

Looking at Galen, Raylan stepped forward.

"Might as well start with the arms and work our way down," suggested Galen from behind him. "That chest is going to be the troublesome part to carry, I bet."

"Yeah, let me grab an arm so you can break it at the elbow," said Raylan, as he knelt next to the stone body.

He grabbed one of the arms, but as soon as he touched it, his fingers went straight through the stone skin and giant's body suddenly crumbled into dust.

"What the—" Raylan scrambled back, wiping his hand clean on his pants. Within moments, nothing but a fine black dust remained, some of it already blowing away in the gentle breeze.

Raylan looked up in surprise at Galen, and opened his mouth but halted, uncertain what to say. Then he gave a small shrug. "Saves us a lot of trouble moving it around," he said, the remark hanging between a question and a statement.

"Fine by me," said Galen, smiling. "I wonder why it suddenly fell apart like that."

"I don't know," said Raylan. "Maybe it's got something to do with those windblasts, or blue light? Perhaps it destroyed the stone's strength from within. How else would it crumble like that?"

"Or… my hits did more damage than we thought," said Galen, as he walked toward the others, holding his hammer high above his head in triumph.

Though Raylan could not see his face, he was certain their heavy hitter was still grinning from ear to ear.

He was about to follow, when he heard Xi'Lao call out in disbelief.

"But—that cannot be!"

He quickly made his way to her. There stood a perplexed Rohan and Gavin, watching how Xi'Lao feverishly flipped through a small book. Mumbling to herself.

"What's going on?" said Raylan, but all he got were two confused looks.

"I found this book in one of the wagons," began Rohan. "It looked important, so I brought it to Gavin to see what it said. But as soon as she saw it," he motioned to Xi'Lao, "she yanked it from my hands."

"Xi'Lao? Are you all right?" asked Gavin, respectfully. "Can you read what it says?"

Bewildered, the Tiankonese woman looked up from the pages, her face whiter than usual. "This cannot be," she said again. "This is all wrong."

She showed them the scribbles in the book. Two different sets of characters, each filling an entire page. She flipped through it, dozens of pages were filled with texts, drawings and diagrams. "This is *my* language," she continued. "The handwriting is horrible, but this is unmistakably Tiankonese. Those other words I do not recognize. They are not your Terran language, or any other written words I know, but I think they say the same things. Look here, and here." She pointed to the page. "The same numbers return a few times on both sides."

"And that is bad… how?" said Rohan, still wearing a confused expression.

Raylan threw a quick look at the text but could not make heads or tails of any of it.

"It talks about army numbers. The number of fighters the Empire has in each province. How many monks there were in the monastery…"

Her words were met with silence.

"Do you not see?" she said, a fierceness now owning her voice. "It must be Kovian—the old language of this region. Someone informed this dark army about the strength and weaknesses of our nation. Someone has betrayed the Empire."

"That's all of it," said Raylan, as a few of them returned from dumping the wagons in the chasm.

"Great. Let's prep the horses and get out of here," replied Gavin. "Raylan, can you do one last sweep?"

With a nod, Raylan took a quick jog around the campsite and the outlying area but saw nothing they had forgotten. The light was already fading when he returned to the group and found Ca'lek on his knees drawing a pattern in the sand. The scout's face had smudges of dirt mixed with blood across his forehead and cheeks.

"What are you doing?" asked Raylan.

"Old hunting custom. When blood ran to ground, my father would always do this tribal ritual to show thanks for a successful hunt and to guide what had stopped living back to the earth to be born again," explained Ca'lek without looking up.

The scout put his closed fists to his forehead and brought his head down to the pattern on the ground. He muttered a few soft words, which Raylan could not fully hear, before getting up and erasing the pattern with his feet. "All done."

"Great," said Richard. "Peadar, call back Kevhin. It's time to go."

Kevhin joined them shortly after Peadar waved him back from his position near the edge of the clearing. "No sign of them yet," he reported to Gavin, who just finished overseeing the loading of the wagon.

The chest and its precious cargo were firmly secured within. Restocked with wood for a slow burn, it would likely keep a high temperature for most of the night.

Gavin hauled himself onto the driver's bench of the wagon next to Harwin, who handled the reins. Stephen was in the back with the chest, the remains of Regis, and the rest of the provisions. As the rest of the squad mounted their horses and turned toward the east, Raylan checked and adjusted the halter of his mount one last time. The mare shook her head and let out a snort.

He stroked the small patch of white fur on her forehead that looked like a crescent moon. "Don't worry, Luna. We'll get out of here now."

Their small group headed out.

Ca'lek took the lead so he could scout ahead when needed. Galen and Peadar followed, each leading an extra horse. The wagon was next, after which Xi'Lao, Kevhin and Rohan took their places, with another four horses trailing behind.

Raylan and Richard would ride rearguard.

As Raylan mounted his horse, Richard guided his steed around and patiently waited as Raylan shifted in his saddle to get comfortable.

"Ready," said Raylan, and they nudged their horses into a walk. "Where did you get those," Raylan asked as he spotted two unfamiliar battle axes on Richard's belt.

Richard freed one and flipped it around. It looked well made, with a sharp, pointed end under the handle. "Not bad, right? They're perfectly balanced for either slashing or throwing. It seemed a waste to throw them away, so I thought I would familiarize myself with them over the next few days." Richard looked up to the sky and took a deep breath. "Something tells me we're going to need all the weapons we can find."

A soft patter of rain started up again.

"Looks like the gods are in favor of us," said Richard with a wry smile. "The rain will wash away our tracks, so for once, I don't mind it as much."

Although Raylan did not have much belief in the gods, he could do nothing but agree. Swaying gently in his saddle, he looked back to the rock formation and beyond, but there was still no sign of the enemy horsemen. As they left the clearing and rode off into the forests again, he silently hoped their luck would hold.

CHAPTER FIVE

Darkness

Koltar Wayler's hastened steps echoed through the empty corridors. The black stone on the floors and walls gave a cold feel to the palace that no fire could warm. Hurrying up the stairs in one of the outer towers, he saw glimpses of the palace exterior through the tall and narrow windows.

He had no time to be impressed by the view; besides, he had seen it a thousand times. The long sleek towers loomed above the different parts of the palace, their sharp rounded roofs giving them the impression of thorns reaching for the sky. It still baffled him how they managed to build such a monstrous structure in such a short time—less than a lifetime ago— though many muttered darkly that the foundation was built on the bodies of those who perished during its construction. Yet, it made little sense, because he knew for a fact there were no bones in or under these walls. Furthermore, for a complex that was less than half a century old, it felt as though it had been there for a thousand years. He had always found it a strange feeling to shake.

The palace was built into the cliffside, the immense structure constructed from very stone surrounding it. Part of the dark mountain slope loomed above, like the wave of stone was about to swallow the dozens of towers that lay at their base.

Partly hidden from view on the north-facing side of the palace, shielded by the other buildings, was a large dome structure—an area accessible to a select few. The dark palace no longer held many secrets for him. From the deepest, darkest dungeon passages to the highest tower steps, he had walked them all… hundreds of times. But even as one of the five High Generals, he had only approached the Dark Vault on a few occasions. His lordship did not tolerate ordinary people in this area, and it was the subject of a myriad of rumors that constantly circulated the palace.

A few years ago, when he was engrossed in a conversation with his lordship, the man had abruptly broken off their talk and dismissed him. He was promptly abandoned in the great hallway that led to the Dark Vault. Seeing his lordship stride toward the main doors, Koltar had soon become aware of the staring eyes around him.

The north side of the palace that housed the vault had its own special army of guards—the 'Darkened'. A Darkened was a foul and scarred soldier. Heavily brainwashed, these were not good men; each of them was stripped of emotion and hardened expert fighters... but most of all, they were extremely disciplined. Koltar had seen them train; they were savage. They were considered the tainted elite, the kind of people you avoid at all costs. Common soldiers and civilians alike dared not stand in the way when one walked the halls. A Darkened could strike down anyone without question. There would be no repercussions. They were not subject to any of the laws but the Stone King's will. They answered directly to his lordship and did his bidding without question, doubt, or remorse.

Disgruntled, Koltar felt the hairs in his neck rise from the memory of the Dark Vault hallway.

The common folk had another name for the guards: The Silent Shadows. While the Darkened were usually not the smallest of men, they could move with surprising speed and with very little sound. But the silent part came from the fact each member had his tongue removed when taking on the position. This ensured none could speak of what they saw or heard. And their discipline was constantly tested, for Koltar knew that any Darkened caught looking into the vault—however brief a glance—would have their eyes burnt out as punishment.

Koltar knew many did not consider him a pleasant man either; he took pride in his ruthless reputation. He easily held his own in a fight and commanded with an iron fist. He was short-tempered which, combined with his fighting skill, made him an extremely dangerous man. But that day near the vault, he had turned to escape the hollow stares of the Darkened. It was not a moment he was proud of.

While walking away, he had heard a low rumbling as his lordship had entered the vault. The sound had resonated in his stomach, trundling like some giant wheeled mechanism.

Wheels busy crushing things, he thought as he turned another corner.

He passed a stairway that led all the way down toward the dungeons. The echoes of muffled screams snaked their way through the narrow stairs and dark hallways. It brought a smile to his face.

Whenever he felt restless, he enjoyed taking on the role of torturer. Not many were cut out for it, but it brought a special kind of calmness to lead someone to the edge of madness with nothing more than physical pain. It was an icy rage he felt when working on prisoners—an internal storm with perfect outer control.

Usually, he pictured his own father sitting in the chair—the abusive thug. It had gone on for years, his mother too much of a coward to stand up to the man, and far too much of a coward to ever consider leaving him. Eventually, Koltar had developed the physical strength to fight back. Despising his mother's weakness, he had vowed to never again give in to fear. Instead, he would instill it in those around him.

He spat on the floor. He often regretted killing his father. Not so much because the man was dead, but because the bastard had not suffered. Koltar had learned from it, taking his time with the prisoners, making sure none expired before he was certain all the information was extracted—and his inner demon stilled.

Some of the prisoners had not seen daylight for years. In the unlikely event one was released, they were often frail, skittish shells of their former selves, unfit to function in the outside world. Freedom was a cruel joke and those released often dove off the drawbridge as soon as they were set free.

Jogging up a small spiral stair, Koltar wondered why his lordship had summoned him. If he was requested in person, it must be of some importance. Perhaps it was to do with High General Setra's return that morning. Koltar was aware of Corza Setra's mission, although the details were few.

His fellow general had left with a sizable force, marching straight along the border of the White North. Koltar had been furious at the time; many of his platoon's experienced fighters had been reassigned to join the march, leaving him to train new recruits to fill his dwindling ranks. It had taken months to get back to a sufficient level of defensive power, leaving their territory weak and vulnerable to intruders.

"Please lord, have mercy. We didn't intend to deceive you. We just love her so much. We… we couldn't let her go…"

Koltar finally arrived at the auditorium. A sniffling woman sat pleading on the floor. A man—presumably her husband—was next to her, holding her shoulders, hugging her, trying to offer comfort.

The couple were huddled before the steps that led to the throne. The seat was made from the same black cold stone as the palace, its polished surface glittering in the light of the many torches and candles in the room. Atop the throne sat his lordship in a black cloak. The black fabric seemed to flow like liquid, constantly in motion. Koltar knew it was made of the world's finest velvet. The inside bled crimson, darkened somewhat by the surrounding black.

Koltar silently took his place along the wall, briefly meeting his lordship's eyes. The man sat relaxed, one leg crossed flat over the other, looking bored at the scene taking place before him. His right hand, completely covered by the cloak, tapped softly on the throne's armrest; his head supported by his other. Perhaps it was all the black within the auditorium, but Koltar thought the man's skin looked unhealthier than usual; nearly ash-gray.

Nobody knew exactly how many years the Stone King had been around, but whenever Koltar's father had tried to beat him to a pulp, the man would always spout some nonsense: "Your grandfather, now there was a hard man. Ruthless, successful and a damn good fighter in the Stone King's army. I'm just trying to keep up the family tradition!"

Koltar nearly spat on the floor again from the memory but stopped himself just in time.

If that were true, the Stone King had to be almost a hundred years in age. However, the man sitting on that throne looked much younger. At a guess, Koltar would put him just past his fortieth year; his long face only just beginning to show lines around his eyes and mouth. They accentuated his lordship's jaw, which ended in a sharp chin. Together with the hawk-like nose, it gave their ruler a stern look.

The king's hair had not abandoned him yet. Long and straight, it was completely white—in great contrast against all the black. Cut just above the shoulders, it was held in check by a simple circlet for a crown. The polished iron ring was heavily engraved with all kinds of etchings and held a single black gemstone.

"Please lord, I shouldn't have let her convince me to try and hide. We didn't know what we were doing. As soon as she was born, she put us under her love spell," the man whimpered.

From the simple clothes they wore, it was obvious the man and woman were peasants. Newcomers to the city, seeking a better life, wealth, away from the dangers of the wilderness settlements. The man looked desperate, his eyes darting between the Stone King and the Darkened standing nearby. The silent soldier had a bundle in his hands; it moved slightly. Small sounds eking from it. As far as Koltar could see, it appeared to be a baby, no more than a week old.

"Please lord, spare our daughter. Don't take her from us. We'll have more children for you!"

The king's mouth twisted. "You know the law! All firstborns are to be delivered to the palace on the day of birth! Disobeying is a serious offense!" His head turned sharply as he looked over his left shoulder. "I know they need to be punished!" he said to the empty space beside him, "you don't have to remind me every damn moment."

He moved his gaze back to the couple. Both the man and woman had shrunk from the sharp tone and icy stare that followed. The infant let out a scream. Koltar saw the Darkened stare down, annoyed.

"We try to make it easy for people," the king continued, "providing midwives that make sure the child is *taken* right away, so you do not need to *give* your child away. It prevents the love spell from taking a hold of you. So, tell me, why did you not send for your midwife?"

"We did, milord! But she was out on an errand and the baby came too fast. I told my wife we had to give her up, but she wouldn't hear of it. She wanted to get away, leave the city. There was no reasoning with her. So what is a man to do but protect his family?"

The man was visibly torn between wanting to save his wife and protecting his child. Tears ran pathetically down his cheeks while he frantically clutched his chest to demonstrate his heartache. "Milord, I beg you, spare my daughter. I'll do anything. I—I'll work the mines for you. Just reunite the child with her mother. She'll die from a broken heart if you take away our daughter now!"

The king's face darkened. "You expect mercy after you knowingly broke the firstborn law? Hiding your wife and child! Pretending you were more special than your neighbors! Believing you have a right to run away and live free of the consequences of your actions!"

The woman started sobbing heavily, while her husband tried his best to comfort her.

"No, my dear man," said the king, with a voice as cold as ice, "you will be held responsible for your actions. Take the child away and give it to the priest."

"No! Please, no!" The woman screamed as she tried to scramble to her feet to reach her child. Her husband held her back with all his strength lest the Darkened cut her down without a second thought.

The woman's wail fell on deaf ears; Koltar did not care. Everyone knew the firstborn law. Introduced nearly a decade ago, it was strictly enforced. With no children of his own—that he knew of—he cared little about this decree.

Few really knew what happened to those babies, but no parent had ever seen their first child again. This couple was lucky they had not been killed on the spot when discovered. Perhaps the midwife intervened. A Darkened would not have bothered to leave them alive. Perhaps that would have been more merciful.

Again, the Stone King turned his head to the left. Koltar had grown somewhat accustomed to it, but there remained something disturbing about the scene of his lordship talking to someone only he appeared to see and hear. Over the years, Koltar had learned it best not to pay it too much attention—or to ask questions.

"What do you suggest we do with them?" the Stone King asked over his shoulder. A moment of silence followed before he grinned. "I like that!" For the second time, his gaze returned to the couple. "I agree that an example is in order."

The king's eyes seemed to reflect the darkness of the palace. Not even the stare of a timber wolf would be considered so lacking in compassion. "Guards! Take them away. Break the woman's feet, so she won't be able to run away anymore. For the husband, cut off one ear so he will be less inclined to listen to his wife's treacherous ideas."

"No, please my lordship! Have mercy!" screamed the man, eyes wide as he stared in disbelief toward the throne.

The woman shivered and sobbed, grieving too much to even take notice. She looked up in shock as the Stone King brought down his covered fist on the armrest of his throne. A deep rumble echoed through the hall.

"Silence!" his voice thundered. "You are hereby ordered to have at least two more children. Both will be handed over to the priests. If you are not capable of fulfilling the task before the turn of the seasons, you will be sent to the mines and more virile contributors will be provided. I am certain the guards would appreciate it. Now disappear from my sight before I change my mind and decide your lives have lost their value."

As the man and woman were dragged away by guards, the man kicked, screamed and begged, while the woman could do nothing more than whimper as tears streamed down her face.

High General Setra entered the auditorium as the couple was dragged out but he, too, gave them little attention. It was nothing he had not seen before. Walking up to Koltar, Corza greeted him stiffly. "High General Wayler."

"High General Setra," Koltar returned, with the smallest of nods.

He had no love, or even friendliness, for his fellow general. Koltar considered the man a weasel and a coward. Slimy, sneaky, treacherous. Corza came from a very different background. Born into wealth, Koltar expected Corza never wanted for anything. The Setra family belonged to the self-proclaimed elite of the city. A tight group of people who were more than happy to use their power to assist the Stone King with his plans. He bet the man's parents were always ready to help their son, even when his sadistic side got him into trouble at one of the whorehouses.

Corza had developed a preference for the newer, inexperienced brothel girls in his adolescent years. Any girl unlucky enough to be chosen would never leave such a meeting unscathed, or on occasion, never leave at all.

Whorehouses that complained about the loss of income were easily bought off. And if that was not enough, an unexpected accident usually solved those problems that coin could not. Koltar had heard the man boast once that whores must be very clumsy with fire, as three whorehouses he attended burned to the ground the two summers past.

It was said Corza was a great battle tactician, but he used none of the tactics Koltar could appreciate. Koltar was more direct, relying on brute force. He felt great discontent toward those using an indirect approach; Corza would rather use poison and deceit instead of a properly challenged duel.

As both men approached the Stone King, his lordship rose with menacing grace and descended to meet them at the bottom of the steps. Koltar glanced at Corza and found the man looked to be a lesser version of the one that left those many months ago with thousands of their soldiers on a classified mission.

Something big was going on, but his lordship tenaciously kept information on a strictly need-to-know basis. This way, no one knew the full plan except for the Stone King himself.

The march must have been rough. Koltar glanced once more at the general. If Corza was an example, it had clearly taken its toll on the men.

Everyone knew once the fat and energy reserves were depleted, the body started to burn its own muscles to keep warm and to provide energy. Corza was a living example. The general looked tired, almost frail despite his tall posture. Taller than Koltar, this made him an interesting sparring partner on those rare occasions the two had practiced their sword skills.

He looks like a man ready to topple over from the smallest gust of wind. Koltar allowed a mocking smile. *His armor doesn't even seem to fit right anymore.*

Both men came to a halt just short of the steps, saluting their king with their hands on their hearts and bowing their heads in respect.

"Lord Rictor," Koltar said to the man coming down the steps. "You wanted to see us?"

"Gentlemen, thank you for coming. Please, walk with me."

The Stone King strode off and led them to a balcony. Stretching an arm to gesture to the city below, he asked, "What do you see?"

Koltar glanced at Corza, wondering if the man had any idea what this was about; but his fellow general remained silent, his gaze locked straight ahead. So Koltar turned his eyes toward the gray city below. The houses went on for miles, until the far end hit the riverside. The buildings were packed tightly together along main streets and narrow back alleys that ran between the cramped blocks. It lacked color as much as it lacked happiness.

People were drawn with the promise of wealth, a chance to rise above their ranks if they served the Stone King properly. Others were grabbed by the Stone King's patrols and forced into labor. The result was that life in the city was hard and often unequal, with much poverty and exploitation.

Once a citizen, one could not easily leave without permission. And despite everything, some still sought the safety of the city. The wilderness on the Dark Continent held many mortal dangers: savage tribes; bandits; forest spirits; long lasting winters and many different predators. One could easily lose their life to a bear, a mountain cat or cunning and cruel wolf packs. And there were some creatures that only belonged in your nightmares.

"I see the city, my lord… and the wilderness beyond," Koltar finally said, uncertain of what else to say.

"Exactly. *My* city, *my* wilderness, *my* world," said Lord Rictor, in a calm voice that held a razor-sharp edge. His head snapped around again. "Yes, yes, your world, too, of course! I have a lot to thank you for, now stop interrupting," Lord Rictor said curtly.

The glazed look in his eyes went away as he turned back to them. "All of this, as far as we can see—and even beyond—is mine. I decide what happens, how people live their lives, what is built, what is destroyed. And when I decide something, I expect this decision to be carried out… successfully. No questions asked. No failures. Now commoners… commoners are thoughtless. They mess up. They need to be motivated, shown the correct way… time and time… again. One can only hope for improvement, but I expect better from my soldiers. Even more so from those that lead them."

Koltar heard Corza swallow next to him. On his periphery, Koltar saw a small pearl of sweat run down the side of Corza's head. Lord Rictor regarded them both, suddenly breaking into fury.

"Decades of preparations, infiltrations, kidnappings, information gathering, building a city and its supporting structures… an army! I bided my time, took it slow, made sure the western lands stayed in the dark and knew nothing of this magnificent realm *I* have built!"

Those last words were spat out, his voice spilling over with tempered rage. He moved so close to Corza's face their foreheads nearly touched. His lordship stretched his neck and back, like a looming shadow stretched across the floor.

High General Setra, now visibly unnerved, did not dare move. Koltar was still in the dark as to what could have inspired their ruler's ire, but he figured the mission had not gone as planned.

"And what do I get in return with one of the most crucial parts of the plan? From one of my most experienced generals? *Failure!*" the Stone King screamed in Corza's face.

Corza broke into a stammer. "Your lordship, please, I-I don't know what went wrong. It should have arrived here days ago."

Lord Rictor's right hand shot up from under his cloak. It grasped the High General's neck and locked it in a crushing grip.

Sometimes, Koltar briefly forgot why Lord Rictor was named the Stone King. It was not his official title. There was no royal heritage or bloodline, but rather a name bestowed by the people out of fear.

What shot out from under that velvet cape, was a lower arm and fist completely made of stone—large, rough and unpolished but as black as the mountain the dark palace was built against. It moved as if it was a living part of Lord Rictor's body, now squeezing tightly around High General Setra's neck.

Koltar almost felt sorry for the man. He had seen that hand smash corners off marbled tables in a rage.

Corza grasped the stone arm with both his hands, wheezing in his breaths. "My lord, I swear. The attack went precisely as planned. We made excellent time moving through the White North… losing only an acceptable number of soldiers… to the extreme cold. The bulk of the force moved south, attacking one of the more… inhabited areas along the coast, drawing the attention of the Tiankonese forces. The monastery fell… within an instant, no match for the… sheer power of our specialized troops."

His voice sounded hoarse; the crushing fingers around his neck making it difficult to speak.

The Stone King closed his fist a fraction more and Corza fell to his knees, gasping for air. Koltar smiled, seeing this man, this *weasel*, squeal like one by the hand of his lordship. But he kept the smile quick; he had no intention of drawing the Stone King's ire.

"Go on," commanded Lord Rictor, releasing his grip slightly.

"We found it, my lord! It was there! We took it and started the special care immediately, as you instructed. We burned the monastery as we pulled out, marching back double time and getting as much distance between us and the Empire before our true intentions were discovered."

Lord Rictor dragged Corza to his feet again and pushed him against the balcony's handrail until the general was leaning dangerously over the abyss.

"Cut to it, Setra, I am losing my patience. So, tell me, where is it now? Why has it not arrived at the palace yet?"

"I don't know, my lord!" squealed Corza as he squirmed in the merciless stone grip. "I sent out a vanguard as soon as we were on familiar territory. I knew how eager my lord was to get the item in his possession, so I wanted to get it safely within city borders as soon possible. We had no indication we were being followed by the enemy, so I sent out a group of our most rested fighters. We even had scouts traveling between the main force and the advance party, for most days."

Corza struggled to draw in fresh air. "I only learned they hadn't made it to the city when we were greeted by a fresh supply convoy, seeking us out on the road. They should've encountered them along the way but didn't. After that, we rushed here to find out what was going on."

Lord Rictor paused, not releasing his grip. Koltar expected this was not new information. The Stone King always seemed suspiciously well informed. He no doubt made sure plenty of people provided him information—all independently and all unknowingly to the other informants. That was what Koltar would do.

Corza's eyes darted back and forth; his lord's silence was probably worse than the furious questions. If Corza did not choose his answers carefully, Koltar expected his fellow general might find himself in need of flying lessons very soon.

"My lord, I swear I don't know what happened. It's High General Wayler's duty to keep our territory secure. We thought we were safe. The unit consisted of the healthiest fighters we had on the march. They were good warriors and shouldn't have been an easy prey for attack. They even had a ghol'm and a clean scroll with them, just in case they ran into problems. We should've seen signs of fighting, if anything happened."

Hearing such a blatant attempt to put the blame on him, Koltar bit his tongue in rage. But the Stone King ignored the remark and inched forward while Corza frantically clawed at the balcony's handrail, trying to find a hold.

"Let me fix this, my lord! I-I know!" he stammered. "It must have been the commander. He must have betrayed us. Y-yes! I thought he was acting suspicious of late. I'm sure of it! Please, my lord, I won't rest until I find out what happened. I'll track them down and bring it back! They can't have gone far with the wagon needed to move the item."

Lord Rictor stopped for a moment, glanced over his shoulder toward Koltar, who had no intention of speaking his preference on the current situation. He did not care what happened to this back-stabbing weasel.

After a pause, which likely seemed like an eternity for those dangling above the abyss, the Stone King spun and threw Corza against the balcony's wall, where the general slumped to the ground, gasping for air. His face was wet from his sweat and his nails were bleeding from scratching the stone handrail, while the marks of Lord Rictor's fingers showed deathly white against his otherwise livid throat. Rubbing his sore neck, Corza looked up with wide eyes.

The Stone King paid him no attention and directed his attention toward Koltar. "I want the northern ocean path closed off at once. Nothing leaves these lands without my permission. You will lead a search party. Find out what happened, and keep an eye on this disappointment," he said, pointing to Corza. "Send ravens to warn the outposts and settlements of the situation, so they can send out scouting units. Then prepare a small force of experienced men. Travel fast and find out where my item is."

Lord Rictor threw a vile look at Corza. "Two of the Darkened will join your group and make sure High General Corza stays true to his word."

"If I may ask, my lord, what will we be looking for?" said Koltar.

"A weapon that will ensure our victory," Lord Rictor replied briskly.

Striding off, he paused next to Corza. "As for you… if it was not so much trouble to replace you during this phase of my plan, you would be at the bottom of that drop. Do *not* fail me again."

* * *

Corza rubbed his neck. Swallowing was painful, but at least breathing was getting a little easier again. He walked the dark halls of the palace. Night was already falling. Koltar had ordered the provisions to be collected, which would take a bit of time, but they would leave at first light.

His mind still raced over the details and all the missing pieces. He slammed open a door which led to a small, dark staircase. *It was not supposed to go like this!*

That idiot Sven must have screwed things up. The commander was *supposed* to be waiting at the agreed warehouse with the chest. They were *supposed* to have taken a couple of slaves and dressed them up as soldiers, making it look like an attack. The item was *supposed* to have been 'lost', taken by bandits; when in reality, it was *supposed* to be safely stored for Corza to use.

He had come up with the idea as soon as he laid eyes on the egg in the temple. With all the decorations, he knew what kind of egg it was, and he wanted it for himself.

Lord Rictor would never have known. Not until it was too late, and he was in control of the dragon. Sure, Corza had expected the loss of temper, but the encounter on the balcony had cut it quite close. For a moment, he thought he would end up at the bottom of the palace cliff.

It must have been a bad day for his lordship.

Corza ground his teeth. When he arrived at the city, he had rushed to the agreed location at the first opportunity he got. But Sven wasn't there—no commander, no chest and no damned dragon's egg.

He nearly foamed at the mouth in fury. Sven would not dare betray him; besides, he did not have the brains to pull it off. This meant something really had gone wrong. If the party was indeed missing without a trace, the egg could be anywhere.

Curses!

He had to find out what happened to that dragon's egg and retrieve it as soon as possible. According to Lord Rictor's instructions, the egg should be close to hatching—perhaps within the month.

Walking down the narrow stairs, Corza turned a few corners and left the palace grounds through a small tunnel that went straight under the high palace walls and into the mountain. The tunnel exited into a natural cave system that had been further dug out for resources.

Standing on top of a large stone staircase, Corza regarded all the workers, running around like ants. Slabs of rock were transported out of the tunnels and brought to the workstations. The network of tunnels was constantly expanding as they searched for high-quality rock formations that could be excavated. The sound of shouting men and dozens of sculptors' hammers and chisels echoed through the different galleries.

Mining underground was already dangerous enough, but the black stone from this mountain was one of the toughest and hardest in the world. It was backbreaking work for the slaves involved, but Corza cared more for the constant resupply of fresh tools that dulled quickly while carving out the large pieces. Working on huge, single-cut blocks, sculptors went through multiple chisels a day; although, Corza hoped the newly improved gem-crafted chisels held up a little better.

Descending the stairs, Corza looked over the hundreds of statues, standing row by row, ready to be transported. Thousands of ghol'ms had already been relocated on regular transports.

These fierce stone warriors had been quite the discovery, their existence made possible by the sacrificial scrolls the Stone King brought forth a decade ago. No one knew how his lordship had acquired the knowledge to make these scrolls, and no one dared ask; but they had been storing the scrolls for a long time.

Halfway down the stairs, Corza passed a dark passage. At the end, the soft light of candles lit a small chamber. He heard the cry of an infant carry from it. Most likely, it was the one he passed in the hallway on his way to the auditorium, but frankly it could be any of the daily arrivals from the city. As he passed, he saw a priest holding the small bundle in his hands, while another just grabbed several scrolls. Corza continued on his way, making sure to steer clear of the Darkened guarding the passage. He had enough troubles. The cry slowly faded behind him until the only sounds were of chisels hitting stone.

The scrolls and ghol'ms were kept strictly separate now, and always under heavy guard. An expensive lesson taught by a slave revolt years ago, when several of the labor force had learned too much about the process. They had obtained a scroll, killing a guard for it, then managed to activate a ghol'm and use it to free themselves from their chains.

In the chaos that followed; the scum activated another two ghol'ms and sent them on a rampage. It had turned into a bloodbath. In the aftermath, tracking parties had attempted to catch the runners but only with moderate success. The two ghol'ms had provided them adequate cover.

Corza had been furious, executing half a dozen guards and changing the system to prevent similar uprisings from ever happening again. Now the scrolls and ghol'ms were transported separately—in small batches and under heavy guard. So far, they had not experienced any more problems.

Today, however, he did not come to check on the manufacturing of the standard ghol'ms. No, today, his interest lay somewhere else.

When he finally arrived at the bottom of the stairs, an elderly man hurried up to him. The man's small stature was made worse by the pronounced arch of his back. He was balding, his skin unnaturally pale with brown specks visible between the thinning hairs.

"High General Setra, is that you?" said the man as he squinted. His nose was large and made him look like a burrowing troll from the old stories. On his hip hung several tools—a hammer and chisels—but also a whip; his scarred hands showed he was well-experienced in using them all. "So good to see you again, sir! Please come, follow me. I'll show you all the progress that's been made. I'm sure you'll be most pleased."

"Foreman Wertel, I have no time, nor am I in the mood for pleasantries. I trust you had no complications in the months I was away?"

Rubbing his hands together, the small man quickly answered. "No, sir, none at all. Just the occasional disobedient slave that refuses to work, but the whip quickly deals with that situation. But those minor details aren't worth your trouble, sir."

"Good, we can skip the normal tour. I see things are well on their way. Do you have any problems with the transports?" Corza asked as they strode past the first rows of ghol'ms. The stone warriors looked impressive and haunting up close.

"They can't keep up with production. More and more statues pile up here, in the main cavern. Sooner or later, we'll run out of space. I can barely turn around at my desk as it is," complained the foreman. "I've sent a request multiple times, asking if the number of statues per transport could be increased, but it was rejected every time."

"Well, let me see what I can do. If the number cannot be increased because of security, I will make sure we get more manpower to increase the number of transports. Now that the main force is back from the march, this should not be a problem. Besides, most of it should be heading south shortly."

"Thank you, sir, it's much appreciated," Wertel groveled.

They passed a slave resting his head on the side of a mine cart for a moment. Corza grabbed the whip from Wertel's belt and let it crack across the slave's back. The man screamed in agony as another four slashes coiled across his back.

"There," said Corza, as he returned the whip. "I feel better already."

As they walked on, Wertel looked over his shoulder, watching nervously as a guard dragged the slave away.

"If the High General isn't here on inspection, can I assume you would like to know about your special project?" he asked, voice hushed.

"That's precisely why I'm here, and I've got little time. Complications have arisen, and I need to know if they're ready to be used. So, stop wasting my time and fill me in on the progress."

Wertel quickly took the lead and led them through a number of narrower tunnels to a small wooden door. Taking out a ring of keys that could rival the set of any dungeon keeper's, he effortlessly located the necessary one and unlocked the door with a loud *clank*. It swung open with a loud, characteristic squeak. Grabbing the torch that hung next to the door, he stepped into the dark room.

Corza immediately followed, ducking slightly to get through the door. The room was larger than he expected, and Corza noticed a large wooden desk to the side with some candles, papers and tools scattered across it. In the middle of the room were two large objects, covered with dirty cloth. As he walked around the objects, Wertel moved to his desk and lit the candles. As the darkness was pulled back by the candlelight, steel bars emerged from the edge of the shadows. Corza slowly approached the cages, examining the two pair of shimmering lights that turned toward him carefully.

Stopping one step short of the bars, he turned his head to Wertel. "Are the specimens still in good health? They seem a little—"

One pair of those eyes charged. Slamming into the bars, a timber wolf snapped its jaws between the irons, barely missing Corza's fingers. As the first tried to take a chunk out of his hand, the other wolf let out a low growl.

Wertel grabbed a steel pipe from the desk and scurried over to the cages, hitting the steel bars and the nose of the wolf. "I'd say they're in perfect health, sir."

"Well, be careful not to wound them. I need them as healthy as possible. How have the statues come along? And were you able to run a test successfully?"

Wertel hobbled over to the two objects in the middle of the room and pulled off the sheets. "Please, see for yourself, sir. I believe they're some of my better works." He even dared to sound a bit proud.

As the sheets slipped toward the ground, two large statues in the shape of timber wolves were revealed. Both were carved in a resting posture, lying on their bellies, front paws straight forward and tail looped back along the hind legs. Their stone heads were held high, proud.

While both very similar, differences in the statues could clearly be seen when Corza regarded them more closely. It was to be expected when carving something by hand.

"It took thirty days per wolf to carve them," offered Wertel.

"The details are exquisite," Corza offered as a rare compliment. "Especially in comparison to the human ghol'ms."

During the original animal testing, Corza had determined that the transfer of the life force was easier if the statue resembled the source energy more closely. This had led to an evolution of how the ghol'ms looked, becoming more detailed over the years. Still, he had made sure the sculptors always left a certain general look with enough spare stone on the statues so the ghol'm could form its own body in the final stages of the life-force transfer. He just had to accept that a small bit of life force was lost during the transformation process. However, for this special project, he had hoped that by making a more detailed statue of the wolves, they would be easier to control in their ghol'm form.

Wertel's face contorted unpleasantly in reaction to the given compliment, like he felt uncomfortable to bring up his next point. "I'm sorry to say the tests could've gone better. The wolf that was sacrificed transferred easily enough into the third statue we made. It did thrash around while settling into its new stone skin, so I suggest finding a spacious place to do the ritual. The person holding the scrolls remained in full command, but make sure no one else comes too close, as it will not spare anyone else stupid enough to approach one of them carelessly."

Both wolves paced back and forth, restless in their cages. It seemed they did not like the look of their stone counterparts, at all. Corza wondered at this; were they aware of what happened to the other member of their pack? Could it be they were intelligent enough to know what was going to happen next?

Do they simply fear it or truly resent it on a deeper level?

The wolves were carved of the same deep black stone as the palace and the other ghol'ms. Corza loved the ominous look it gave them. Wertel had captured the long legs and pointed muzzle perfectly. Timber wolves could easily grow bigger than the average height of a human. It put their sharp, flesh-tearing teeth right at face level, a very intimidating fact for anyone facing these beasts. They were relentless hunters, one of the reasons Corza had chosen them. They could easily jump fallen trees, small walls and other obstacles, often without slowing their pace.

Their normal prey consisted of the larger species of deer that roamed the wilderness, but they were known to attack huge bears, if the pack was hungry enough.

Corza knew wolf packs hunted together, swapping out the front positions to more rested members of the pack if one tired. Prey could be followed for days, constantly showing themselves, spooking the prey. Being chased without a moment's rest, their victim would eventually collapse from exhaustion, making it an easy kill. He hoped the wolves would show the same instinct after the ritual, so he could use that renowned tactic to track the whereabouts of the dragon egg and make sure the people responsible for stealing it were torn to shreds.

"And that's not all," Wertel said, after a moment's hesitation. "It seems the wolf was unable to track the scented trail we set up. It was what we expected; the nose was unable to pick up any scent at all. I think it still had its old memories or instincts, because it looked thoroughly confused without a working nose. After some time, it seemed to accept things more as they were and was able to hunt successfully, if the prey remained in visual range. It showed cunning in its methods, but solely used its eyes to seek out the mark and kill it."

Corza slowly walked past the black wolf statue, letting his hand slide along the stone skin. "That's unfortunate, but it will have to do. Anything else I should know?"

Wertel gave a wry, toothless smile. "Don't lose the scrolls."

Corza gave him a blank stare.

"I mean it. Their animal instincts take over and they go on a rampage if they aren't controlled by the scroll master's thoughts. The human ghol'ms seem to at least retain a little bit of intelligence. They carry out their task and simply go dormant if their scroll is lost; but these wild animals are different."

"What a troublesome flaw." Corza shook his head in disapproval.

Wertel nodded quickly. "You're right, sir. But can't nothing be done about it, I'm afraid." Clearly wanting to move the subject away from such failure, he quickly asked, "When would you like them to be ready, sir?"

"Right away, we'll leave first thing in the morning. Take the wolves to the sacrificial chamber and get the scrolls prepared. I want you to hand deliver them to me as soon as they're done. The statues can be loaded up for transport right away. I'll send six guards to escort them."

"As you wish. If you could please follow me back to the main cave, then I'll get things moving along, so they're sent out as soon as possible."

While they returned to the main entrance, Corza's step felt a little lighter.

With the wolves and the guards, I should have a strong enough force to break from High General Wayler's group, if needed. But first I must find that egg; until I do, I can't risk anyone finding out my plan. I'll use Koltar and his men to track down those bastards that stole my egg; and once they have outlived their usefulness, Koltar won't know what hit him. As for those Shadows… they'll be no match for my wolves.

He chuckled as he started up the stairs, which immediately triggered a jolt of pain in his bruised throat. Rubbing his neck again, Corza silently cursed the Stone King.

CHAPTER SIX

Lost

"DO YOU NEED more wood?"

Raylan snapped out of his reverie and saw Harwin standing next to him, arms full of dry wood. "What?"

His mind had wandered again. Ever since they had retrieved the chest, he felt strangely drawn to the egg. Unfortunately, they had little time to rest, as the group wanted to stay on the move as much as possible. Tonight was an exception though; everyone needed a well-deserved break to replenish their energy.

Harwin gave a laughing grunt. "Well, you're miles away it seems. I said, do you need more firewood… to keep the egg heated?"

"No thanks, it's pretty filled up already. If you have wood left over though, put it in the wagon, as our stock is running low."

Raylan had devoted himself to helping Xi'Lao take care of the egg and make sure the chest's temperature was kept high enough. The egg had often been the topic of conversation this last week, and today was no different.

"But what if it tries to eat someone?" Rohan asked from the other side of the camp.

"You still on about that," said Galen, cocking his head.

"She already said there weren't a lot of reports of injuries during a hatching in those old scrolls of hers," Kevhin put in. "But who knows, it might think *you* tasty."

Rohan gave his fellow archer a fake laugh.

"I just want to see it fly," said Peadar. "I can't imagine such a large creature take to the air. It must be a sight to behold! Does anyone know if it will have feathered wings?"

"I don't think so," said Rohan, hesitantly. "Wings like sails in the stories, remember?"

"Oh, yeah. Well, it could be feathered sails…" said the youngster, his voice trailing off in disappointment. Then he added with new enthusiasm, "I wonder if it can outfly a pigeon, then. Maybe we should hold a race!"

"Let's focus on getting back safely first, Peadar," said Richard, who was helping him prepare their evening meal. "We're still a long way from home."

The remark immediately dampened the mood again.

Xi'Lao emerged from the forest with a couple of freshly-filled waterskins slung over her shoulder.

"Is there anything else you can tell us about the dragons hatching, Xi'Lao?" asked Kevhin, who spotted the Tiankonese woman entering their little camp.

"I would not dare to assume I know what to expect," she said tactfully, her step faltering. "So much info has been lost that your guess is as good as mine."

"Hmmm, well, that's no help at all," said the archer as he scratched his head.

Xi'Lao looked at him blankly.

 "Uhh, sorry, I did not mean it like that. I-I just meant th—"

"Richard? Xi'Lao? Can you join me here for a moment?"

Raylan turned to his brother's voice, but Gavin was out of sight, so he watched Xi'Lao make her way to other side of the camp, leaving a stumbling Kevhin behind. Rohan rolled his eyes at his fellow archer and gave a soft push against his head while adding something that was too soft for Raylan to hear. A smile flashed across Raylan's face, but disappeared as soon as his thoughts settled back on Xi'Lao's answer. She kept saying she did not know much else, but Raylan did not feel she was being entirely honest. He had thought about confronting her on it but in the end, decided his time was better spent taking care of their precious cargo.

"Well, I'll believe it when I'll see it," said Galen, after a moment, when Richard and Xi'Lao were both out of sight as well. "How are thing coming along, Peadar? Do you need any help with the food?"

The rest of the conversation trailed off to a different topic, the words fading into the background as Raylan refocused on the chest.

After a while, a slight shuffling walk announced Harwin's return from the wagon.

"How's the leg doing?" Raylan asked.

"Well enough, it doesn't really hurt, just a bit stiff. We cauterized the wound to limit the chance of infection and it seems to have done the trick. I'll be skipping along in no time," Harwin said with a grin. "How about you? You doing okay?"

"Yeah, but it's good to get some rest."

"It looks like you're quite fond of that thing," said Harwin, pointing at the chest. "Are you worried about it? Or just wondering what it will look like?"

Raylan closed the lid on the chest and secured the metal clip the best he could. He wished he had another lock to secure it with. "Both, I guess. Who wouldn't be curious about such a creature? But it's more than worrying or wondering. There's this warm glow in my chest. It's strangely soothing, even in this cold, unknown land. I mean… I'm still miserable with all the cold rain, don't get me wrong," he said with a small smile, "but I can't compare the feeling with anything I know. It's almost the way you feel when you're young, being hugged by your mother, feeling safe but in a different way."

Raylan let out a sigh. "It's hard to explain…" he broke off embarrassed. Why was he telling the grizzled old soldier any of this? *He must think I'm being daft.* Raylan shook his head. "Maybe I'm mistaken. For starters, I barely remember my mother. Let alone what it felt like being hugged by her. It's probably just the heat of the stones and wood or something, nothing more."

Harwin frowned. "Your mother died young?"

Raylan's heart contracted in sorrow for a moment. He lowered his eyes and gave a short nod. "She died when I was very little. A disease swept through the city, both me and my mother got very sick. Somehow, I pulled through, but my mother was too weakened. Gavin and I had some trouble adjusting after that."

Crouching, Harwin came down to Raylan's level. "Sorry to hear that, I didn't know. I heard the commander had a rebellious phase when he was younger, but he never really talks about his family."

Raylan's eyes darted to his brother's direction then back to Harwin. "Her face floats up in my dreams sometimes," he said, grateful for those moments of remembrance when he woke up, but it always meant he had to suffer the unshakable sadness and loss then too. "And I truly miss her, but Gavin took it… differently. Perhaps because he was older when it happened. He had a lot of anger issues and our father was left trying to raise two boys on his own. He was very strict—it wasn't a very good combination."

He chuckled in remembrance. "It didn't stop Gavin from picking fights. He took on bullies, angry customers, even protected our workshop cat against stray dogs. It always got him into trouble, and me too, if he managed to drag me into it. I've lost count how many times we had to help around the workshop to make up for things."

Harwin gave an amusing grunt, before replying in a more serious tone. "It's tough to lose someone so young. We hope our loved ones will be with us forever, but reality is often much crueler." He spat on the ground as if to insult said reality. The bearded soldier put a firm hand on Raylan's shoulder, before getting back to his feet. "Well, no matter what it is with this egg, I'm sure you'll find out sooner or later."

Harwin gave a soft smile that made Raylan wonder what kind of life the man must have had. He was aware the old soldier had served in the army for more than twenty years already, but that was about all he knew about him.

As Harwin hobbled away, Raylan stood, letting his curiosity lead him. "How about you? You seem to be in a good mood a long way from home."

Harwin looked back. "What do you mean?"

"Well, isn't there anybody waiting for you back home?"

"I've served in the army for nearly half my life. The army *is* my home," said Harwin. "Ain't no use having someone waiting for an old hand like me all the time. Ain't no fun for them either."

"…I guess not," Raylan said. "Then, you must have seen a lot, over all those years. Are *you* curious about that dragon and what it will look like?"

"Damn right I am. This is the stuff that keeps the world interesting and worth living in," replied Harwin. "Though, I must admit I would probably have been very skeptical about it being a dragon, if we hadn't just been fighting a living statue less than a week ago. Now, I figure, anything is possible. And whatever it will turn out to be. It's bound to be a story to share."

The old warrior stretched his neck for a moment, before a grin painted his face. "Now come on, Kevhin brought back a great-looking deer of sorts and it looks like Galen and Peadar are almost done preparing it. We won't be going hungry tonight." Harwin slapped his stomach with both hands as he walked away. "How's that meat coming along, boys?"

Raylan followed, happily letting his stomach drive out the more confused feelings inside. He was starving.

As the group had moved south, it slowly got warmer. It was still cold, but the rain was less frequent, and ground vegetation had increased, much to the pleasure of the horses.

Their little caravan had followed the path Richard had found at the bottom of the hill, but it had soon led nowhere. As they could not risk turning back toward the enemy's forces, they resolved to slowly travel further south; which meant cutting through the forest using the horses, swords and much sweat. They were only making a few miles per day, at most; but after a couple of days, they still had not seen any of the black soldiers and it was not likely they were moving toward an inhabited area. But Gavin had warned them there was no way to be sure. Even without enemies from the north on their heels, they still had to watch for any backcountry patrols. And they had to remain vigilant, as the ground was treacherous to travel on; it would be disastrous if one of the horses missed a step and broke a leg.

Raylan was glad to see Gavin was recovering well. It took a couple of days before his brother's headaches had stopped, after which traveling by wagon had become a little easier. His bruised ribs seemed to be another matter. Gavin grabbed them every now and then—his face wrenching in pain—but he assured Raylan and the others they were bothering him less and less.

Although the squad had little trouble functioning, it was still good Gavin was fully assuming the leadership role again. Before they had found the enemy transport, tension had run high between some of them. The weather, their hunger and the fact they had been searching for months had brought morale dangerously low. A strong leader did not just ensure things got done more efficiently; he also kept everyone's focus on the more important things, like working together.

Raylan spotted Gavin, Xi'Lao and Richard standing at the back of the wagon, looking over one of the maps they had brought with them.

"See what I mean? These are useless," said Gavin as he threw the maps on a pile together. "No one has ever traveled this far inland and returned to tell about it." He scrutinized the sky. "Judging from the sun, we're still traveling south by southeast, which means we're moving further away from the coast. Problem is, without any reference points, it's impossible to tell where we are."

Xi'Lao studied the map, following the coastline with her finger as Richard checked another.

"What do you suggest we do?" asked Richard.

"We can't risk going back without knowing what we're up against," said Xi'Lao. "And without knowledge of the area, we'll just be moving around blindly. At least along the coast we'll get a sense of how far south we have traveled. Maybe we can find a boat. Or even construct one ourselves and take to water?"

"That won't do us any good," Raylan cut in.

"What do you mean?" asked Xi'Lao as the three of them turned to face him.

"These coasts have no known harbors. And in the offchance we encounter any people that are fishing, it's likely the boats will be too small to hold us all. And building one from scratch… unless you know how, that won't work either, since none of us know anything about it. The Great Eastern Divide won't be some calm lake water that you wish to cross. Storms might show up; even slightly rough water can be a problem if the vessel is not seaworthy."

Xi'Lao looked back to Gavin, disappointment flashing on her face before she regained her composure. "You're right, we hit some pretty rough weather when sailing to Aeterra from the Empire, and it was not even storm season."

"And it's not just that," said Richard, "but the only one here that has any sailing experience is Raylan. I wonder if we would be able to correctly handle a ship."

Raylan looked around the camp. "We would have enough deckhands, but it won't matter without the right ship."

Xi'Lao mouth twisted in frustration. "Okay, but what can we do? We cannot keep going south. We will just get further and further away from our home."

"Well, like I wanted to explain before we were interrupted," said Gavin, giving Raylan a sideways glance. "I think I've got a solution, but it will require some planning."

That glance reminded Raylan of how much his brother had changed from rebellious to annoyingly serious when he joined the army. When they were younger, it never used to bother Gavin if Raylan spoke out of turn or voiced his unrequested opinion. But times had changed. The more they had spent apart, the more Raylan had felt abandoned by his older brother, leaving him stuck in the workshop, helping their father. And if Gavin showed up—often unexpectedly—he had acted all high and mighty, telling Raylan it was his duty to help their father and the kingdom.

"Before leaving on this assignment, we discussed multiple strategies with the war council," Gavin continued. "Things rarely go as planned, and I had no intention for us to get stuck on this continent without alternative routes home."

Raylan looked at his brother. "So, what's the plan to get us out of here?" he asked still irritated.

"Two of the remaining pigeons we have aren't bred in the capital, but Azurna."

"How does that help us?" Xi'Lao said.

"Azurna is one of our most eastern harbors in Aeterra. Its closest to the Dark Continent. On a good wind, a ship could get to the western coast of these dark lands in three or four weeks. The idea was to have a ship ready in Azurna that could depart on short notice and cross the Great Eastern Divide to pick us up. We'll send both pigeons out carrying the same message. As soon as they know we're cut off from returning home over land, they'll set sail to come and get us."

He pointed on the map. "The western point here has a rock formation called the Drowned Man's Fork. Three giant pillars rise out of the sea, towering high above the water. It's a landmark recognizable from both land and sea. Instructions are to put down anchor there for a moon cycle, or two, if possible. During that time, we've got to make our way toward that most western point overland. Once we arrive and spot the ship, we'll create a large fire with the dried herbs to signal them in with yellow smoke. They'll pick us up, we'll depart right away and return to Aeterra by ship," Gavin said.

"And what if we don't arrive before those two cycles have passed?" Raylan asked, already knowing the answer.

"They'll assume we were killed in action and return home. We'll be on our own. That's where the planning comes in. I need to figure out where we are to estimate how long it will take us to get to that most western point. Trouble is, without landmarks we only have the coast to rely on. Following the coast, however, would be strategically unwise as we would limit our movement should we encounter enemy forces. Here, we can move around in all directions to escape detection."

Xi'Lao frowned. "So that means you want to hold course and stay away from the coast," she said, coming to the same conclusion Raylan had. "But you're looking for higher ground to have a better view of the coastline to determine where we are?"

"Precisely, I want to go to the higher mountains toward our east and then go parallel to the coast. The mountain ridges should give us a better view of the coastline. Hopefully, by seeing the coast on such a scale, we'll be able to determine where we are. Perhaps we'll even spot the Drowned Man's Fork."

Raylan had to reluctantly admit he was impressed. During their ride here, it had not crossed his mind at all how they would be going back. At first, he had been focusing on how much he did not want to be there. Then his thoughts had been mostly preoccupied by the possibility of encountering enemies they would have to fight. And after that, his mind had been filled with thoughts of the egg and the unborn dragon. He had just assumed they would ride back after the fight without any problems. He realized how naive he had been. It seemed his brother's reputation for strategic planning in the army was well deserved.

"As soon as we know where we are, we'll release both pigeons at the same time. It will increase the chances of our message arriving in Azurna. So, get some rest tonight. I want us to be on our way again, toward those mountains, at first light."

With that, Gavin packed up the most detailed map and put it inside his cloak and asked Richard to put away the rest. "I'm going to check on Stephen."

"Hold on," said Raylan, as his brother walked off. He caught up with him on the other side of the wagon. "You didn't have to embarrass me like that in front of the others," he said as he grabbed Gavin's arm.

"Then don't interrupt."

"I just wanted to help," Raylan countered.

"Sometimes helping means listening and doing what I say, instead of speaking your mind."

Raylan instantly felt his face flush in anger. "If you don't want my opinion, why did you request me on this squad then? I didn't even want to be here."

Gavin looked at him in that brotherly all-knowing way, that he used to hate. "I was trying to protect you, you birdbrain."

"Protect me? I only had a few weeks left of my draft and then I would've gone back to the sea! To sailing. But no, you had to drag me all the way out here, to this miserable, cold place."

"You've got no idea what you're talking about," snapped Gavin. "I asked them to let you stay behind when they suggested you for the squad. But they said all the reserves were going to be sent to Forsiquar as a show of force, including you. Do you want to throw yourself against the walls of that city over a simple lord's squabble?"

For a moment, Raylan did not know what to say. His brother's eyes were burning fierce, scolding him with unsaid words. He had no idea they had been planning to extend his service again. His placement had already taken longer than he expected when he was drafted two years back.

"I-I," started Raylan.

"That's what I thought," his brother interrupted.

"Listen, the political importance of this mission is gigantic. It's not every day an official emissary of the Tiankong Empire reaches out to the Aeterran king for help," continued Gavin. "Had our army not already been preoccupied with things at Forsiquar, the king and council might have sent a much larger force. Instead, we get a chance to prove ourselves. As a squad, and as individuals."

There had been little information available of what had happened behind closed doors when Xi'Lao arrived at the court. All Raylan knew was that the meeting lasted two days as she had explained how an army of unknown origin had crossed and survived the barren region of the White North and infiltrated the Tiankong Empire, leaving devastation in its wake before claiming the dragon egg the Empire now so desperately sought to retrieve.

"Besides, the mission was a long shot. There was a chance we wouldn't encounter anything at all, which wouldn't have been so bad either. With no enemies to fight, the danger to this squad would be minimal—*you* would be safe, instead of stuck in a siege without me. We would've done our duty for the court and showed the Tiankong Empire that Aeterra was willing to help."

Gavin suddenly fell silent, as his eyes briefly darted over Raylan's shoulder. "So, I took you with me. And I'm not sorry, not even with how the mission is going. It's what we do. We follow orders. I'm just sorry it turned out to be more dangerous than I had expected. Now, I just want to get this done. Get this egg, and us, back home in one piece. And I would appreciate it if you didn't make me regret taking you along, while doing so."

With that, his brother turned his back to him and stormed off.

Irritated, Raylan spun the other way only to see Xi'Lao standing behind him near the back of the wagon, watching Gavin stride away.

"I am glad he is okay again," she said, calmly, as if the whole argument had never taken place.

"Yeah, seems like he's back to his regular old self," said Raylan, annoyed. He squirmed under the silent scrutinizing look Xi'Lao gave him and relented with a sigh. "No, you're right. It's good he's recovering. I just wish he was a little less *him*, sometimes. Do you know if he still has headaches? That might explain his mood."

"None that I can tell, but I am not sure if he would show it if they still bothered him. He does not like it when people doubt his fitness to lead."

"He sure is someone who likes to be in control," Raylan said with a smirk.

This time Xi'Lao gave him a smile. "I think that comes with the territory. Control means safety. Your brother is very dedicated to keeping us safe, which I think is a very admirable characteristic."

When she looked in the direction Gavin had headed, Raylan thought he saw the faintest blush on her cheeks. Feeling a bit uncomfortable discussing his brother with her, he quickly tried to change subject. "How's the treatment of Stephen's leg doing?"

She looked back at him and shook her head. "I am not sure. At first, he felt fine and his skin was not torn. I saw no sign of damage on the outside."

"But…?"

"But his leg is still swollen after so many days. The skin looks inflamed and feels hot to the touch, so I am afraid he has an infection." She shook her head. "The traveling is not doing his leg any good, it needs to rest and to be cooled by fresh water. I have been searching for herbs I recognize but no luck so far. I am afraid that if this keeps up and the infection goes into the bone, we might have to take off the leg…"

Raylan looked at the campfire where Peadar was stirring the cooking pot. Stephen sat next to him on the ground with his leg resting high on a rock. The swelling had made it necessary to take his armor pad off. Right now, he was cooling it with wet rags while he traded words with Gavin. The leg seemed to leech all color from Stephen, leaving his face pale and clammy.

Raylan ran his hand through his hair and sighed. He had enjoyed his talks with Stephen during their ride north—the scout had been a cheerful traveling companion. After the fight with the living statue, they had all called him lucky for getting off light. Now, Raylan was not so sure. He often heard Stephen grunt and groan from the wagon as it bumped over the nonexistent road. During the nights, the injured scout tossed and turned in his sleep, soaked in sweat, which in turn cooled him down so much that he would wake shivering in the coldness of the night. This landscape was harsh for men that were healthy; it was brutal for those with injuries.

"How is the egg doing?"

Xi'Lao's question brought his mind back to the present situation.

Raylan shrugged. "Honestly, I've got no idea. I think it's okay, but I haven't got any experience with such a thing. Thank you again for trusting me and letting me help take care of it. It must be a great honor to have such a task, I expect."

Raylan knew Xi'Lao still checked on the egg to make sure things were going well and nothing was forgotten. He often saw her slip off into the wagon after sundown and right after he had tended to it; he took no offense, completely understanding her concern. Although no one would have considered the egg still viable, it had been guarded for generations and, from what he understood, was strongly intertwined with the Empire's culture and society. To have a living, breathing dragon soon return to their world must be of great importance to the Empire. As official diplomat, Xi'Lao would be compelled to ensure all went well. The pressure of such responsibility probably weighed heavily on her shoulders.

"I've got one concern, which I wanted to talk to you about," said Raylan. "Or rather, I wanted to ask. When we discovered it in the cave, the eggshell had been soft, almost like smooth supple leather; but now, it feels like the shell is much harder. It is losing some of its color, too. So, I was wondering if you've got any idea if we're doing something wrong."

Xi'Lao sprinted to the chest, opening it. She ran her hand over the top of the egg. The shell was a lot stronger and thicker than before.

Raylan crouched next to her; as she bit her lip. "See what I mean? Do you know what's happening?"

Running his hands along the egg, the creature inside tapped the inside of the shell where his hand lingered. Xi'Lao had given up telling Raylan not to touch the egg, as she must have seen he was not totally in control of himself when he did. She had said to him that in those moments, it looked like his mind wandered. Besides, the egg did not seem to be harmed by it, and the dragon often reacted positively to his touch.

She turned toward him. "From what I have read in the scrolls, it is normal for the eggs to harden before hatching. As the dragon grows bigger on the inside, the body gets closer to the edge. The hardening of the shell helps protect the unborn dragon from injury," she said as she frowned.

"What is it?" said Raylan.

"It is the journal we found while clearing the camp," she said as she pulled the small handbook from an inside pocket. "There is this diagram that did not make much sense. But now, I think it talks about the time till hatching."

"And what does it say?"

"I am not entirely certain, as this part is not all written in Tiankonese," she said as she looked up the page and studied it in detail. "But if I have this right, it means we have less than a moon-cycle before it will hatch."

"Less than that? But-but that will never be enough time to get it back home! Do you know what will happen when it hatches?"

"Not precisely, all I know is that the dragon will be very hungry, and we will need to have food for it once it comes out of the egg. I read about special herbs being burnt during the hatching ceremony to dull the dragon's senses somewhat; stifle its hunger. Though I have no idea which herbs they were, or if we could find them here in a climate so different from the Empire's."

"Food we can do," said Raylan. "But it would be best if we're far away from here before it hatches, don't you agree?"

"I will talk to your brother about it," said Xi'Lao, her worried look never entirely abandoning her.

Raylan looked back to the egg, gave a short tap with his finger in response to the dragon's tap inside and whispered. "Just wait a bit longer, little one. Now's not yet the time."

Closing the chest, they joined the others at the fire as Raylan silently pondered their little chat. What was this worried knot he felt inside? He was sure Xi'Lao had more on her plate than him, with all this going on. He had little to do with the Empire and their heritage. So why did it feel like a ton of rocks weighed down on his chest? Why did his heart race and his hands shake if he thought about this creature coming into the world? And why was it all replaced with this serene calmness as soon as he touched the egg? It did not make sense.

He finally put his thoughts aside when Peadar called everyone over for the food. Only then did he notice the atmosphere was strangely relaxed. Kevhin and Rohan were complimented on their kill and Peadar on the cooking. Richard walked off to give Galen his share of the meal and Xi'Lao took the place next to Gavin to start up a light conversation with him, undoubtfully choosing to keep the discussion of their latest discovery for a little later in the evening. His brother's face cleared visibly when he saw her take her place. It was like a gathering of friends instead of a group hiding from danger. Leaning forward to fill his bowl with steaming stew, Raylan let out a sigh. If possible, he wanted to enjoy the moment while it lasted; grateful for the small break of the more pressing things in the world.

CHAPTER SEVEN

Hunters

KOLTAR SAT FROWNING on his horse. Beside him, High General Setra sat astride his own mount as they surveyed the large clearing. Corza looked miserable and had been in a bad mood all morning. Koltar expected the man had not anticipated returning to the wilderness so soon.

This, however, was not the reason Koltar sat deeply in thought. He had been surprised when they met up with a small transport on the first day; even more so, when Corza had gone to great lengths to convince him they needed the extra men and special cargo he had prepared.

Going back to the palace empty-handed was not an option, so notifying Lord Rictor about Corza's curious scheme was out of the question, but he was wary of the men Corza brought with him. He knew almost none of them and when he requested to inspect the cargo, Corza respectfully declined, stating the cargo had been packed up securely to ensure no damage would come to it.

It only added to Koltar's suspicion, but he did not want to let something escalate between them, so he bit his tongue. Waiting was not his strongest virtue, but he was no dumb brute who rushed into a situation with limited information. He would never have made it to his position had he not forced himself to have patience now and again.

Neither had spoken much to each other over the following days, but Koltar had ordered his men to keep a close eye on Corza's additional soldiers.

A soldier strode up to them, spear and torch in hand, and a short sword strapped across his back. Stopping a few steps short of the horses, he planted his spear in the ground and brought his fist to his chest to greet them with a small dip of his head.

"High General Wayler, High General Setra, we've found them. The wagon tracks we discovered this morning led to a small chasm to the south of here. I sent some men down for a closer inspection and there they were. The low light made it difficult to see, but we counted thirty-nine soldiers and three wagons at the bottom of it—as well as the remains of a sacrifice."

"Fucking idiots," Corza growled. "How could they be so incompetent as to be taken by force, especially with a ghol'm in reserve."

Koltar ignored him and addressed the soldier. "Commander, I assume you've been able to determine which way the item was taken?"

"My scouts are pretty certain they continued west from here."

"Pretty certain?" Corza mocked the commander. "I was under the impression your scouts were the best in the city, and you give us 'pretty certain'? Your men's skill reflects poorly on you, High General Wayler."

Corza's face was all smirk.

Koltar let the jab slide, but his subordinate quickly bowed his head and stared at the horse's feet.

"High General Setra," said the scout commander quickly without raising his eyes—clearly not wanting to be a disgrace for his commanding general. "The road coming in from the cliff has only one main path, which I understand was used by the main force's wagons coming into the clearing. It's unlikely the enemy took that road, or your force would've undoubtedly run into them. No other tracks were found leading away from the clearing, except for the path west. It goes further into our territory and not only did we use it this morning, your own force traveled across it as well on the way to the palace. This, in combination with the past days' rain, makes it hard to be absolutely certain."

Corza's face returned to a scowl, but he said nothing.

Koltar took another look around the clearing. "Get everyone ready and send two men ahead to scout along the wagon trail we came in on. They must have veered off at some point. We'll leave as soon as all are mounted. And inform the Darkened."

The scout commander's face twisted in disgust at hearing the Silent Shadow's name. Once again, he pounded his fist over his heart before turning on his heel. He began shouting orders to the closest soldiers and Koltar was pleased to see two mount their horses immediately and gallop away. The remaining soldiers scrambled to put away the pots they had taken out to make some lunch.

Koltar turned to Corza. "How did your force not notice something was wrong when they passed through this clearing?"

"What was there to notice?" Corza countered, annoyed. "There were no bodies or signs of fighting. And why would we look for a group of soldiers that were supposed to have already arrived at the capital at that time?" Corza stared back at him with a conceited look on his face. "Besides, where were your troops? Are you not charged with keeping our territory free of infiltrators? Where were the patrols, the scouting parties, the check posts?"

Koltar's jaw stiffened while his eyes shot fire. "When you left, you took half my defense force with you, without even properly notifying me. I have spent months training recruits to take their places. I finally got to a point where my soldiers could cover the entire territory again, and his lordship sent them off down south to join up with the southern garrisons," Koltar snapped. "I barely have enough soldiers to secure the capital, let alone to station checkpoints near the cliff. So, don't you dare use my troops as an excuse to hide the fact that this is a making of your own incompetence! You had the item and lost it. You have no one to blame but your own shortsightedness."

Corza's face reddened, but after a moment he gave Koltar a small smile. "Well, I'd say it's about time to put that cargo of mine to some use. Would you care to have a look?"

Corza guided his horse toward the cargo wagon without waiting for an answer. From the corner of his eye, Koltar saw one of the Darkened instantly follow. They were not letting Corza out of their sight, as per Lord Rictor's orders. Koltar always made certain one of his own soldiers did the same, but in this case, he followed the general himself.

Arriving at the wagon, Corza barked commands at his soldiers. The crates, too heavy to be lifted, were carefully rolled off the tailgate of the wagon under Corza's watchful gaze. Once safely on the ground, a soldier took his axe and gently pried them open.

Koltar cursed when he saw what emerged. *That weasel has some nerve to bring these abominations.*

He had not seen any ghol'ms in this sinister wolf shape before, only those that resembled a human. He had never needed to use one on their home territory, but he was fully aware of the devastating power ghol'ms possessed.

"What in the King's name is the meaning of this?" he said. "I wasn't aware we had a new type of ghol'm. What do you plan to do with these?"

Corza took his time dismounting. "Now that we have a trail to follow, it's best to ditch the wagon," he said. "It'll only slow us down. These two beauties are more than capable of keeping up with a galloping horse. If an enemy group is in possession of the sacred item, they need a wagon of their own to transport it. We'll be able to catch up with them in no time at all—if we don't lose the trail. But such a heavy wagon is bound to leave tracking clues everywhere, so even *your* scouts should be able to find them."

Corza dug around in his saddlebag until he finally pulled two sacrificial scrolls from its depths. The parchment of the scrolls was stained with blood.

Koltar's mood darkened. He had no objection to the extra power a ghol'm gave to their hunt, but all that power at Corza's disposal did not sit well with him.

"Can they move faster than a normal ghol'm then? You know how slow they are when they're not fighting. They've got that awkward stride, and it takes forever for them to move between the forest trees."

Corza gave him a bored look, but Koltar knew he was right. It had surprised them when the first test ghol'ms showed a complete difference in speed during a fight and normal travel. Their smartest people had tried to find a solution, but in the end had to accept it as an awkward flaw. Koltar theorized that in combat one's energy was completely different from their normal state of mind. That combat buzz one felt during a battle had the power to take away fatigue, pain and doubt. He figured it triggered a complete change in how the ghol'ms moved. A change perhaps even influenced by the one controlling the scroll. It was one of the reasons the ghol'ms were transported on wagons rather than letting them walk.

"Not to worry, High General Wayler," Corza said, "for these creatures, there's no difference. There's only the hunt. Now, if you please, stand over there. This could get a bit dangerous and we wouldn't want you to get hurt."

The sarcastic tone in Corza's voice was barely noticeable, but Koltar was fully aware of its presence. Turning his mount around, he put some distance between him and the stone wolves. He was still shocked at the size of them. Both were immense; a good deal larger than their real-life counterparts. During their patrols, Koltar and his men had plenty of encounters with the timber wolves these statues clearly represented; he had a healthy respect for these killing machines of nature. Combining that ferocity with the strength of a ghol'm did not seem very wise to him.

Without further delay, Corza walked between the statues and stopped at the back of their necks. He raised the scrolls, one in each hand, and started mumbling an incantation. Koltar heard the hum of the resonating scrolls while a faint blue glow originated from the parchment. In one swift motion, Corza brought down the scrolls; their sharp points hitting each wolf statue accurately between the shoulder blades.

The blue light immediately increased to a bright sparkling flare, as the resonating sound increased, making the horses toss their heads and scuff at the ground. Corza's clothes flapped in the wind created by the sound, and he braced himself for what came next. The final bursts came nearly simultaneously as the blue energy rushed into the statues before expanding in a ring of light, as the booming sound echoed along the forests. Birds around the clearing took to the sky with protesting cries.

Wrenching the scrolls free, Corza returned to his horse and put some more distance between himself and the black wolves. Koltar observed the tense look on Corza's face; it seemed his fellow general did not precisely know what to expect.

The hairs on Koltar's arm rose at the sound of stone cracking. Small pieces crumbled to the ground. One wolf first turned its head sideways, and then back, to stretch its neck. The other looked down as it ripped lose its front paws. Large claws extended from the end of the paws as both tails broke loose and swept back and forth a couple of times. The cracking grew louder as a muffled growl became audible. Koltar frowned as the entire jaw formed, and their mouths split open, revealing razor-sharp teeth. Their two large canine fangs were nearly half the length of Koltar's lower arm.

The wolves had an eerie appearance, with little color difference between their skin and their fangs. Their eyes glowed blue in their hollow sockets. It was like the entire beast was a shadow, which made it difficult to see the details clearly. There was a small difference in size between the two. The larger was almost fully formed and seemingly ready to get up; the smaller one was currently snapping its head backward, trying to bite its own tail.

Arching its head back, the howl it threw at the sky was like nothing Koltar had ever heard. He knew well the howl of a wolf, but this sound was like the echo from within a cave, bouncing off the stone walls, amplifying itself. Koltar felt it resonate through him. Instantly, he was back at the black palace near the vault, where that rumble had sounded so familiar and so unnatural at the same time. He wondered what the Stone King hid in that dome.

The smaller wolf reacted to the howl and added its own. Ripping its paws lose, it stumbled to the side and crashed into the larger wolf. The impact was all that was needed to set the beast off. In an instant, it snapped sideways and threw itself viciously onto the smaller creature. Its jaws closed on the back of the other's neck as the sound of stone scraping over stone cut through the air. The smaller wolf rolled away, taking the larger one with it, and at once put in a counterattack.

Neither wolf did any real damage to the other with their teeth, or their claws; but Koltar had no doubt they had enough power to bite through a man's arm, leg, and perhaps even a torso, with ease. The wolves tumbled over each other, scrambling to their feet and launched into another attack. They crashed into a large boulder, the force of the impact splitting them up again.

The smaller one dashed to the side, using the side of a large boulder to get behind its foe. But the larger wolf immediately switched to keep its competitor in front of him.

The smaller wolf lunged at the bigger one's throat but was pinned by the full force of its larger rival. Unable to move away, the smaller wolf finally yielded into a submissive position.

The larger wolf lowered its head and let out a low growl, at which moment one of the soldiers came around the boulder to see what all the ruckus was about. Instantly, both wolves forgot about their squabble and jumped at the unprepared soldier. He barely had time to raise his spear as the two pitch-black wolves pounced on him. The larger wolf closed the full length of its jaw over the soldier's torso, its enormous canines piercing all the way into his stomach, while the smaller wolf sank its teeth in the man's left femur, tearing the leg off at the hip. The soldier died so fast, he had no time to scream.

* * *

Fascinated by the spectacle, Corza failed to suppress an immense grin. His creations were more marvelous than he had dared to dream. The fact the soldier had been one of Koltar's men made it all the more sweet.

That's what you get when you call me incompetent.

When the wolves noticed their prey had stopped moving, they quickly lost interest. Perhaps they had no appetite to feed. They backed away and looked around, seemingly confused, taking in their surroundings for the first time. They spotted both Corza and Koltar observing them. The larger one turned and started stalking toward them. Head held low, teeth bared.

"Corza! Don't you have any control over them?" Koltar roared, as he drew his sword from his side.

Corza did not bother answering. He kept his eyes on the approaching wolf. The smaller wolf was now following closely in its tracks, as they simultaneously increased their speed. The distance between them and the wolves closed rapidly, as Corza tightened his hands around both scrolls.

Wertel better be right, or I will have his head.

Koltar's horse moved nervously from side to side, seeing the wolves come at them. Any untrained horse would have been long gone, but even the trained warhorses had trouble following commands with ghol'ms nearby, and these were no normal ghol'ms. The wolves were fast, athletic and even more intimidating than any normal ghol'm—or wolf. It was a wonder their horses had not thrown them yet.

"Corza! You better tell me you have a way to stop these things! You bastard, say something!"

But Corza did not turn around. His eyes were locked on the larger wolf, counting under his breath. Both creatures were in full run now, mere moments away from pouncing. Corza considered, for a split second, letting the wolves tear through Koltar, right there and then; but that would mean instant chaos. One of Koltar's soldiers might get away in the panic and inform Lord Rictor, and that would complicate things. Besides, he only had eyes on one of the Darkened before he ordered the crates opened, which meant the other might be able to take him out unexpectedly. Reluctantly, he decided to wait for a more opportune moment.

* * *

Koltar clenched his sword, ready to slash at whichever wolf dared attack him first. But just before the wolves were on them, Corza's voice bellowed clearly through the air.

"STOP!"

Both beasts skidded to a halt, stopping right in front of Corza. They looked at him, cocking their heads left and right, not fully comprehending why they broke off their attack.

"Lie down!" Corza ordered in loud voice, and both stone wolves sank to the ground.

"Excellent, this is working out perfectly, I would say," Corza said to no one in particular.

"You son of a whore. You let those things tear up one of our soldiers for nothing." Koltar forced his horse to move in closer to Corza and the wolves.

His fellow general turned. "One of *your* soldiers, to be precise. You better be careful about what you call me, High General Wayler. We would not want the wolves to lose control again. Who knows what could happen…"

With the slightest movement of his finger, Corza let the wolves rise, after which they moved to either side of him, strategically positioning themselves between both generals. The largest wolf was nearly as tall as Koltar's own horse. Its hollow eyes stared at him from just below his horse's eye level. The smaller one lowered its head slightly and let out a small growl.

Not willing to push his luck in a situation like this, Koltar cursed. He forced himself to turn his horse around then looked over his shoulder. "Trust me, High General Setra, I'll remember. Now if you can keep them under control, let's see if they can truly keep up with the horses. I'm sure you wish to catch these thieves as quickly as possible."

Koltar gritted his teeth as he rode off to whip the men into motion. These wolves would be trouble and not something he would easily be able to get rid of. High General Setra had become a much more dangerous person to contend with.

Raylan sat back and let his stomach settle with a sigh. It had been a while since he had eaten such a satisfying meal and he gladly suffered the aftermath of overeating. He closed his eyes and sighed again. When he opened them once more, he saw Xi'Lao approaching.

"I need your help," she said.

"What's wrong?"

"Stephen's leg is getting worse. I need to do something, or it will be too late."

"Okay, what do you need me to do?" he asked, getting to his feet.

"Find as much of this moss as possible," said Xi'Lao, as she pulled a small pluck of green out of her bag. "It looks similar to the moss back home that is known for its disinfection abilities. I want to make a paste out of it for Stephen's leg."

"Sure. Where did you find that?" said Raylan.

"I came across it after we ate. It was on the shady side of a tree. Mostly in very wet spots… but that is not really a problem here," she said with a small smile.

Raylan headed toward the surrounding trees, searching each for the moss. As he crouched, the echo of howling wolves resonated through the hills. He wondered if they were greeting the first stars of the night, or perhaps they were sending a warning they were on the hunt.

Better hurry up and get back. We shouldn't let the fire die out tonight.

He quickened his search, finding the moss he was looking for and picked as much as he could carry before returning to camp.

Xi'Lao began making the paste as soon as he returned, asking Raylan to stay with Stephen until she was ready. The scout had slipped into a restless sleep, tossing and turning as sweat ran down his face, talking incoherently.

"Ready," said Xi'Lao.

"What do we do now? Just smear it on?" asked Raylan.

"No, I first have to relieve pressure from the infection, get the leg as clean as possible… which means making a hole to let the bad stuff out…"

"You're going to *cut* him?"

"It's the only way to get the infection out," said Xi'Lao. "I will prepare my knife in the fire. Can you please wake him and put this dagger's handle between his teeth? It will prevent him from biting off his tongue."

"Won't that cauterize the wound too fast?" asked Raylan, as he accepted the sheathed dagger.

"I will let it cool first, but the fire is needed to cleanse the knife, so using it does not add to the infection while we try to get rid of it."

Raylan woke Stephen as gently as possible and was met with a groggy gaze. It seemed their injured friend had been almost living in another world. Xi'Lao explained what they had to do as best as possible, but Raylan doubted Stephen understood any of it.

"Okay, put the handle between his teeth and grab his shoulders. Richard? Can you hold his other leg? Gavin, put pressure on the thigh of his injured leg."

With the three of them holding Stephen down, Xi'Lao removed the knife from the fire and waved it around to let it cool. As she made the incision, Stephen moaned painfully; but under the circumstances, Raylan thought he remained impressively quiet. The cut was deep and about an inch long in the thickest part of the swollen leg. A white fluid came gushing out, and a stench like rotten eggs filled the night air.

"All right, that was the easy part," Xi'Lao said. "Now grab hold, I need to push out as much of the wound's fluid as possible."

As she put pressure on the leg, the reeking, white fluid flowed out, mixing with blood from the freshly made cut. Stephen jolted under their hands, screaming from the sudden torment. It was like the pain burned away all the haziness from the scout's mind as he briefly looked straight at Raylan with crystal clear eyes. Stephen bit down hard on the wrapped handle as a tear ran down his cheek. Xi'Lao pushed on the leg for a second time, resulting in another muffled scream.

Stephen drew a few short breaths, tensing under the pressure Xi'Lao applied. Then his body went limp as his eyes rolled back in his head.

Xi'Lao continued to drain the rancid fluid, which was now starting to slow.

"Raylan, check if he is breathing!" she said. "Put his head slightly to the side and make sure he does not swallow his tongue. Gavin, I am almost done with this. Can you get the pot with boiling water, some clean rags and the medical paste for me… oh, and the cleanest bandages we have, too, please."

As she put the paste on Stephen's leg and wrapped it up, Raylan finally allowed himself to sit back. For the first time, he noticed his own heavy breathing. It had taken more energy than he expected to keep the scout pinned down during the procedure. He rubbed his shoulders and neck, trying to loosen his cramped muscles.

Xi'Lao wiped the sweat from her forehead and sat back as well. "Thank you all."

"Will he be all right now?" asked Raylan.

"We will have to see. I have done all I can, so all we can do now is wait. Time will tell, sooner or later, time will tell…"

As Stephen stirred in his sleep, Raylan looked up to the stars, listening to the wolves howling at the moon again.

They seem closer… I wonder if they caught their dinner for today.

CHAPTER EIGHT

Cross

SMALL ROCKS CRUMBLED away from the wheels of the wagon, before falling into the depths. The horses snorted as they put their weight forward to keep the wagon in motion. Over the last three days, they steadily gained altitude while moving southeast. The forest had opened up, which made traveling with the wagon a bit easier. Even more so, when they eventually moved above the tree line.

The mountain range they approached was less intimidating than the peaks of the White North, which faded out of sight on the horizon. But it was still a dangerous road to travel. Crumbling paths, sheer drops, and sudden wind gusts made for too many close calls.

For once, the rain held off, which was a blessing. The temperature had slowly risen as they left the cold north behind, but it dropped again now that they traveled higher in the mountains. Raylan was glad that riding behind the wagon kept him somewhat sheltered from cold mountain wind.

Closely following the wagon, he quietly studied Stephen, who sat with his back against the chest. The scout was trying to keep his leg raised and as motionless as possible, which was not an easy feat on the winding mountain slope.

"Loose gravel," came a warning from Ca'lek in front.

"Slow and steady everyone," Gavin immediately added in a loud voice from the front of the wagon. "Once we get to the southern slopes, we should see enough of the coastline to check for the Drowned Man's Fork and possibly send off those pigeons."

The path they traveled, if one could call it that, weaved alongside the mountain; always climbing, but—so far—without any difficult or dangerous switchbacks. Until now, it always provided enough footing for the wagon to continue onward, but Raylan doubted it had ever been a proper road at all. If it had, it must have been ages ago, and there was no indication of any recent travels.

"How's the leg doing?" Raylan asked.

"Actually… I think it's doing a little better now," said Stephen, as he grabbed hold of the chest next to him as the wagon hit an unexpected stone. He gave a lopsided smile. "…it feels a lot less swollen and hot today. Though it still hurts like hell when I try to move it."

Stephen tried to put on a more genuine smile; but Raylan noticed pearls of sweat form on the side of the scout's head.

"Does the cut still look clean?" Raylan asked, a hopeful tone in his voice.

"It looked clean this morning. I'm hoping we'll be able to wash it out again with some boiled water tonight. Xi'Lao said enough moss was collected to apply a fresh paste to the wound."

"Don't worry, we'll make sure to get it done," said Raylan.

He was glad to see Stephen did indeed have more energy today. The color had somewhat returned to his face, but it was still quite early in the day and traveling would take a lot of energy out of him before they stopped for the night.

As they came to the top of the slope, the path widened enough for Raylan to ride up to the front of the wagon and keep pace beside it. Gavin looked straight ahead, checking the quality of the road as they slowly rode into the shadow of the mountain again. It looked like this next dip in the path would be the last one before they passed over the summit of the mountain and moved from the northern slope onto the south side.

Raylan silently regarded his brother for a while. They had not brought up the argument again, and he thought it best to leave it be.

"How's it looking?" he asked as casually as possible.

"Once we pass the mountain ridge and reach the south side, I expect we'll see the western coastline run south for quite a distance," Gavin said. "I'm just hoping the weather stays clear. I'm sure you remember how easy those things can change in the mountains."

"Ha," said Raylan, picking up on his brother meaning. "I remember how lucky we were when we snuck out of the city to explore the mountains behind Shid'el." He grinned at their own stupidity at the time, glad to be reminded of days where they were getting along.

"We were so damn fresh back then. That storm really came out of nowhere and pinned us on the side of the mountain without any warning whatsoever."

They had sought shelter under a rock overhang; but the rain soaked them in moments and, together with the wind, froze them relentlessly.

"I don't think we would've made it, had the skies not cleared as fast as they had clouded over," said Gavin. "That wind was what stayed with me most. It came swirling in, bringing the rain with it, as if the drops were tiny little ice-cold blades."

A cold shiver passed through Raylan at the memory. Luna shook her head, twitching her ears, as if the same chill passed through her body, too. "Not even the nights in this forsaken place felt as cold as I felt back then. Father was so glad we weren't hurt that he completely forgot to punish us," he said.

"You maybe," said Gavin. "As the eldest, he gave me an earful after you fell asleep. It was my duty to protect my little brother, which meant to be smart about those things." His brother gave him a small smile. "Yeah, we were pretty stupid," added Gavin. "Sometimes, I wonder how we managed to reach our twenties at all, but here we are."

"Not that we find ourselves in a very safe situation now…" said Raylan, as he gave a twisted smile back.

"Let's hope the south side of the mountains gives us a little bit more warmth and hospitality than the north."

Raylan noticed they had begun climbing again and looked up ahead. He watched as Ca'lek rode on to check out the top of the slope. The wind tried to cut beneath his shirt; pulling his cloak close, he urged Luna into a trot. The upward path seemed safe enough, so he passed Xi'Lao and Richard, who had been riding at the front of their little caravan behind Ca'lek.

Looking over his shoulder, he called back. "I'm going to meet up with Ca'lek and see what the other side brings us," he said, after which he put his heels in Luna's flank, taking off in a canter.

He reached the top shortly after Ca'lek did. At the sound of his approach, the scout turned. "No enemy movement to report. Also, Gavin will be pleased we'll be able to start checking the coastline from here on out."

Luna circled on the spot as he regarded the terrain further south. The unfolding landscape had a dark beauty to it; he had never seen anything like it before. Toward the east, the mountains continued to stretch out, slowly turning to the south and eventually lowering into rolling hills. Large forests covered the land, the dark pines holding most of the high ground, the deep green slowly mixing in with the richer colors of the deciduous tree species at the lower altitudes. The forests they had seen in Aeterra, even while riding north, always seemed brighter, in a way. Here, it looked like the trees swallowed every bit of sun. The absence of reflected light made the forest look like a dark green ocean that stretched across the land.

He observed their path going down, it would not take them long before they encountered the first tree stumps again, which was a good thing. Once they were below the canopy, it would shield them, somewhat, from enemy eyes. Following the green sea of leaves toward the west, the horizon shimmered in the daylight. The forests somewhat lessened toward the western horizon; but in most places, it looked like the trees reached all the way to the coast. The Great Eastern Divide's glimmer only added to the already magical feel of the scenery.

"Amazing," he mumbled.

"Just keep your eyes open. Don't forget we're in enemy territory."

"I know we're in a bad spot; but these moments just make me love being out of the city, seeing lands almost no one has seen. It reminds me of the open oceans. It always feels so liberating to have all that space around me. I mean, just take a look. Have a real moment. Take it all in and say to me that you don't find it amazing."

The scout looked at him with a smile before turning back his gaze at the valley. "What I see are difficulties. Dense forests which will slow our traveling to a crawl again. No clear indication if there are any settlements out there that we need to avoid. And the area looks like it can sustain bigger wildlife."

"Well great, hopefully we can hunt again," Raylan said, optimistically.

This time Ca'lek looked at him and raised an eyebrow. "It also means the predators have more food, so they will likely be bigger and more abundant. We'll need to have constant fires during the night to ward off any unwelcome guests which, in turn, means we'll be easier to spot by the enemy."

Raylan let out a groan. "I suppose you're right…"

He was aware of the danger of predators living in the world. Back in the city, he had heard stories about big striped dog-like creatures, or large cats with enormous teeth that roamed in the wild territories south of Aeterra and the large bears up north. He just never considered nature as evil and dangerous. Animals were just behaving on instinct—you could not fault them.

Trying to shield his eyes against the shimmer, he followed the coastline south, but he could not spot any three-pointed rock formation along it.

"Have you found the Drowned Man's Fork? I don't see anything that looks like it."

"No, but the shimmering water makes it difficult. With the sunlight against us, we won't be able to see much detail from this distance. It does look as though the coast is bending toward the west on the southern horizon, which could be the horn Gavin was talking about. The Drowned Man's Fork should be at the end of the horn, at the western-most tip."

Looking down the slope again, Raylan frowned. "Hey Ca'lek, do you think we need to cross that bridge?" he asked, pointing at a large arch a ways to the east.

"I don't know if I would call that a bridge…" Ca'lek remarked. "From the looks of it, the path winds down in that direction." He stood in his stirrups. "I can't be entirely certain because of the elevated terrain, but I'm pretty sure the path turning around that far side of the slope down there is the same one we're on. If that's the case, it's likely we need to cross that rock arch across the ravine."

The rock arch extended over a large ravine about a third of the way down the mountainside near the tree line. It looked like a giant had brought down its sword, cleaving straight into the slope, splitting the mountain open in a deep chasm. The sound of rushing water a distant hum. The higher side had a sheer drop into the depths while the other, across the arch, had eroded more gradually over time. It sloped away from the path before stopping abruptly and dropping away. Raylan pictured the strong currents running in the depths of the ravine. Rocks and raging water were never a good combination.

"That arch looks awfully thin. Do you think the heavy wagon will be able to get across it?" said Raylan, hoping that the scout's eyes could spot more detail than his own.

"Impossible to tell from here," Ca'lek said with a shrug. "The distance makes it hard to be sure but I don't see any other way across. And it is much too far to jump, even for the horses, so it will have to do."

"It will probably be a good idea to take a rest on that small plateau just before the arch. We should probably take a moment and check how strong that crossing is, then go across one by one," said Raylan.

"Look at you, taking your time to assess and plan. You know, Raylan… you're smarter than you look." Ca'lek gave him a large smile. "And I agree… but you'd better go tell your brother and see what he says."

Raylan pulled Luna's reins and moved toward the north side of the mountain again and spotted the wagon nearing the final stretch to the top. Calling out toward the forefront, he waved his arm to encourage them over. "Come on everybody! You got to see this!"

The bone-chilling howl that answered froze Raylan's arm midair. The howl was so unnaturally hollow, without any warmth, it made the hairs on his neck instantly rise. Xi'Lao and Richard both turned to see where the strange sound came from, as Luna shuffled her feet nervously.

A black shape emerged from behind the last hilltop. The dark silhouette resembled a wolf, one much larger than Raylan had ever seen before. As it stood atop the hill, it threw its head back and let out a second, deep howl that echoed against the mountainside. A deep rumble—like thunder—resonated beneath the sound. At once, Raylan knew this was no ordinary wolf. His realization was enforced when numerous men on horseback came into view, speeding along the path they had been traveling now for days.

"Soldiers!" Raylan shouted at the top of his lungs. "Move!"

Xi'Lao and Richard immediately put the spurs to their horses as Gavin cracked the whip at the animals harnessed to the wagon. The enemy troop was still a good distance removed but the wagon would not be able to outrun them for long. They had to get to the rock arch as soon as possible. It was the best possible place to set up a defense.

He turned in his saddle. "Ca'lek! The stone arch, we need to make it!"

The call to action was all that was needed for Ca'lek to turn Aine and gallop away.

As Xi'Lao and Richard flew by him, Raylan shouted. "Keep going! Follow Ca'lek!"

The wagon took longer, but luckily it had already been quite close to the top. As Raylan turned Luna toward the south side of the mountain, he noted the large wolf was joined by another—larger again—and both jumped into motion, running along the path toward them. Their speed was incredible. They would be on them in no time at all. One last look and he counted at least twenty enemies riding toward them. Raylan kicked Luna into motion as the first shouts of enemies encouraging their own horses reached his ears. He quickly caught up with his brother, and the wagon.

Shouting at Gavin loud enough for the other riders to hear, he yelled, "A stone bridge ahead! We can make a stand there. It's our only chance! They won't be able to attack us all at once!"

Galen and Peadar passed the wagon as soon as the path grew wide enough. Stephen was cursing in the back as it bounced roughly over the rocky path downhill. Behind the wagon, Harwin, Rowan and Kevhin led the spare horses from the encampment. The frightened animals had no trouble keeping up after hearing the wolves howl.

Approaching a bend in the path, Gavin used all his expertise to prevent the horses from careening out of control and slipping off the path into the depths. The wagon tilted dangerously on two wheels through the turn. Raylan heard a loud bang and, judging from another cursed outcry, it was Stephen being thrown into the side of the wagon.

As both wolves crested the top of the path behind them, the larger one broke off the pursuit, diverting to its left, running along the mountain ridge, out of sight.

The single wolf charged down the path, the horsemen coming just across the hill behind it. The group had already closed the gap between them by half. The wagon slowed them on the winding road; the lone horses could not go faster without the risk of slipping off the path.

"We can make it!" he shouted to Harwin and the two archers, trying to make himself believe it. "Keep going!"

Around him, Raylan heard shouts hastening the horses to full speed and beyond. As they approached the stone arch, Raylan saw how thin it truly was. The thinnest part stretching across looked more than thirty feet in width before it thickened again at the other side of the ravine. It looked very unstable and so narrow the wagon might not fit across it at all; and if it did, the weight of it and the cargo might destroy it altogether.

"Gavin! I don't know if the wagon will be able to get across!" Raylan shouted above the thundering of hooves and the rattling of the wagon's wheels.

"It'll have to!" Gavin shouted back.

His brother understood perfectly well they stood no chance fighting the enemy on this side of the ravine. They needed the bottleneck of the bridge to fend off their pursuers. Kevhin and Rowan would be able to take positions on either side to loose arrows, while Galen and Richard could guard the bridge's path.

A loud thud sounded on Raylan's left side. An arrow stuck in the back end of the wagon and, an instant later, another whirred by his right ear. Glancing over his shoulder, he spotted the enemy's archers riding at a dangerous speed, gripping their horses with just their thighs, pulling back their bowstrings to fire off another volley.

Most of the arrows never hit their targets, as the movement of the horses and the distance made it challenging for the enemy soldiers. Rowan and Kevhin both retaliated but directed their attention back to riding once they noticed the distance made hitting anything almost impossible; they did not want to waste the arrows. Unfortunately, the enemy archers did not seem to share their concerns.

Raylan whipped his head round at the cry of one of the spare horses; it had been unexpectedly struck in the hind leg. Its pain could almost be felt as the scream of fear rose from the animal's throat. The horse bucked and nearly dragged Harwin, who was holding the reins, out of his saddle. Unable to figure out which reins were from the panicking horse, he let go of all of them. The second spare horse, suddenly with the freedom to move in any direction it wanted, swayed dangerously toward Raylan, almost pushing him and Luna over the edge of the path.

"Hiyah! Hiyah!" Raylan shouted, to encourage Luna and scare off the other, which was now out of control.

The terrified beast slid back into formation between the riders, not daring to slow with the black wolf giving chase. Without a human to carry, it started to overtake those in front, moving into the lead.

The wounded horse, crippled, limped to a halt, unable to put any weight on its hind leg. As the enemy group drew nearer, the animal went into a frenzy of fear, trying to get out of the way. But the wolf did not attack, it simply ran past without paying the distraught animal any attention. The riders did not seem to care either but as they sped by, the wounded horse kicked back and knocked the legs from under a passing steed.

Both horse and rider crashed to the ground, but his fellow soldiers gave it no notice and sped by the wounded man. The gap shrank to less than five hundred feet.

The wagon jolted into the air ahead; another rain of curse words streaming from within. Raylan duck low to the saddle as dry wood flew out of the back, tumbling over the path but in their frenzy none of the horses seemed to notice the pieces of wood that slammed into their legs and bodies.

Raylan's thoughts went to the egg. A knot formed in his stomach. He swallowed hard. Unsure whether this was entirely his own emotion; he hoped the egg remained safe with the rough handling.

As the path bent around the final mountain slope, the stone arch came back into view. Before making the turn onto the natural bridge, it opened onto the small plateau they had spotted earlier. The mountainside rose straight up, giving the feeling they rode along the walls of a grand castle as they tried to make it to the drawbridge.

We're going to make it. We have to make it.

Raylan watched Gavin take the wagon left, making as wide a turn as possible to steer it directly onto the stone arch. Ca'lek, Xi'Lao and Richard were already speeding toward the stone arch, maneuvering into a single line to pass over its narrowest part and divide their weight as evenly as possible.

As Raylan urged Luna onto the plateau, a shadow shifted at the top of his vision and every fiber in his body reacted to the threat. He reined in the mare as the giant stone wolf landed on the plateau, shaking the ground. It was in front of Ca'lek, Xi'Lao and Richard's group and pounced on the horse Harwin had released. Stone and flesh slid and crashed to a halt directly in front of the bridge. The wolf turned toward them, its paws firmly set on the dead horse. It let out an icy howl in challenge.

Ca'lek's mare, galloping at full speed, reared away from the wolf. Unable to maintain her balance, Aine crashed down, throwing Ca'lek from the saddle as she slid toward the edge of the cliff. The horse screamed as she tumbled down into the fast currents below. Ca'lek scrabbled at the ground, trying to slow his momentum, but the edge came up dangerously fast. His legs went over the brim as he finally snagged his fingers into a rent in the stone, stopping his involuntary flying lesson with a sudden jolt. For the second time, the scout found himself dangling above the depths.

Richard jumped of his horse as soon as it slowed enough and grabbed the scout by his arm. He managed to pull Ca'lek back onto the plateau, but from there they had nowhere to go.

The wolf cut off their only escape route; but it did not move to attack either Richard or Ca'lek, who were a mere ten feet away. Instead, it paced back and forth in front of the bridge, growling at the horses, which all shifted nervously. The wagon slid to a standstill as Gavin steered the horses full circle to prevent the weight of the wagon from forcing the animals too close to the wolf. One of the wagon's wheels looked dangerously crooked, but it seemed none of the axles were broken.

Xi'Lao had her knives in hand, as Galen and Harwin each pulled their swords. Galen's war hammer would be too slow for mounted fighting, so he kept it strapped to his back. Ca'lek, completely covered in scratches from sliding across rock, pulled his sword as Richard drew his newly acquired battle axes from his belt.

Raylan had his sword in hand and turned Luna as the second stone wolf and the enemy riders came pouring onto the plateau. The wolf halted at the path's exit, as the riders flowed to each side, surrounding their squad.

Richard and Ca'lek were driven back into the center of the circle, the enemy archers aiming arrows at them while the other soldiers stretched their spears forward. Several soldiers dismounted and pulled their swords, until they were surrounded by at least thirty-five hardened-looking soldiers.

Raylan saw his brother stand on the jockey box to survey the enemy force, perhaps searching for the leader. Raylan instantly spotted the commanding officer, or rather officers, as they rode onto the plateau. Both men wore clearly visible golden diamonds on their chest. The four golden diamonds shaped in a larger one were in strong contrast to their armor, which was dark gray and black. The armor itself looked to be of a very high quality, multiple layers of darkened metal formed a dark chest guard. Shoulders were of fine metal plating and the arms were protected by darkened leather. Black gauntlets protected hands, while they wore strong leather boots. On their lower legs, the same dark metal plates as their thighs, with leather running beneath them. It all looked strong but flexible. Their helmets held a Y-shaped opening for their eyes, nose and mouth. Although the helmets had a similar design, Raylan noticed a difference in the eye openings, which probably meant they were specially made for each individual.

As one of the men spoke, Raylan saw the black wolf, which had been standing near the path's exit, move between the two men's horses and sit. The other man, who had not issued the command, looked down; a mixture of anger and disgust briefly flashed across his face before he composed himself again and looked Raylan straight in the eye.

Raylan's observation was confirmed when one of the soldiers broke from the circle to report to the two in charge. However, two more soldiers behind the leaders drew his attention. These two were something else entirely. Their faces were hideously malformed; a skull only half covered in flesh. Their dark eyes were as cold as Raylan expected the White North to be on a cloudless night. They gave no emotion, no thoughts for Raylan to read, just emptiness. It reminded him of the eyes of the great flesh-eating fish sometimes caught during one of his long sea voyages. He would keep an eye on them for as long as he could.

"Sit!" commanded Corza to the stone wolf closest to him.

As it moved between them, Koltar could not hide his disgust as he looked down. It seemed the scrolls were key to commanding the beasts and Koltar had looked for a way to strip Corza of at least one of the parchments, but the wolves had been a constant obstacle for him and his men. He did not know if it had been Corza's original plan, but they protected the general day and night, and Corza made a special effort to rub Koltar's nose in his fellow general's new-found security at every opportune moment.

He threw Corza a look. "What are you grinning at?"

"Oh nothing, I'm just glad *my* wolves could help you fulfill your duty of capturing this enemy intrusion."

Koltar scoffed. He let his horse step forward and shouted in his best Terran language. "You're completely surrounded! Drop all your weapons!"

The Stone King had made it a custom for all commanding soldiers to learn the language of the larger enemy territories, for spying, interrogation and—

less likely—negotiations. Koltar estimated his Terran was quite good, but the language of the Tiankong Empire was a completely different story. It was structured so differently from their own spoken language, only a handful of commanding officers had been able to master it sufficiently.

Normally, he would have attacked the enemy as soon as he found a way to secure victory—and they currently had a strong advantage—but Corza insisted they capture and interrogate them to see how much they knew about their plans. He hated to waste an opportunity to take the enemy out, but acknowledged the fact that information was more important.

Maybe it was for the better, as the Stone King had told him nothing about this so-called weapon they were retrieving. Corza had not graced him with any information either. He had reached a decision to hold back his urge to fight and to use the opportunity to gain more insight in what was going on. What was this relic? And why it was so important to the Stone King and that snake Corza? So, here he was, talking instead of fighting, and disliking every moment of it.

For a brief instant, he wondered if his Kovian accent was too thick, since the enemy riders all stared at him blankly. Raising his hand, he signaled all his soldiers to take a step forward with their spears. He was about to give the order to charge, when the nearest enemy soldier turned his head toward the wagon. The soldier looked young and had thick brown hair and dark brown eyes. He saw a small nod from the other soldier on the jockey box.

"The leader," Koltar mumbled to himself.

One by one, the enemy soldiers lowered their weapons, although none threw them on the ground.

Looks like they're not ready to give up just yet. Koltar spoke in a calmer tone but still loud enough so all could hear him. "There's no way out. You only have two ways of getting off this terrace, you can fly or—if you prefer—you can swim. Both paths are guarded by one of the most ferocious creatures you'll ever see in your lives. Trust me, you don't wish to find out what kind of damage they can do. So, I say again, lay down your weapons."

"My father used to say, any man that needs to tell you to trust him, is likely not to be trustworthy."

It was the young soldier with the brown hair that spoke. Koltar looked at him. Two brown eyes stared back at him.

He doesn't look afraid. If he is, he's hiding it well.

"Sounds like your father's a wise man, but that doesn't change the fact you have no way to survive this without surrendering. We're here to claim back that which you've taken, and you'll be brought before the Stone King

111

to receive his judgment on the matter. Drop your weapons, step away from the wagon and prepare to be secured for transport."

A horse in the back was briskly ordered to move to the front. Koltar, admittedly, was surprised to find a woman as part of the enemy group. Women were strictly forbidden in a Doskovian army and for good reason; not many survived an encounter with the Doskovian soldiers that set out to have fun. And those that did often wished they had not. It was one of the reward structures to keep the men in check.

The woman glared furiously at him. "You cannot claim back what you have stolen in the first place! You had no right to take it!"

Does this group have no regard for the situation they're in? Maybe they're a suicide squad on a desperate mission?

"It belongs to the Tiankong Empire!" continued the woman. "It is our heritage! You had no right to just go in and take it! You even had the nerve to burn down our most sacred monastery!"

"Raylan, stop her!"

The shout came from the commanding officer on the wagon. Koltar saw the brown-haired soldier turn toward her.

"Xi'Lao, calm down! What's gotten into you?" He tried to put a hand on her shoulder to hold her and her horse next to him.

She shrugged the hand away. "No, you do not understand! They have to pay for this!"

Laughter in the background drew their attention. Corza was chuckling in his saddle. "No right? Ha! Those idiots had no idea what they were doing. It would've been a disgrace not to take it! They had it for hundreds of years and still had no clue of its real value. One of those strange, old monks even had the nerve to tell us to go away—until my dagger sank into his stomach. They told me he was the master of the monastery, but all I saw was a frail, weak old man. If that was your Empire's most holy person, I can't say I was impressed."

The woman called Xi'Lao let out an angry cry and kicked her heels into the flanks of her mount. The soldier next to her shouted, in surprise, as the horse jumped straight toward Corza's position. As she grabbed one of the smaller knives on her belt, Koltar maneuvered into her way. It was more instinct than the will to defend his fellow general. Koltar could not care less about Corza being attacked, or even killed for that matter, but he would be damned if he would let a woman get past him. He saw the dagger fly before it left her hand, going straight for Corza's throat. He blocked the blade's path with his gauntlet and it clattered harmlessly away.

The woman shifted her next attack toward him. A dagger in her right hand came at him in a horizontal arc from the left, but he grabbed her wrist midair and twisted until she could not hold on to the blade anymore. The knife fell toward the ground, as a second already moved into her left hand again; but this too was stopped by his iron grip. Both their horses were locked, side by side, pressing his leg strongly into hers. The animals turned around each other as Koltar firmly held her wrists in a painful twist.

One of his soldiers stepped in and used the back of his spear to hit the woman sharply across the ribs under her raised arm. Knocking her out of her saddle, she made an awkward twist, before slamming to the ground.

"You're lucky your leg got unpinned, or it would likely have broken," said Koltar.

Scrambling to her knees, with an arm for support, she coughed deeply while holding her ribs, trying to regain her breath.

Koltar dismounted and strolled around his horse. The young soldier with brown hair tried to push closer with his horse, but Koltar's unit was shielding him with their spears.

"Xi'Lao! Are you all right?" called the youngster.

"Raylan, is she all right?" A shout from the wagon.

It was the second time Koltar heard the names called out. *Xi'Lao and Raylan.*

Ignoring the woman, Koltar walked past her and stepped directly in front of the soldier that knocked the woman from her horse. He pulled back his arm, closed his fist, and punched the soldier—full force—on the nose. The man dropped to the ground, spear flying from his hands. "Don't ever attack without my direct order!" he roared. He dragged the woman to her feet by her hair. "I see you like knives. Mind if I borrow one?"

He plucked a knife from her belt and held it across her cheek. "Shall I carve up your pretty face for a bit? Or shall I start a bit lower?"

He moved the knife down, hooked it under her leather armor strap and cut it off. The breast guard snapped free.

The female soldier struggled, as he saw the others of the squad shift around and the commander jump down from the wagon.

"It seems you have some fans. Why not give them a show?"

He put the knife under the fabric of her shirt and tore downward, ripping it open and half exposing her breasts and stomach. She grasped the fabric and put her hands across her chest, a natural reaction, to protect her dignity.

"Don't you touch her!" shouted the commanding soldier, near the wagon.

Good. Now that I have their attention, it's time to create some goodwill and get some answers.

He walked the woman through the group of spearmen and shoved her toward the one brown-haired soldier.

Dismounting, the young man knelt next to her, supporting her.

"Raylan, was it? You better keep her in check. I'd prefer to transport you all back to the palace unharmed, but I won't tolerate any further foolishness. Now, how about you tell me what kind of weapon you're actually moving in that wagon."

The soldier next to the woman looked at him in disbelief. "You mean you don't even know?"

"I know you've got a dangerous weapon hidden in that wagon. I'm asking for details. I believe I haven't been unreasonable until now, so how about you keep your smart remarks to yourself and answer me directly… before I order my men to pierce a few new holes in you."

The young soldier looked back to the wagon for a second. "It's not a weapon, it's a—"

"Enough! I grow tired of this," shouted Corza. "Clearly, they aren't prepared to go quietly, men prepare to attack!"

Corza signaled his men, who immediately readied their weapons and repositioned themselves.

"Now, hold on! I'm still talking to them." Koltar raised his voice in anger, turning toward Corza.

"You've wasted enough time, High General Wayler. I need to get that relic back to the palace as soon as possible, and I will not tolerate your idle chitchat with the enemy," Corza sneered, impatiently.

Looking back to the group, Koltar saw those that had repositioned themselves already, swords and axes raised and at the ready, arrows aimed and eyes alert. But that was not all—something was not right. Corza's men had repositioned themselves strangely. Their positions did not make sense from a tactical point of view. This way, their direct line of attack would be blocked by their own men. No, not their men, *his* men.

It only took Koltar a heartbeat to recognize the danger; but by that time, Corza had already given the order. Launching the attack, High General Setra's men impaled several of Koltar's loyal subordinates before his voice had a chance to rise from his throat.

"Defense rear!"

CHAPTER NINE

Hatch

KOLTAR WAS IMPRESSED by the immediate response of his men to the surprise attack. They had been well-trained. But it was clear who had the upper hand. Koltar's men had always outnumbered Corza's troops; but, a third now lay bleeding on the ground, while the rest were pinned between two enemy fronts.

Koltar growled and spun to face the son of a bitch that had turned on him, only to see the stone wolf coming at him in full speed. While his vision focused on this direct threat, Corza's grinning image faded into the background. His muscles tightened when he saw the wolf leap toward him, jaws spread open like some razor-sharp monster from a nightmare. The image of his own soldier being shredded to pieces by those jaws flashed through his mind.

His fighting spirit rose. No choice, have to evade. There's no blocking this.

He rolled backward and pushed his sword horizontally into the wolf's jaws, while putting his feet on the beast's belly. Even with the weight of a stone statue, momentum made it easy to throw the wolf behind him, extending its jump. The wolf tumbled across the plateau as Koltar scrambled to his feet and ducked below his horse to the other side.

In the meantime, Corza had focused his attention on the two Darkened who had been behind him. Four of Corza's men had engaged them, but two were instantly struck down. The Darkened were almost unparalleled in fighting skill, and it was clear that Corza's men were no match for them. Corza smashed his horse into the tumult and slashed off one of the Darkened's hands, while it was in mid swing.

Koltar jumped back on his horse as he saw the wolf scramble to its feet. It bit a nearby, unlucky soldier in the leg, from agitation. The soldier's flesh was torn from its bone as the wolf violently shook its head. He quickly scanned the battle and noticed the other wolf circling the wagon.

Those beasts need to be taken care of. I need those damn scrolls.

He redirected himself toward his fellow general and kicked his horse into a charge.

As Corza turned, he spotted Koltar moving toward him. Obviously recognizing the danger of having both Koltar and the two Darkened still alive, he called the second wolf over to assist with the two Silent Shadows. It tore through the group like a storm. Knocking Corza's own men aside, it pushed one of the Darkened to the ground and ripped his head off while the torso was pressed to the ground by its massive forepaws.

Koltar reached Corza's position just before the Silent Shadow's head rolled across the plateau. The wolf let out a victory howl before picking his next victim. As Corza turned to block his attack, Koltar noticed just how much the march through the White North had taken its toll on his fellow general. The movement to block was sluggish; but as Corza raised his sword, he also threw himself backward in the saddle, dodging Koltar's incoming strike.

His attack did not hit any flesh, but that had not been Koltar's intention. His weapon's tip snagged the side of Corza's armor and cut the leather strap that secured the pouch with both the wolf scrolls in it.

As the pouch tore, Koltar saw both scrolls sticking out, but they remained clamped under Corza's armor. Pushing off from his horse, Koltar threw himself toward the traitor before Corza had a chance to recover his balance. They slammed the ground. Both scrolls broke free from the fall and bounced across the rocky surface of the plateau.

"You imbecile, they'll rampage!" screamed Corza, as he jumped to his feet to retrieve the fallen scrolls.

Koltar kicked his leg out, tripping Corza, who fell flat onto the ground with a heavy grunt. Corza's sword came slashing backward so fast Koltar barely dodged it. Using the created opening, Corza scurried toward the scrolls.

Both wolves were now on full rampage. The smaller wolf let out a howl, joined by the deep resonance of the larger one. Their instinct taking over, the wolf spotted one of Koltar's soldiers still upon his horse. Running straight for the horse's position, the wolf growled. All color disappeared from the rider's face, as he turned his horse, bolting away.

Outrunning the wolf proved impossible. It jumped full force into the side of the horse, its jaws closing around the soldier's leg and the horse's neck in one bite. The force of the attack slammed the trio into the rock wall at the side of the plateau. The panicking soldier screamed out in terror, as he lay trapped under the weight of his horse—one leg pinned and shattered by his mount, the other ripped off by the wolf. The wolf, however, did not pay him any attention, as it was completely concentrated on ripping the horse's intestines out of its belly.

In that short time, the larger wolf completely devastated the group of soldiers surrounding it. Both Corza's men and the remaining Darkened were nothing more than a pile of limbs and guts. Pieces of bone and flesh hung from the wolf's sharp teeth as it regarded Corza and Koltar from a distance. The wolf watched as the two men continued to struggle.

The wolf stalked slowly toward its previous master's position. It shook its head and let out a rumble.

Koltar panted heavily as he turned and saw the traitor head for the scrolls. The large wolf began its approach, completely ignoring him and focused solely on Corza. Perhaps it felt Corza was to blame of his unnatural state.

Koltar regarded the devastation the wolf left behind. *Total carnage…*

The stone animal dropped its head and shoulders, stalking low to the ground. Its tail stretched down, its ears flattened against its head as it slowly advanced on the unsuspecting Corza.

Koltar realized his opponent could only reach one scroll in time. He jumped to his feet, dashing for the other, which had landed near the edge of the ravine.

Behind him, Corza picked up the scroll and finally looked up. The wolf that was ravaging the crushed horse and soldier suddenly raised his head and looked at his new master again. Koltar heard the traitor swear, as Corza realized the scroll in his hand belonged to the farthest wolf instead of the one approaching him from the side.

"They're mine!" screamed Corza as he dashed after Koltar, trying to reach the other scroll. Then he shouted commands to the wolf. "Attack him! Kill Koltar!"

Koltar dove toward the scroll, grasping it as he slid across the ground. The smaller wolf was coming for him at high speed.

Now how do I control it? "Stop that wolf!" he screamed.

The large wolf instantly came out of its stalk and moved to intercept the smaller wolf as Corza lunged at Koltar and made a grab for the scroll.

The wolves collided heavily, less than sixteen feet from where Koltar and Corza were fighting. Flying splinters cut Koltar's cheek as black stone shattered from the wolves' skin. The crash made the incorrectly positioned larger wolf tumble sideways, slamming into the men with full force. Koltar made a grasp for Corza's armor as they rolled across the plateau. He felt his grip slip on the scroll as Corza yanked it from his hands. Trying to recover the scroll, he stretched his arms toward that double-crossing weasel. He felt strangely light, trying to reach out…

He saw Corza hanging from the ledge, but once more something was off. It seemed surreal. He could not remember seeing Corza slide over the edge. The distance grew wider, and more daylight was engulfed by dark rock walls. Then, it dawned on him.

It's not Corza that has gone over.

Daylight quickly slunk to less than a hair-thin slit as the sounds of the battle was drowned out of his world by an increasing thundering roar.

As he reached the end of his fall, the sound of the impact was completely washed away by the deafening roar of the water. A small salamander, clinging to the wall, was the only one that heard his voice, bellowing with rage, rise above the noise of it all. He screamed the name of his betrayer, just before he was swallowed whole by the wet darkness.

Raylan supported Xi'Lao, checking if she was okay, while keeping one eye on the soldiers. He wondered why she lost her cool like that. She must have known it would provoke them into action while they were clearly outnumbered. She was lucky they did not kill her for it. They all were.

As he tried to guide her away from danger, all hell broke loose.

He had no idea what was going on, but he recognized an opportunity when he saw it. As the enemy soldiers turned on each other, he dragged Xi'Lao to her feet. "Move! Get on your horse!"

As he pushed her into the saddle, she slumped forward, still not able to fully straighten up. He grabbed the reins and pulled her horse, while running toward the wagon.

An enemy soldier moved in from his right. It happened so fast that he was unable to position himself between the attacker and the incapacitated Xi'Lao. As the soldier raised his sword to strike, a crossbow bolt pierced the man's neck. Raylan spotted Stephen through a hole in the canvas. He must have been following everything from inside the wagon, peering through the many holes and cracks in the canvas. The injured scout smiled at Raylan and stuck up his thumb through one of the other gaps, before quickly reloading the crossbow.

Kevhin and Rohan both fired their arrows, taking out two of the enemy archers aiming for their group, while the remaining Doskovian archers were too busy with their internal conflict.

Coming up to the wagon, Raylan yelled toward his brother. "Gavin! She can't ride!"

"Switch with me! I'm a better rider than you!" urged his brother.

As Gavin took his place behind Xi'Lao and took the reins, Raylan jumped on the coach box. Richard and Ca'lek were fighting some enemy soldiers near the edge, but the biggest obstacle was still that huge stone wolf. Raylan did not like the look of that thing, at all. *It looks worse than the human rock statue from before.*

Kevhin and Rohan shot off another two volleys, this time at the large wolf who had been guarding the stone arch bridge. With ease, the wolf dodged them all, except for the last one, which it caught between its jaws and snapped it like a twig.

Galen and Peadar were using the spare horses as a barrier, encouraging the nervous animals to kick backward at any soldier attempting to approach them.

"Take the wagon across the bridge," he heard his brother shout. "We need to break through."

"How? There is no way we're getting past that wolf," Raylan replied.

"We'll have to ram it. The wagon is the only thing that might be heavy enough to break through. We need to make use of this chaos. Now go!" ordered Gavin.

Cracking the reins, Raylan forced the frantic horses into motion. He used all his strength and skill to keep the horses from careening out of control. It seemed futile; the animals did not dare move any closer to the wolf. Unwilling to let the wagon pass, the wolf began to circle, scaring the horses away from the stone arch. Raylan drew his sword, following the black nightmare with his eyes. But with one hand off the reins, the horses immediately stopped obeying their master and started pulling away from the unnatural danger. Raylan now had to turn around to keep the wolf in sight.

He'll come as soon as he's in my blind spot.

As Raylan tightened his muscles, readying himself in case the wolf decided to attack, Gavin guided himself and Xi'Lao behind the wagon, staying out of the wolf's direct line of sight. Using his horse to block the wagon's horses, Gavin tried to keep them from turning their backs to the wolf, as well to keep them pointed toward their only escape route. If the horses decided to circle on the plateau, they would never be able to get out.

The wolf almost disappeared behind the back of the wagon as Raylan tried to keep it in view, when suddenly, it shifted its body toward the wagon. Had it noticed Stephen… *or is it going after the egg? Panic rose hard and fast.*

Crouching, the wolf got ready to launch itself at the wagon. Raylan knew it was impossible, but he could not help himself. He shouted anyway. "Stephen, get out of there. It will be on you in seconds!"

But instead of jumping into the wagon, the wolf raised its head sharply, twisting to look across the battlefield. It darted off in an instant, throwing itself into the tumult of men, fighting near the path entrance.

"Now!" he heard Gavin shout. "Everyone, go! This is our chance."

Raylan dropped back onto the wagon seat and snapped the reins hard to get the horses moving. Richard and Ca'lek were already making a break for the stone arch on foot, while Kevhin and Rohan turned their mounts around and set off in the same way.

Galen sent Peadar ahead, while kicking a soldier in the chest, who attempted to pull him from his horse. The spear, which the soldier had thrust at him, was locked under his massive arm, as the kick dislodged the soldier's hold on it. He swung the spear around in one hand and threw it with a short, powerful motion into the chest of another soldier coming toward him.

Gavin, who had moved ahead of Raylan and the wagon, reached the stone arch. Tightly holding on to Xi'Lao, he raced across. Richard and Ca'lek had just reached the other end and were looking back to see if everyone was following.

Kevhin and Rohan galloped across, the thundering hooves of their horses echoing across the ravine. Peadar followed with two of the spare horses and Luna in tow. With each small group passing, cracks in the stone arch lengthened by a few inches—the cracking sounds barely noticeable because of the stomping of hooves.

Just before he turned the wagon onto the stone bridge, Raylan saw Harwin and his mount cut in front of him to get to the other side. He had no idea where Harwin came from… he had lost sight of him as soon as they were surrounded; but judging by the blood on his face and armor, he must not have had a clear path to retreat across the bridge.

A rock bounced the wagon partly into the air, making it thump down its heavy weight onto the rocky surface of the arch. The wheels were a mere finger's length from a very steep drop. Leaning over the side, Raylan peered down into the abyss. Pieces of rock broke off the natural bridge and tumbled into the depth below.

"It's cracking!" he heard Richard shout ahead of him.

Harwin just passed the waiting duo at the other end, which meant only he and Galen were left to reach the other side. He had no time to wonder about

Galen though, as he saw a crack originate under the wagon and shoot out across the length of the stone arch all the way to the point where Richard and Ca'lek waited. Snapping the reins feverishly, the horses jolted, increasing their speed even more. He saw foam running from their noses and mouths, their eyes stretched wide open, as the panicking animals both tried to push away from their side of the abyss, with the poor result that they only ended up working against one another.

Finally, hurtling past Richard and Ca'lek, Raylan let out his breath. He had made it in one piece and with the egg nonetheless. Keeping up his speed, Raylan passed Gavin and Xi'Lao, who seemed to be sitting a bit straighter.

"Keep going!" was the order.

He followed the path as it bent to the right. Looking across the ravine, he noticed the two enemy men who had addressed him, locked in a fight near the edge of the cliff. As the wolves clashed, he saw them tumble, and one of the men rolled off the ledge from the momentum. He was unsure which of the two soldiers it was, but he saw the remaining person scramble to his feet, looking around and noticing the wagon across the ravine. Unable to fully hear the rampage, it was clear the man was very unhappy with the fact the wagon was on the opposite side. Pointing toward the stone arch, Raylan saw him shout something, as both wolves sprang into action and stormed straight to the narrow crossing.

In the meantime, Galen reached their side safely; but the stone arch developed even more cracks along its length, as another large piece of rock broke free and dropped into the raging water below. As their heavy hitter reached the other side, Gavin called out to him.

"Dismount! Let Ca'lek take the horses!"

In one fluent motion, Galen jumped from his horse, making room for Ca'lek, who was up on the saddle before the horse had fully come to a stop, urging it on again.

"Ca'lek, get out of range of any archers. We need those horses," ordered Gavin, his voice carrying across the distance.

As the path turned right, it slowly ascended. The weight of the wagon, in combination with the nearly exhausted horses, had slowed them to a walking pace. If he did not want the horses to die from exhaustion—or stress— Raylan had to give them some breathing space now. They were far enough from the battle to be safe; but Gavin would not approve of him stopping completely, so he let the horses slow down to a walk instead. Standing on his jockey box, Raylan peered back. Gavin dismounted and set Xi'Lao onto the path, commanding her to get to safety.

Raylan saw his brother run toward Richard and Galen. While on the other side, the two wolves stormed across the plateau toward the bridge. Some of the soldiers closer to the arch moved in as well, clearly with the same intent as the wolves—to cross the bridge.

Gavin gestured wildly his arms, while shouting and running toward Galen and Richard. The latter sprang into action and thrust the back end of one of his new axes into the crack that had formed across the stone arch. Galen took his war hammer from his back and started hammering at it right away, as Gavin encouraged him on. The clear clang of metal hitting metal rang out against the mountain slopes. After the third hit, a loud crack rent the air, and Raylan saw a large part of the arch shift in its place. Another two hits and the arch started crumbling, a large boulder falling free and crashing into the ravine.

With its stability gone, the stone arch gave off a series of loud cracks as it broke off, piece by piece, creating a gap of twenty feet.

The soldiers stopped dead in their tracks but could hardly turn around as the remaining commander and his two wolves were now right behind them. The commander, who had reclaimed his horse, was furious. Riding back and forth, shouting at his troops, he seemed to order the men across the gap. At first, none of the soldiers seemed crazy enough to attempt the jump; but when both wolves were steered toward them, one of the terrified spearmen did a run-up and launched himself across. As he plummeted down into the chasm, his scream discouraging the remainder of the soldiers to give it a try, no matter how big the wolves were.

All the while, Richard and Galen were on the other side, watching for arrows. Gavin turned and signaled Kevhin and Rohan back. They fired off two arrows, which struck one soldier in the neck, making him keel over backward and disappear into the depths of the ravine. A second was hit in the arm, as the group of soldiers tried to escape out of range. As they turned to flee back to the plateau, their commander ordered both wolves to make the jump.

Crashing straight into the fleeing group, another two soldiers lost their balance and were thrown aside by the first wolf making the jump, their screams quickly disappearing into the depths.

Just when Raylan reached the top of the hill with the wagon, the wolf soared across the gap. A new piece of rock broke off the stone arch where the wolf pushed off for the jump. Landing heavily, the wolf came to a screeching halt a few feet from Richard, Galen, and his brother. It pounced directly onto Gavin as if given a direct command. It seemed the enemy commander wanted to take out their leader, to weaken them. Seeing the wolf land heavily on his brother,

Raylan resisted the urge to turn and help him; he knew he could not leave the dragon egg and the wagon alone. Gavin would never allow it.

Some nights ago, when Xi'Lao opened up a little about the dragon egg, she made it clear the importance this egg had for the world, or rather, how catastrophic it would be if it fell into the wrong hands. The historical information on dragons led her to believe they were creatures of great power. Gavin gave her his word to defend the egg at all costs. This included keeping it out of enemy hands, even at the risk of losing the lives of everyone in their squad. It was the honorable thing to do. Their task now solely consisted of getting the dragon's egg back to Aeterra, where it could be kept safe until the king officially handed it over to the royal family of the Tiankong Empire.

Peadar circled the wagon, nervously.

"Come on Raylan. What are you waiting for? We have to keep going."

"But Gavin…" Raylan protested, as he could not turn his eyes away, no matter how much he wanted to.

Fortunately, Galen did not hesitate to act. As the wolf snapped its jaws left and right of Gavin's head, his brother dodged the incoming attacks as much as possible, using his swords to divert the razor-sharp teeth.

Approaching from the flank, Galen came in swinging his war hammer low. Hitting the wolf just behind its foreleg, he used all his power and speed to push the wolf upward. Being pushed sideways on to three legs, the dark terror turned its head toward its unexpected attacker, snapping at him.

Grunting loudly, Galen pushed harder, his muscles bulging, straining under the weight of the stone wolf. His efforts were rewarded, as the movement of the wolf—and Galen's forceful push—toppled the stone wolf onto its flank. However, as it rolled over and lost its footing, its hind leg swapped Galen's feet from under him.

Raylan wanted to shout out a warning, but the words were unable to leave his throat, as the scene played out beyond his control. Losing his balance, Galen stumbled forward together with the wolf. Raylan watched in sheer horror as both the living statue and the man disappeared into the dark chasm, on their way to meet the white, foaming, swirling waters at the bottom.

His brother and Richard dashed toward the edge, only to watch their comrade disappear into the depths.

The second stone wolf came flying through the air, landing heavily on their side of the now broken stone arch. This one completely ignored the men on the bridge and immediately started running toward the top of the path.

It was coming for the wagon.

"Raylan! Snap out of it! What are you waiting for? It must be coming after the egg. Go. Go. GO," shouted Ca'lek, who was just reaching the top with the two spare horses in tow.

Raylan dropped onto his seat and whipped the reins to spur the horses on again. *How the hell are we going to outrun this thing?*

Although the path sloped down again, it still followed the ravine. As the first trees swished past, the stone wolf all but overtook the wagon. Raylan tried his best to keep ahead of the dark creature, but the horses were near their end, and one of the wheels wobbled, dangerously unstable. The wolf did not seem tired at all. It passed all the others on the path and came straight for the wagon.

The wolf snapped its jaws at the back wheels. Harwin and Peadar tried to draw its attention, but their efforts went unrewarded. Ca'lek rode up front, shouting back to Raylan, in case the path did anything unexpected, and trying to keep Raylan informed about the wolf's whereabouts. Raylan had no time to look for himself. The wagon pulled heavily in the turns as the weight of chest, firewood and Stephen shifted from side to side.

Likely noticing that attacking the wheels did not do enough to stop the wagon, the wolf shifted to the side of the speeding vehicle. Its black shape ran so fast, it looked like its eyes were leaking, as the cold blue light seeped from its sockets like smoke.

Pulling away from the wagon slightly, the wolf suddenly slammed its full body weight into the side of it. Wood cracked under the power of the attack, but the wagon's momentum prevented it from tipping. Another two attempts did not do much either; the wagon's weight worked in their favor, for once.

"Rock left!"

It was Ca'lek's shout from the front. A huge boulder sat on the path's left side. Raylan carefully steered to his right, approaching dangerously close to the edge of the path. An idea sprang to life. Correcting the wagon's course, he steered as narrowly past the boulder as possible. If he was not able to squash the wolf between the wagon and boulder, at least it would have to slow down, dropping behind them.

The wolf, however, did not slow at all. It sped up.

It was still not running at full speed? Raylan bit back his horror at the sound of the running stone paws drawing closer.

The wolf ran up the left side of the mountain slope and leaped to the top of the boulder. From there, it launched itself directly toward the wagon… there was no escape.

For the second time since the conflict started, Raylan saw a wolf pass over his head like a dark shadow of death. There was nothing he could do as a chaos of fangs and claws threw itself directly on top of the pulling horses. Crashing toward the ground, the legs of both horses snapped like twigs, and the entire wagon began to roll. A disarray of flesh, stone and wood crashed down the slope. Raylan was launched into the air, barely missing a dead tree stump on the way. Slamming into the ground, he slid on his side into a stone boulder. With his heart pumping pure adrenaline, he jumped up at once, watching the remainder of the wagon continue its downward crash.

The steep slope was littered with small boulders and trees; the ground filled with the fallen needles of those forest giants. It had softened Raylan's landing, but also made the ground a slippery slope all the way to the ravine's edge. The wagon smashed into a large boulder with the sound of shattering wood and bending metal. The horses' limp bodies rolled along the slope. Raylan heard the wolf growl in anger, as it got tangled up in the reins and four pair of legs. Its heavy stone body was dragged along by the dead weight of the horses and rapidly approached the edge of the ravine; but that did not concern Raylan in the least. Before he actually saw the stone wolf disappear over the edge, his focus was drawn to the wagon. It had split open upon the rock, throwing Stephen and the chest out of it.

Raylan frowned as a second, bandaged person flew through the air, until his mind caught up to the fact that Regis' remains had been in the wagon as well. Raylan was moving before Stephen hit the ground, next to their diseased, wrapped-up comrade. The chest followed not much later; its busted lock sprang open from the impact. The dragon's egg launched out of its wooden confinement and instantly began tumbling down toward the ravine at incredible speed.

NO! The word more mental scream than sound.

Sprinting down the slope, trying to make an impossible choice, Raylan felt despair rise inside of him. Save the egg or save his comrade? Both were on course to end up plummeting into the abyss. It seemed like it did not matter which he chose, as the distance was only increasing no matter how fast he ran.

The dragon's egg picked up speed, tumbling, bouncing off the ground for small moments at a time, until it skimmed off a dead branch lying on the ground. The change of course sent the egg flying directly into the thick trunk of a tree, where the egg shattered. Raylan's breath caught in his throat; his eyes wide in a mixture of terror, despair and disbelief. As pieces of the egg's shell flew past the trunk, he saw the dragon smash backward into the tree.

Its body hit the wood with such force, pieces of bark flung into the air. Raylan saw its limbs, its head, and what he would later recognize as its wings, whipped around the trunk. It let out a high yelp on impact, before sliding to the ground. There it remained, still, at the foot of the tree.

A large shape blurred past him. *Harwin.* The man had forced his horse on a suicide run down the slope, chasing after Stephen—who still slid toward his doom.

Regis' remains were the first to reach the end of the slope. Launching into the darkness of the ravine, its silent flight the only funeral it would ever receive.

Stephen tried his best to slow down. He grasped desperately at the ground but ended up with nothing but loose needles in his hands a dozen times. He reached the rocky ground at the end of the slope, and as the edge approached, he was only capable of preventing his premature exit from this world at the very last moment. Launching off the edge, his hands finally hooked onto a sturdy tree root, stopping his momentum just in time to be left dangling with nothing but air and raging water beneath him.

As Raylan neared the spot where the dragon lay, he dropped to his knees from exhaustion. His head was thumping, making him feel hazy as he dragged in deep breaths. He looked up and saw Ca'lek and Harwin, racing toward the edge. Harwin turned his steed as he approached the spot where Stephen held on for dear life, and jumped off his horse. The veteran warrior slid to a halt, his heels in the dirt, and dove forward on the rock with his arms stretched forward to grab Stephen.

Harwin grabbed the scout's hands in an iron grip as they slipped from the root. Stephen tried to pull himself up but lacked the strength.

"Someone help!" grunted the old shield warrior.

Ca'lek arrived, and with Harwin, pulled Stephen onto solid ground.

"Thanks," said Stephen, his voice weak.

"I've been there, my friend. I know the difference a helping hand makes," said Ca'lek, with a smile.

Harwin just gave a short scoff, patting Stephen's shoulder.

Raylan returned his gaze to the young dragon. Its pale-yellow body lay motionless between the roots of the tree. Wanting to approach, Raylan tried to stand but his head spun and his vision blurred. He put his hand to his head, and his fingers came away sticky, bright red blood painting his skin. It was the last thing he saw before all light and sound disappeared from his world.

CHAPTER TEN

Life

"*T*OO... EARLY...*"*
Who's there?
"*Not... ready yet.*"
Ready for what?
"*It... hurts...*"
Where are you?

Raylan's fingers cramped on a tiny ridge of cold, wet stone. His breaths echoed hollowly, but it was too dark to see. The only light, a small circle above that beckoned him upward. Below him, nothing but darkness, and the soft drip of water falling in a puddle. Panic strangled him. How did he get here? He shifted his foot; increased pressure on it, trying to give his fingers some rest.

"*It's cold...*"
What's cold?

He still could not pinpoint from where the voice came.

Are you at the top of the well? You need to help me. I'm stuck down here.

"*I cannot... too weak. Need... you.*"

There was a buzzing in his ears and his head hurt like hell. He managed to climb another few steps. His muscles burned as he pushed himself to keep going.

"*I am... hungry. And cold... so cold.*"

"*Hold on,*" Raylan called out, uneasy.

A desperation flowed through him, and he forced himself to move faster. Feel his way up. The light grew as he neared it.

"*Get away from me. It hurts!*"

The sudden outburst echoed through the well. Raylan now moved dangerously fast, trying not to think about the possibility of slipping and falling. He swore he felt the voice's distress. It urged him onward... upward... toward the light.

I'm getting closer. I'm almost there...

"*Hurry...*"

As Raylan finally reached the top, the light blinded him for a moment. He blinked a couple of times as his eyes teared up. Above him, the treetops came into view; blurry at first, then more focused. He groaned.

"Easy now."

He looked sideways and saw Xi'Lao, sitting next to him.

"Where..."

Cutting him off, she said, "You are safe. You collapsed and blacked out. You hit your head pretty hard from what I can tell. Fortunately, we stopped the bleeding."

He held his hand to the side of his head, where the pain radiated, then lifted his head to find the dragon.

Misinterpreting him, Xi'Lao quickly continued, "The stone wolf went over the edge. Stephen seems okay, for now. His hands are pretty raw, and he has quite a few black and blue spots. But he is quite talkative. I am most concerned about his leg. It took another big hit and dirt has found its way into his wounds."

"*Where are you?*"

The voice in his head came at the same time he heard an unfamiliar animal sound not far from him. He sat upright despite his head's objection. He could not quite place the small growl he heard right away; but he certainly recognized the voice.

Looking at the tree some feet away, the dragon stood on its legs, shivering. Its sleek body gracefully curved. Nervously, it swayed its head back and forth at the people surrounding him. Those not injured—or not looking after Raylan—moved in on the dragon as it awakened. It snapped its jaws at whoever came too close, hissing and growling. Its head scanned left to right, trying to keep everyone in its line of sight. Its left wing hung strangely limp at its side. It did not look like it was able to move it.

Getting to his feet, Raylan staggered forward on wobbly legs. "Stop it. Leave him alone. You're frightening him!"

"What? Him who? What are you talking about?" Gavin said.

Raylan pushed Richard and Ca'lek, who had been closest to the dragon, away. "Back. Give him some room." He turned around and dropped to his knees. "Easy now... it's me. I'm here."

The dragon turned toward him. It blinked anxiously with its inner eyelids. Raylan stretched out his hand as slowly as he could. Still trembling, he reached all the way out. He let his open hand hover in front of the dragon's head.

"Careful, Raylan. It nearly took Peadar's hand off when he tried that before," said Richard.

The dragon slowly stretched out its neck, as he limped a step closer. His head was sleek, with deep sockets in which the most beautiful eyes swirled. It looked like the eye consisted of three smaller pupils, spinning around like sparkling vortexes. A tear, around the vortex, ran a small stream of black to the edge of the iris, which was a stunning deep yellow. The color changed, slightly, as shades of gold and orange moved when the eye refocused. His neck was flexible, protected by a series of spikes forming a flat collar that started at the jaws and went over the top of his head. The spikes had, what looked like, hardened skin stretched between them.

The pale, yellow skin had scales cascading over each other. Differing in size, here and there, the scales covered most of his body, except for a softer belly area and the inside of his legs. He was about the size of a large street dog, if not for his long tail. The dragon could easily be picked up if one wanted, but one look at his mouth would make anyone reconsider. Two large fangs and a row of sharp-looking teeth lined his mouth; some showed even when his jaws were closed.

Raylan held his breath as the creature inched closer. Halting just before him, the creature looked at Raylan, flicking his forked tongue through the air. For a moment, Raylan was afraid he had completely misjudged the situation… of course, the voice was not real, and the feelings was just confusion from hitting his head. He was probably about to lose his hand to an unknown beast.

His thoughts were interrupted, by a single gesture of complete acceptance and innocence, as the dragon stretched his neck forward and slid his head into the palm of Raylan's hand. The dragon closed his eyes at the first touch. The feeling was indescribable as it rushed through Raylan in a tidal wave of warmth. The hairs on the back of his neck stood on end as he felt the warmth go up his spine, arriving at his head. His surroundings brightened as he saw the sunlight increase in density. Colors became more vibrant; sounds more intense.

As the voice entered his head, clearer than it ever was, he knew there would be no going back, nor would he ever want to.

"*You are mine, and I am yours. My name is Galirras.*"

The bond was made. He realized he would do anything to protect this creature. The connection felt like a multitude of love, although love was not the right word for it. It was different from love between humans; the word love was too limited to describe it. Love was fleeting, unnatural butterflies in your stomach. This was rooted much deeper. It was as if this creature, this beautiful being, had always been a part of him, and he of it. Raylan could not imagine it had ever been different, while clearly, the reality was that he had not even known about such a possibility this morning. It felt as natural as breathing or moving your body without thinking. It was there in the world, and he had no choice but to accept it.

"It is too early. I was waiting for you. What took you so long? I do not feel well." The last words came out as a soft whimper.

"I'm sorry. I didn't understand. I still don't. Please, help me understand," said Raylan. He moved closer to the dragon, putting an arm around him.

"Who are you talking to?"

It was Peadar, who moved closer, seeing that the potentially dangerous situation was disarmed when the dragon showed his acceptance of Raylan.

Raylan looked at him, confused. "What do you mean? Can't you hear him?"

"Get him away," shouted the voice in Raylan's head.

Galirras turned his head around and snapped his jaws at the curious Peadar.

Raylan felt the dragon tremble beneath his touch. He quickly stroked along his flexible neck, whispering soothing words. "It's okay. He's a friend… they're all friends. You're safe here."

Galirras quickly put his head against Raylan's arm. *"You are nice and warm. I am so cold… and hungry."*

Raylan looked up at Gavin. "Can we make a fire? He needs warmth. And food. Food would be good. I think I have some dried meat in my pack, still." His brother hesitated. Raylan kept his eyes locked with him. "Please."

It was enough for Gavin to decide not to intervene. "Let's do what he says. Ca'lek mentioned an overhanging rock a little further down the path. It will provide us with some basic shelter. Harwin, you, Rohan, and Kevhin go and prep a fire. After that, you two go hunt," said Gavin, pointing to the two archers.

In the meantime, Xi'Lao passed Raylan his dried meat. Holding it in front of the newly hatched dragon, Raylan spoke softly. "Here, eat this. It's not much, but it's all I have right now."

Galirras flicked his tongue along the dried meat, sniffing it carefully. Satisfied by the smell and driven by his hunger, he scooped up the piece and swallowed it whole.

"More. Is there more? I am still hungry."

"I'm sorry. It's all I have, little one," Raylan said, regretfully.

As the others started their climb up the slope, to make the preparations for the fire, Harwin turned and called out. "One of the horses became untangled and did not go over the edge with the stone wolf. It was already dead, but we should still be able to use the meat."

Raylan looked Galirras in the eye. "Would that work? Do you eat horses?"

"I do not know. What does it taste like?" he asked, curiously.

It seemed to Raylan that the young dragon had somewhat recovered now that he had eaten a tiny bit, since Galirras looked around with a sudden jolt of energy. Raylan pointed out the carcass of one of the horses that had pulled the wagon. It lay some ways down, near the edge of the ravine. As soon as he had spotted it, Galirras moved toward it. Pushing off, he did what came naturally and spread his wings, but then let out a yelp of pain.

"Something is wrong. I want to fly. Why can I not fly?" Galirras exclaimed, in a panic.

Raylan quickly moved forward, sitting next to Galirras again, to see what was wrong. He noticed the position of his left wing was all wrong. It appeared not to be in the same spot as the right wing, and it looked swollen at the place where it was attached to the dragon's body.

"It's your left wing, little one. It must have been injured during the wagon crash. We'll need to let Peadar have a look at it." Noticing a nervous feeling in his gut that was not his own, he quickly added, "It really is okay. Peadar takes care of all our birds and has experience keeping our animals healthy. He knows what he's doing. He studied under the royal animal maester back at Shid'el. He'll help you get better, I promise."

Feeling Galirras give in some, he beckoned Peadar, who had moved away to give them space. "It's alright. He'll let you come close now."

As Peadar came closer, he slowly crouched next to Raylan and Galirras. He carefully picked up the wing. Galirras let out a low rumble from his throat. Peadar instantly froze.

"It hurts."

"It's okay, little one. He needs to have a look. He'll try not to make it hurt too much," said Raylan, soothingly, while nodding for Peadar to continue.

"Fascinating, I've never seen anything like it. The bone structure is like a bird's, but much more solid. There is a lot of strength and flexibility in the framework of the wing. The skin is flexible and thin but seems very durable."

"Can you see what's wrong?"

"It looks like the joint near the shoulder has been badly dislocated. It must have happened during the crash. Luckily, none of the bones seem broken.

But we'll need to set this upper bone correctly into its socket, or it will never be able to use its wing."

"His wing…"

Peadar looked at him, confused.

"You said it, he's a he…"

"How do you know?"

"I just do. His name is Galirras. He told me."

"It… he talks to you?" said Peadar, looking at the completely unknown animal species in front of him.

"Up here," said Raylan, tapping on the side of his head. "I don't yet understand it myself."

"Stop talking. I am hungry," squealed Galirras, while squirming underneath Raylan's arms.

"I'm sorry. Please, hold on just a while longer, little one." He turned back to Peadar. "Quickly tell me… the wing, how do we do this?"

"There's no easy way. We need to stretch it and let it pop back into the socket. There's a lot of muscle, even if he's still small. We'll need to use some force."

Raylan felt his stomach turn as he explained to Galirras what was needed. The little dragon did not understand why they had to hurt him to heal him. He asked Raylan if they could let it be.

In the end, Raylan could do nothing but ask Galirras to trust him. If he ever wanted to use the wing properly, it had to be done. It took Raylan's most soothing words, while stroking the dragon's neck and jaw, and using all his warmth and open friendliness, to win over Galirras. Eventually, Galirras reluctantly gave in, but not until he had been bribed with another two pieces of dried meat that Xi'Lao offered from her own rations.

Raylan sat and took the little dragon in his arms, locking his legs around the dragon's shoulder. He made sure the other wing was properly folded up against the dragon's side, while holding Galirras' head gently but securely in his arms. He saw Galirras' tail nervously twitch back and forth.

"Will it hurt?"

"I'm afraid so, little one; but it must be done, if you ever want to use that wing. I wish there was a different way. Please, be strong. We'll do it as quickly as possible."

Peadar excused himself to Galirras, before pulling the wing outward and moving the bone up. Gripping it securely with two hands, he pushed his weight backward to maneuver the wing into its correct position.

Galirras let out a long whine as Raylan felt the poor creature tremble from the pain. He whispered more soothing words and his heart ached at the pain they were inflicting on the little dragon.

"Sssh… it's okay, my brave one. You're so strong. It will be over soon. Try to hold on a little bit longer. You can do it."

It seemed to take ages as Raylan held Galirras firmly locked in his arm. He felt the little dragon squirm, surprised by the power this little creature already had in his body. He had seemed so weakened, but now he felt the large muscles move beneath the scaled skin. Finally, with one last yelp from Galirras, the bone shot into place.

Peadar quickly took a step back, to give them some space again. Raylan slowly loosened his grip.

"Are you all right? Does it feel better this way?" he asked.

"It does not hurt… that badly anymore," Galirras said, as he swung his head around, nudging the wing carefully with the top of his nose.

Raylan let out a sigh of relief, when he suddenly saw Galirras sink through his legs, going limp. Raylan felt all the energy drain from the dragon's body.

"No. Galirras? Wake up!"

Raylan immediately lifted the head that had ended up on his leg. He looked up to Peadar. "It must have taken too much energy to reposition the wing. He needs food. We need to get some food in him. Where's that dead horse?" he asked, fear tingeing his voice. He looked around frantically and began to stand up.

"Hold on. Stop, don't move. We first need to tie his wing, securely, before you start dragging him around," Peadar quickly interrupted. "The wing needs to be supported—and then completely rested—for at least a couple of days for it to heal properly, I expect. Let me grab some of the weapon belts."

Raylan held Galirras close as Peadar sped off toward the wagon wreckage to grab belts. As he pulled him closer, he noticed the little dragon felt colder than before. Xi'Lao, who—along with Gavin—followed things from a distance, seemed to sense the same thing as she came over with one of the fur coats to put around Galirras.

"Thanks," Raylan said, quietly.

"Just keep him close and give him your warmth. We will get some food in him and get him to the fire they are preparing, soon," Xi'Lao replied softly.

As soon as Peadar returned, he carefully and skillfully put the wing in a resting position against Galirras' flank. He secured it with two weapon belts, one around the shoulder and torso and the other around the waist of the little dragon.

"It's the best I can do at the moment, but at least you can move him now," he added, apologetically.

With Galirras firmly in his arms, Raylan got to his feet. Slowly, walking downhill toward the horse carcass, Raylan made sure each step had a firm foothold before he placed weight on it. He felt the dragon breathe heavily, as if in a deep slumber. The reality that Galirras might be too weak to survive, coming out of the egg before he was ready to hatch, dawned on Raylan more with every step he took. His heart felt heavy when they finally reached the dead horse.

As he carefully put down Galirras, he spoke clearly. "Here is the horse, little one. Please eat. You need to eat. You need the strength."

There was no reaction from Galirras.

Picking up the dragon, Raylan put him on the horse's stomach. "Here, feel it. It's still warm. You've got to eat, please."

A low rumble rose from Galirras' throat, as the smell of the dead horse entered his nose and sparked his senses. But he was still too weak to lift his head, barely having the strength to flick his tongue outward.

As a last resort, Raylan grabbed his sword and stabbed it deep into the horse's carcass. Slicing open the entire belly, the guts spilled out. Throwing his sword to the side, he took his dagger from his belt and feverishly slashed the inside of the horse. Its blood was still warm enough to flow; sluggish though it was.

Cupping his hands, he caught as much of it as possible. Lifting Galirras' head with one hand, he let the blood trickle into the dragon's mouth. Raylan saw most of it spill out of the corner of his mouth, but Galirras' eye crept open and swirled around, trying to focus.

Another handful of blood elicited an approved rumble from the weak dragon, after which, it slowly shifted his head. Raylan used the opportunity to cup blood with both hands, increasing the amount of blood poured into Galirras' mouth.

Slowly but surely, the dragon drank more, waking from an almost comatose state. *"More… I need more."*

"Don't worry. I'm here for you. Just drink. Use your strength to eat, you need the energy."

Raylan took his dagger and cut off a small piece of muscle from the horse's hind leg. Cutting it up smaller, he put the pieces in Galirras' throat, allowing the little dragon to instantly swallow them.

With each bite, it seemed the little dragon became more alert. He moved his tail first, then his legs. Eventually, he had enough strength to lift his head, and to crawl across the horse and take a few bites by himself. It still took effort

134

to tear off the meat from the horse's bones, so Raylan helped rip up the meat for him. After a few bites, he sank down again.

For a brief moment, fear raced through Raylan; but then the now familiar voice in his head said, *"So full... so sleepy..."*

He stroked the back of the dragon's head. "You did well, little one. Go to sleep. I'll keep you warm."

It took Raylan the remainder of the afternoon to carry Galirras back up the hill, as the dragon entered a deep slumber. Raylan stopped frequently to check if Galirras was still breathing. He kept the creature as close as possible, wrapped in the fur coat Xi'Lao had given him.

The sun was making room for the moon, and by the time they arrived at the campfire, night had fallen completely.

Exhausted, Raylan sat against the rock wall as close to the fire as he could manage. He was careful not to bring Galirras into contact with the open flame, but figured the dragon could withstand more heat than a human. As an egg, Galirras had lain unprotected on hot stones and embers.

Gavin had worked with Peadar, cutting up the remainder of the horse, taking big parts with them to the fire. They agreed they would save large parts for the dragon but prepared a well-sized meal for them all. They did not know if tomorrow would provide them with the opportunity to eat.

The group was quiet while eating. The events of the day weighing heavy on them all. Not only had they lost Galen, they had seen an amazing new creature come into this world. They had encountered the black stone horrors for a second time. Unnatural things that were hard to accept.

"What were those damn things?" said Peadar, in a soft voice. "If I hadn't seen them with my own eyes, I would have laughed had another told me such a story."

"I don't know," said Kevhin, "but I think we were lucky to get away from those things. Those wolves seemed a lot more savage than the stone statue we encountered. There really was a wild animal somewhere in that stone body."

"Galen wasn't so lucky," mumbled Richard, his head dropping.

"Did you know him from before?" said Gavin.

"Not before, no. But we grew up in the same region in Aeterra. We knew a lot of the same places." A sad smile rose to Richard's lips. "He could be damn funny."

Raylan traced the scar on his arm and thought back to the heavy-hitter's victory pose as the man walked away from the crumbling statue. A chuckle, broken and dismal, caught in Raylan's throat.

"And now he's gone," Richard continued. "He didn't deserve that. Not to mention, we lost Regis' remains, too."

Silence fell, only the soft moaning of Stephen broke the hush. The fall had not done him any good. He seemed fine, at first, but now it looked like the fever—together with his restless sleeping—had returned.

Raylan looked at his brother and Richard. "What happened, precisely? I was too far away with the wagon to see it clearly. What about the skinny guy that was calling the shots? And the remaining enemy soldiers?"

"The soldiers backed off after the wolves jumped the gap," Gavin said. "I expect they'll either try to circle round or try to bridge the gap. Either way, it should hopefully take them some time... although we'll remain at a disadvantage as long as we're in enemy territory."

"What about Galen?"

Gavin looked him in the eye and shook his head. "I was pinned by one of those monsters. Thought I was a goner, for sure. But the wolf seemed to be unfocused, looking away from me a couple of times. Still... if it hadn't been for Galen, I wouldn't be here, that's for sure."

"It happened too fast," added Richard. "Before I could react, Galen rushed in. He lost his footing when he pushed over the wolf. They both went over the edge into the ravine... by the time I looked down, he was already gone..."

Raylan had no words that would provide Richard any comfort. They had all gotten to know each other well during these months, traveling as a small, tight group under difficult circumstances. Sure, there had been friction, especially after their food supplies had begun to run low. They had damn near given up when Ca'lek and Stephen came across the tracks of the Doskovian soldiers. But they were there for each other and losing a second member of their squad made the reality of being far from home, and safety, hit hard.

Raylan looked down at the sleeping dragon on his lap. "I bet he would have been amazed, if he saw Galirras."

"Is that what it's called?" asked Kevhin.

Raylan nodded, slowly. "*It* is actually a *he*, and he told me that's his name. I have no clue how someone knows his own name when being born, but maybe that's normal for dragons."

"Then... you understand those growls and hisses it—I mean, he makes?" said Kevhin, with a frown.

"It's not like that. I mean, I hear the growls, too; but it's more like a voice, reaching my ears from inside my head. Sometimes, I also feel if he's nervous or afraid."

136

Raylan looked at Xi'Lao. She had been very quiet since their escape from the wolves. "Do you know anything about this, Xi'Lao?"

She looked up to her name, but clearly had been too preoccupied with her thoughts, and looked at him quizzically.

"Do you know why I can hear Galirras? Or why he knows his name without someone giving it to him?" repeated Raylan.

Xi'Lao shook her head firmly, holding her bowl of horse-meat soup. "No, sorry. Like I said, I only know some basics from the scrolls I read while at the palace." She rose from her position. "I'll go check on Ca'lek, and bring him some soup for his watch," she said, and left the campfire circle.

"What's wrong with her?" Raylan asked Gavin, after she left.

His brother shrugged in reply. Raylan wondered if she was still bothered by the impact the spear had on her ribs, or perhaps something else was wrong and she was just trying to dodge his questions. He pulled some of the rocks surrounding the fire closer to Galirras, increasing the warmth they received. Raylan heard him breathe in irregular intervals and, every now and then, saw one of his legs spasm as if the little dragon was in a fevered dream.

One by one, the members of the group went to their sleeping places, until it was just Gavin and Raylan left by the fire.

Throwing some more wood on the fire and switching out the cooled stones with hot ones, his brother sat next to him. "You should get some sleep, too, little brother."

Raylan shook his head. "I don't want to leave Galirras or move him away from the fire. I think he needs the warmth of the fire, so I'll stay here."

Gavin gave Raylan a look he knew well. "Everyone on the team needs to be fully aware of the dangers surrounding them, and tired people make mistakes."

"I can always sleep with my back against the rock," Raylan conceded.

"Do you think he'll make it?" said his older brother, nodding at the little dragon.

"I don't know... he seems really weak. He kept saying it was too early. I didn't understand at first, but I think he meant it was too early to come out of the egg."

"He looks quite pale. Has he awakened since he ate this afternoon?"

Again, Raylan shook his head. "No. I was wondering if I should try and wake him."

"I would let him sleep for a little while longer. Perhaps try to feed him some of the soup and cooked meat, later. It'll probably warm him up inside. Just let me know if you need anything."

As Gavin moved to stand, Raylan grabbed his arm. "What will we do now?"

Gavin retook his seat. "What we came here to do. Retrieve the sacred relic of the Empire."

"But it's not a thing anymore. He's alive, able to think and to communicate. You can't just ship him off," objected Raylan.

"I think our original mission has changed little. Bring back the stolen relic. But instead of the egg, I think we should get Galirras back to the Tiankong Empire. They can decide what will happen to him from there."

Raylan shifted uneasily. He did not like the sound of that at all. What if they took Galirras away from him? The Empire was far away, and everyone knew they did not look kindly on strangers trying to enter their territory. Xi'Lao had said it was not uncommon to execute foreigners that tried to get in and he knew the stories from his sailing days. What if he was denied entry? What would happen to Galirras?

"For now, let's focus on going south and finding the Drowned Man's Fork," Gavin said. "We only have eight horses left and ten riders—eleven, if you count your new companion. Some people will need to share their rides. On the other hand, we'll be able to travel more quickly now without the wagon, getting away from the path, and perhaps, losing our pursuers."

His brother poked the fire with one of the sticks they had gathered. "Unfortunately, Peadar said one of the Azurna pigeons broke its neck in all the chaos this afternoon, so we'll only have one shot to get word back to the harbor, requesting pickup by ship. It's going to be a big gamble."

Raylan felt Galirras stir on his leg. The soft, irregular breathing rumbled deep in his chest. "I really wish Xi'Lao could tell us more. She's so difficult to gauge. I know she's on our side in a fight, but she's always dodging my questions and acting mysterious. She's been distant with everyone except you. You two seem to have hit it off."

"She's an interesting woman," Gavin admitted, with as much grace as his blushing permitted. "…but she is often as much a mystery to me as to you, little brother."

"Okay, so perhaps you can enlighten me about her reaction this afternoon. What the hell was up with that?" Raylan said, slightly irritated. "She showed complete disregard for the situation we were in and lost it. It was nothing like her. I mean… normally she's so in control. It's a wonder most of us got out of there at all."

Gavin stayed quiet for a moment, just staring into the flames while Raylan stroked Galirras' neck to give some comfort, while he waited for his brother to answer.

Gavin let out a deep sigh. "I'm sorry. You'll have to ask her yourself."

138

"Oh, come on. You know I can keep a secret."

Gavin shook his head. "It's not my place to say. You should ask her. Earlier, she said she needed to talk to you, anyway; so, you'll get the chance soon, I reckon. I've got a feeling she'll open up more now that Galirras is here." Getting to his feet, he gave Raylan's shoulder two taps—it was one of their father's supportive gestures from when they were younger. "I'm going to check on the watch and then turn in. I'm up for early morning watch duty."

For a while, Raylan was alone with Galirras by the fire. He woke the little dragon up and fed him some boiled horse meat soup, thickened with the blood they collected from the carcass. Galirras ate everything, although it seemed he was almost sleep…eating. He did not react to any of Raylan's questions, and his eyes were constantly swirling around, unfocused, and his tail made little involuntary jerky movements.

By the time Galirras slumbered again, Xi'Lao joined him by the fire.

"Hey," said Raylan.

"How's he doing?" she whispered, trying not to disturb their sleeping comrades.

He noticed her accent more when she spoke softly. It never bothered him before; but now, he felt annoyed by it. It reminded him she was not of his homeland, and it made him wonder if she had a different agenda, a secret one.

"He ate quite a bit again, just now, but it takes a lot out of him," he replied, pushing his thoughts to the side.

Galirras grumbled, as if to confirm the statement.

Staring into the fire, Raylan remained silent. He did not feel like talking to her, afraid of what she might say.

"I—I think I owe you an apology," she began.

Raylan looked up, surprised by the admission "What for?"

"My outburst this morning… it was—was not how I normally am."

She was stammering, slightly, as if she suddenly had trouble with the foreign language. It made her sound vulnerable. Raylan's irritation evaporated. He saw a person who felt very much alone and in need of a friend.

"It's okay, you know," he said, thinking on his next words. "Gavin told me to ask you what caused your outburst. I'll understand, if you don't want to tell me."

"It is not that… it is just that this is difficult to talk about. I am not sure anyone would understand. We are from very different cultures. I was afraid it would turn people away, but I see now that not telling is probably worse."

"I think you're a valued part of this group. You've been searching relentlessly for Galirras' egg since the beginning, never once complaining about the hardship of the journey. And, you definitely held your own in a fight. I

believe you've helped this group come this far, together with my brother, but…
I've still got a gnawing feeling that you're not telling us everything."

Xi'Lao was silent, for a moment. "It is true. I have not shared all the
information I have, but I have my reasons for that." Instead of telling him that
reason, she looked him in the eye, as if sizing him up. "Can I ask you a question?"

"Errr, sure."

Xi'Lao's tone turned very serious. "What do you plan to do with Galirras?
What do you think will happen?"

Raylan was immediately on guard. Was she testing him? Checking to see
if he would try to take away the Empire's property? Besides, it was strange to
hear the question he had been asking himself for the entire night, said aloud.

"Honestly?" said Raylan, trying to decide if he should speak the truth or tell
her what he thought she wanted to hear. In the end, the truth seemed easiest.
"I've been asking myself that very same question. I think he'll have to decide
for himself, when he is well enough."

"That is not good enough. Galirras will look to you for a lot of things,
knowledge about the world, right and wrong. Your opinion will weigh heavily
on his decisions. So, what will you do?"

"Really, I've got no idea. At this moment, I just want Galirras to survive. It
scares the hell out of me that he might not make it, which is weird, because
I've known him less than a day."

"What if he lives? What do you think should happen?"

"Should happen? Get out of here, of course. Away from those living statues,
away from those people trying to kill us. Keep him safe… I guess."

"And after we get out of here and return to Aeterra?"

Raylan's frustration grew. He was not any closer to any answers to the
questions he had asked himself this afternoon. "I just don't know. We'll have to
go report to the king and the council on this mission. He'll want to see a real-life
dragon for himself, I reckon. As long as I can stay with him and protect him."

"It might not be your choice, in the end."

"I know, but I'll try everything within my power, so we'll not get separated.
He'll need protection from people who mean him harm. He's still so fragile.
People might try to use him for their own good."

Apparently satisfied by his answers, Xi'Lao gave a small nod and continued
the conversation. "I'm glad you're taking this so seriously. I think you have a
good heart, which I feel will take responsibility for Galirras, even if the road is
not an easy one. Therefore, I would like to ask you to come with me to the
Empire. Actually, I think you will need to," said Xi'Lao, with a small smile.

"Why's that?"

"Because I have a feeling Galirras will not go unless you go, too. You say that you always had a feeling about me not telling you everything, right? Well, I think it is time I tell you what I know."

Raylan nodded. Maybe he would finally get the answers to his questions.

Xi'Lao bit at her bottom lip, as though trying to find the right words. "See, the stolen relic… Galirras' egg—I just… it is more personal than you might think. It is not just the Empire's safety and honor that is involved. My full name is Xi'Lao Wén. The old master, the one that skinny, blatantly insulting wretch was talking about this afternoon, the one person who was responsible for protecting the egg, his name was Lai'Ping Wén—Grand Master Wén they called him. My grandfather."

Raylan's mouth dropped open, and it took a good few moments to find his words. "What do you mean, your grandfather? Were you at the place that got raided? The monastery?"

"No, I was never there. I mean, I have been there when I was younger. My parents died when I was very little, so I never really knew them. My grandfather raised me, at the monastery. However, I have been living in the capital these last several years." She pulled up her knees and put her arms around them. It made her look much younger than Raylan knew she really was. Tears filled her eyes. "Sometimes, I wish I had been there. Perhaps I could have done something, saved my grandfather. But the reality is, if I had been there, more than likely, I would be dead, too."

Raylan did not know what to say, precisely. He could relate to losing a parent while still little, but it seemed her entire family was taken from her.

She looked at him, apologetically. "That is the reason I snapped this morning. Here was this loathsome bastard claiming to have killed my grandfather, like he was announcing he had a slice of bread for breakfast. I could not take it. I wanted him dead… I still do. For my grandfather. For the Empire. For my family's honor—dead!" Her hands clenched to fists. "But I know we have more important things to worry about, especially now, with Galirras out of the egg. We have to get him to safety, away from enemy hands. Who knows what they plan to do with him."

Raylan could not agree more. "So… why you? If I may ask. What about other family? No brothers, no sisters?"

She shook her head. "No. I was an only child. There is my mom's sister, but she lives in the south of the Empire, away from the capital. We do not talk often."

"I'm sorry. That… must be lonely."

Xi'Lao gave him a little smile, but he felt the sadness behind the mask. "The problem is, although my grandfather was killed the night of the raid, his dishonor—by failing to protect one of the Empire's greatest treasures—befalls the entire family. I refuse to let that stand. I want to restore our family name. Make sure my grandfather gets the respect he deserves for his dedication, his life in service to the Empire. So, I begged the Emperor to give me a chance to head out and restore my family's honor by retrieving the egg…"

"…But things are a lot more complicated now," added Raylan, seeing more of the whole picture.

"Exactly. With a live dragon, we will have all kinds of people chasing after us. They will want to capture Galirras and to use him. It might be for a good cause; it might be for something extremely bad. I think it is safe to assume our pursuers do not have the best intentions for him. I expect they will not be the last to try and get their hands on Galirras."

"I won't let them."

"I know. I believe you. But you'll need all the help you can get. Let's find our way back to Aeterra and then continue on to the Empire. It will be the best place for Galirras, I'm sure of it."

"What makes you say that?"

"Because of our history. The information I told you about dragons… it is actually only the tip of the iceberg. The Wén family, our life's work—our destiny—was to collect and keep any and all information on dragons for the use of the Empire. For centuries, my family maintained the official dragon archives in the nation's capital and kept positions of great honor throughout the Empire.

"But, over the generations, the family has been dwindling, for more than a century now… diseases, accidents, old age, disputes about our sacred duty. I am… the last in my bloodline, and responsible for the archive. I have been educated in the knowledge of dragons, as was my father before me, my grandfather before him, and his father before him, going back all the way to the time when dragons roamed the skies by the hundreds, even thousands."

Raylan's head spun with the idea of so many dragons living in this world. Coming back to the point, his reaction was one made of insecurity. "So, all this time, you've been playing dumb? What if I did something wrong? What if I did something to hurt Galirras?"

"Look, I am sorry. I did not mean to offend you; but I needed to know, first, how everything would play out. I had a feeling you would link with the dragon once it hatched, but I could not be sure."

"What do you mean link?" He pinched the bridge of his nose; more questions kept arising. "Please, Xi'Lao, tell me what you know. You've got no idea how frustrating and confusing this all is."

"I will, but even I do not know everything. We are not in the Tiankong Empire. We are on the run and in constant danger. It is not what you call a nice and stable situation to figure out how to best approach this new creature and his needs. The historical archive might provide some guidance, but it will not be even close to the real situation, not to mention it is thousands of miles away. I am afraid we are mostly on our own in figuring things out."

Xi'Lao shifted to make herself more comfortable. "Okay, let me start at the beginning. A thousand years ago, the Empire flourished in what we called the golden age of dragons. Man and dragon lived side by side in society. Some dragons remained wild and lived in the vast faraway areas where few humans went, some worked together with humans of their own choosing.

"Dragons were a common sight during the day, in markets, in farming fields, in fisheries, and even in mines. The creatures came in various subspecies that shared common characteristics but differed from each other in many ways. This was not always the case. One or two ancient scrolls speak of men fighting beasts, in those dark times before the golden age; but we know little of those times, as nothing was recorded at the time.

"The royal family often had one or more rare dragon species in their surroundings, which was considered an honor for both dragon and human. Protecting the royal family was the responsibility of the Drakk'maru—the Dragon Guard. Dragons and their chosen riders, who excelled in both aerial and ground combat, would be given the honor of serving the royal family as part of the Drakk'maru, an honor which was rarely passed upon."

Xi'Lao fell silent, seeming deciding what to tell next. "But, the current archives only date back about two hundred years. The scrolls from that time tell of a major disaster hitting the Empire and, in particular, the dragon population. Things are not completely clear on what happened, as almost all scrolls—and other recorded materials—were destroyed in those turbulent times."

She stared into the flames as she continued. "There are multiple theories, from epidemic diseases, to dragon rebellion, to invasion. But the truth is, no one knows for certain anymore. The only fact that remained was that in a matter of months, dragons vanished without a trace from everyday life. The Empire was plunged into chaos as multiple factions tried to use the confusion to make a grab for the throne. High lords that had recruited their own armies fought each other, constantly. Villages were wiped out. Cities burned for days. It is estimated a third of the Empire's population did not live to see the end of those troubled times… it took decades before the rightful heir to the Emperor's throne returned and a more peaceful era began again."

"And all this happened because of the dragons vanishing?"

"We are not sure, but the dragons had been a form of regulation in conflicts. They were sentient beings that understood the society of humans but could remain completely impartial. They often mediated between rivaling factions, coming up with peaceful solutions, if possible. If a peaceful way could not be found, they sometimes were referees, making sure battles were fought honorably."

Raylan shook his head. "It's hard to imagine such a world existing so many years ago." He looked down and tried to imagine how Galirras would fit into such a society. "Can we go back for a second? You mentioned a link between dragon and human? What's that about?"

"Sometimes, it happened that a newborn dragon chose to link with a human that is present at the hatching event. This would not always happen, as it is, in some ways, the dragon's choice. But if it did happen, the partnership created was often capable of exceptional things. Detailed information on linking was kept strictly on a need to know basis, and off the record, as it was passed on from generation to generation. Often, people said, they had strong indications on what the other was experiencing or feeling; but that was never officially confirmed. Many in service of the Drakk'maru were said to be linked with their dragons; but this, too, was just recorded in the scrolls as rumor, without evidence."

"I wonder if that was what he meant by 'you're mine'," Raylan whispered.

"What was that?" Xi'Lao asked.

"It's nothing. Just something Galirras said when he first put his head in my hand. He said, 'You're mine, and I'm yours'. I had no idea, at the time; but I now know, for certain, that's the moment I knew I would protect him with my life."

Xi'Lao's face brightened, for a moment, as if given a wonderful present on a bad day. "Would you mind telling me more? I had not even thought about it, but the current situation will give me a chance to record events firsthand. I know I have not been fully open with you, until now; but any information could become vitally important down the road. It would be an honor if I could record your experiences with Galirras. Would you not think?"

Raylan gave this some thought as Xi'Lao retrieved a small paper scroll and charcoal from her pack. He no longer had the notion that Xi'Lao was holding anything back. She had already proved herself a valuable source of information, and he agreed they were not in a 'normal' situation. He could really use someone to talk to about all these new experiences with Galirras. It would provide him with a different perspective, one that was likely based on the only knowledge of dragons in the world. So, he put his trust in her, and told her about the feelings he encountered after the hatching, his dream of being in the well, and all the other events that took place that day.

Xi'Lao quickly scribbled short keywords as they talked deep into the night, until Raylan was too exhausted to keep his eyes open any longer. Calling it a night, he settled down to sleep, the little dragon tucked safely against him.

CHAPTER ELEVEN

Wind

Raylan felt that he had only enjoyed a moment's sleep when they broke camp at first light. While everyone quickly finished the previous day's leftovers, Galirras was fed as much as he could swallow, while Raylan kept him by the fire until it was time to move out.

Peadar crafted a cloth sling for Raylan to put around his back. The small dragon was carefully lowered into it, together with several of the warm stones from the fire. The added weight was a strain on his shoulders, so Raylan partially rested the sling in front of him on the saddle. He hoped the stones and his body heat would be enough to keep the creature warm until Galirras could maintain his own temperature.

For the next couple of days, the group traveled away from the path, covering their tracks when they could. They came across a few enemy patrols, but thanks to Ca'lek's scouting skill, they were able to stay hidden. Clearly, word had been sent ahead, as the enemy patrols seemed to be systematically checking the area. But the forests were vast, and they found plenty of places to hide from searching eyes. The enemy leader was not seen amongst the parties they encountered. They had no idea how much time the skinny man needed to circle back and come after them, but it was unlikely he would give up. The internal conflict they had witnessed only showed how determined he was to get his hands on Galirras.

The small dragon mostly slept deeply during their travels, but Raylan made sure they stopped as often as possible. Now that they had crossed the mountain ridge toward the south side, the rain fell less frequently, making it easier to stay warm and to find dry wood for a fire. Richard had shown him how to quickly build a small, almost smokeless, fire. It provided Galirras with much-needed heat and gave them a chance to reheat the stones before continuing southward again.

He would wake Galirras to eat, after which the dragon would often fall asleep again, drowsy with a satisfied stomach.

The landscape slowly changed as they left the high-altitude mountains behind. The forests became slightly denser and more colorful than in the north. A ray of sunlight would often shine through the branches, or in a clearing, providing beautiful light displays. As insects put on aerial shows, enjoying the sunlight, hungry birds nosedived to feast on them. Other wildlife was seen more often too; but somehow, the forest still looked empty.

With the constant pressure of their pursuers, they did not often have time to hunt for big game. With the minimal time available—and the fact that Galirras consumed at least five rabbit-sized servings, five times per day—it was difficult for Kevhin and Rohan to keep up with the demand for fresh kills.

While Raylan was glad the dragon seemed stable and kept eating whatever was offered, Stephen had more and more difficulties. The fever still stalked him in his sleep. The cut on his leg was now festering, no matter how much they cleaned it.

"I do not think the moss paste is doing anything, anymore… maybe it never did," said Xi'Lao, at the campfire on their third day.

"But the first day the swelling was almost completely gone, and the fever broke," said Raylan.

"I know… it must have been the cut that released the infection from his leg. Perhaps, if I had not put the paste on it… maybe it is my fault," said Xi'Lao.

"We knew it was a long shot, and it might have been the fall from the wagon… I just wish we could do something to help him now."

Stephen had not eaten anything since the day before. Drinking was quickly becoming a challenge, too. Richard sat behind Stephen during the travels, trying to prevent him from falling off the horse; but eventually, they had to stop and set up camp in order to give the wounded scout some much-needed rest.

Raylan looked at him, twitching and turning under the blanket. His face had lost all its color again, and he was quickly losing weight. They tried to break the fever with clothes dipped in cold mountain water again, but it did not seem as effective as before.

That night, Raylan found himself, once again, watching over someone fighting for his life. He had just fed Galirras his last meal of the day and put him next to the fire, surrounded by warm stones. He picked up one of the drinking bowls and tried to make Stephen sit up to sip from the cup.

"Come on, Stephen, you need to drink."

The scout did not seem to hear him. His eyes moved back and forth, rapidly, under his closed eyelids, as he softly murmured in his sleep. "No… ah… let go… get… get away…"

"He's been like that the entire evening. It sounds like something is chasing him in his dreams," said Peadar, who took care of Stephen most of the night. The young animal healer had hollow eyes and wore a hopeless expression.

"Can you help me get him up? I really think he should drink something," said Raylan. But the moment he touched Stephen's shoulder, the scout shot up and clutched onto Raylan's shirt.

Stephen's eyes were wide, staring straight at him, but Raylan got the impression that his sick friend was not seeing him at all, or anyone else for that matter. Then, the scout spoke to him. "They're coming. The crumbling darkness is coming. Everyone… all… we're all going to die. You must stop it, Raylan. You must—must stop the darkness."

Stephen slumped back again, retreating into his feverish dream. For a moment, Raylan could not shake the eerie feeling Stephen's rambling had given him, but he put the bowl to the scout's lips, carefully trickling some water into his mouth.

"Get well soon," said Raylan, before leaving the scout in Peadar's care. He nodded to Xi'Lao, who came by to check on her patient.

Sleep did not come easily to Raylan, but he must have found it somewhere because he awoke at early light to some sort of commotion near Stephen's bed.

He quickly rose but as he approached the scout's bed, he saw Xi'Lao shake her head at Gavin and close Stephen's eyes with her fingers. This cold wilderness bed became their friend's final resting place.

Raylan felt a lump in his throat. Ca'lek cursed the three gods of combat for taking one of them, again, after such a struggle. Raylan saw him stomp off, probably to cool off and to mourn in private. Everyone gathered around their fallen friend, and for a moment, there was no pursuit, no enemy trying to chase them down and capture them. They just mourned their friend with the respect he deserved.

After what happened to Regis, and due to the loss of the wagon, Gavin decided Stephen would have his last resting place in these strange lands, under these foreign trees. Raylan and Richard prepared a grave, which they marked with a small pile of stones. The grave was simple and was made a part of the forest as much as possible. It was the only way to prevent anyone from discovering it and disturbing their friend's peace.

With the final stones in place, they all found themselves silently lost in thoughts. It was the first time they had a moment to stop and reflect on their fallen comrades. Gently, Harwin's deep voice sang the words they all knew. First softly but stronger along the way, the old warrior started a final goodbye… not only for this fallen friend in front of them, but for those lost along the way as well.

"Stretching fields, drifting clouds…"

Ca'lek, who returned to show his respects, joined with Richard; their deep voices blending well with Harwin's.

"Beacon white on mountain side…

"Watch over us, as we ride out…"

As the others followed their example, the song filled the sky as a message to guide the fallen home.

"A guiding light for all to see…

"And should we fall far from your side…

"Allow us all, to find our way…

"Back to your warmth, where we will stay…

"To rest our blades, hearts and souls…"

The days after Stephen's death, they spoke little. Raylan reflected on the mission. Why them? Why did the Empire not send their own squads with Xi'Lao? Was it a punishment? Did they not expect anyone to succeed? Were they all expendable? What about Galirras? Would he be expendable, too?

But on the tenth day after the hatching, if one could call it that, Raylan's thoughts were interrupted when Galirras unexpectedly opened his eyes. The group was still riding as it was in the middle of the day.

Raylan felt him stir in the sling, just before he heard Galirras' voice inside his head.

"*What's happening?*"

"We're still riding. Go back to sleep."

Ca'lek, who rode beside Raylan, raised an eyebrow in question.

"It's Galirras," he said, with a quick smile. "He's awake."

"*I smell horse.*"

Looking down into the sling, he said, "That's because we're on one."

"*Can I eat it? I'm hungry.*"

"No… you can't."

"*Why not? It smells great, much better than those small things I ate earlier.*"

Luna neighed as if she fully understood what they were talking about it.

"Those small things are called birds, and we need the horses for our travels. Now just go back to sleep; we've still got a while to go. When we take our next break, I will wake you for your food."

Raylan felt Galirras tuck his head against his side, and soon felt the little dragon relax again.

He was glad Galirras woke by himself. Over the next few days, he woke more often and stayed awake much longer. His scales darkened, a little, and lost its softness, somewhat. The scaled skin began to feel pleasantly warm to the touch—much warmer than his own skin—which meant Galirras was regulating his temperature more easily. Raylan and Peadar checked his wing multiple times, encouraging him to open it. Peadar was astounded how fast the swelling disappeared. The cuts Galirras received from his violent hatching were also healing at an incredible rate. Still, every time they moved his wing, Galirras complained that it was painful, and he could not move it further.

According to Peadar, it looked fine and was healing great. Raylan wondered if the wing truly still hurt, or if Galirras was afraid to stretch it out completely. If Galirras was in any pain, he did not let it ruin his appetite. The meat did him well, it seemed. Raylan swore he had already grown ten inches in length in the last two days.

On the seventeenth day, they circled back, dodging two large patrols. Raylan had just made his fire when Galirras got to his feet. He moved around, more and more, during the breaks—stretching his legs, walking around the fire, grooming himself. His talk became livelier, too. Raylan saw him turn his neck and nudge the wing that had been dislocated.

"How does it feel?" Raylan said, hoping the answer would be different today.

"It does not hurt much," said Galirras.

"Can you stretch it out?"

Galirras stretched his wing outward. The framework of bones spread as the thin membrane between them slowly unfolded. The yellow-brown color reflected the sunlight on his body's scales, almost giving him a golden sparkle.

For a second, Raylan thought today would be the day his wing would go past the critical point, but Galirras flinched and tucked his wing back against his flank again.

"It will not go any further."

"Come on, you just have to try. I know you can do it," encouraged Raylan.

Once again, Galirras started to spread his wing. He slowed when he reached the familiar point. Raylan saw the muscles trembling under his scales.

"That's it, just a little further. You can do it."

But the wing refolded abruptly, as Galirras whimpered. *"It is no good. I will never be able to fly."*

150

His head hung low as he lay down next to the fire. *"Are Kevhin and Rohan back yet with my food?"* he asked, disgruntled.

"Not yet," said Raylan. Noticing Galirras' mood change, he added, "Perhaps… you should try to hunt some for yourself."

That got his attention. He saw Galirras' head snap upward. *"I can?"* he asked.

"Well, you seem to be moving around better and better. I'm thinking it will help you build up more muscles. Sitting around, riding on a horse won't help much, so why don't we go and see if we can catch our own food."

"But how can I hunt without flying? It feels wrong to stay on the ground," said Galirras, sulking slightly.

"I'm sure you'll manage," countered Raylan. "You've got four legs, don't you? With sharp claws, right? But okay, if you want to just sit here and wait for Kevhin and Rohan to get back, that's fine by me."

"No, no, I'll go!" Galirras said quickly, as he got to his feet.

Raylan informed Gavin they would be going for a quick hunt. As he returned, Galirras paced on the spot, like an overly enthusiastic kid on his name-day.

"What did he say? Can we go now?" he asked.

"He's fine with it, as long as we're as quiet as possible," he answered, but Galirras did not hear the last part, as he darted off between the trees. Raylan ran to catch up.

They spent some time moving amongst the trees, Raylan stressing the importance of keeping a low profile in the forest. Taking the task very seriously, Galirras adjusted his movements. As Raylan followed, the dragon seemed almost like a stalking cat. A very large cat, nonetheless, with a long neck and an even longer tail; but the elegance of his low movements was fascinating to watch.

Galirras attempted to chase down a couple of birds, but they were too quick to be taken by surprise by such a large predator.

During the small trip, the dragon's movements improved before Raylan's eyes. Where the wobbly trampling of its claws scared away birds—or small game—in the beginning, Galirras had already figured out how to move his claws along spots that were more solid, making less noise. His movements became more precise and coordinated. Instinct took over.

Over the next few days, Raylan and Galirras went hunting during each break. On the second day, Galirras came close to biting a tuft of fur from a rabbit's tail. The day after that, another rabbit seemed to get away, as it ducked into a hole in the ground at the last second. But Galirras, annoyed that he had not caught anything the first two days, did not give up that easily.

Digging wildly with his two front claws, he tore open the hole. Raylan clenched his hands, in anticipation.

The rabbit jumped from its hiding spot in a bid to escape, but Galirras was prepared. He snapped it out of midair and shook his head violently for a moment, ripping the rabbit apart. Pieces of meat dangled from his teeth as he feasted on the small creature.

As Galirras fed on his very first kill, Raylan swore he saw a grin on the dragon's face. He had not seen many big predators feed after a kill, and he was slightly taken aback by the gory scene and the ferociousness of Galirras' eating.

Misinterpreting Raylan's stare, somewhat, Galirras looked at him. "*Do you want some? You can have a leg, if you want.*"

Raylan chuckled. "No, thanks. It's all yours. That was an excellent kill, so enjoy it. I'll eat something back at the camp."

Walking back, Raylan felt the adrenaline of the hunt, and Galirras' excitement still rushed through him. As they arrived at camp, Peadar offered Raylan a bowl of meat soup, but he had some trouble finding his appetite again. He wondered if it was due to the excitement or the dragon's sloppy eating.

Galirras continued exploring during the breaks. He even started to walk with the group while they were traveling, which probably was a good thing, since the dragon was rapidly increasing in weight and was becoming too big to ride on his horse's back. The mounts, which had now been around Galirras for several weeks, were adjusting surprisingly quickly. As they were not currently on his menu, they seemed to tolerate the small dragon quite well… at least for now.

The exercise benefited Galirras. The dragon's shoulder and leg muscles increased, but it worried him that Galirras rarely used his wings. The bands around his wing—to keep it stationary—had been taken off more than a week ago, but his wings remained tucked tightly against his flank. Raylan thought it was partly because they would get in the way of his walking.

As he grew stronger, Galirras ventured away from the group to seek new challenges. At one point, during one of their hunts, Raylan found Galirras twenty feet above ground, climbing a tree with his sharp claws. He was on his way to a bird's nest to devour the eggs it held.

At the end of the twenty-third day after hatching, Kevhin rode up next to Raylan for a bit. They had not seen any patrols for the last four days, so Raylan hoped they had outmaneuvered their pursuers for the time being.

"The trees keep getting bigger ever since we crossed the mountain chain; but man, these are something else. Look at the size of them, they're huge!"

Raylan had not paid much attention to their surroundings. He had been keeping track of Galirras' movements. When he looked up, in reaction to Kevhin's voice, it was the first time he truly noticed the size of the trees in this forest.

"I wonder how old they are," continued Kevhin. "They must be at least a thousand years old."

"Amazing," mumbled Raylan, awestruck. "When did they get so big?"

"Ha, you've been daydreaming, man. The forest has been widening for the last two days. The tree's roots have been taking more room as they get taller. Look at that one over there. I bet if we all hold hands, we wouldn't even reach halfway around it!"

Raylan saw what Kevhin meant. The trees grew further from each other, providing plenty of space for their horses to pass through the forest, even with all the large roots running across the forest floor. Some roots were higher than Raylan, sitting on his horse. It looked like he was riding along a brown wall, until the root dropped into the ground, at the end. The ground was covered with moss and needles, almost completely dampening the sound of their horses' hooves. The needled leaves seemed to be three or four times the size of the needles up north. Stones broke through the surface every now and then, looking like islands in a green and brown sea.

"They look like giants in comparison to the trees at home. Even the ancient forests of Lash don't have trees this big," said Raylan.

Rohan joined them. "And these go almost straight up. Look at how far they rise before the first branches. The trees in Lash grow in almost every direction, their branches and roots are like squirming snakes. Hey, remember our training missions there, Kev?" said the archer.

"How much fun we had moving around in those trees?" added Rohan, a sparkle in his eyes.

And although Kevhin acted as if he had not heard the hinting tone in Rohan's voice, the playful remark was not entirely lost on Raylan. He often wondered what the bond between them was. Rohan never appeared unnecessarily far from Kevhin and vice versa.

Lately, he noticed more gestures of affection, similar to those he increasingly saw between his brother and Xi'Lao. Small things, like a hand lingering a little longer than usual on a shoulder. He wondered if any of the others noticed, but he did not think anyone else paid enough attention to such small details. Since his link with Galirras, he spotted such subtle things more and more. Something about the connection with the dragon gave him a deeper appreciation of all things, and an eye that was even keener than before.

Coming from the Dahalaes region, Raylan knew both archers met well before their army training. He had figured they were kept together because both had such exceptional archery skill. But now he wondered if there was not more to it. Perhaps they wanted to be together.

"*Why would it matter?*" said Galirras, who had been following Raylan's thoughts.

Raylan shrugged, and then answered the dragon in his head. "*It wouldn't... to me, at least. I mean, I don't mind at all... on the contrary, I'd be happy for them, if they enjoyed each other's company to that extent, especially being so far from home. However, having relationships within the army is not tolerated. There are no official sanctions for same gender preference; but any relationship, discovered within the same platoon is broken up. Usually, by reassigning one partner to prevent conflicts of priorities. So, while I don't mind at all, I don't know if they'd want other people to know.*"

"*Why is that? It is not as if they are hurting anyone... right?*" Galirras said.

"*No, not at all, and I don't always agree with that rule. Unfortunately, same gender lovers are heavily frowned upon by some. You often hear about such people being ridiculed, beaten up, or worse. They're ignorant and small-minded people that do those things. I mean, who gave them the right to judge how others should feel?*"

Shocked at his careless remark, he looked over at Kevhin to explain what he was talking about; but the words stuck in his throat, and it dawned on him what had just happened.

"*Hold on... Galirras, did you just read my thoughts?*" Raylan thought, in his own head.

"*No, I just listened to them. Why?*" responded Galirras.

"*And... did I just reply to you without actually speaking?*" Raylan thought the unspoken words.

"*Yes, why do you sound so surprised? You did it before, in the well,*" said the little dragon.

"*The well? I thought that was just a dream. Xi'Lao mentioned this telepathy thing earlier, but I thought it only meant that I could hear your voice, not the other way around. It might have been hurtful and, at the very least, inconsiderate of me to speak like that next to Kevhin and Rohan.*"

"*Well, no one can hear you, except me. So, no worries there,*" said Galirras, cheerfully.

"*Can you hear anyone else?*"

"*No, why would I? You are the only one that is mine.*"

"*So, since when are you able to hear my thoughts? Can you hear me all the time?*" Raylan wanted to get all the details right.

"*Only when I'm close, otherwise you become too soft to hear. And, only if I choose to listen, of course. Why? Did… did I do something bad?*"

The thought of doing something that Raylan would not approve of made the dragon's voice a little shaky.

Hearing the reaction, Raylan quickly adjusted his tone. "*No… no, little one, not precisely. It's just that I'm not used to sharing all my thoughts so openly. Most people would like to keep their thoughts their own, I guess. Sometimes, people think over multiple things before deciding on what to say or do. I would not want you to misinterpret anything.*"

"*Oh, but I do not judge,*" said Galirras quickly. His voice was a mixture of hurt and disappointment now. "*But if you want, I can stop. I mean, I will stop listening.*"

Raylan felt awful for his tone. It seemed to be completely natural for Galirras to communicate in such a way. And he always enjoyed talking to the little dragon. At least now, their conversations will not draw the looks of his comrades when it seemed like he was having a one-sided conversation.

"*No, sorry, it's okay. I just overreacted a bit. Just promise me that you'll ask me when you don't fully understand something. Aaaand, I might need some time to get used to having another perso… I mean, a dragon in my head,*" he added, with a chuckle, while he winked at Galirras, walking to his left.

A warm feeling instantly streamed through him, filling him with a content and happy sensation.

That night, they made camp in the shelter of one of the giant trees, where its roots shielded the light of the campfire and acted as a barrier against any cold wind.

Gavin and Xi'Lao retreated together, while Richard took first watch. The rest of their group sat around the campfire, enjoying the warmth, when Kevhin continued the conversation about the trees.

"Seems like these trees are all reaching for the stars. The branches look like a giant ceiling, so thick I can't see any clouds or sky at all."

"In a way, they remind me of the roof of Shid'el's High Cathedral," said Peadar. "I used to spend hours looking up at the paintings on the ceiling there."

"*What is a cathedral?*" asked Galirras, looking upward.

"*It's a really big house of god. This one is in the main capital of our homeland, and it's huge,*" thought Raylan.

Galirras looked at him. "*What is a god?*"

Raylan could not help but smile at the dragon's continued curiosity. "*Many people believe this world, and all that's happening, is the work of an all-powerful entity. But, there are different ways to believe. Some people think it's just one being, others say there are many of them."*

"And this god... lives in the cathedral?"

"Not at all. They say god is everywhere. God isn't actually a physical being. People go to the cathedral to talk to god, but it is more like talking in their heads... maybe a little like you and I do."

Galirras thought about this. *"So, this god talks back in their heads? Perhaps... it is a dragon!"* he exclaimed. *"If it is, can we go look for him?"*

Raylan let out a laugh. When the rest looked at him, wondering what he was laughing about, he explained how Galirras wanted to meet a god as he thought it might be a dragon.

"I don't know if gods actually exist," he continued, aloud, to Galirras. "It's hard to prove their existence. Not many people seem to get a direct answer when they talk to god. The ones that claim they do, often seem not fully right in the head. But who knows, maybe they speak the truth. But—"

"I've seen plenty of things in my life that would suggest no gods are in this world, son," Harwin rumbled. "And if they are, they're heartless bastards, at best. I say give me a beer above a god, any time," he said, and spat in the fire.

"Actually, for my people, everything has a god. A tree, a rock... the tiniest of grasshoppers," said Xi'Lao. "We believe the life energy flows through everything. All things are connected but represented by their own god."

"And you have other forms as well," said Raylan. "During my travels, I've met a few men from the southern Water Clans who believe in a single ocean goddess that provides them with all they need. And Ca'lek here often mentions his forefather's greatest hunters are referred to as gods, right?"

"True," said Ca'lek with a nod. "Our stories are filled with those that outgrew their flesh shells and led the tribe with unseen hands."

"I do not get it. If god is everywhere, and people talk to god in their heads, why does god need such a big building as Peadar describes?"

Raylan went over this point, from multiple sides, after which he finally thought, *"That's indeed something to think about. Perhaps people, who believe in the same thing, like to come together and share that belief."*

Galirras went over this in his head. *"Do you believe in god, Raylan?"*

It was an innocent question, but the topic somehow seemed to be linked, in his head, with his mother's death. Strangely enough, he did not really feel the emptiness he usually felt when thinking about his mother. Instead, the pleasant warmth of his link with Galirras was present.

156

"*No, not really. I've always been more of an 'I believe it when I see it' kind of person. I don't know when that started, perhaps around the time my mother died. We were a loyal, church-going family, until my mother passed away. Gavin always got very upset about the subject of god after her passing, so eventually we stopped going. I don't know if he still believes, and blames god, or that he lost his belief because of certain things. For me, it matters little; gods may or may not exist, but I care little for them.*"

The dragon grew silent, in a different way, after that. It seemed he was deciding if he should ask his next question. After a while, he did. "*Will I ever know my mother? And, are there any other dragons?*"

Raylan wondered when the little dragon would ask such a thing. He tried to come up with a suitable answer, in preparation, but never really succeeded. "*I'm sorry, but I don't know about your mother. In our kingdom, dragons are just a myth, as if they never really existed in the first place. Xi'Lao says dragons vanished from this world a long time ago. She said no-one thought they'd ever be back. But now, you're here... so I would say that makes anything possible.*"

This seemed to cheer Galirras up, a little. He returned to the initial topic, trying to wrap his brain around the concept. "*So gods might, or might not, exist but some people say that god exists. How do you know if someone is telling the truth? I mean, if someone told me they had seen dragons, how would I know they speak the truth?*"

Raylan had no real answer for that. "*I think you go with your gut feeling.*"

"*What has my stomach got to do with any of this?*" said Galirras, confused.

"*It's a figure of speech, it means you feel it in your core... your wisdom, if you believe someone is telling the truth or not. Besides, there is nothing wrong with believing in something, it only becomes a problem if that belief actively becomes an obstacle for someone. If a person believes he'll live forever by only eating bird eggs, no one will bother him. But if someone starts forcing other people to only eat eggs because of that belief, it will become a problem. Belief should never be forced onto someone. It has to be free choice.*"

Raylan gave it some more thought. "*Sometimes, if you'd really want something to be real, it is not so much 'belief' but 'hope'. There is a difference. Either way, belief can be a powerful thing, even if that belief is based on a false truth. For example, the people who spread belief in a god, usually enjoy a certain level of power. They're the same people who run gatherings at a cathedral, or similar smaller houses of god, like churches. Some people think these church leaders will do anything to keep that power, including making people believe in some higher being that does not exist...*"

Galirras stayed quiet for a while and Raylan wondered what was going on inside that quickly growing, scaled head of his. Would the dragon think it wrong if anyone would want to make you believe something that was not true? But his winged friend seemingly decided to let the topic rest, for a bit.

Instead, Galirras looked up toward the branched roof again. "*Can we climb up and have a look around?*"

Raylan put his hand on the dragon's snout and spoke aloud. "I'd love to, but I don't think we'll be able to. We don't have any good climbing gear with us, and we don't have your claws to help us climb."

"What'd he say?" asked Kevhin.

"He asked if we could climb up into the trees. But unless we grow claws like him, I reckon we won't get up there." Looking upward, he added. "That said, the view must be intense!"

"Totally!" agreed Kevhin with a grin.

Later that night, when most of them were already asleep, Raylan put his hand on Galirras' neck. The dragon slept calmly. It looked like the restless nights were all behind him—apart from the occasional dream hunt. In those dreams Galirras clattered his jaws from excitement, like a cat ready to catch a bird. Raylan rolled up next to him, enjoying the warmth of the fire on one side and the natural high temperature of the dragon on the other. Trying to fall asleep, his mind went over the conversation of that evening.

Perhaps, in the old days, dragons were seen as gods. Who knows, he might even be right.

He closed his eyes and smiled. As he fell asleep, he heard them again. For the first time in days… the sound of wolves. The howls, echoing through the night's sky, seemed awfully close.

Galirras burst into a full-on sprint. The small deer he spotted, unfamiliar with a dragon as a hunter, hesitated before recognizing the danger, then dashed away. It was all the time Galirras needed. As he ran past one of the large tree roots, he pushed off and leapt through the air. Shooting out with his claw, he slashed the deer's hind leg from under it. The animal came crashing down, tumbling from its momentum. As it slid to a stop, it only had a split second to let out a high cry before the dragon sunk his teeth into its neck and put the animal out of its suffering.

"*My biggest one yet!*" he said with pride.

"Well done. That jump was very powerful. It almost looked like you were flying," complimented Raylan, who came running up.

"Well that would even be easier, I think. They would not hear me approach, if I could fly and glide through the air…" he said with a small gloom in his eyes. *"But, this is good enough. It's exciting to hunt on foot."*

Raylan had given up asking him to use his wings. Galirras did not want to put in the effort anymore, it seemed. In the meantime, he had also learned to stay behind Galirras while he hunted. The dragon quickly learned to walk stealthier than him. By staying too close, Raylan would only scare away potential prey. And with a kill in sight, Galirras still got so excited he sometimes forgot Raylan was there and knocked him over during a pursuit.

As Galirras tore into the soft belly of the deer, Raylan knelt beside him. He had somewhat gotten used to seeing him eat, although he still found it messy. Then again, some of his companions in their squad ate in a similar way. The dragon was growing fast. Standing next to him, Galirras' head already came well above shoulder height. His body filled out with muscles and stretched out from head to tail the dragon was easily the size of one and a half men.

They had been traveling through the giant tree forest for several days now. The trees started to vary in species. The ground held various leaves next to an abundance of thin needle leaves. Despite the differences, all trees still had massive trunks towering upward. And although the branches of some trees twisted with complexity through the air in comparison to the straighter branches of the needle trees, there were still very few low branches… it often felt like walking in a hall of pillars.

As Galirras became more adept at hunting, he and Raylan took over some of the hunting trips from Kevhin and Rohan.

"Would you like to take a leg back to camp? Maybe even two?"

The dragon sighed heavily. It had been a successful morning hunt, perhaps because they went out before dawn.

"I think that'll be a great idea."

As Raylan cut through the hind quarter of the deer, Galirras moved to the side. He lay down on a flat slab of rock, which had been warming up in a rare ray of sunlight falling through the canopy.

Raylan tied the two hind legs together and slung them across his shoulder. The group would not go hungry today.

As he approached Galirras, he found the dragon staring intensely at a spot on the ground. Another ray of sunlight touched the ground, not far from the stone slab Galirras sat on. In the beam of light were three leaves twirling, moving around each other in circles, almost dancing.

Raylan looked at the leaves, mesmerized. He frowned, something striking him as odd. He saw no other leaves moving, no branches swaying, nothing. There was no wind this morning as they stood in the dim light of the forest.

"That's odd," he said, aloud.

Galirras looked startled, as if he had not seen Raylan approach. Immediately, the leaves dropped to the ground.

"*What is odd?*"

"There's no wind at all, yet those leaves moved as if touched by it."

"*That was not the wind. I think that was me.*" Even Galirras sounded a little surprised at his remark.

"What do you mean, that was you? Can you do it again?"

"*I think so.*"

As he returned his gaze to the leaves, Galirras raised his head, in concentration. Front legs crossed, head raised, the dragon looked both focused and relaxed as the end of his tail twitched occasionally.

After a moment, one of the leaves started trembling. Shortly after, another two leaves began to shift. The movements increased, until all three leaves suddenly lifted in the air, as if carried by a breeze. The leaves swirled around, just above the ground, sometimes touching the green moss, sometimes flying to the side. But each time, some invisible force pushed the leaves up into the air, or back into the odd dance.

"That's amazing! How are you doing this?" Raylan wondered.

Looking at Raylan, the dragon beamed with pride. Right away, the leaves scattered, as if hit by a gush of wind, and fell to the ground. Galirras let out his breath. "*It takes a lot of effort, but I am getting better at it.*"

"What do you mean?"

"*I have been practicing.*"

"But how can you move them without touching them?"

"*I am touching them… in a way.*"

"I didn't see you move. How can you be touching them?" said Raylan, who grew more confused and more interested.

"*I touched the air around it. At least, I think that is what I did.*"

"The air? But how? You can't even see the air…"

"*You cannot?*" asked Galirras, as he turned his head and twirled his three pupils at Raylan, in wonder. "*When I look at things, I see little sparkles flying everywhere. They light up and fade away quickly, like flowing water sparkling in the sunlight. I see them better in direct sunlight. It's harder to see them in the shadow of the trees.*"

"It must be a dragon thing," said Raylan, "but what does that have to do with the leaves moving?"

"Well, I thought the sparkles looked pretty, so I wanted to catch them. But my claw moved right through them, or perhaps the sparkles flowed around it. I tried several more times, but it had no effect. So, I started watching the movement of the sparkles. They were random, at first, but I noticed a few days ago that if I concentrate on them, they started moving in the same direction. The more I concentrate, the faster they move."

"So, you are able to move things by moving the sparkles?"

"Not at first. One night, I noticed the flames of our campfire got larger, if I moved the sparkles toward them. I saw I could push against a flame and make it bend. That got me thinking what else I could move. I was not successful, until I just moved these leaves today."

"And here I thought you just liked to look at the flames every night. Who knew you were doing such an amazing thing."

Galirras yawned. "It is very tiring to do. I would like to go back to camp and sleep for a bit, if that is okay."

"That's fine. We got enough meat for today's meal," said Raylan. "Besides, I want to ask Xi'Lao if she knows anything about thi—"

A low growl rumbled from behind Raylan.

He turned slowly to find a dark brown timber wolf, head lowered, teeth bared. The animal let out another deep growl, staring Raylan in the eye as two more wolves skulked from behind the tree. The soft snapping of a branch had Raylan glance to his left. Another wolf circled in.

Seven wolves. Surrounding them from all sides.

The smallest one was as big as Galirras.

"What do they want?" said Galirras, as he rose to his feet.

"They must have been drawn here by the smell of your kill," Raylan whispered as he held out a hand to Galirras. "Make no sudden movements, there are too many of them. If we're lucky, they'll only want the deer remains…"

With slow, careful movements, Raylan shifted his hand to his shoulder, lifting the string with the two hind legs. The brown timber wolf let out another deep rumble and took a step forward.

"He must be the alpha… the leader of the pack," said Raylan, more to himself than to Galirras.

Another wolf moved up beside the alpha and was greeted with a quick snarl and a snap of the jaws, before the wolf's yellow eyes focused on Raylan again. By now, he had the deer legs in his arms. Trying to make no sudden movements, he dropped the pieces in front of the wolf, where it landed with a heavy thud.

The wolf brought his nose down and sniffed. As it looked up at him, Raylan hoped their offer had been accepted. But then the alpha leapt, jaws open…

CHAPTER TWELVE

Friends

Raylan's muscles were more prepared than his mind. A blend of instinct and training forced them to react to the oncoming danger. He threw himself to the left, drawing his sword. The wolf adjusted its trajectory but overshot him; its jaws snapping closed on nothing but air. Rolling across his shoulders, Raylan further increased the distance between them. His sword swished through the air in full swing as he rolled to his feet. He hoped to slash the wolf's neck, but the animal reacted too fast. Shifting sideways, the blade only nicked the alpha's ear.

The animal gave an angry growl, before it moved forward to pounce once more. The moment it launched itself, Galirras stormed in from the side with a deep roar.

"Stay away from him!"

With his mouth stretched wide, baring all his teeth, Galirras crashed full force into the predator's flank. The dragon showed an unrelenting ferociousness that topped the wolf's own. Raylan felt his friend's burning desire to protect him from the attacking pack, as the dragon slashed his claws into the wolf's ribs and sunk his teeth into its back. Unfortunately, the long rigid hairs of its fur protected the timber wolf against the heavy attack. Flipping around on the spot, the wolf tried to lock its jaws on Galirras' neck, but only managed to reach his shoulder. Despite the rapid growth Galirras had gone through over the last few weeks, the wolf still had a size advantage over him. The dragon let out a short yelp, before clawing furiously at the alpha's nose and eyes.

Raylan wanted to move in to help, but he had no time to focus on anything but his own safety. The remaining six wolves had followed their leader's example, although less aggressively and more opportunistically. One snuck in an attack to see if Raylan would react, while another made use of the reaction to see if he left an opening.

To his side, Raylan heard another loud yelp that drew his attention. Thankfully, it was the wolf who cried out after Galirras' claw scratched it directly in the left eye. The other wolves used the moment to close the gap on Raylan in an instant.

Raylan, noticing his mistake, tried to slash the incoming wolf across the face, but the wolf caught the sword's tip in its jaws and held it tightly between its teeth. A smaller, black wolf jumped for Raylan's unprotected right calf. His only option was to let go of his sword and take the wolf on barehanded. Before he could, a strange whirring sound swept through the forest followed by the *toink* and loud *thud* Raylan knew well from traveling with Kevhin and Rohan. The black wolf, moments away from putting its teeth into Raylan's leg, was thrown to the side by the force of a black bolt hitting its ribs.

Raylan expected to see one of the archers—hell, perhaps even both—with their crossbows at the ready again; but the sight was much stranger and completely unexpected. Two figures came down from the trees above via a tall rope—or cable—reaching all the way into the lower leaf canopy. Their faces were covered by leather masks and hoods. They held one-handed crossbows, which looked awfully small for the punch they packed. As one reloaded, the other shot a bolt into the hind leg of the wolf with Raylan's sword. It promptly released the blade, and leaped away from Raylan, whimpering. As the two figures reached the ground, the whirring stopped. Both pulled on levers, before firing another salvo. One hit another wolf, the other barely missed, burying itself deeply into a tree trunk.

Shouts sounded in the distance.

"Raylan! Where are you? Answer us!"

"Galirraaaas!" another joined as the voices closed in rapidly.

The alpha wolf, which Galirras had been fighting, raised its head, ears erect. With an unknown danger coming from the trees, along with the shouts of at least a handful of people quickly approaching, the odds turned against its pack.

As the wolf broke off the fight with the dragon, Galirras chased it, for just a few steps. The dragon stopped before he lost sight of Raylan. It looked like he was not about to leave him alone in such a dangerous place with unfamiliar men.

Walking slowly and deliberately, Galirras returned to Raylan's side. Blood ran down the dragon's shoulder where the wolf had bitten him, but it did not seem to bother him much. Moving in front of his human companion, he kept a steady eye on the two mysterious men with their strange backpacks and ropes going up into the trees.

Running footsteps approached. Richard, Kevhin, Gavin, Xi'Lao and Ca'lek all came skidding around one of the large tree roots.

Kevhin noticed the two strange-looking men first and aimed his crossbow in less than a heartbeat. The others, with swords and knives in hand, slid to a stop, spreading out around the unknown danger. One of the two men turned and aimed his crossbow at the arriving party, while the other kept his gaze on Raylan and Galirras.

"Who are you?" demanded Gavin. "Put down your weapons!"

"Hold on, Gavin. They helped us," Raylan said.

Gavin was not that easily convinced. "Tell us who you are. Do you understand me? We have you outnumbered, so lower your weapons and let us see your faces."

Gavin squared his shoulders. Behind him, the others of their squad nervously shifted their feet, their eyes locked on their unfamiliar company. Raylan saw the larger of the two men slowly shake his head at Gavin, gesturing with two fingers at his own eyes and then pointing behind the small group up in the trees.

The strange whirring disrupted the sounds of nature once again, as three additional people slid down from the trees. One twisted around a large tree trunk, running along it, spiraling downward until he reached one of the root plateaus. Another halted halfway down along the trunk, and rested his feet on the bark, while balancing his crossbow and taking aim. The third dropped just to the right of Gavin.

The distance between them was close enough to be dangerous, but far enough to be reactive to any attack Gavin might attempt. Raylan saw his brother shift nervously, back and forth, trying to decide the best course of action.

"Listen to me, Gavin," said Raylan. "They really helped us. There were wolves, big ones! They helped chase them off. I don't think they mean harm. They're clearly not the men we fought before."

Gavin did not move an inch. This was enemy territory. What were the chances that they would find allies, or friendly people, this far from home? It was his duty to protect everyone, not to expose them to any unnecessary risks.

The man, who had made the gesture to them, slowly lowered his crossbow. One hand in the air, palm forward, he slowly put the crossbow down on the ground with his other. Turning, he gestured for his companion to do the same. The other man rolled his eyes, before he, too, lowered the crossbow. The other three soon followed.

Raylan saw his brother and the others relax a little. Once everyone lowered their weapons, the one who had put down his crossbow first, pulled off his hood and mask. Underneath was a man with a rugged beard and long dark brown hair tied back in a ponytail. On his cheek, a large scar that looked like someone had branded him. It was shaped like a closed fist.

The man looked at Raylan and broke into a big smile.

"Who are you?" Raylan asked, even though it was unlikely the man understood.

"Someone who's overjoyed to hear free people speak the language of his motherland in these uncommon lands after so many years!" he replied, to Raylan's surprise. His grin grew even wider.

The man had a thick accent but definitely spoke Terran. "You speak Terran?" Raylan said.

"Ever since I was little."

"You're all Terrans?"

"No. Some are from here, some are Southerners. Me, I'm Terran... it's a nice mix of things. But we all have one thing in common."

"Oh, and what's that?"

"We're all former slaves of the Stone King."

At this, the others removed their hoods, showing different skins tones, but all wearing the same burn mark on their faces. As he studied them, Raylan noticed one of them was a woman. The look in her eyes carefully sizing him up as she held her hand firm on her crossbow.

"Slaves? From who? And how did you all end up here? How did you survive?" Raylan fired off question after question.

"Easy there, mate. You'll have plenty of time to get to know us, I expect. You and your lizard."

"He's a dragon, not a lizard."

"A dragon? You don't say. I thought those only existed in stories."

"Not anymore, as you can see."

"Interesting!"

The man looked at Gavin. "You're the commander, correct?"

"Indeed I am, and you are?"

"The name's Sebastian, but my friends call me Seb. I would like to invite you back to our base. I believe our council would be interested in meeting y'all."

"Why's that?"

"'Cause they're the curious type and it's not every day we run into fellow Terrans in these parts. In fact, we never thought anyone would get this far without being killed or captured. As you may have noticed, this part of the world isn't exactly safe. We spotted a soldier patrol half a day's walk from here yesterday, so I suggest we start moving. Since no one knows we're here, I assume they're looking for you guys. There are more of your people nearby, right? I think we better get them and be on our way."

"Hold on, how do you know there are more of us out there?" Gavin said, his shoulders tense once more.

"We came across your group a few days ago and have been following you ever since. You didn't seem like normal soldiers, so I got curious. Imagine my delight when I heard you all speaking my native language around the campfire at night. But we can talk later. Let's get everyone somewhere safe, first."

Sebastian whistled and motioned upward to the woman and the farthest man. They pulled a handle on the side of the strange contraptions on their backs, and pushed off hard, descending all the way to the forest floor. As soon as they touched it, they pushed off, forcefully, while pushing the handle the other way. The metallic whirring filled the surroundings as both man and woman shot into the air to the lowest branches. Raylan could not believe his eyes, and he felt Galirras share his feeling of awe, in his head.

"*What is that?*" said Galirras.

"*I've got no clue,*" replied Raylan, privately.

Sebastian called out to the younger guy who had landed close to Gavin. "You take the high road, too, Twan. Tell Otis and Danai to follow us and keep an eye out for trouble. We'll be heading for the stables. Ivar and I will stay on ground level, so unclasp us when you get topside."

The one called Twan, released his lever and pushed off just as the others had done. With crazy speed, he shot upward, disappearing into the lower canopy.

"Ivar and I will walk with you all, if that's okay. Safe grounds are not far from here. If we pick up the pace, we should make it to the stables by nightfall."

A different whistle came from above, signaling the cables dropping. Both men pulled the lever to partly rewind the cable, allowing the remaining length to crash on the ground next to them. Picking up the end of the cable, the last of it disappeared neatly in the strange contraption on their backs.

"Ready when you are," said Sebastian, his grin still wide.

The camp was quickly broken up, and they were well on their way before the sun hit its highest point of the day. The others in the camp were as surprised as the rest to see friendly faces so far from home, although an overall wariness was present in each member of their group.

Sebastian and Ivar took the lead. Every so often, they would make bird calls with their hands, which were then echoed back from the tree branches where the rest of their group were following. Raylan tried to spot them up amongst the branches, but rarely saw more than the occasional shadow moving between the leaves. The members of each group kept careful eyes on their surroundings, making sure they were not getting surrounded or walking into a trap.

Raylan and Galirras were in the middle of the group. Together with Gavin, who walked next to them, they kept an eye on their new friends.

"I wonder how long they've been out here," Raylan whispered.

"Who knows? They seem a little bit too well equipped though to be recent slaves. I wonder where they got all the gear."

"Maybe it was payment for luring us into a trap."

Raylan looked warily at his brother.

"*They do not seem like bad people. Not like the other people who stole me. They do not smell of blood, and they talk differently, too,*" remarked Galirras in Raylan's head.

"That's doesn't mean anything, Galirras. The most brutal assassin can dress up nicely and wash himself before going to hunt his target; but in this case, I think you are right… they do not feel like bad people."

Gavin looked at him.

"Galirras said they don't seem like bad people. I tend to agree… if they hadn't shown up when those wolves attacked, who knows what would have happened," Raylan added with a shrug.

He looked behind them to see if the rest were still keeping up. Peadar and the others were on their horses, but Raylan was glad that Gavin decided to walk with him and Galirras, for a bit. "It was a good thing one of you heard the wolves attack; but I think you would've arrived too late, if it hadn't been for Sebastian and his men."

"We never heard the wolves," said Gavin.

"What?" said Raylan, while looking at his brother.

"I said we never actually heard the wolves. Never saw them either."

"But how's that possible? You all came rushing to our aid when we were being attacked. Did you hear Sebastian and his men with those weird backpacks then?"

"No, actually, I think it was Galirras that called us…"

Raylan dropped his gaze to Galirras, who had a blank look on his face.

"*I think so, too,*" the dragon said happily, after a moment. He seemed very pleased with himself, this morning.

"You never told me you could do that."

"You never asked, either. Besides, I'd never tried something like that before. We were in trouble, so I think I sent out an unfocused call for help. I think these strange tree people might have heard it, too."

"If that is so, others might have heard the same call," said Raylan.

"We'd better be on guard for any enemy patrols, especially if one is as close as this Sebastian mentioned," he added, while quickly explaining things to Gavin.

Raylan was silent, for a bit, going over this new information.

"Would you be able to talk to the others like you do to me?" he said, finally turning to Galirras.

"I do not see why not, now that I think about it. It is different from our link, which is effortless. Before, with the others, I really did not focus on their minds at all... nor did I hear any of their thoughts. I just pushed my own 'voice' out there. With some practice, I am sure I will be able to do it again."

"Great, let's try it out with Gavin here."

"Try what out?" Gavin said, a frown forming.

"To see if you can hear me again," said Galirras, after some concentrating.

Gavin smiled. "Ha, so it was you! I recognize the sound your 'voice' from before... if one can call that sound... you're still fading in and out, a bit."

"Gavin is not the only one that can hear you," said Xi'Lao, who had been walking close by.

Yet the others did not seem to react at all.

"I think Galirras can only send out an unfocused signal, strong or weak, when he speaks to other people. He cannot direct it, like he does with me," said Raylan.

"Which would mean, if he talks to one of us, he talks to all of us," added Xi'Lao, as if she made a mental note. "Like a normal person talking out loud."

"Well, in any case, that took me completely by surprise," said Gavin.

"It can be a little disorienting at first, right?" Raylan laughed, punching his brother on the shoulder.

Raylan saw Galirras make a small misstep, something that he'd not seen him do for several days already. "Was that difficult to do, Galirras?"

"It takes some concentration. I will have to get used to it. I am sure it will become easier, with practice," said the dragon.

"I suggest we keep this within our group, until we know for certain who we can trust," Gavin spoke, softly.

Raylan gave a small nod.

"Agreed. We'll practice with other people later this evening. We've got to keep an eye on our surroundings, for now... and we wouldn't want Galirras to trip," he added, with a wink.

"Hmpf, I would never trip!" Galirras snorted, as both brothers and Xi'Lao laughed, heartily.

The day went on without incident. As the sun began to set, Raylan started to wonder how long they still had to walk. They had been moving south most of the time, meaning they were going in their preferred direction, at least.

"Sebastian, how far do we still have to go?"

"You can call me Seb, you know. And not much further. In fact, we should see the entrance any moment."

They had been walking uphill for some time, the ground becoming more stone than dirt. To their left the hill rose into a big rock formation as they moved along its stone walls.

"Here it is," said Sebastian, after another quarter mile.

"I don't see anything at all," replied Raylan, looking at the dead-end cove in the stone wall that Sebastian had been pointing at.

"Just have a closer look."

Raylan and Galirras walked toward the end of the Cove.

"This doesn't look like stables, at all," said Raylan.

"What do stables look like then?"

Raylan pictured one of the many stables he had seen in Shid'el and presented the image to Galirras, in his head. He was really getting used to this sharing of thoughts. Galirras had to ask less and less about things he did not know, as he would just pull up the reference from Raylan's mind when discussing the subject. It worked like a charm.

"They're not stables in the traditional sense. Just go closer, you'll see what I mean," said Sebastian.

Moving forward, Raylan was looking at all sides. There seemed to be nothing but rock wall and plants. Coming to the far end of the cove, he noticed a small irregularity in the wall. Upon closer inspection, he pulled away some of the shrubbery and discovered a hidden passageway. It was large enough to move a horse through if you took the reins. A person would never find it, unless you walked all the way to the end. The natural flow of the cove completely hid the entrance from sight and as the ground consisted of solid rock, there was also little fear of leaving footprints behind that would expose the secret entrance.

170

Peadar joined them after dismounting. "I'll go have a look," he said, after Sebastian invited them to go further.

After a few minutes, he returned. "Raylan, come on, you've got to see this. It's amazing."

Following Peadar, they entered the rock formation, one by one. The horses fit perfectly, as did Galirras, as long as he kept his wings folded. Turning a corner, the passage quickly opened up. What Raylan saw could have come straight from a children's fairy tale. The scene was magical in the last rays of sunlight. A large clearing completely surrounded by stone walls. Open at the top, it was as if someone had scooped out the inside with a giant spoon. The ground was filled with a green, grassy field as well as crops where most of the sunlight shone during the day. On the shady side, large bushes of blackberries ran along the wall. At the top, the high edges of the stone walls were colored orange and deep red from the setting sun. It gave the grass a golden shine, which slowly turned to deep dark green as night took over the sky.

At the far end were two horses in a small, fenced, part of the hidden cove. Next to them were Twan, Otis, Danai and another unknown man, speaking softly. As soon as they saw their travel party enter the clearing, they broke off their conversation, and Twan sauntered over.

As Gavin moved next to him, Raylan felt his brother tense. If this was a trap, this would be an ideal moment to let it spring.

"Twan, is everything prepared?" asked Sebastian.

"All taken care of Seb. Their horses can join the others. There's plenty of grass for them to eat. We've just started a fire and are about to cook some stew with some shrooms and forest potatoes."

Sebastian turned to Raylan and the rest. "Welcome to our stables," he said, spreading his arms wide. "This man here is our head of stables, Borclad. He doesn't speak much Terran, but that won't prevent him from being a fine host for us weary travelers. Unpack and make yourselves comfortable, we'll be safe here from the patrols for the night. Tomorrow, we'll go and see the council. I'll bet they'll be surprised to see y'all."

They all followed Sebastian, and Raylan saw his brother relax a little.

As the rocky bottom surrounding the hidden cove prevented large trees from growing too close, a large part of the heavens was visible. Rows of clouds slowly drifted by as more stars winked to life in the darkening sky.

The group slowly relaxed as good food was offered and people had time to talk, taking turns telling each other their stories.

Galirras was slowly swirling some leaves around, letting them dance above the flames of the campfire. Every so often, a leaf would come dangerously close to getting burned, but he always managed to blow the flames away before the leaf would incinerate. When he got bored with that, he started splitting the grass with the wind, drawing figures which lasted mere moments.

At the same time, he also spoke with Gavin and Xi'Lao to practice multitasking and improve on his concentration. After the earlier introduction that day, Xi'Lao was delighted that Galirras was able to communicate with her directly and used every discreet opportunity to ask him hundreds of questions about what it was like to be a dragon.

Eventually, he grew tired from the extended bouts of concentration. He moved closer to Raylan and fell asleep with his head on Raylan's lap.

"*Sleep well, little one, you did great today. Soon, your head will be too heavy to sleep like this; you're growing so fast. I won't be able to call you little one for much longer, either.*"

"*I don't mind being called little, not by you, at least,*" answered Galirras.

He yawned, involuntarily showing the rows of sharp teeth lining his mouth. As Raylan looked at him, he noticed Galirras' head had gotten wider. His neck had also become more muscular. Next to the large horned comb, smaller horns were now growing along his spine. His scales were increasing in size, too, and the color of his skin was approaching more of a golden brown, moving away from the pale yellow he was when he came into this world. It seemed to him that Galirras was slowly leaving his frail build behind and growing into a much stronger dragon.

Raylan looked at the folded wings. The membranes had gotten thicker and sturdier. The bone structure of the wing had kept growing, but the muscles around the shoulder area still looked underdeveloped due to Galirras' refusal to test out his wings.

Softly scratching Galirras above his eye ridge, Raylan noticed Sebastian staring at them. "You don't seem to be afraid of him," said Raylan. "None of you, actually."

"You forget we followed you for a number of days already. I saw how everyone was around him. I figured as long as we don't get on your bad side, there would be nothing to worry about. Don't get me wrong, he looks like a fierce beast, but you seem disarmingly friendly with him."

"But you didn't seem surprised about seeing a dragon, either. It makes me wonder if you have seen creatures like him before."

"No, but I saw plenty of strange creatures when I was sailing as a young lad. Huge fish, monsters with many tentacles, some were almost half the size of the ship itself. So perhaps meeting a dragon didn't seem all that impossible to me," Seb said, shrugging one shoulder.

"Perhaps someday you can tell me about those other creatures you saw," said Raylan, yawning.

Sebastian smiled. "We'd better turn in for the night. Tomorrow, we'll need to focus on the road while traveling and that's best done when well rested."

Raylan did not need much convincing; it had been an exhausting day. He started to make himself comfortable, when he turned back. "Hey, Sebastian."

"Yeah?"

"I never thanked you for this morning. If it hadn't been for you and the others, Galirras and I would've been in real trouble. So... thank you, I owe you one."

CHAPTER THIRTEEN

Treetops

Raylan saw Galirras squeeze through the tunnel in front of him. The dragon had to partly walk over the wall to fit through the narrow passage. After some discussion, they had left the horses behind in the care of Borclad.

The cove, where they spent the night, had another exit in the back. It led through a series of narrow tunnels that barely accommodated the ever-growing Galirras. The dragon had awakened well rested. During breakfast, he happily exaggerated to Gavin and Xi'Lao about his hunts the previous day and how he protected Raylan from the wolf, which, he swore, had been at least twice his size.

They had been walking upward for some time when they turned a corner and saw light at the end of the corridor. Stepping into the open air, Raylan heard Galirras, in his head.

"*It is a dead end. Where do we go from here?*"

It took a moment for his eyes to adjust before he saw what Galirras meant. They walked onto a rock terrace, just big enough to fit their group and higher up than Raylan would have guessed. It seemed the lower branches of the trees ran on the same level as the terrace.

"*I've got no clue,*" he answered.

He approached Sebastian, who was waiting for everyone to exit the cave; but just before Raylan could ask what was going on, the man started to speak.

"All right, things will now get a bit tricky, so listen up. Your boots will only get in the way from this point. Since I don't have any spare leather ones with me, you'll have to go barefoot from here on."

"What do you mean barefoot? Where are we going?" asked Gavin.

"Up there."

Sebastian turned and pointed at one of the massive branches that had grown from the trunk straight onto the rock terrace. From the ground, the branches had already looked big, but this was something else. The branch was so wide it could almost be called a road; two people could easily pass each other without touching or falling off for lack of room.

"What? The tree?" asked Raylan.

"It's much safer than traveling on the ground, especially now we're reaching the soft, sandy parts of the forest. Better tie your laces together and hang your boots around your neck. You don't want to drop them while walking up there," Sebastian said with a smile.

At that, the man jumped onto the branch and walked toward the trunk of the tree. Once above the precipice, he turned around. "It will probably take us a good deal of the morning to reach our settlement, so let's get moving. But watch your step... some places can be quite slippery."

They saw no choice but to follow. Taking off his boots, Raylan was the first to step onto the branch. The tree bark felt cold to his skin; and he felt every crack, bump, and cavity on the soles of his feet.

Galirras followed Raylan onto the branch. His claws dug into the bark, allowing him to move easily over its surface. He looked down and instinctively stirred his wings. Using his tail for balance, it looked like Galirras felt as sure of his footing as he would on the ground.

It did not take Raylan long to get accustomed to the feel of the tree either. His years at sea allowed him to develop a confident stride while the ground constantly moved below him. As the branches swayed ever so softly from the wind, he saw the others were less happy with their new high road.

Xi'Lao and Gavin seemed to be doing okay. Peadar walked uncertainly, his legs shaking. Raylan heard him mutter his dislike of heights. The young lad made sure he kept close to Twan, who assisted people in the middle of the group. Both archers and Ca'lek found their way okay, but Harwin had some trouble with parts of the path. Otis and Danai helped him constantly, as he muttered that men were made for walking on solid ground. Richard closed the ranks. He did all right, but walked slower than the rest, suggesting he was only a fraction less nervous.

The morning flowed by slowly as they systematically made their way from branch to branch. Sometimes, sliding down to a lower crossing branch; other times, climbing higher. Often, they walked all the way to the center of the tree, moved around the trunk, and continued to another branch on the other side.

The party was happy to find steps carved into the wood from time to time, creating crude stairs to move around on. Some were wide steps; others were nothing more than chunks taken out of the side of the massive tree trunks. The latter proved quite a challenge for Harwin and Peadar to get across. But Sebastian made certain everyone was safe as each was secured with a rope and spotted by two others during each crossing.

Galirras was enjoying this new adventure, clawing around on the branches and tree trunks, chasing small lizards or insects living in the canopy. It was like they entered a completely new world. As empty as the forest was on the ground, the trees were buzzing with life. Life that made excellent snacks, according to the dragon. He had seen some sort of black squirrels, caterpillars, centipedes as big as an arm, lizards, and spiders; but also larger animals, like the thing that looked like a climbing badger—small furry creatures living in holes—and the large eagles they came across earlier. Raylan was sure lots of other animals remained undetected. Most were harmless, but Sebastian meticulously checked each handgrip hole thoroughly to make sure no poisonous spider or other harmful insect occupied it.

Galirras moved more swiftly than Raylan felt comfortable with. Sometimes, he was two trees over. Then, all of a sudden, he was above them, moving along a higher branch before disappearing from sight again. He always climbed though, never jumped, tried to glide, or use his wings. Thankfully, his movements looked confident, and Raylan had not seen him make a mistake… yet.

Their progress was slow. They often had to wait for the entire group to move along one of the tree-trunk steps. Their feet were getting numb from the cold, which only increased the chance of a mistake.

Waiting for the last of their group to cross, Raylan wondered how Sebastian knew where to go—all trees looked the same to him.

"There are small carvings in the bark of the trees. Just keep an eye on Sebastian and you'll see it."

Raylan looked up to Galirras, who clung to the tree some twenty feet above them. Following his advice, Raylan noticed Sebastian's hand slide over the bark of a tree trunk when they set out again. On closer inspection, Raylan spotted a small symbol carved into the trunk, clearly put there to indicate which way to move forward.

Walking behind Sebastian, Raylan noticed the flexible leather boots their guide wore. The soles appeared to have a rough surface, increasing grip on the tree bark as much as possible. Each of their new friends, Sebastian included, had strapped on that strange backpack again. The device covered more than their entire backs and had a hook sticking out of the top. They looked heavy, but Sebastian did not seem bothered by the weight at all.

"Hey, Sebastian? What are those packs you're carrying? How do they work?" Raylan asked, when they were walking next to each other across an especially wide branch.

"These things? They're our stolen life savers."

"Where'd they come from?"

"We got a few of them some years ago during one of our warehouse raids. The guys that went out on that trip didn't know what they were, but they decided to bring some back with them just in case. Best choice ever. Once back at base, one of the older men recognized the devices."

Sebastian hopped onto another branch. "We didn't know it at the time, but Old Luke is a real tinkerer. He told us he and a younger slave had been working for a group of weird people. These people did nothing else but try and come up with all kind of strange contraptions and devices. He said he'd never seen metal like the one they worked with in those workshops. It was both very flexible and strong."

He extended a hand to pull Raylan up. "Apparently, Old Luke had very steady hands in creating the smallest things. His job was to build the contraptions they'd think of and help them test it out. It was only luck that he'd been with us in the mines the day we made our escape. Normally, he worked somewhere in the palace, but he'd been sent to check on a delivery of some sort."

"He built them?"

"Parts of it, I believe. He took one apart to take a closer look and worked out how to use it… might've even made some adjustments. At the time, we were still forced to move around on ground level, which was dangerous. We'd lose people to predators or quicksand, especially at night."

"So, how do they work?"

"He showed me once how this strange metal band is curled up inside. That band is attached to a rope. Pulling the rope tightens the band inside, allows the rope to retract if let go. I've got no idea how that strange metal keeps its curled shape. I've never seen anything like it before in my life. Normal iron is dull and heavy, but this metal has a strange greenish glow over it and feels incredibly light. It's almost like it has no weight at all."

A strange fussy animal crossed their path. Twice as large as a squirrel, its head resembled that of a mouse, but it had a large, cat-like tail. Intrigued by its appearance, Raylan followed it as the creature shot up the tree trunk and disappeared into a hole. He turned to find Sebastian had already walked on and hurried to catch up. "So, what…?" he said, when he caught up with him. "You just hook it to something and jump down?"

Sebastian laughed. "That's pretty much it, yeah. It took me a while to get the courage to do so, though."

"But how is it you don't smash into the ground?"

Sebastian pointed to either side. "See this lever? That's the brake. Pull it and you stop the rope from coming out. The dial adjusts the tension on the metal curl, allowing you to adjust for higher or lower heights. It's not without fault though. Jump from too high a branch and you'll end up dangling helplessly in the air. Or adjust the tension wrong and you'll hit the ground hard. It took us a lot of trial and error to get things right. Poor Crippled Claude will never be able to walk right again."

The former slave shrugged. "But we wouldn't be able to do without them, now. Once we figured out how they worked, we were able to come down from the trees wherever we liked, giving us the element of surprise and a much safer travel route in this forest of giants. We went back several times to steal more before they caught on to them disappearing and moved the stockpile away."

"Unreal," Raylan said with a shake of his head. "I seem to run into impossible things all the time of late."

"Ah, it seems we're almost there," said Sebastian, pointing ahead.

A rope bridge connected two of the trees in a place where none of the branches crossed each other. As they moved across it, Raylan looked down, expecting to see a massive depth, opening to an unwelcoming ground down below. But he barely saw the ground at all. Branches and leaves ran under the entire bridge. It kept everything out of sight to anyone on the ground who would look upward, by chance.

They crossed another five rope bridges, each hidden from the ground before they were eventually greeted by a dark-haired man with a large bow on his back, and two short axes at the ready, perhaps in case the rope bridge would need to be cut.

At least that's what I would do.

Sebastian greeted the man with a slap on the shoulder and something said in a non-Terran language. The man pointed toward them, asking him a question. After some back and forth, Sebastian threw his hands in the air.

"Oh, come on, Ratjic! They're kullah," Sebastian said. "Guests! From my homeland! We've been on the road for weeks, and it was a long trip. I want them to meet with the council."

"It seems like this man doesn't like us entering the village," said Galirras, as he jumped down from his high spot where he had been waiting.

The guard gave a short outcry and grabbed for his bow. Sebastian quickly put his hand on Ratjic's arm, pushing down the bow. He added something in the unknown language.

The guard looked bewildered, taking in Galirras and their entire group from head to toe, for some time.

Finally, the man called Ratjic said something to Sebastian as he gestured to Galirras.

"Excuse me. I am not a lizard!" said Galirras suddenly, as he swung his head close to the guard.

The guard jumped back, even Sebastian and his companions had a look of surprise on their faces. Most of their own group had been introduced to Galirras 'speaking' during the morning travel. Harwin had happily grumbled about the surprises in the world. Kevhin and Rohan briefly talked about hunting prey with him. Peadar on the other hand got startled and almost lost his balance. He gave everyone quite a scare by almost plummeting to the ground, but afterward had been delighted to talk to the dragon about all kinds of things like the biology of his body. Ca'lek had shown the least surprise, as if he had expected the possibility of communication all along.

"You understand what he's saying, Galirras?" asked Raylan.

"They were talking the same language when I was in the egg."

"You were aware of the outside while you were in your egg?"

"Of course, I felt you, did I not? Words reached my ears, images flowed into my head. I think that's how I learned."

"So, you *can* hear other people's thoughts? Are you able to hear his thoughts now?" said Xi'Lao, who had come to see what was going on.

"No, I cannot. Everything turned much quieter after Raylan became mine and I became his."

"But he couldn't have understood you. You spoke Terran, just now," remarked Raylan.

"I spoke to him in his own dialect. I merely just spoke to you in your own language, too."

Galirras looked apologetically at Xi'Lao, for a second. "I am sorry, Xi'Lao. I do not speak the language of the Tiankong... not yet, anyway. I would have liked to speak to you in your native language, too."

"You silly magnificent creature," said Xi'Lao. "Though I would love to have a conversation in my own language again, there's no need to apologize for any such thing."

Raylan saw she was trying not to lose her reserved posture and not to laugh out loud. It made him feel good that Galirras was getting along with the other members in the group. The guard, who looked at them having a conversation, relaxed for only a tiny fraction. He turned to Sebastian and spoke quite briskly.

Galirras stepped forward, but not directly at the guard, trying not to look threatening. "It is not my intention to frighten anyone. If it means that much to everyone, I have no problem waiting somewhere on the outskirts of the town. But there is no need to insult me."

That finally seemed to do the trick. They agreed that Galirras would follow higher in the trees and wait at one of the empty spots Sebastian would point out.

As they passed the guard, he looked every single member of the group in the eye, his face stern. Only the man's companions, like Twan and Otis, received a smile and greeting, welcoming them back to their home. Danai gave Ratjic a hug as she passed, but Raylan thought it looked more friendly than romantic.

The village soon came into view on the other side of the tree. The sight was amazing. Platforms, large and small, were constructed on the higher branches. The first huts were small and older; but as they got farther into the settlement, the buildings became larger and appeared increasingly sturdier. Full stairs, with handrails, had been constructed in many places, allowing for safe passage between each part. Some platforms even had troughs with dirt, where plants and berries seemed to grow.

Several platforms were connected by the same kind of rope bridges they had crossed earlier, since the distance was too great for normal stairs. Torches were positioned on most platforms, but none were lit during the day.

"You know, you might actually be some kind of large lizard," remarked Raylan to Galirras, privately, as they walked on.

"Really?" Galirras looked back at the guard with a hint of guilt. *"Maybe I should go back and apologize, then."*

Galirras shifted uncomfortable, sitting on the platform. Next to him were all kinds of boxes and piles of wooden planks. At the other side were some woven baskets smelling of fish and dirt. But the scent was not the problem.

They had only been there a short while, but news had spread quickly through the small treetop village; and a group of spectators rapidly formed, every single one making sure not to venture too close. A handful of small boys and a dark-eyed girl stared at him. The boys dared each other to approach. Something that should not be that difficult, or scary, in Galirras' opinion.

It was his first time seeing small children. They looked in all aspect human, but their dimensions were off in some ways. One of them with blond curly hair had arms and legs that seemed very long in comparison with his torso; and this other child with short spiky rugged hair carried around a head that was way too big on those small shoulders. They also seemed to be much rowdier than the full versions of humans.

Raylan and his brother were talking to Sebastian, when he noticed the group of spectators making way for a small delegation. Two women and a man approached with slow, well-measured paces. Raylan, who was used to the Shid'el's council, had imagined something slightly different when Sebastian talked about their council. Back home in the capital, 'The Thirty' were influential men put in place to represent the common folk and to act as guidance for the king. It seemed an odd thing to call these three a council, though he admitted they looked old enough to fit the image.

One woman looked like his old neighbor near his father's workshop, and she had been a great-grandmother with more grandchildren than two hands could count. This woman looked anything but feeble though. She had strong eyes and held her gray-haired head high as she took in the scene—locking her eyes on Galirras with interest when she saw him.

The other woman and man seemed a bit younger but were easily twice Raylan's age. The small, well-rounded woman looked like she enjoyed a good life, but the deep facial lines told of a hardworking past and most likely the present. The man's face showed the same hardness, though much of it was hidden behind a black beard speckled with gray. His tall build made him an impressive presence even at his age. The one thing that was not covered by his facial hair was the slave mark burned in his cheek. Both women had one, too, though the elderly woman didn't have the symbol on her cheek but on her left hand. The mark was so faded it must have been there for a very long time.

"Sebastian, welcome back," the man began, when the trio was close enough. "How did it go?"

"It's been a long but good couple of weeks. The new trails are marked. One leads to a promising fishing pool. We did some maintenance on two bridges on the track to the stables, but the rest was still in great shape."

"What about the food storage?" asked the round woman.

"Ann, Jarod, can't you see we've got more important things to discuss? We've got guests," the elderly woman said, cutting her short.

"More important? What is more important than feeding every mouth in this village? Food stock has already dwindled ever since we lost part of it in that last spring storm. We can't have people go hungry. It's not good for morale," said Ann.

"You're always hungry," replied the elderly woman. "I, for one, would like to know who these people are before we discuss anything of a sensitive nature."

"Svetka's got a point, Ann. My apologies for rushing in like that," said the man called Jarod.

"Perhaps we should talk somewhere a bit more private?" suggested Svetka.

After some polite official introductions, they were invited to a small meeting space a little bit higher up in the tree. Raylan joined Gavin and Xi'Lao, attending the closed meeting with the small council and Sebastian. They were sure to have questions about Galirras, so Gavin wanted Raylan present to represent their unusual companion.

"Why have you brought them here?" said Svetka.

The question was directed at Sebastian; it seemed, for now, she was completely ignoring their party, which Raylan found quite rude.

"Because they're from Aeterra, just like you, and Jarod. They could help us fight. Or perhaps can help us get back home," Sebastian started.

"Home? Child, I've long forgotten my home. These dark woods feel more like home than any far away kingdom will ever be again. Who knows what has changed after all this time. And how can you be so certain? It might be a trap. They might be here to kill us all when we least expect it," she replied, glancing their way.

"No," said Sebastian, shaking his head. "I don't believe that. They were being chased by the dark troops. I saw them looking for them, everywhere."

"And you brought them here? What if the enemy followed them?" added Ann.

"Dark troops have been known to speak Terran perfectly, if properly taught. Did you actually see them fight the dark troops?" asked Svetka.

Sebastian held his tongue on that one.

"It seems to me you have endangered everything we've built these last years by guiding these strangers here. If we're discovered, we'll have nowhere else to go. Not to mention, bringing this unknown ferocious looking creature into our midst, the like no-one has ever seen before."

The old woman's voice sounded like she was scolding her grandchild.

"It's called a dragon, and he's a member of our group," Raylan interrupted.

"Silly child, don't be absurd. There are no such things as dragons. It's important for young people to know the difference between the real world and fairy tales."

"Well, this fairy tale is tr—" began Raylan, when he was interrupted.

"We really mean your people no harm, ma'am. I can assure you this." Gavin held up his hand to keep Raylan quiet. "We found ourselves stuck behind enemy lines after carrying out our mission and we're currently trying to find a suitable way home to bring this whole ordeal to a close."

"How'd it come to pass that you're stuck here?" This time, it was Jarod asking the question.

"We came on horseback rounding the northern bays of the Great Eastern Divide. Our journey has taken us many moons from our safe haven. Before we could return, the road home was cut off by the Doskovian army coming in from the west and we were forced to travel south, escaping detection. We're looking for the Drowned Man's Fork. I was hoping perhaps you've heard of it?"

"And you can fight?" Jarod asked.

"We can hold our own," stated Raylan, without permission.

"We've had some close calls, and I'm sad to say not all of us made it," continued Gavin, ignoring Raylan's rudeness.

"And this pet creature? No known animal looks like that, not even in these ancient woods."

"He's not a pet! Like I said, he's a dragon, and as far as we know, the only one of his kind," blurted Raylan.

"Good sir, council members, please feel at ease," Gavin said. "We have no intention of staying longer than necessary and have no plans to put pressure on your resources. If we hadn't run into Sebastian here, we'd have never met your community at all, I expect. We welcome your help, even if it's only advice. We don't want to be a bother to anyone, so perhaps we can show our value in a way that can gain your trust?"

"Hmmm, I was just thinking the same thing. Maybe we should give them a chance to prove their value to us," Ann remarked.

"What do you suggest?" said Svetka.

"Well, we really do need to restock our food supplies. They could join Sebastian and retrieve food from the newly-discovered storage."

"Would that be possible, Sebastian?" asked Jarod.

"The help is more than welcome. The depot is lightly guarded, and with the extra hands, we could be in and out without anyone knowing."

"So, leader, what do you say about this chance to prove yourselves?" said Svetka.

The three of them had a short discussion before Gavin gave their response. "Not all my men will be fit enough to join. We're willing to lend you a hand with those who're capable. In return, please let our wounded rest and gain back their strength. I hope this will convince you we're who Sebastian says we are."

"We'll see. Another thing, the beast stays here. I don't want that thing roaming around in the dark, allowing it to get the drop on us. He will be put under constant guard until you return."

"You can't do that. He'll have to hunt!" exclaimed Raylan.

The old woman looked at them sternly. "Fine, we'll see if we can catch some birds for him."

Raylan was furious. They did not need this. They should leave and let these tree dwellers to their own fate. He was about to give this woman a piece of his mind, when Gavin held up his hand again to urge him to calm down.

"We agree to your request. My men could use another good night's rest, but those who will join Sebastian will be ready to go at first light."

"Wha—" began Raylan, but his brother's fierce eyes told him to keep his mouth firmly shut.

They left the meeting room shortly after that. Raylan was unable to bite his tongue any longer and turned to Gavin. "Why the hell did you do that? We can't leave him here alone. Galirras won't like it at all. And neither do I, for that matter."

"*You* need to learn when you're supposed to keep your mouth shut. Running your mouth at the one person that might be able to help us get home quicker—think on this, for a moment. We're within enemy territory. We've got no idea how far we still need to go. We need allies. *You* need to follow orders. No, actually, *I need* you to follow orders. *You* need to explain to Galirras this is how it'll be. Once we get back from this food-run, we can continue to our destination with the help of these people. The sooner we do this, the sooner we can head home."

"We could easily fight our way out. They're not soldiers, they're probably untrained at combat, even though they outnumber us," objected Raylan.

"And then what? We're back where we started. Lost on a continent that wants us dead. No, our best chance is to gather information from the locals, and this is probably the best, if not the only chance we're going to get. No discussion."

Raylan did not like it one bit. Xi'Lao looked at him with pity in her eyes. "I can stay with Galirras for you. I can protect him. It will give us some time to talk uninterrupted," she said.

"I'm letting Harwin and Peadar stay behind, too," added Gavin. "Peadar can make sure the pigeon gets its strength back for the flight home. Harwin can assist Xi'Lao if there's trouble. And don't forget, Galirras isn't that helpless either."

That evening Raylan felt restless. He had informed Galirras of what they would have to do the next day. As expected, Galirras did not like it one bit. Not only would the dragon have to stay put, which would force him to stop moving through the trees, a thing Raylan knew he enjoyed immensely, but his winged friend would not be allowed to stay by his side and protect him from possible danger. The latter being the dragon's point of greatest concern. It took Raylan the entire evening meal to talk Galirras out of throwing a fit, and no amount of meat seemed to help this time—not that there was much meat to appease the angry dragon.

They were forbidden to go hunting and were under strict orders from his brother to follow that rule. The golden-colored tree pheasant he had been served, while being a beautiful bird to see, was hardly a meal for the dragon. Raylan was glad he had eaten his fill the day before. It meant Galirras would be fine for a couple of days with less food. Many large predators went without eating for days before killing their next large prey. Then again, the dragon was still growing—inches every day—and probably needed all the food he could get, so Raylan had given his own meat to him as well. Afterward, he had also asked Xi'Lao to look for ways to get additional things for Galirras to eat.

Now, dissatisfied with how things were going, Raylan was walking around the wooden pathways and rope bridges—trying to clear his head. Richard, who had noticed him moping around, decided to tag along. And although Raylan was not in the best of moods, he welcomed the distraction from his own grinding thoughts.

"I wonder how long we'll be gone," said Richard.

"Should be less than five days as far as I understood. Four, if we can get the food on the night we arrive at the depot. Or so I was told, at least."

Raylan did little to hide his disagreement with the decision made.

"I'm sure Galirras will be fine. No one would dare approach him, if he wouldn't let them. He's as tall as you and me already, just standing normally. Before you know it, he'll be the size of two horses. Who knows how big he'll eventually get."

"I worry about him though," Raylan said. "He knows nothing of what men are capable of. And those wings… he really needs to exercise them, but he won't do it." Raylan let out a sigh.

"Have you tried convincing him?"

"A bunch of times already. He just won't listen. He needs to decide this on his own or he'll be stuck walking for the rest of his life."

As they were walking past a small cottage, they heard a loud crash and yelling inside.

"I don't need more ointment. What I need is to stretch my legs. I've been lying in this blasted bed for weeks," the voice roared.

Raylan and Richard looked at each other, in surprise.

"I know that voice!" said Richard, excitedly, as he sprang toward the door and threw it open.

It took a second for their eyes to adjust to the low light in the room. A single primitive oil lamp burned on a table. There, in the corner, was a small bed, occupied by a large man. A man, not in a particularly good mood, who smiled when he spotted the new arrivals.

"Galen!" Richard shouted.

A woman's voice screamed, in Kovian, something Raylan guessed meant 'get out' or perhaps 'who are you and what are you doing here?'

"That's one of our companions," said Raylan, pointing at Galen.

"How did you get here?" Richard asked Galen.

The woman called out and immediately two guards showed up in the doorway, forcing themselves in.

A few moments later, both Gavin and Sebastian showed up, finding six people arguing in two different languages. A panting Peadar was standing next to them. Apparently, he had seen Raylan and Richard burst into the door and figured Gavin would be needed if they did not want things to end badly.

"Quiet!" hissed Sebastian, after which he said, in Kovian, "You three know better than to raise your voices during the night." Translating the words for Raylan and the others.

The two guards and the woman quickly fell silent.

"And you, Raylan… Richard, I expect you take the safety of this settlement into consideration by refraining from shouting where sound can carry through these woods for miles on windless nights like this," said Sebastian.

"Someone tell me what's going on," said Gavin.

Raylan just pointed behind the guards' backs. Following its direction, Gavin spotted Galen, lying on the bed.

"Galen?" He shook his head. "How's that possible?"

"Who's that?" Sebastian asked Raylan.

"He's one of our companions. We thought we lost him a while back, when we were attacked by a group of Doskovian soldiers," he answered.

"It's good to see you all," said Galen, "but can someone explain to me where we're at? They haven't told me anything, since I arrived here. They didn't even seem to speak Terran."

"Where'd this man come from," Sebastian asked the woman in the local language, "and why is he tied to the bed?"

The woman looked at Galen, before speaking to Sebastian, who nodded as he translated.

"She says Aanon's scouting party brought him in a few weeks ago, just after I left. They found him floating in the river, west of here, more dead than alive. He didn't look like a Darklander—the armor was all wrong—so they brought him here. They thought he might be an escaped slave, but he has no mark on him."

Sebastian frowned as he listened to the woman before continuing. "At first, it didn't seem he'd make it, but he slowly got better. He's been fighting fever-dreams and he wasn't eating much, so it took time for him to regain his strength. Apparently, his mind only just returned to this world when the fever broke a few days ago."

The woman looked at Galen, for a moment, and continued speaking to Sebastian.

"According to her, his body was black and blue, scrapes all over and a nasty cut on the back of his head, as well as along his back. They had to restrain him, or he would have thrashed around so much in his fever that he'd likely end up breaking down the house and falling to the ground."

"Well, I think it's safe to say he won't fall off anymore, so release his binds please," said Gavin.

The woman objected, although less forcefully than before.

"She says Aanon told her not to let anyone get close to him until he got back," translated Sebastian. "I'll take responsibility for it. This man is obviously a companion of our guests. We should treat him like one, too. If Aanon has a problem with that, just send him my way when he gets back," said Sebastian directly to the woman.

Galen rubbed his wrists after the woman removed his binds. Getting to his feet, he took an uncertain step, holding on to the bedpost.

"Do you remember what happened?" asked Raylan.

"I remember the stone bridge and those damn black wolves. I remember falling, using the wolf to break my fall in the river. After that, it all went black and cold. I must have lost consciousness right away." He groaned. "But, as you can see, my body remembers. I may have been lying here for weeks, but I still feel like I've gone through the laundry wringer."

Galen gladly accepted a shirt the woman handed over, and all of them saw the large bruises and cuts he had on his back and chest as he changed it with the one he was wearing. Some had healed—more or less—but the bruises still looked awfully painful. He winced as he dressed. "And I think I might have broken a few ribs in the process."

Gavin, who had told Raylan only a few days ago how he had been glad to finally breathe somewhat normal again, sympathized with him.

"Well, now that you know you're amongst friends, why not lie down again and let your body recover. I'll ask Xi'Lao to come by and inspect your ribs. We'll likely move on in a few days, so rest up as much as possible."

"Thanks, but I really need some fresh air first. I'll go back to bed after I've taken a stroll."

"I'll join you," said Richard, "loads of things have happened." When Galen was out the door, he turned to Gavin and the others. "I'll make sure he stays out of trouble—and gets back to bed as soon as possible."

Walking away, Raylan saw the relief on Richard's face. One of their second-in-command's closer friends had not been lost after all. And Raylan had to admit it lifted his spirits, too.

"*I am glad he is okay. I would like to meet with him, once he is up for it,*" said Galirras.

Automatically, Raylan looked toward the platform where his friend lay. He saw Galirras look back up at him.

"*That's right, it all happened before you came out of the egg, so you've never met Galen. I think you'll like him. And you'll have some time to get to know him while the rest of us are running this errand.*"

"*I wish I would be allowed to go with you,*" said Galirras, as he laid back his head, sulking over the situation.

"*Me too, but you'll be safe here. Don't worry.*"

"*I told you, it is not me I am worried about. What if those wolves come back, or the soldiers find you? I will be stuck here, unable to do anything…*"

"*I'll be fine. We'll be taking the high road, staying out of sight for almost the entire way. And I trust Sebastian. He looks like he knows what he's doing. Besides, Gavin and the others will be there, too,*" said Raylan, trying to assure him.

"*That is true, but they are still not me… nobody can protect you better than I can…*"

"*You might be right, but you can't be there for me all the time, little one. You've got to believe in other people too. Trust that they know what they're*" *doing and don't take any unnecessary risks. And you know how my brother is, he won't leave anything to chance."*

"*I still do not like it very much,*" said Galirras.

"*You and me both... you and me both. Hey, perhaps you can use the time to practice your wind dancing more. You can show me what you learned when I get back.*"

It was the best he could think of to keep Galirras occupied while they were gone.

CHAPTER FOURTEEN

Food

THEY LEFT AT dawn. After a short good-bye, a total of ten set out on the food run. Sebastian led the group of tree-dwellers. Twan, Otis, Danai and Ivar were all ready to head out again, although Ivar complained they had just returned and needed a break.

Raylan, Gavin, Ca'lek, Rohan and Kevhin formed the other half of the expedition. Gavin decided that Richard, as second-in-command, would stay in the settlement to keep Galen company during his recovery and to hunt, near the village, in the treetops. They all received a set of the rough leather shoes, allowing them to move around more easily on the slippery tree branches. There were bound to be edible animals around, or maybe some bird's eggs. In any case, Richard promised Raylan he would find something that could be given to Galirras, in case it was needed.

Peadar let out a sigh of relief, when Gavin told him to stay behind. The youngster explained the platforms gave him the feeling of being on ground level, so he could—hopefully—fool his head into thinking he was not frightfully high up in the trees. He would take the time to carefully check on the last remaining bird, and to get it well-rested. He could also assist Xi'Lao in case she needed help treating Galen's wounds.

Without any wounded and those afraid of heights to slow them down, they moved much faster than the previous day. They made good time toward the enemy's food storage, partly thanks to Sebastian, who gave Raylan and the rest tips on how to move quickly but safely through the trees. They learned to recognize slippery spots and rotten bark, and how to keep the weight on their legs while climbing to different branches.

They crossed from one branch to another by rope, multiple times—not all of which could be called 'bridges'.

"Where did you guys get all the rope you use, anyway?" Raylan asked Sebastian, while they were waiting for the last three people to cross a single rope crossing between two branches.

"Originally, we used rope we liberated from our captors. They only lasted a few months, at most. It was dangerous around the settlement. I think it was the mold. The ropes would get too moist and never properly dry again because of the canopy."

"And now?"

"A few years ago, we found a sort of plant growing high in particular trees. Its growth was stringy, with lots of small threads you could pull loose. Over several weeks, the women with weaving experience learned how to process the plant without destroying its strength. They spend all day making these ropes. They're even in our descenders," Sebastian said, pointing to his backpack. "If done right, the rope is almost as strong as an iron chain, but much lighter. It made the packs easier to carry and we were able to increase the length of the cable."

"That's what you call them? Descenders?" laughed Raylan.

"Fits the function, doesn't it?" returned Sebastian with a grin. "Anyway, I didn't come up with that one."

"You ever encounter anything dangerous in these trees?" asked Raylan.

"Well, at this height, anything that can startle you is dangerous."

"True, but I meant like animals or something."

"Well, the spiders and small tree scorpions can be difficult. If you are far from the antidote plants, the swelling after the bite, or the sting, can make tree travel quite difficult. Various snakes seem to be around, but only one of them is poisonous—that we know of—the other kinds tend to strangle their prey." He glanced around the canopy then returned his attention to Raylan. "Some animals can be aggressively territorial. You don't want to disturb a borrowing bee's hive during your climbing. Twan had his arm go numb for two weeks after being stung a few dozen times last summer when he accidentally disturbed a hive. He spent a good week in bed before the fever and the swelling went down."

"It seems to me Galirras is the biggest predator in these forests, or will soon be, at least."

"The eagles might challenge him from the sky though. During their breeding season, they'll attack anything that comes too close to the nest. Wolves are one of the biggest predators I've seen, although Ivar and Otis swear they've seen bears walking around which were almost as large as two men standing on each other's shoulders."

Hearing about the eagles, Raylan thought about Galirras' reluctance to fly, but decided not to confide it their newly-made friend just yet. He took a step forward and looked down to the forest floor, but he could see little through the branches.

"Did you guys encounter any of them when you first came to the forest?"

"Bears? No, luckily they seem very shy. Wolves, unfortunately, were a different matter. We've lost a few people in those first weeks and were constantly hunted by a small pack of them. The cove really saved our lives back then. But the wolves aren't the worst that live in these forests."

"They're not? What can be worse than giant wolves with rows of sharp teeth?"

"Sand devils… it's part of the reason I revealed myself to y'all, besides saving you from the wolves, that is."

"I've got no idea what a sand devil is."

"Be glad about it. They're the stuff of nightmares, at least for those who call this forest home. Locally, they call them *kzaktors*, which means something like burrowing blood-critter; but we ended up with sand devil in the Terran language, mainly because these creatures look like they come straight out of hell. We'll be crossing their territory in a bit, but we've seen them to the south, too.

"While we traveled through the area, we noticed the wolves gave up pursuit. We thought we'd caught a lucky break, never thinking about what made the wolves retreat. Then, the first night, people started disappearing. They seemed to vanish into thin air, until we started to find ripped off limbs in different places. One time, we all heard this horrific scream, but searching only turned up a few stumps of flesh which might have been fingers."

Sebastian's face paled from the memory. The thought alone made it hard for Raylan to swallow.

"It took us two days to figure out something was taking these people at night, so we set up men to guard the camp inside, in addition to the ones already on the perimeter. That night, two of the men were doing their rounds when a movement in the sand drew their attention. Something shifted under their feet in the loose sand."

"A sand devil?"

Sebastian nodded.

"One of the men suddenly sank into a sandpit and started screaming. By the time his friend pulled him out, both lower legs were already gone. Because of the scream, everyone saw the creature pop up for the first time." Sebastian shook his head, his face still pale. "Its body was like a giant centipede, the length of a man. It rose from the sandpit to thrust itself onto its denied meal.

192

Its head had rows of beady eyes on each side, with four small antennae on the top of its head. Its mouth split open in four directions, showing a gaping hole with rows of small, razor-sharp teeth lining all the way into its throat. Next to that horrible mouth, it had two enormous pincers, while it had six larger and dozens of smaller legs all the way down its body. It ripped right into the thighs of its victim with those pincers."

Raylan looked at him in disbelief. "You can't be serious? Something like that exists?"

"I swear it's the truth. Everyone started panicking and running, but the blood-soaked sand and the screams only attracted more of the blasted things. Another three people were grabbed before the rest of the group ended up on a rock formation."

Raylan glanced down again but those patches of ground he *could* see showed nothing out of the ordinary. "You must have been terrified. How did you all escape?"

"After two days and nights on the stones, someone finally got up the nerve to test their reaction to a stick. We noticed they were a lot less active during the day. One of the creatures tried to grab the stick but fell back screeching. It seemed like the light hurt their eyes. And, its movements slowed considerably during the daytime. So, we took advantage of the daylight and made a hasty escape. Most swore never to go back."

"I can only imagine," said Raylan, trying to process the information as the last of their group safely made it to their side. If Sebastian had not shown up, who knows what such creatures might have done to their group, or Galirras.

They spent the night on a large branch with a flat surface near the trunk. With a small campfire after a long day's walk, Raylan quickly drifted off to sleep. His last thought was of Galirras, and he wondered what the dragon had done that day.

They got an early start the next morning, and after the lunch break, Sebastian informed them they were making good time. They should reach the food depot before the sun set too low. He praised them for the quick study they were with walking in the trees.

"It's like walking on the deck of a ship," said Raylan, once they were on their way again. "I quite like it."

"I've made that comparison myself, a few times," said Sebastian with a smile.

"That's right, you mentioned before you saw many strange creatures when you were sailing. Is that how you ended up here? By ship?"

Sebastian gave a small nod. "Yeah, that was many summers ago. My father put together a crew to discover untouched riches at the other end of the Great Eastern Divide."

"Many failed at making such attempts," said Raylan.

"But that didn't stop him. There was plenty of trade to do in Aeterra. My old man said that ever since the end of the Great War merchants were one of the pillars that carried the kingdom forward. But I think he was looking for something else. Something to put his name on. And it didn't look like he would find it in the midlands."

Raylan knew that last term well. After the Great War ended almost a century ago, the nickname for their kingdom had stuck as people started to look outward for opportunities. It did not only refer to the geographical location of Aeterra—centered between two oceans and continents—but was also related to the fact that the warring parties had come together and met in the middle to establish a truce. That truce turned into long-term peace as families strengthened bonds through marriage and cooperation. Aeterra had prospered, allowing settlements to flourish for decades. The recent trouble in Forsiquar was the first big conflict in years.

"I'd served on his ship ever since I was twelve," continued Sebastian. "I was one of the ship's best rope climbers, apart from this one little kid on our last trip."

"So, what happened?" Raylan asked as they made their way around a large, knobby trunk.

"I was fifteen when we set sail. For weeks, we followed the coast of the Dark Continent, looking for a good spot to land. But the rocks were vicious and the currents treacherous. One day, heavy weather forced us to find shelter in a bay. During the night, we were raided by a large group of heavily-armed men. They were covered—arms, chest, face—in tattoos. Most of the crew were killed that night... my father amongst them."

"I'm sorry to hear that." It was the only response Raylan could give.

"It was a long time ago..." said Sebastian, giving a smile that showed no happiness.

"They took the younger ones with them and torched the ship. They didn't even check for valuables... just torched it and let it burn." Sebastian's jaw clenched. "Those who hadn't been killed, the wounded, were left to the flames."

"Where did they take you?"

"We ended up with a small group of prisoners in a crammed city. An immense palace loomed over it. As black as a starless night with dozens of towers and bridges between them. I'd never seen stone like that before in my life. The city was strange, like every person living there was afraid. You could taste the fear in the air."

Raylan hopped on a large branch and offered his hand to Sebastian to help him up.

"Did they keep you in the city?"

"No, we didn't stay there long. They moved us to work deep in some mines, not allowing us to breathe fresh air for days. It was hard labor, filthy and unhealthy work. Lots of people just gave up in those dark tunnels. The light of life never returned to their eyes. By the time we finally managed to escape, I'd left my childhood years behind me. It'd been almost four years since I'd seen the sky…"

Raylan could not imagine being stuck underground for so long. He needed the open sky. He loved the freedom of the open ocean, surrounded by nothing but miles and miles of possibilities to go where you wanted. Those tunnels would have felt like a death sentence.

"When we broke out, I tried to take as many of those bastards' lives as I could, but I could've done more; the problem was we had no real weapons and, more importantly, we needed to get out quickly if we wanted to live. I think we were lucky to make it out alive, and I intend to make the most of it."

"They didn't come after you?"

"Of course they did. We were relentlessly hunted by the dark forces. Some were caught. We split up into smaller groups to avoid mass capture. Most of us were far from anywhere we'd call home, and the mountains and the forest proved a dangerous place with all the wolves, bears and other creatures. It was nothing short of a miracle we found that cove when we did."

Sebastian grabbed Raylan's arm to hold him back. He pointed at a snake that slithered across the branch they were on. "Let's give it a moment."

Raylan crouched to give his legs some rest.

"You never wanted to return to Aeterra?"

"Wanted, yes. Could? No. Our group consisted of not only men, but women, children, and the elderly. They would never have survived such a long journey, especially under the constant fear of being recaptured. When we stumbled upon the clearing, most of us were exhausted. I think we might have lingered too long. Some of us got too settled. It felt safe, and most of us didn't want to give up that feeling."

"How did you survive?"

"By doing what was necessary. We hunted, gathered, scavenged, stole, built, you name it. We stole from enemy outposts, but only if there was little chance of being discovered. It has been difficult, but most are able to find happiness in just being alive. We even had a few new additions over the years, some freed slaves but also a handful of newborns."

Sebastian walked ahead a few steps, checking their route across the branch. "It's clear."

"They were never able to find you?" said Raylan as they continued their way.

Sebastian shook his head. "We've been very careful, only taking the risk of exposure if it was really necessary. The sand devil territory has worked in our favor for all these years, I expect. The nearest enemy outpost that we know of is a week's walk from here. This food storage depot is fairly recent, I believe. It's the closest we have to our settlement now. The last few seasons, it's been easier to move around and raid things like stockpiles and warehouses. The patrols have barely been present, for some time now. Maybe we've just been forgotten."

Sebastian's face grew darker. "I've been asking for more direct action. I want... I *need* to hit them where it hurts. I tried to convince the council that now was the time, but I've received a lot of protest. Their fear of being discovered is still greater than their desire to get even, or to help the other slaves still left in the mines. Some seem to have forgotten how awful those mines were. Perhaps running into you means I can convince everyone to take the next step, to fight back, to secure our freedom or, at least, to return home to Aeterra."

"I don't know about that. We're in more than a pickle ourselves, at the moment. We've been on the run for weeks. Aren't you afraid of drawing attention by helping us?"

Sebastian shrugged. "I'm sick and tired of playing hide and seek all the time. I want to act but I can't force them to join me, and I can't do anything alone. I guess we'll see when we get back."

"It seemed like Svetka wasn't really looking for a way home. She seems like a... difficult woman," said Raylan.

"It can be challenging to reason with her, sometimes, but she has the best in mind for the entire village. She's very well respected and one of the key people that made it possible for us to escape during the slave riot."

"So, she was a slave, too, right? Why doesn't she have the mark on her cheek like the rest of you?"

Sebastian stayed quiet for a moment, a range of emotions flitting across his face. "It is the practice used for women who are used as entertainment for the soldiers," said Sebastian, eventually. "She doesn't often speak of those times, but she has spent a lot of nights in unwelcome company, with no means of refusing. It's one of the main reasons she helped organize the uprising. Not every woman would be able to live through such days without losing herself."

The sun was setting slowly when Sebastian signaled them to quiet down and huddle up. He pointed out a small cluster of buildings below them in the distance, surrounded by a wooden wall. Two sentries were visible in front of the gate, but no soldiers seemed to be on the walls.

As they moved closer and circled around the compound, Raylan pointed out a few horses present on the inner yard.

"They weren't there some days ago," said Sebastian.

Now that they were closer, they heard men laughing and some flute music playing. Sebastian pointed to one of the back structures. "That's the food storage depot."

"How are we going to get there now, with all these people around?" asked Raylan.

"We'll have to wait until things quiet down. Once the night turns toward morning, we'll have a better chance of getting in unseen."

"So, how will we get in," said Gavin. "I'd like to know the plan before we get started."

"We will use the trees to get as close as possible. I would suggest we work in teams of two, like we normally do. Instead of hooking the rope to the branches, we will leave the pack up in the trees and hook the rope to our harnesses. One person in the team will be in control of the descender. That way the sound of the pack's moving parts will be kept to a minimum up in the trees. The other person will hook the rope into his harness and will be lowered into the compound.

"Once on the ground, any sacks of food will be hooked on the rope and lifted into the trees. The signal will be three short pulls to start manually reeling in the rope; in the meantime, the person on the ground waits, in hiding, until the rope is lowered again. Depending on the food we find, we should get a full-size sack for each person to carry back to the settlement. We will focus on grains and slow spoiling food."

"Also," Danai started, "if we find any seeds whatsoever, we take those, too, if only a couple of hands full. The garden platforms can use some fresh crop seeds."

Sebastian nodded. "After we have enough sacks, the men on the ground will be reeled back up—one by one—to minimize any noise, and then we're off."

"It's not a bad tactic," said Gavin, "if you can stay hidden. What is your fallback plan?"

"We've never had any trouble before," Twan said.

"Not good enough," said Gavin with a shake of his head. "You need an exit strategy in case things go wrong. And where is your entry point, precisely? As far as I can see, there is no other door besides the one in the front of the food storage depot and that faces the inner yard."

"Why don't we go in through the roof?" Raylan suggested, scanning the complex. "No one is on the walls. They don't have a tower. The roof is not that high, and there is a latch in it on the far side. It will be out of sight of the main gate, and the lighting is low… there should be enough cover of darkness to stay put. One or two people can be lowered into the hatch, and then they can pass the food up onto the roof. The others can hook them up to the cables."

"You took the words right out of my mouth," said Sebastian, smiling.

"As for your exit strategy," Sebastian said, turning his attention to Gavin. "Enemy contact means getting out of there as soon as possible. The rope should be ignored, if possible; we don't want to risk them knowing we move through the trees. Retreat on ground level toward the west, back in the direction of the settlement. It won't be easy to keep up in the trees, but we'll try to cut ahead and set up a cover ambush with our crossbows."

Gavin frowned in thought; an expression Raylan knew well. "That's not much of a reassurance," Gavin finally said.

"We all know it's a risk, but it's how we've survived for a long time," said Sebastian. "We know what we're doing."

"And who'll go down into the compound?"

"I want two of us up in the trees, so that we have those with experience control the descenders if anything goes wrong. Three of you can help man the other descenders and move the food out of the way as it is brought up. The other two will need to come down with us. It's up to your lot to decide who that'll be."

"I'll go down," said Raylan, right away.

"I have no problems with heights either… not anymore, at least," said Ca'lek, volunteering.

They spoke some more on the precise details of the plan and spent time practicing knots, tying the cable and using the mechanisms of the descenders. They used the remaining time catching up on sleep until it was time to move. Otis offered to take first watch.

By the time the moon had fallen halfway in the sky, the sounds from the compound had finally died down. Everybody was getting ready. Raylan secured the cable to his harness and stepped up to the edge. It took his mind some time to convince his body to take that final step and hang into the harness; but before he knew it, he was dangling a hundred feet above ground. It was a strange sensation to have no control over your movement, and he watched Rohan control the lever that let him descend softly toward the compound.

They landed on the roof of the food building with the softest of thuds, something to be admired as the person doing the lowering was quite a long way from there. They unhooked the cables and passed them to Otis and Ivar. Raylan, Ca'lek and Sebastian moved toward the hatch in the roof to get it open. As they pried the blade of a sword into the crack in the hatch, the wood creaked loudly. They all froze, and Raylan instantly felt a rush of warmth flow over him as his palms turned sweaty. No reaction was heard. They pushed open the hatch and quickly lowered themselves into the food building, disappearing out of sight.

After his eyes adjusted to the dark surroundings, Raylan saw there was a lot more food present than they would be able to take with them.

"Why is all this food here?" he whispered.

"You've got these kinds of food stores all over the roads of the Dark Continent, although most are far from the coastal areas. They're used to feed soldiers on patrols, to act as food reserves or as temporary stops for traveling replacement forces. They're usually very well stocked and too good of an opportunity to pass up."

They quickly chose the sacks for the first haul and lifted them up through the hatch in the roof. Otis and Ivar hooked them and gave the signal to reel in the first ones. Raylan saw the sacks disappear into the darkness with little fits and starts. Sebastian had been right though; no whirring sound was heard from the packs nor from their people up in the tree.

Working in the back of the storage depot, they moved quickly, checking crates and sacks for the most useful food to take. After the second haul, Ca'lek returned to the trees again, slowly ascending. Shortly after, Otis and an extra sack on Ivar's cable went up. Then Ivar and another sack.

Checking two of the last crates, Raylan and Sebastian found a big sack with seeds. Grabbing two empty sacks and tying them together to hang around their necks, they scooped in as much seeds as possible.

As they walked to the back of the storage depot, a loud clang startled them. They heard the door open and barely jumped behind a few stacks of crates in the back of the storage room, before two dark silhouettes entered and closed the door.

The sound of a fire stone sparking was heard and a soft flame came to life, illuminating the room. The two men started a discussion in Kovian, which was, from the sound of it, quite heated. One of the men had his sheathed sword in hand. The conversation got so fierce, he slammed his sword, *bang*, on top of one of the crates and left it there while his hand wildly moved through the air, emphasizing his words. The sound made Raylan slowly move sideways to peek between the crates to see what was going on. He saw Sebastian do the same. As the two soldiers came into view, both their eyes grew wide with recognition.

On one of the men's armor, Raylan saw the small diamond-shaped emblem, twinkling in the oil lamp's light. As the soldier turned, the light also illuminated the soldier's face. It was the skinny commanding soldier they had faced at the stone arch.

What the hell's he doing here?

The argument went on for some time, while Raylan tried to keep his heartbeat from growing too loud, forcing himself to take slow, shallow breaths. Finally, the commander and the other soldier concluded their discussion, blew out the lamp and slipped out the door again.

Raylan and Sebastian each let out a breath, simultaneously.

"We need to get out of here. That's the guy that has been chasing us all this time," whispered Raylan.

"The long, skinny one?" asked Sebastian. After a confirming nod, he added, "That… was Black Death Setra. If he is chasing your group, you're in some real trouble. Corza Setra is one of the most ruthless High Generals in the dark army. You have no idea what kind of evil he is. He was often in the mines, experimenting on slaves. I even heard their screams when I was working in the farthest tunnels."

"Yeah, well let's not hang around and allow him to find us," said Raylan, as he boosted Sebastian upward through the roof hatch.

He was about to jump up, when the clang of the door startled him. As he turned around, Corza burst inside and reached out to pick up his sword from where he left it on the crate. The High General froze as he saw Raylan standing there.

"You!" The Kovian word close enough to Terran for Raylan to understand.

Raylan briefly glanced at his sword, which still held the hatch in the roof open. He would never get it out fast enough, and he would expose Sebastian and the cables, too.

Raylan glared. No other choice.

He broke into a run. With the hatch not being an option, his only way out was through the door the High General blocked. As Corza scrambled for his sword, Raylan charged at him. Grabbing the small sacks with seeds from around his neck, he hurled them at the general's head. Corza dodged out of the way. Hitting a crate, the sacks ripped open sending an eruption of small seeds through the air.

With his sword too far away now to be of use, the general went for his alternative, a long straight-pointed dagger from the side of his belt. As Raylan slammed his full weight into Corza, he felt a sharp pain cut along his leg. The enemy commander crashed sideways into the crates, and within moments, Raylan was through the door.

Outside, he quickly scanned his surrounds, his thoughts racing to keep up. *No other soldier? He must have returned to the main house.*

His hand pressed on his leg, blood ran down his skin under his pants. He did not have time to stand around and wait for Corza to call for help. He had to find a way out.

One of the horses whinnied nearby and Raylan hurriedly limped in its direction. As he crossed the inner yard, he checked over his shoulder and saw Sebastian ascend into the trees. He barely had time to make a quick gesture to move faster, when Corza came running out of the building, screaming things in his native language.

Raylan had never untied a horse so fast. He had to hop a few paces, as the horse sped toward the gate; and he barely got into the saddle, as his leg gave way. As the sentries entered the courtyard to see what all the shouting was about, Raylan spurred his horse straight past the two surprised guards. He was out of the gate, and into the forest within a heartbeat.

Distance, I need distance.

As he steered the horse through the forest, the shouts of his pursuers were accompanied by the barks from dogs. Things went from bad to worse.

Raylan ran the horse to the point of exhaustion, but could not outrun the hounds on his tail, nor his pursuers on *their* tails. He had no idea where he was going. He circled back several times, trying to escape; but every time, the dogs kept up with his change in direction. And they were gaining on him.

Three riders came into view, led by the dogs. The sound of the horses echoed through the forest, as their hooves stomped through the soft layer of needles on the ground, running past the trees and rocks. When he looked back again, the dogs were right there, snapping at the horse's legs.

Raylan pulled the reins to steer away, but instead of the given command, he felt himself suddenly launched forward as the horse stumbled and crashed, headfirst, into the ground. Raylan tumbled a few times before sliding to a stop. Scrambling to his feet, looking for the dogs that had been following him, he felt a jolt of pain in his leg and instinctively pressed his hand on it again. His horse must have tripped over one of the dogs, or perhaps missed a step.

There!

Two dogs with wide thick heads raced toward him. Their white, short-haired pelts glimmered in the moonlight. As they approached the horse, one dashed around it and one jumped over the fallen animal. Blood was visible under the horse as it thrashed around, trying to get up. Raylan braced himself, automatically reaching for his sword; his hands finding an empty belt.

Corza and two other soldiers on horseback charged around one of the bigger tree roots. The dog that had leapt the fallen horse had barely touched the ground when a spray of dust funneled in the air, swallowing the hound. The high-pitched yelp made the other dog hesitate, then it, too, disappeared into an explosion of sand and dust.

Before the riders could react, their horses saw the danger and skidded to a halt. The lead horse had too much momentum and toppled forward, throwing its rider.

"Kzaktor!" shouted the soldier still on his horse, as the other scrambled to his feet.

Raylan saw the creature clearly. It rose next to the second fallen horse in a cloud of dust, and dug its enormous pinchers into the soft belly of its prey. Sebastian's description had not done it justice. The creature was a squirming bundle of teeth, legs and ring-shaped body pieces all stuck together. The horse's shriek was cut short, and as soon as it stopped moving, the horror dove back into the ground.

Corza and the other man struggled to keep their horses under control; the animals were mad with fright. Corza was thrown backward, out of the saddle, while the other soldier was flung sideways. His foot was still stuck in the crampon as the horse took off. Raylan watched as a trail of sand shot after the stampeding horse, the soldier dragged helplessly across the ground.

Another sand devil shot from the ground and killed Raylan's horse, while the three remaining men stood frozen to the spot. Raylan searched for an escape. A rocky formation, only forty feet away, could be a safe-haven.

But will I be able to reach it?

Corza's subordinate yelled and ran, panicked. The sand shot toward him as he sprinted away. Raylan dashed the other way, his injured leg screaming for reprieve. Shifting right, to dodge a patch of moving sand, he used a few small rocky spots to keep off the sand as much as possible. With one final jump, he reached the larger rock formation, completely out of breath. Checking behind him, the sand moved beside the rocky edge of the boulder.

Safe.

As he dropped on his back, panting, he remembered he had not been alone. He shot back to his feet, looking for Corza. The High General had apparently followed Raylan's example, seeing as the soldier had volunteered himself as bait by running. However, Corza had ended up on one of the large tree roots nearby.

They stared at each other; the distance was less than a hundred feet but it might as well have been a hundred miles. Raylan took another look around. What became of the soldier, he did not know but he could guess.

Raylan would not be safe here forever. The sun would soon rise, and if what Sebastian told him was true, Corza would be able to come at him as the burrowing critters became less active. The High General had the clear advantage—he still had his sword, and Raylan's leg obstructed free movement.

It was Corza who broke the silence. "We meet again, young soldier. I believe Raylan was your name, right? It's clear you've got nowhere to go. Why don't you give up and come with me, quietly?"

Raylan did not answer as he felt his anger rise.

"What's with that look? Have I done something wrong?" Corza said, laughing. "Tell you what, if you tell me where you hid the egg—I'll let you go. No harm done."

"You must be insane, if you think that I'll give anything to you," Raylan answered, scanning the rock formation he was on.

"Ah, he speaks," Corza taunted. "How did you get here, then? Where are your friends? Did my wolves get the better of them?"

Corza was still grinning.

"Not really," Raylan said with an indifferent shrug. "Your wolves are at the bottom of the river, somewhere."

Anger rose on Corza's face; the man's jaw locked tight. Raylan spotted a few small rocks led around the tree roots, out of sight of Corza's prying eyes.

As he jumped off the other end of the rock, Raylan balanced himself on the small stone patches. Skipping from one to another, he heard Corza call after him.

"You can't run far, boy! I'll find you. That egg will be mine, and I will put you so deep in the mines, you won't see any sunlight for the rest of your life."

Moving around the corner, he saw that Corza was right. As he stood on the last stone, there was nowhere else to go. Even the tree roots were no help there. But he refused to return and give that weasel the satisfaction.

Let him wonder where I'll be. Once first light breaks through, I'll just have to make a run for it.

"Raylan, you'll never make it," Corza shouted. "Before long, reinforcements will be here. The kzaktor will be dormant again, and I'll have my hands on you faster than a whore can lift her dress for a bag of gold."

As the night went on, Corza kept yelling at him, trying to get a reaction. Raylan almost spoke up a few times, but bit his tongue, looking everywhere for a way out.

As the moonlight began to fade, small patches of sky started to show its morning colors, he was ready to make his move. He picked up a rock and threw it some way out. Instantly, the sand snaked toward it and the rock was swallowed into the ground. He would have to wait longer.

As he let out his breath, slowly trying to think, his ears registered a soft sound.
"Pssst…"
Raylan's head snapped around, but he did not see anything.
"Pssst, up here."
The language was poor Terran. It was Otis, dangling along the side of the tree, only fifteen feet above. A smile broke out on Raylan's face.

Without a sound, Otis went back up into the tree. Once up there, he lowered the cable, allowing Raylan to attach it to his harness. He gave three small tugs to the cable and immediately the cable tightened as he was lifted off his feet.

As he ascended toward the lowest branch, he kept close to the tree trunk, so Corza could not see him. The sun was coming up, and by the time he pulled himself onto the branch, several new riders were approaching their position.

Corza finally left his safe refuge, ordered one of the soldiers from his horse and mounted up, right away. They moved around the tree where Raylan had waited the entire time and found nothing. The general was furious.

"Find him!"

Corza barked orders as the soldiers sped off in different directions. While Raylan followed them with his gaze, Otis quickly packed up his backpack and quietly motioned Raylan to follow.

Corza wouldn't be able to find him any time soon.

It was midmorning by the time the group reunited.

In order to find Raylan, they had split up to cover more ground. One of the descender carriers was always in visual range of any person that did not have one, but they ended up spreading out farther than intended. By following the noise of the chase, they had set out in the most likely direction, trying to keep up with the horses.

"It was a good thing you circled back a number of times, or the distance would have been too big to bridge," said Sebastian. "We can't move very fast away from known tree paths. Traversing at different heights and searching for suitable routes to follow takes time."

Otis added some words in Kovian, making Sebastian laugh.

"What?" said Raylan.

"It was Corza's own shouting and taunting that had helped Otis locate you on the far side of the tree," said Sebastian. "Guess his anger is good for something else except inflicting pain."

Raylan laughed, sheepishly.

His brother grabbed Raylan by the back of the neck and pulled him forward, touching foreheads. "You just have a knack for getting into trouble, don't ya little brother?"

Raylan flashed an apologetic smile. "Sorry about that…"

"Just be thankful you didn't end up in Corza's hands," remarked Sebastian as they redistributed the food haul into equal loads. "I promise you, you wouldn't have liked the company."

"Do you know more about him?" Raylan asked. "Like I said, he's the same person who attacked us some weeks ago. He turned on his own group before sending out these monstrous wolves made of stone after us."

"Stone wolves? Are you sure they were made of stone? Were there ghol'ms, too?" Sebastian asked, worry clear in his voice.

"Ghol'ms? What are ghol'ms?"

"Stone statues, black as night, but they move. They… live," Sebastian explained in a whisper, while searching for the right words to describe the walking terrors.

"Svetka once said her father told her a story when she was little… before she was captured and made a…" he gave a knowing nod. "Her father used to travel a lot when she was younger, coming back with all kinds of stories. This particular one was about an ancient religion in the southern regions of the mid-continent."

They drew their packs onto their backs as Sebastian continued. "This religion had a guardian of red clay to protect the innocent from harm. But the guardian was corrupted by the men who sought power and it went on a rampage. It was eventually calmed by a peasant woman with the purest devotion to the religion's god. The guardian then crumbled and formed the mountain that oversees the red earth plains in that region."

Sebastian nodded to Otis to lead the way, and they moved off quietly, Sebastian continuing once more in a whisper. "That guardian was called 'gholem' or 'ghol'm'. That's where we think the name comes from, but these things are no guardians… they're too good at destroying, well, everything."

"We fought a stone warrior before encountering the wolves, if that's what you mean," said Raylan, his voice hushed, "but we saw only the wolves; no stone warriors were there when he tried to capture us. Why? Who *is* he precisely?"

"Like I said, that's High General Setra. Black Death, Corza Setra. He climbed the ranks by killing and backstabbing, and, apparently, because of his skill with strategic planning. Or so everyone told me in the mines. He's got no regard for human life, whatsoever. Especially if that life is in the way of whatever he wants at the time. He visited the mines and quarry often. And after each visit, new stories of terror would always buzz around in the tunnels."

Sebastian looked over his shoulder at them and let out a sigh. "You've made yourself a dangerous enemy, especially if he's got it in for you personally. This man has experimented on humans to find out what makes us tick and how to greatly extend suffering in the process. He is thought to have created the ghol'ms, although I personally think he just took credit for someone else's work."

"He created them? How can a man even do that? Is it some kind of magic?"

"It might as well be. No one knows how it works, precisely. But by piecing things together from stories, we know life is taken to give life to the statue."

"We've seen this. One of the soldiers sacrificed himself before the statue started to move," said Raylan.

"Well, that's not what is normally done. They can sacrifice anybody to get the statue moving."

"How do you know all this?" asked Gavin.

When Sebastian turned to look at him, there was an emptiness in his eyes. "Because they forced us to make them. That's the purpose of the mines. It's a ghol'm production site…"

Both Gavin and Raylan fell silent at this point. The idea of more of these statues being created somewhere was a very unpleasant thought, and it was clear Sebastian did not feel entirely comfortable talking about it.

"We better pick up the pace," said the former slave. "We still have a long ways to go."

CHAPTER FIFTEEN

Sacrifice

GALIRRAS LOOKED UP at the sky. With the wind gently blowing through, leaves parted enough for the stars to be seen every now and then. He heard people speaking softly. The nighttime meant minimal lights and low sounds. Most of the people in the tree settlement remained indoors or went to sleep early.

The young dragon tried to do the same, but he could not sleep anymore. He had just woken from a dream and felt restless. He did not know precisely what he had dreamed about, but it felt like he was awakened by a song.

He had been feeling uneasy ever since Raylan left. It was very pleasant to talk to Xi'Lao and he had enjoyed meeting Galen, earlier that week. But they were merely brief distractions from the fact Raylan was not here.

Galen had told Galirras all about surviving the wolf attack. The dragon heard the story before, multiple times, from different people, but he did not want to be rude and interrupt. The large man grew tired after his recollection of events, and Richard had coaxed him back to bed—to rest up and to be ready, in case they would be leaving when Gavin, Raylan and the others returned.

The problem was that Galirras was not allowed to move at all. His body grew restless and it became more difficult to find a comfortable position on the platform. He was under permanent guard even when he slept, but at least they were not constantly pointing their crossbows at him anymore.

On the first day—after Raylan left—he had tried talking to the guards, but they had ignored him, either out of a sense of duty or out of fear. He had half-expected the fear, which he still found strange because he did not seem that scary to himself.

For the last few days, Galirras had put a lot of effort and practice into improving his wind manipulation, being careful he was not seen. He was mildly pleased with the amount of progress he had made, although he still got tired quicker than he would have liked. Playing around with leaves and flames had become relatively easy, so as a challenge, he had searched for something bigger. He had found it, when he saw the children playing with a ball made of straw.

Asking them over, they had given in to their curiosity; though, some of them needed a little convincing. They had approached the edge of the platform, where they threw the ball to him from a safe distance. He had nudged the ball back a few times with his head, making sure it did not accidentally end up falling off the platform. Just when the children became more comfortable with him, Svetka had shown up and rebuked them for coming close to such a dangerous animal. They had darted away at the first sound of her voice and left their ball in their rushed retreat.

From that moment on, Galirras had used the ball for practice. At first, it had not moved at all, so he experimented with different streams and approaches, using larger areas of air to funnel into a tighter stream. After an afternoon of practice, he had been able to move the ball at least six feet. But during the night, after he had slept, he improved his technique some more and easily directed the ball all around the platform.

Having now mastered the movement of the straw ball, Galirras found himself alone—and still confined to the platform—for the fourth night in a row. He absentmindedly pushed short bursts of air out of his nostrils, manipulating the moving air into small bubbles and rings of sparkles. The shapes got bigger as they floated upward. He tried different techniques and speeds of moving air. He wished others could see the shapes he was able to make, but it seemed Raylan was not the only one who did not see the small sparkling air particles. In fact, none in their group were able to see it.

Perhaps it really is a dragon thing.

Galirras felt his stomach rumble and shifted to his other side. He wanted to hunt. They had given him some small game, but now he wished he had not eaten everything at once. He could use a nice, juicy deer. His stomach answered with another rumble and saliva dripped from the corner of his mouth.

For a moment, he considered waking Richard to ask for more food but decided against it in the end. Instead, his attention was drawn to high-pitched beeps, which seemed to be coming from some small-winged, furry creatures. They differed in size but were rarely larger than the kinds of birds he had eaten before. He tried to grab one out of the air, but it somehow dodged him at the last moment. He tried a couple more times, but the small creatures were either too fast or were able to steer clear of his jaws.

Driven by his curiosity, and his hunger, he tried different things. He now tried to hit the animals out of the sky with a quick thrust of air from his nose. It took several tries before he timed it right. Finally, he hit one of them, but the small thing was able to stabilize its flight and fluttered past him.

Now, he tried to use a bigger air push from his throat. Taking care not to make too much sound, he breathed in deeply and gave a short thrust. He used his wind-force to speed up the bubble, hitting one of the flying fur balls in the side. The creature spiraled out of control. It crashed into the tree and, missing the platform, careened down into the darkness. Galirras tried again, missing his target. A third time gave him another hit, but the animal bounced off into the depths, again, thanks to its momentum.

Galirras looked around to see if anyone was still around. Being late in the night, or rather, early in the morning, he saw both guards had dozed off at the edge of the platform. He silently stood and moved toward the tree trunk. As he dug his claws in the bark, he climbed upward as quietly as possible, keeping a constant eye on his guards for any movement.

Slowly, he moved higher and higher until he was above the flying creatures. Just like before, he took a deep breath and sent out a burst of air, which he sped up. As the air hit one of the larger creatures from above, it twirled straight down, hitting the platform with a *thump*. Quickly, Galirras let himself slide back down toward the platform, checking if the guards were awakened by the sound.

He scooped up his kill and laid back down on the platform. It was more hair than meat, but the satisfaction of the kill and the pleasure of being able to move around, if only for a moment, made it taste like a five-course meal… which, according to Raylan and the others, was supposed to be delicious. Galirras had heard them talk about it multiple times around the campfire during their travels, even if he was no step closer to figuring out what precisely a five-course meal was.

It was late in the afternoon on their fifth day away, and Raylan and the others were still not back. Galirras was hungry again. Even with his nightly snacks, he was not eating enough to quell his hunger. He wanted to go hunting, to get a nice, juicy deer… he would settle for a badger. Even a couple of rabbits would do. But he promised Raylan not to cause any trouble while they were away.

That night, he had dreamed again of the singing. It sounded very distant, soft, as if sung behind mountains and forests. It was as if the sound was carried on the smallest of wings, like those little animals he had seen flying around when hunting with Raylan.

What had he called them? Buttered fleas?

He felt like he knew the song yet had no memory of it.

While he was trying to remember how it went, he felt a familiar, warm presence enter his mind. He immediately raised his head to look around.

Richard and Xi'Lao, who had been sitting at the edge of the platform, both stared at him.

"They are back!" Galirras said to them. "I can sense Raylan. He is back."

His tail twitched back and forth from excitement. He stretched his neck to look at the edge of the village. Xi'Lao and Richard both rose and walked to the rail for a better view. They saw people moving, heard soft shouts and saw guards using hand signals with one another. The children ran toward the entrance of the village.

Xi'Lao almost stretched her neck as far as Galirras did. The children arrived at one of the last platforms, when a group of men walked into view. Gavin was amongst the first. And Galirras watched as her face broke out in a smile and she let out a sigh of relief. She seemed almost surprised at the realization she had been nervous about his return.

"There is Raylan. I can see him," Galirras shouted to pretty much anyone who listened.

As the group approached the platform, Galirras dashed forward, greeting Raylan.

"Careful, careful, watch the tail. You're going to push someone off, by accident," laughed Raylan. He took his friend's head in his hands and put his forehead against Galirras'. "*It's good to be back, little one.*"

Richard shook their hands. Xi'Lao seemed almost too shy to touch Gavin, only briefly squeezing his hand and giving a small smile.

"*You're hurt,*" said Galirras, as he sniffed the blood on Raylan's leg. "*What happened?*"

"It's nothing, just a scratch. Otis already stitched it up and it is healing fine. There's no need for you to worry," he replied.

The council came out to greet them and to see the result of their trip. Sebastian walked them through everything, while a few men went through the sacks to catalog what was brought in. They had some more potatoes, and seeds that could be planted for crops. One sack contained dried and salted meat. And several sacks had grain, which could be used to bake bread. Overall, not a bad haul. It would help the village bridge the time until the new crops were ready to harvest.

The council allowed them to hold a small, festive dinner that evening to celebrate the return of everyone, including Aanon's group who had returned the previous day. It had been a long time since everyone was in the village at the same time, apart from Borclad who remained in the stables; but he preferred solitude over company.

"Can I suggest," began Raylan, who saw an opportunity to let Galirras hunt, "that Galirras assist with getting extra food for the festivities. If we're allowed to hunt, we'll bring back a deer or some rabbits for stew or a spit roast. I think everyone would enjoy that."

The council was reluctant but saw no real reason to object. The meat would be welcomed, but they did insist Sebastian go with them. He would show them the hunting ground, or so they said. And keep an eye on them for the council, Raylan expected.

After Raylan briefly spoke with Xi'Lao and Richard to get an update on their time in the village, they set out for the hunt. As the sun lowered toward the horizon, the plant-eaters came out to forage, which made it an ideal time to search for prey.

Guided by Sebastian, Galirras and Raylan walked through the village to the far end of the platforms. He saw that the village had been experimenting with growing crops up in the trees, building large platforms to hold a few feet of soil. Sebastian told him it had taken a long time to get the soil up so high, but they were finally ready to have more localized crops. It would cut back on the traveling to and from the stables. Another platform they passed had been designed to collect water streaming down the trees when it rained. It ensured there was enough water for people to drink, unless the rain held off for a long time; but then the small lakes in the forest would provide a steady water supply. Now, a second water platform was being built, which would be used for crop irrigation.

They took two descenders with them, while Galirras did it his own unique way and, soon enough, they were standing on solid ground again. It was the first time Raylan controlled one of the packs by himself, but he found it surprisingly easy to handle. They hid their descenders behind some shrubbery, making sure it could be reached quickly in case they encountered enemy troops.

"I'll go check on some of the snares while I'm here. Someone should have set some this morning," said Sebastian. "Be sure to keep track of where you are in case you need to make a hasty retreat."

And with that, he walked off.

"It's nice to see someone trusts us, at least," Raylan remarked to Galirras.

"*I would like it if he would come with us. Do you think that is possible?*" asked Galirras.

"I don't know. He's got responsibilities in this community… I expect it will depend on their council, on Gavin and on what Sebastian wants."

"*I guess you are right… maybe I can ask him, later.*" He brightened up a bit, anticipating the meal he was about to have. "*Thanks for going hunting with me, right away. I was getting really hungry.*"

"I know," laughed Raylan, as he gave a quick tap on the dragon's lower neck. "I could barely think about anything else because of your stomach. Now, let's go catch a nice, juicy deer for you to eat your fill and we'll see if there will be anything left after that to take back."

It did not take long for Galirras to track down a group of large deer. He just used his nose and tongue to follow the smell. He moved silently onto one of the large tree roots and launched himself from the high ground, taking down a large buck. While he killed it with a quick bite to the neck, Raylan heard one of the does let out a cry. As he followed the sound, he found the animal had broken a leg in its panic to get away from the unknown predator. Taking out his knife, Raylan gave the animal a quick, merciful death.

"I guess you got two birds with one stone," he said to Galirras, who in turn looked at him, confused.

"*I thought these were called deer, where did I get a bird? Can we bring it, too? Richard told me he quite liked the taste of the colorful birds that live here.*"

"Sorry, just a figure of speech, my friend. But I think this doe will be very welcomed for the festivities tonight."

While Galirras started on his meal, Raylan gutted the female deer, cutting off the best parts to take with them. This time he kept an eye out for any wolves that might think of scoring a quick meal.

He gave the parts he would not take back to the village to Galirras. As they finished, Sebastian returned with two fresh rabbit kills and a small, slender rodent Raylan had not seen before.

"Can I ask you to take the antlers back with us? They can be used for any number of things back in the village," suggested Sebastian, after seeing Galirras' leftovers.

Galirras quickly broke off the antlers, so Raylan could pick them up.

As they walked back to the spot where their descenders were hidden, Galirras' attention was drawn to a soft scratching sound. It seemed to come from behind one of the large trees on the left. Without saying anything, he crouched down and slowly crawled toward the other end of the tree. Raylan and Sebastian looked at each other, frowning.

Disappearing from view, Raylan began to move after him, when he heard Galirras call out in surprise.

"Raylan, Sebastian, come look. There is some really hairy kind of animal here. Oh! There are two. They look like small, hairy rocks," said Galirras, excitedly.

Raylan sped up his pace, while Sebastian came running to see what was going on. As they turned the corner of the large root Galirras had climbed over, they both froze dead in their tracks.

Galirras jumped down next to them.

"Look, it's like they are playing a game to see who can push the other one over first. I wonder if I can join in."

As Galirras started to move forward, Raylan grabbed him by his hind leg. "Wait!"

Looking back, surprised, Galirras saw Raylan stare wide-eyed at the two young bears that dug and scratched at the bottom of the tree. The young bears were at the base of the tree, surrounded by the large wall-like roots. As the three of them looked at the two playing cubs, Raylan noticed they entrapped both small bears by simply standing there.

Perhaps small was not the right word for the two young bears which, from the look of their fur, could not have been more than three seasons old. They were almost up to waist height when standing on four legs. Both bears were now looking at the trio with curious interest, making small noises.

Sebastian turned, scanning the surroundings.

"Where's the mother?" said Raylan, softly.

"We need to get out of here," whispered Sebastian.

"Why? It looks like fun. I want to see if perhaps I can win their game. I bet I am stronger than them, since I am bigger. Can we not stay for a little while?"

"You don't understand Galli—" Raylan began, when a thunderous roar cut off the sentence midway.

All three spun, startled by the abrupt sound. In front of them, a gigantic bear stood snorting and grunting, looking directly at them. She swayed her head back and forth, while scratching the ground with her forepaws. Each paw had five razor-sharp claws, easily three inches long, which were ripping up the ground with no effort at all. Her fur looked dark brown with patches of black in it. Large scars were visible on her snout and face.

The mother bear grunted and moved a step forward, lowering her head.

Galirras looked at the bear in awe. She was the biggest animal he had seen up till now, even bigger than the wolves they had encountered. He felt the anger resonating from the bear. Her breath swirled around in the little particles of air at increasing speed. The wolves had just wanted them for food, for which Galirras could not fault them, of course. One needs to eat. This felt more like a personal anger, as the bear seemed to have a problem with them that was not driven by hunger. It made him wonder what he should do.

"We're standing between her and her cubs. We need to move but slowly. Don't antagonize her further," hissed Sebastian.

The young bears, hearing their mother's call, happily cried out to greet her. It was the only motivation the huge bear needed, and before any of them could even back away, the large bear came at them at full speed.

Recognizing the oncoming danger for Raylan, Galirras immediately shot in front of him.

"Don't!" Raylan yelled, but Galirras refused to move, shielding both Raylan and Sebastian.

As the charging bear approached, Galirras took in air and let out a deep roar of his own, trying to imitate the bear's previous roar. As he had never let out a real growl, or any roar like that before, he was not sure if it would be enough.

* * *

Raylan looked at Galirras taking a stand. His roar sounded low, vibrating deep in his throat. Raylan gripped his knife with one hand, while his other clutched the pointed antlers of the deer Galirras had taken down. He wished he had not left his sword back at the food storage depot, but the knife and antlers were better than nothing if Galirras required help.

The bear, visually confused by the gesture of a creature she had never encountered, slowed her charge, but her motherly instinct seemed to drive her forward. The urge to protect her cubs was not so easily discouraged.

As the bear walked toward them, she let out her own deep roar, this time much longer. It sounded like she was challenging Galirras. Slowly, Raylan and Sebastian moved to the side, away from the cubs. But they were blocked by the large wall of tree root on both sides. Galirras inched sideways, to keep them out of the view of the bear as much as possible.

Up close, the bear was even bigger than she had first looked. Galirras was slightly longer, but only because of his tail. Besides that, he was much skinnier than the rugged-looking bear. The sheer volume of the animal was incredible, her roar made full use of her mass to show Galirras she would not back down from protecting her young.

Galirras raised himself on his back legs and let out another deep roar which did not fully follow through. The bear was winning this standoff. Having seen enough of the dragon not to be impressed, the bear focused her attention on Raylan and dashed forward, intent on mangling the smaller threats. Again, Galirras shot in front of her, showing his flank, trying to look bigger than he was. Raylan and Sebastian now had their weapons in hand.

The bear, seeing she would have to take out Galirras first, was right on top of him. As she raised herself on her back legs, the bear seemed to grow at least six feet. Now showing her total height, she was nearly the size of two adult men. If she chose to bring all her weight down on Galirras with her forepaws, he would surely be crushed under the sheer force of her.

"Galirras, watch out!"

* * *

Galirras barely heard Raylan's words. The dragon, slightly panicked by the bear's display of power, was completely taken over by instinct. Driven by the need to protect his own, he took another deep breath, and rose on his back legs for the second time. As he stretched, he unfolded his wings in one powerful push. As they spanned outward, they spread to their full length with a loud snap. Galirras dramatically increased in size.

The movement of his wings created turmoil in the air. Sensing, more than seeing the flow of the air, Galirras let out a third roar. Where before he had always reached out to move the wind, this felt more like his entire core pushed outward at once. He felt himself push his roar forward, using the turmoil his wings created to amplify it.

* * *

Raylan had to jump back, along with Sebastian, to get out of the way of the unfolding wings. Both seemed stunned to see the magnificent scene in front of them. As it began to sink in that Galirras now showed his full wingspan for the first time, Raylan immediately felt warm pride and happiness swell inside him. The little light of day there was seemed to glint off the dragon. He saw the silhouette of his wings clearly and the framework of the bones spanning the length of the membranes. Galirras was no longer this small, helpless dragon and Raylan was certain the image would never be forgotten by either him or Sebastian.

The roar sucked him back into reality, as he literally saw a ripple in the air move forward. The bear, taken aback by the sudden increase in size of her opponent, felt the rush of air hit her body. It was not enough, by far, to topple the bear but the force gave rise to confusion and seemed to knock away any desire to get into a direct fight.

By now, the two young bears had moved along the other tree root, approaching their mother from the side. Their small grunts and peeps appeared to sway her to leave the conflict where it lay.

As the bear dropped to all fours, she snorted at Galirras, clearly not sure what to make of it all. But with her cubs now safely behind her, she turned and guided her young off into the forest.

Sebastian got his voice back first. "That... was a close call."

Lowering himself, Galirras folded his wings. He seemed to follow the bears with his eyes, until he was not able to see them anymore. "*I still do not understand why she was so upset. I just wanted to play with them. It is not like I wanted to eat them. I just ate an entire deer,*" he said to Raylan, privately, turning around. "*What's wrong?*"

Raylan looked at him, smiling while tilting his head. "You just spread out your wings for the first time... you know that, right?"

"*Oh! You're right. And it did not even hurt at all,*" Galirras said, excitedly.

He jumped around in circles before he turned his head, staring at his wings. He spread and folded them a couple of times, moving them back and forth and up and down. He bent his neck and pushed his nose against the wing that had troubled him so much.

"*Nothing, no pain, no obstacle. It is like it never had any problems to begin with.*"

As Galirras tried out his wings, Raylan felt the breeze created by the movement. They already shifted a lot of air and did not seem to have any weak moments in the strokes.

Galirras jumped off the ground and tried to keep himself airborne—it was not a great success.

"It will take some time to build up your muscles, and strengthen your wings," said Raylan. "You should practice as much as possible to make up for time lost, I reckon. But for now, let's get back up to the village and bring back the doe for the festivities. They'll be wondering where we are by now."

By the time they returned with the meat, the preparations were already well underway. Before long, they found themselves with pretty much the entire village on one of the large platforms, enjoying a simple but tasty dinner. People sat on the floor of the platform in small groups, chatting, softly laughing, always aware of the danger of sound carrying through the air. Luckily, the wind had picked up a little, which gave them a little bit more freedom, as the leaves and trees created a constant rustle, washing out the noise made by their feast.

Raylan understood the danger of being discovered but could not help feeling restricted by something so constantly present. For a moment, he yearned for his sailing days, where a strong storm would test their wills; but would also allow them to scream their anger, frustration, and excitement to their fullest, without anyone ever being bothered by it. The wind obliterated it all.

"If I keep growing and train my wings, I might be able to take you up into the sky. I cannot imagine any place feeling more free and unrestricted than up there with nothing more than sun, moon, stars and wind," Galirras spoke softly to him.

Even after his successful hunt, they made him stay on the storage platform. Raylan objected at first, but Galirras told him he was fine with it. He was so excited about training his wings. He preferred the open space instead of being cramped next to all the villagers.

Raylan felt a trickle of excitement flow through him. It felt as if Galirras had been suppressing the urge to take to the sky, completely, when he was under the impression his wings would not function. Now that it might be possible, he could not hide his desire to get up there as soon as possible.

As the entire village was present, the platform was not big enough to hold everyone. There were small groups of people sitting on the walkways leading up to the community platform, as well as in a few of the small buildings along those paths.

Raylan saw Sebastian sitting next to a man he had not met before. They seemed to be in a heated discussion.

That must be Aanon. Raylan remembered Sebastian's description of the man.

Further down, a building was used as the community kitchen, with women walking in and out carrying dishes of stew, rice, and a fruit Raylan had never seen before. The fruit was small, oval and dark in color. The taste was sweet, and it had a large pit in the center.

One of the women, who had been serving the food, explained that they grew near the larger trees that contained the vines used for all the ropes. They were not easy to reach as they grew all the way in the top of the trees, bathing in the sun, so only the most experienced climbers could get to them. The fruit had been a welcomed addition to the local diet, as not much fruit grew in this region. Mostly small nuts and forest roots had sustained them up to the point of the fruit's discovery.

Raylan was listening to the woman answering one of his brother's questions, when a commotion at the other end of the platform made him look away. A woman's wailing was heard from within a small group of people. She was screaming words, crying and hitting some poor man on his back with her fists. Several bystanders tried to calm her down and hold her back.

As Raylan and his brother approached the scene, they recognized Richard being the one assaulted. He made no attempt to fight back and looked as surprised and as baffled as the bystanders were. The stream of words the woman yelled, slowly changed into a soft muttering as she dropped down on her knees and was hugged and consoled by one of the other women.

"What's going on here?" Svetka's voice cut through the air.

The council had been sitting in a far corner with a select little group—it had been invitation only.

Richard looked around; all eyes were on him. "Don't look at me," he said, "I've got no clue what just happened. I was just taking a piece of meat from her platter when suddenly she started screaming at me and pounding my chest. I didn't understand a word of it. She's not speaking Terran."

Svetka sneered at the sobbing woman and then called out to her. Startled, the woman looked up and spit out a flow of words, rapidly. It took Svetka several questions to get a clear picture of what had happened, as the woman was beside herself and sobbed uncontrollably every couple of words.

At the end of it, Svetka looked at Richard as if judging his worth. She had taken time to talk to all members of their group, to get a good understanding of the situation and their intentions; and it seemed she had accepted them, more or less. Now, however, her look was full of suspicion.

"Did you, by any chance, use a knife when selecting your piece of meat?" she asked, calmly.

"Of course, its good table manners, isn't it?"

"May I see it, please?"

Richard glanced around for a moment before picking something from the ground. Turning back, he flipped a long metal object in the air. He deftly caught the blade tip and stuck out the handle to Svetka.

The blade was an uncommon design. It was long and straight and twice the length of the handle, which was covered in strange markings. The handle was a faint blue color, and it seemed to have been made from a bone of some sort. The blade looked more practical for stabbing than for cutting, as it had four sides to cut with, constructed together in a long, crossed point. The blade's metal was dark gray, with lines of lighter metal gray flowing in it, from the creation process most likely. It was a very unusual blade.

Raylan frowned. That's the same blade Corza had on his belt.

He was still a bit surprised about all the details he seemed to pick up, even when he was focused on something completely different, like fleeing for his life.

Carefully, Svetka reached out her hand. Raylan noticed it was trembling slightly. She picked up the knife and looked at it. The color disappeared from her face. Raylan noticed several other people, who laid eyes on the knife, breathe in sharply, in surprise.

"Where did you get this?" the elderly council member asked, softly, as she turned the knife in her hands.

"What does it matter?" Richard answered.

Svetka's eyes filled with fire as she lost control of her emotions. Her head jerked up and she looked Richard straight in the eyes. "It matters because this knife represents a lot of suffering and sorrow for a lot of our people. Now tell me where you've got it from, or I'll have to remove all of you from this settlement, immediately."

"I took it from one of the dead Doskovian soldiers, weeks ago. The blade struck me as uncommon, so I thought it would be a good souvenir. I thought, if I were lucky, it would bring me a pretty penny, once I sold it back home."

"What's wrong with it?" asked Raylan.

"It was used to slaughter innocent children—infants, not a day old. That's what's wrong with it!" said Svetka with such force that all chatter on the platform fell silent, at once.

Richard did not know what to do or even where to look.

She turned to Gavin. "Gather your men and have them wait on the platform where your beast is sleeping. The council needs to talk to you and your representatives, right away, in our chambers."

As Richard was sent to round up the remaining members of their group, Raylan found himself following his brother toward the council chambers for the second time in their short stay.

"*Everyone is gathering here. What is going on?*" Galirras asked from afar.

"*I don't know, yet. Something must have offended Svetka. She looks like she's about to burst into flames,*" Raylan replied.

Svetka waited, deadly silent, back turned toward them, until Jarod and Ann arrived. They talked amongst themselves, in hushed voices, speaking the local language. It was a heated conversation. Sebastian was fetched and brought into the discussion—or rather, told what would happen. Their newly-made friend's face showed shock and anger, as he forcefully disagreed with what was said to him. But Jarod called him to order, forcing him to simmer down.

Only then were they allowed to approach the council to hear what had been decided.

"Commander," Svetka began, speaking directly to Gavin. "The council has made its decision. On the subject of your requested support, this village declines. We ask you to head out first thing in the morning."

Raylan could not believe his ears. After they followed all their little rules, helped them get extra food, and nearly ended up caught—or worse—in the process, they were throwing them out?

"What? Why?" His brother beat him to it. It seemed he was just as surprised and just as annoyed as Raylan.

"Please, would you not reconsider?" pleaded Xi'Lao, at the same time. "We could really use your help, and the wounded could use more rest."

Sebastian stood silently to the side, his head held down, in shame. With his original reaction hijacked by his brother, Raylan tried the politer approach.

"Honored council members, if it's possible, can we please hear your explanation? We did everything you requested. Surely, you must have a reason for not coming to our aid?"

Svetka looked at him as if he had offended her with his polite tone. "I already had my doubts about bringing you all in, and it seems I was right. We fear you all have brought instability to our settlement. Your presence is dividing our people, while the most recent event has completely shattered the little trust you all had built up within this community. People fear your true intentions and the danger you all might bring upon this settlement. That's why we would like you all to leave, sooner rather than later."

"Does this have to do with that strange dagger Richard had?" said Raylan, already forgetting his polite efforts.

This time Jarod spoke. "That dagger is a Roc'turr... a sacrificial dagger. It is used in a certain ceremony to bring life to the ghol'ms."

"Ghol'ms?" said Xi'Lao, looking confused.

"That's what they call the living statues we fought," Gavin explained.

"Aye, living statues, but they do not start like that. They need the sacrifice of a human being to be brought to life," Jarod continued. "Life in the mines was never easy, but Black Death Setra had a knack for making it almost unbearable. Hundreds of slaves were killed in experiments with the ghol'ms. Some bled out slowly over days, until death followed; others were killed instantly, stabbed in the heart. They tried everything they could think up to see what would work best... they would use scrolls to transfer the light of life from the person they murdered to the ghol'm they created."

Svetka and Ann fell silent. Tears welled in their eyes. Sebastian had no courage to raise his head and look them in the eyes. It seemed he knew what Jarod would tell next.

As the tall, bearded man continued, his own voice became less stable, emotion flowed through it. "After all these tests, mutilations and killings... they eventually found what they were looking for. The younger the sacrifice, the longer a ghol'm would function. They began to take children from the mines, some who'd never even seen a tree outside, and to drag them into these chambers. Screams... day and night. Blood ran out from under those doors."

Xi'Lao held her hands in front of her mouth, unable to utter anything that made sense. Raylan saw her hands trembling and tears build in her eyes. Raylan noticed Gavin slightly inch closer to her.

"Some tried to stop it, but they were only killed in the process. We had no strength. We were outnumbered. Then one day, the sound of a newborn baby was heard through the tunnels. One of us had survived long enough to complete her full term; and even in the most miserable of circumstances, the newborn baby girl brought a smile to the face of her mother..."

Tears freely flowed down the women's faces now, as they stood silently staring into nothingness. Xi'Lao softly shook her head, trying to reject what was yet to be said. Raylan felt a knot in his stomach as it tightened, fearful of where this was going.

"Corza was present in the mines that day..." continued Jarod, as his tone suddenly became very flat. It was as if he was distancing his being from the words he was about to speak aloud. "He strolled over. As if it was the most normal thing in the world, he came up to the new mother, looked at her in disgust, and spoke the words 'Take it away and begin the sacrifice ritual immediately' to one of his soldiers.

"Two men, who jumped at them with rage, were cut down immediately, and the infant was ripped from her mother's arms. Everyone heard the child crying for her mother, all the way up the stone stairs to the sacrificial chambers.

"The mother was screaming, pulling out her hair, scratching out her eyes in despair, right up to the point where the crying of her daughter suddenly stopped. It was the end for her. She dropped on the ground, unwilling to move or get up. After kicking and whipping her without success, the soldiers dragged her away. It was said she died the same night."

The silence in the hut held weight, dropping Raylan's shoulders.

"I was her midwife of sorts in all this," Svetka eventually said. "That was the day I swore I would get as many people out of there as possible. It went from bad to worse. Corza must have been pleased with the result of his infanticide, since from that moment on, all first born babies were taken away from their mothers and murdered, used for ghol'm scrolls... not only from slave mothers, but from any mother living under the Stone King's rule.

"It took almost another four years before we were successful in escaping. I have seen too many children taken from their mothers, too many hearts broken. Your presence here has brought all of that back."

She pointed at the door. "That woman on the platform, she was one of the last that had her baby taken from her. Every day I regret that we couldn't save her little boy. Instead, her little boy saved us. The scroll which had sealed the boy's light of life was retrieved during our revolt, and we used it to let a ghol'm come to our cause. Corza was there that day and I would have happily sent the ghol'm after him, but the situation didn't allow for it."

Their group was silent, searching for words that would never be enough.

"I'm sorry... sorry we've brought back these terrible memories, but can you not see we're on the same side here?" said Gavin, eventually.

"Are we? Even if you are not directly an enemy, will you save us? Are you planning to attack the Stone King's army? Rid the world of his evil? Or perhaps take us all to safety, back to Aeterra? A place where some of us don't even wish to go as, despite everything, they feel this place is their home? No, I'm sorry, the decision has been made. You *will* leave our village and be on your way in the morning."

"At least tell us if you know how to get to Drowned Man's Fork," Raylan said, frustrated.

"I'm sorry. I can't help you there, either. Few of us have ever been to the coast, and this place you describe is not known to any of us."

And with that, they were kindly but firmly escorted out by the guards. Raylan saw that Sebastian stayed behind. The former slave had not uttered one word during the whole ordeal.

"What now?" said Xi'Lao to Gavin.

"Little we can do. Let's inform the others and then get some sleep. We'll head out at first light."

CHAPTER SIXTEEN

Hope

THE NEXT MORNING, Raylan and the others found themselves escorted out of the settlement as dawn broke. The friendly atmosphere was all but gone; the few people that were up and moving around avoided them, whispering behind their backs.

Raylan was thankful Galen had most of his strength back, so he seemed fit to travel. Luckily, they did not have to walk much; when they were lowered to the ground, one by one, they found their horses waiting below together with Otis and Danai.

"Seb told us to bring the horses down last night. Sorry to see you all go," said Danai, apologetically.

"We put a new sword in your pack, since you lost yours at the food storage…"

"Where's Sebastian anyway?" asked Raylan.

They had not seen him since the council meeting last night. Danai shrugged. "We left last night while it was getting dark. I've not been up yet, this morning."

Raylan wondered if he would be able to say good-bye to him, but as soon as they had prepped the horses, Gavin told them to move out.

"*I would have liked to say goodbye,*" said Galirras, while stretching his neck as he stood on one of the tree roots, his swirling eyes checking between the trees.

"*Me too,*" said Raylan, solemnly.

Over the past few days, it felt like they had been friends for years, and he was sorry to leave the man so soon.

The sun climbed in the sky as they navigated the forest at a walking pace. Ca'lek took up his scouting duties, accompanied by the archer duo.

"Where are we headed now?" Richard asked the question everyone had on their minds.

"We'll continue south and head for the coast. I see no other option to find the Drowned Man's Fork," said Gavin. "We'll increase our scouting efforts to make sure we're not surprised by Corza and his men. And, let's hope the coastal area has little patrol activity."

Galirras used their travel time for flying practice. He looked for high tree roots to jump from, spreading his wings and gliding down. It took a few attempts, but he soon seemed to get familiar with the weightless feel and started correcting course with his head, wings, and tail. By the end of the day, he was experimenting with using a few wing strokes to get from tree to tree without touching the ground.

After a friendly request from Raylan, the dragon put some distance between his practice and the traveling horses, since the unfamiliar flapping of the wings made them nervous. Peadar's mare seemed to have difficulties with the large shape gliding through the air, making Gavin fear for the pigeon on which their escape still very much depended.

Raylan took up position between Galirras and the group, making sure the dragon would not lose track of them in his enthusiasm. He challenged Galirras to reach certain heights or to stretch for hard to reach landing spots as a sort of game and found himself constantly surprised by how fast Galirras adapted to different circumstances. The most difficult challenge looked to be gaining height, as the dragon's muscles were just not yet strong enough to provide the powerful strokes needed to ascend. And landing on a vertical surface like a tree trunk proved difficult, too; his first attempt resulting in a loud crash as Galirras had been unable to turn his body enough to grab hold of the bark properly.

That evening, Galirras used his newly acquired gliding skill to almost effortlessly catch two large boars and a deer. They split one of the boars, half for dinner and half for their rations. And Galirras was hungry enough to eat the deer and half of the second boar, saving the other half for his breakfast.

It was an exhausting day, with all the flight practice, and before long, both Raylan and Galirras were in a deep sleep around the campfire. They had made certain to set up on one of the rock formations. Hearing the stories about the sand devils, Gavin did not want to take any risk, even if he was unsure there were any in this area.

"Raylan..."
Raylan felt a nudge in his side. His head was still groggy from sleep.
"Raylan, wake up. Something is coming."

This woke him up right away. He checked around and saw most of the group still sleeping. The campfire was now just embers, barely giving off any light. As the morning had not presented itself yet, it took some time for Raylan's eyes to adjust to their surroundings.

He and Galirras had taken last watch, but he had dozed off against the dragon's warm skin. Galirras had not minded, he had not felt sleepy anymore; and besides, he had much better night vision, so it seemed only logical he would keep an eye on their surroundings.

As Raylan carefully drew his new sword, ensuring not to make too much sound, he turned toward the rustling leaves and the occasional snap of a twig. He thought about waking the others, but one of the bushes on the edge of the rock formation started to move as something approached.

A shadow stepped out of the shrubbery; human-shaped. Raylan's grip tightened when a face came into view of the smoldering, dim campfire.

"Now is that any way to treat a friend?" Sebastian said softly.

"Oh!" Galirras let out in surprise.

"Seb? What are you doing here? You nearly gave me a heart attack," whispered Raylan.

"Did you come to say goodbye to us after all?" asked Galirras.

"No, I've not come to say goodbye. If it's all the same with you, I would actually like to come with you."

"Really? What about the council and the village?" asked Raylan.

"They'll be fine without me, I'm sure. And, to be honest, I couldn't stay there anymore after they threw y'all out."

"But how were you even able to find us?" Raylan whispered.

"Ha! Well, it's not that hard to follow Galirras' tracks once you know what to look for. Although he did throw me off when he suddenly started to cover larger distances without tracks on the ground, until I realized he would want to use his wings after yesterday."

"Oh, that is clever!" commented Galirras.

"I shall wake the others," said Raylan, but Sebastian stopped him.

"If you don't mind, I could do with a bit of sleep, it's been a long run. I'm sure Gavin and the others will be just as surprised in the morning."

"Of course. Take my spot by the fire. Galirras and I will finish our watch."

In the morning, Gavin and the others happily welcomed Sebastian to the group.

"I'm glad you'll be accompanying us. We can use your knowledge of the area, especially since we have no idea where to go at the moment," said Gavin.

226

"I believe I can help you with that, too," said Sebastian, smiling widely. His lower lip showed a bloody crack, he had some scratches on his jaw, and his left eye had a deep blue mark under it.

"After you left, I went around asking people about the Drowned Man's Fork. I was having little luck, until someone told me to speak to Aanon. He knew of three pillars rising from the sea. He'd only seen them from afar, but he reckoned it could only be what you all were looking for."

"Did he know how to get there?" said Gavin.

"Aye, we're to follow the river, which lays some ways to the west, for about ten days southward until we hit a big lake. From the lake, we move due west toward the coast, which should get us to the cliffs in two or three days. From there, we should see the pillars on a clear day, out in the distance. He estimated it would take another couple of days to get there over land, depending on the terrain."

It was the best lead they had in a long time and after some debate, Gavin decided to send out the bird to Azurna. It was a big gamble. If it ended up not being the Drowned Man's Fork, Gavin imagined they would have to look for an alternative way home, perhaps trying to make their way all the way up north again.

They had a long way to go; but even if it would take them twice as long to get there, the timing would still work. They could still meet up with a ship, as the vessel would be ordered to wait for several weeks. Not wanting to risk staying in one place for too long while the enemy was still looking for them, Gavin decided it was time to go. They all ate a quick meal and prepared to set out again.

"So, what happened to your face?" Raylan asked Sebastian, once they were on their way.

"This?" he said, pointing at his jaw. "It's nothing. Aanon didn't agree with me leaving. Said I needed to come back or he would not let me leave at all. He believed we have a responsibility toward the settlement. I believed they did not deserve my dedication anymore. We ended up… talking it out."

"Just because of us?"

"Nah, I think it was a long time coming. You being forced to leave… it was just the final straw, I guess."

"What about Otis, Danai, Twan and Ivar?"

"I had a chance to say goodbye to them. They all have their own reasons for staying, for which I don't fault them. But my place isn't there anymore. I think Galirras and you will have an important place in this world, and I want to be there to witness it firsthand."

"Well, I—for one—am happy for you to join us," said Galirras, who had been following their conversation.

227

"Me too!" added Raylan cheerfully. "Now let's go and find our way home."

Sebastian was given Xi'Lao's horse as she joined Gavin on his. As the group set out toward the river, Raylan rolled his shoulders to let them relax. He smiled, letting out a sigh. He felt motivated by the group's renewed hope and looked forward to leaving these lands behind.

Days later, Raylan found himself looking out over a large body of water, idly scratching the healing wound on his leg. There was little left of his optimistic feeling. They had come upon the lake that afternoon and—tired as they were— decided to take a rest in one of the more hidden parts on the forest's edge. It had been a stressful trip; they had run into multiple patrols, had to fight their way out of two encounters and were forced to hide in a cave for three days surrounded by enemy movements, without little more than the rations they carried and a small waterfall trickling in from one of the cave walls. Galirras' appetite had eventually forced them to look for prey again. After which, they were finally able to sneak away, when they found an opening in the enemy's perimeter. All in all, it took them a good fifteen days to get to the lake.

Behind him, Galirras splashed in one of the shallower pools, flinging fish from the water with his claws. He had enjoyed a great bath when they arrived; Raylan had gotten some branches to scrub him down. He was getting so big, it would have ended up quite a task if everyone had not jumped in and helped, at one point.

The dragon had loved the attention. He was not used to taking baths and reveled in the fact that his scales were getting cleaned to the point that sunlight would sparkle off them, showing a deep copper-like color. He now wanted to show his gratitude by catching dinner… and getting the occasional snack himself.

The exercise and practice Galirras had accomplished during their days of travel showed clear results in the build of the dragon. His flight muscles had increased dramatically, giving him a more buff look; although it did not seem the dragon would ever lose his lean build. Raylan thought his head had grown a little wider again, and a few ridges of scales now had a more prominent presence on his face.

The scales on Galirras' back seemed to have hardened, while the sides of his belly still remained reasonably soft. The skin would be tough to damage, Raylan expected. The hardened skin on his spine gave the dragon added protection from head to tail. Raylan would not necessarily call them spikes as they did not break the skin; it looked more like an extra-thick layer of scales that formed a natural armor without losing its flexibility.

Finally, his tail had gotten longer as he grew, and the end of it had widened, as a thin membrane stretched from one side of his tail to the other in the shape of a rugged oak leaf. Slowly but surely, Galirras had grown considerably larger than Raylan. When sitting up, with his front legs on the ground, Galirras was now a good four heads taller and a great deal heavier.

The lake was one of the biggest ones Raylan had seen. The distant shore was barely visible from this side. They had not seen any settlements nearby but remained on guard.

"You're not going to believe this!" Peadar shouted, as he came running up.

"What is it?" Raylan asked, turning around.

"A pool with warm water. It is bubbling up from ground. It's too hot to even touch!"

That made Raylan curious. While Harwin and Kevhin stayed with Galirras and made sure the fish he caught were cleaned and prepped, the rest followed Peadar up a small creek to the spot that had excited him so much.

Small pools of water bubbled on the sides of the riverbed. Some smelled like eggs gone bad, while others seemed to have no scent at all.

"We have got something like this at home," Xi'Lao said. "They are spread throughout the Empire. We call them hot pools. Our public bathhouses are built on top of them if possible, providing excellent bathing opportunities." She moved along the creek, seeming to search for something. "This will work," she said, and started to move some rocks around. "Can someone please help me with this?"

Raylan hopped over a few stones and helped her drag a bigger one toward the stream. Before long they had created a natural dam, and the flow of water was partly redirected to one of the deeper bubbling pools. As it overflowed, the mixed water dead-ended in an even deeper pool downstream.

"See, we can use the dam to control the flow of water into the deep pool. With a bit of experimenting, we should have a very comfortable water temperature to bathe in after dinner," she said with a smile.

In fact, a few of them were already in the warming pool before dinner was half done. The heated water did wonders for their aching muscles. They were exhausted after riding for days, weeks, without proper rest.

As the sun began to set and the group prepared for the night, Raylan went back to the hot pool to soak in the water for a while longer. As he approached, he heard soft talking from the direction of the bath. A dusky sky made it hard to see where he was going, so he stepped carefully, trying not to lose his footing. As he rounded a bend, he stumbled upon his brother kissing Xi'Lao intimately in the hot pool. The sight caught him off guard and made him miss a step, almost ending up face forward in one of the other pools.

"Uh… sorry… didn't mean to… uh… interrupt," he said, as he quickly straightened himself and then hurried back to the campfire.

"Oh shit… Raylan… wait," he heard behind him, as his brother got out of the water and moved across the stones to catch up with him.

"Hold on!" he heard his brother say, as he was halfway back to camp. He reluctantly stopped and allowed a bare-chested Gavin to catch up with him.

"What? I said I was sorry," Raylan said, somewhat annoyed.

"It's not that. I wanted to check if you were alright. I'm sorry you had to find out like this."

"What do you mean?" said Raylan, puzzled.

"Well you know… me and Xi—we've gotten to know each other pretty well."

"Okay…" said Raylan.

He had a feeling where this was going, as he waited for his brother to find the words. Normally, Gavin was never so uncertain when speaking.

"Look, I know you've been spending quite some time with Xi'Lao, and I just wanted to be sure that us being together doesn't create a problem."

"And you ask me this now? After… and not before," Raylan said, in his most earnest tone.

"I wanted to tell you—but with everything going on, it never seemed like the right… moment," stammered Gavin. "When you talk about her, you seem very impressed with her. I-I was afraid you might have similar feelings toward her… which clearly seems to be the case by your response."

Raylan kept his expression in check for a little while longer, then broke into a big smile. "Ha! Relax, I'm just messing with you," he said, as he placed a hand on Gavin's shoulder. "I'm not interested in Xi'Lao that way—at all. She is an intriguing person who has great knowledge on dragons. Knowledge that I need and appreciate very much, I might add. If I'm to gain any insight into how to live with a dragon, I can use all the help I can get. She's a great friend and comrade… frankly, I think she is a great woman, just… not for me."

"So, you're not bothered by it at all?" Gavin said to him with some residual disbelief in his voice.

"None whatsoever! In fact, I think you two are great together, and I know you both have Galirras' back and mine."

"You can count on that," said Gavin. "But why did you speed off at the hot pool, just now, then?"

230

"Well, it's one thing being okay with my brother's choice in women, but another to witness that intimacy at work. Besides, falling flat on my face didn't help much either," said Raylan, adding an embarrassed laugh.

"So, we're good?"

"We're great, no worries. Do me a favor? Let me know when I can take my bath. I'll be back at the fire… or along the lake, if Galirras wants to practice some more."

He walked off, letting out another laugh as he heard his brother's sigh of relief. Heading back to the campfire, he felt Galirras tingle in his head.

"*You did not need to let him sweat like that, did you? You knew almost right away what he was afraid to say to you… did you not?*" said Galirras in Raylan's head.

"*Hehe, you caught me… but I couldn't help myself. It's not every day that I have the upper hand in our conversations… I guess the kid in me just wanted to enjoy it, if only for a bit. But you're right, it wasn't a very nice thing to do.*"

Coming back to the lake, the sky was reflected in the lake's calm surface. As the clouds broke apart above the lake, stars filled both the sky and the water. The moon was barely a sickle and, if not for the stars, it would have been a very dark night. Along the lake were the outskirts of the ancient forest. The trees had gotten smaller these last few days as they moved south toward the lake. They were still some of the biggest trees Raylan had ever seen; but were, by far, not as massive as the trees in which the tree settlement had been built.

"*You want to meet me at the river exit and do some flying practice?*" he asked Galirras.

"*Sure! I will be right there,*" said the dragon, sending a burst of happiness that Raylan was as interested in his flying as he was.

As Raylan watched the moving of the water, he heard the now familiar swishing of wind and snapping of the leathery skinned wings. Galirras sat down next to him.

"Hey, that went a lot better. You didn't even slide that far on the ground."

"Thanks. If I tilt my wings a bit more, I can actively slow down before touching the ground."

Most of the flying came naturally to Galirras; but certain things had taken some time, since he had spent such an extensive time walking on the ground, neglecting his wings. The positive side of it was that Galirras had plenty of power in his hind legs, enough to launch himself into the air and for his wings to get enough room to lift him off the ground. Raylan decided to send him out above the water to practice controlling his low altitude flying.

"See how low to the water you can fly without falling in. Be careful not to tip your wings in the water, or you might end up taking another bath."

As Galirras jumped up, Raylan noticed a flow of air pulled his hair forward just before the wind gush of beating wings pushed it the other way again. Being familiar with the movement of wind from his days on sea, something inside him made him curious.

Galirras sheared across the water. Barely having to move his wings, he glided a small distance above the water, close enough to touch the water surface with a claw if he wished. Suddenly, he pulled upward, going up a few wing beats, before spinning across the length of his body and going in for another dive. Even so close to the water's surface, he was able to make sharp turns. Every time he did, a ripple formed on the calm surface. Looking closer, it seemed as if Galirras was creating a bow wave, if he got close enough to the surface—which seemed strange as he did not actually touch the water.

The sound of grinding pebbles made Raylan look around to see Xi'Lao approach him.

"If you want, you can take a bath now," said Xi'Lao, with a light blush on her face.

"Thanks. I'll head over in a bit."

She lingered for a moment, without saying a word.

"Was there something else?" asked Raylan, when he noticed her staying.

"I wanted to thank you. For the support you give your brother," she spoke softly. "I know you both do not always agree, but I see he cares a lot about you."

"Thanks," said Raylan, after thinking for a moment. "I'm glad he took me along on this mission after all. Not just because of Galirras, but I didn't really leave on the best of terms with him and father, when I left home. This, at least, gives me a chance to undo some of that damage."

"What do you mean?"

He saw nothing but genuine interest from her, so continued. "I don't know. I guess I was younger, more stupid," he said. "I hated the mundane chores at our father's workshop, but Gavin's pushing to be drilled and grounded into a soldier wasn't much better. So, one night, I just left—toward the promise of the endless seas. I snuck out of the house, made my way to Eore and boarded the first ship heading west that would take me. I sent father a letter to apologize from Eore's harbor, before I departed toward the Arosh'ad islands, but we've not spoken much over the years. I don't think Gavin ever truly forgave me for abandoning them—or fully understood, for that matter."

He kept his eyes on Galirras, as he let the words flow out.

"But you are different now," came the dragon's thoughts into his mind.

"When I look back at it with what I know now, I'd like to think I would've done things differently," said Raylan out loud, half in response to his scaled friend's remark.

He looked back at Xi'Lao with an apologetic smile, but she merely stood there, politely listening. It seemed she felt no need to pry deeper.

"He is doing well," she said after a while, gesturing at Galirras.

"Yeah, I think he's really making up for lost time. His wing muscles have almost tripled in size from the looks of it."

"So, is there anything wrong? You were watching him pretty intensely when I came to get you. His wings are all healed, right?"

"Yeah. I'm not worried about that anymore. He seems to have good control over them, and he hasn't mentioned any pain since the tree village."

"But?"

Raylan glanced at her. "Galirras told you about his ability to manipulate wind, right? How he could move leaves, make them dance above the fire?"

Xi'Lao gave a nod. "He showed me. It was hard to believe at first, but he moved the leaves precisely where I told him to. He gets more amazing by the day, it seems."

"I agree with that… I think he might be using his wind power to add to his basic flying skills. There! See how just before he turns the water surface is disturbed? I think he is creating his own counter wind to slow down, then he pushes sideways with the wind while turning in the direction with his wings. It allows him to make very sudden and sharp corners. It's a whole other aspect to his power."

"That is incredible," said Xi'Lao, after observing the dragon's turns for a while. "I wonder what other powers will show up over time. But he most certainly does justice to his name already."

Raylan raised an eyebrow. "What do you mean 'does justice to his name'?"

"I realized the other day after he told me about seeing the wind and controlling it. His name in the old dragon tongue would most likely come from *ga'li roras*. If I remember my grandfather's teachings of the old language correctly, it would freely translate to 'catcher of the winds', or 'manipulator of air'. It seems to fit him perfectly, I would say."

Raylan looked back at Galirras. The explanation of his name made him see a whole different being. The dragon had stopped being helpless some time ago, as he constantly increased in size. But somehow, now, he did not just see the physical presence of his friend, he saw all Galirras' potential— what he might become… and it was incredible.

As he saw Galirras turn toward shore, obviously tired from his flying lessons, he could do nothing more than feel admiration for this magnificent creature that had chosen to bond with him. And as he smiled, he spoke the dragon's newfound name under his breath.

"Windcatcher…"

The next morning, their brief relaxation quickly came to an end. Harwin, who had been on watch, spotted two small boats coming down the coast, filled with two dozen soldiers. Before their group was discovered, they quickly broke up camp and retreated into the tree line, heading west toward the ocean.

"I could have taken to the air to attack them," said Galirras. "It is such a shame we have to leave this place so soon."

The dragon had thoroughly enjoyed the hot pools, even bathing in the ones that were much too warm for any human. It had not bothered him; in fact, he said the heat had warmed his body through and through for the first time since he was born. He had never noticed because of the climate here, but now he felt as if he had been cold the entire time. He had told Xi'Lao that this discovery led him to believe that dragons greatly enjoyed the heat, and he was reluctant to pass this up.

"And how would you do that? Attack them," asked Raylan.

It was clear the dragon had not thought that far ahead. He was getting bolder with his increased size, but Raylan was not yet comfortable letting his precious friend be on the front lines.

"Perhaps I could have come in low. Topple the boat. Surely, they would drown, or at least have trouble reaching land, where you could have been waiting to kill them."

It surprised Raylan how easy the dragon suggested killing. Although he could hardly blame the dragon for it. Galirras had seen little else in his life except people chasing people and man trying to kill man.

"And what if they have archers? Shoot arrows at you? Or perhaps you underestimate the size and weight of the boat and you end up in the water with them? What then?" Raylan asked. "Besides, I rather avoid killing people if I can. People should strive to work together and conquer shared challenges to better themselves and the world, not be at each other's throat."

"But you have killed people to get to me, have you not?" said Galirras, cocking his head.

234

"If there had been any other way, I would have gladly taken it; but for one thing, I didn't want to fail my brother, and after I found you, I'd do anything to keep you from harm."

Raylan tried to figure out how to precisely say what he needed. "I'm not saying that you shouldn't defend yourself or protect someone you care for if needed, but that doesn't mean it's okay to outright kill someone. You should never stop looking for better solutions. When you look at these kinds of problems, perhaps there's a way to avoid a direct confrontation. A way to prevent casualties... whichever side those are on. You would almost forget that we're the invading enemy here. We have our reasons, good reasons if you ask me, but to them we might seem like the aggressor."

"I don't agree," Gavin interrupted. "Our being here is a direct result of their attack on the Tiankong Empire. They're the aggressor and we're the reacting result. Besides, sometimes a preemptive strike will remove a threat before it can become real, saving a lot of lives. Who knows what Corza and the Stone King would have done with Galirras under their control." Gavin looked the dragon in the eye and gave him a small smile. "But Raylan is right on one thing, Galirras. You're currently too valuable to be put at risk if such an easy alternative is available. Besides, if the boat patrol disappeared, it would only draw attention, give away our position, and possibly our direction of travel. We better stay hidden as much as we can and get home as soon as possible."

That proved easier said than done. The group had to take their time moving to the coast. They came across two enemy encampments along the lake, forcing them to circle back and find an alternate route.

By nightfall on the sixth day, they were looking for a place to camp when Ca'lek and Sebastian returned from scouting.

"We're here! We're at the coast," said Sebastian.

As they rode out of the forest, Raylan could hear the distant crash of waves. The forest had not become any brighter and dusk set in early under the trees. But when they emerged, the view of the Great Eastern Divide was spectacular. The setting sun painted the sky orange and red, going into a deep blue where the night sky was gaining ground.

The ocean burst onto the rocks sixty feet below them. Often overhanging above the water, the cliffs were too steep and dangerous to climb. Along the entire coast, the steep rocks acted like a natural barrier, making it hard to find a good place to reach land. The height of the rocky shore seemed to vary as much higher cliffs were seen in both directions.

Toward the south, the land bent westward. Filling a quarter of the horizon with steep cliffs, it suddenly stopped where the landmass turned back on itself. The multiple levels of trees and forest layers would suggest it was more mountainous than flat. Unfortunately, no sign of the three giant pillars rising out of the sea was seen.

"Perhaps Aanon was lying…" Sebastian began, before he stopped himself. "No, no, he couldn't have. I know him. I'm certain of it. He might have hit the coast more toward the south, hit on higher ground."

"It seems clear that's the landmass he was talking about," said Gavin, pointing to the cliff turning west. There's no such thing in the north as far as we can see. So, south it will be."

Raylan had explained the sea to Galirras, about how far it stretched, but after the lake the dragon was still surprised by the sheer vastness of the ocean.

"*How can it reach so far? Where does all the water come from? You do not see any land at all! How long would it take to fly to the other side?*" asked Galirras, inside Raylan's mind.

Raylan tried his best to provide answers. "Our fastest ships can go five to six knots, which would take about three weeks to make the crossing, if they maintained their maximum speed at all times. You could probably fly faster, but you wouldn't find any land to rest on for at least a week, I reckon. So, unless you can stay in the air for at least seven days, I wouldn't recommend trying to fly it," Raylan replied.

"*And there is another ocean just like this on the other side of your kingdom?*"

"Indeed. The Great Western Divide lies on the other side of the mid-continent. Aeterra spans all the way from west to east."

As the sun set, darkness slowly took over the world. In his enthusiasm, Galirras stretched out his neck over the edge of the cliffs, trying to see as far as he could. Suddenly, he let himself drop off the cliff. Using a wind gush from the waves crashing below, he immediately ascended with a few heavy beats of his wings. Circling with short turns, he was up in the air—at least three hundred feet—before any of them had time to call out.

"*What are you doing? You might be spotted!*" Raylan called out, telepathically. Gavin hurried over, urging him to call Galirras down.

"*I just want to see how far it goes! Besides, I do not see anyone around. And, even if they were, I doubt they would be able to see me in this twilight.*"

This was true. Raylan had trouble keeping Galirras in view, as his shape became smaller and fell away against the dark sky. And he knew what he was looking for.

"Well, please come down, anyway. You're making the others nervous," said Raylan.

Galirras did one more turn, before he set his descent. But just before he dove back down, he stopped in midair, the strong strokes of his wings keeping him almost stationary. Raylan knew Galirras was using his wind manipulation to give himself a strong headwind up there, or perhaps, he had found an air current to redirect and enhance, slightly. It allowed Galirras to stay in the air—virtually still in one spot—without having to frantically flap his wings. His wings stroked—steady and powerful—in a turning fashion, pushing air not only downward, but also forward.

"I can see it!" Galirras called out to all of them, as he hung there hovering. "I can see the three peaks!"

He dove forward, rapidly descending toward the water. Turning the length of his body back toward the cliff, he pulled up and used the upward flow of wind to approach the edge of the cliffs and landed neatly next to Luna. The horse whinnied, due to the sudden approach from below the cliff; but Raylan had learned to keep the reins short around Galirras.

"I saw the Drowned Man's Fork," Galirras said to Raylan and Gavin. "It is behind that second peak from the right. It looks like they are part of that hill, but that is just the low light and the twilight playing tricks on your eyes. I saw them, three pillars rising from behind it. Does that mean we can get out of here?"

"Let's hope so," said Raylan, as he gave a quick stroke along Galirras' neck.

Gavin had already turned toward the rest. "Let's make camp nearby, quickly. We'll head out for the fork at first light. It's about time we leave this place behind."

Corza sniffed deeply, forcing himself to carefully put down the small glass flask he had in his hand. He squeezed his eyes closed and tilted his face toward the ceiling for a moment, giving the drops time to do their work. When he opened them again, he began to pace his room.

After the stone arch collapsed, he and his men had taken the long way 'round, falling back to one of the forest forts to get reinforcements. He had taken a moment to inform his dear leader, Lord Rictor, about the unfortunate demise of High General Koltar Wayler at the hands of their enemy, and to ensure that he would not rest until this group was caught and brought to justice before the Stone King.

He slammed his hands on the desk thinking back to the dark palace's balcony. The bang spurred a soft whimper from behind him.

They had been chasing the group for weeks. Sometimes losing track of them, but then a patrol would spot them—or go missing—and give them an indication of where the enemy squad had been. And yet, they still had not been captured.

He grabbed his Roc'turr and walked over to the young woman that stood tied to the side wall in his room, hands above her head. She was sobbing, silently, clearly afraid to draw attention to herself.

Corza put his hands on her ragged dress and ripped it from her body. "A girl as impure as you has no need for modesties like clothes," he hissed.

The girl whimpered. According to the soldiers in the harbor, she was one of the regular girls, tending to the needs of the soldiers and, apparently, quite good at it.

"How dare you try and seduce me when I'm not in the mood," Corza continued.

He took hold of her left breast and squeezed as hard as he could. The girl let out a pained cry. He had to admit, she had a pretty face. He would have to do something about that later.

"See, I still don't understand how he could have vanished into thin air that night, out in the forest," he growled as he dragged the point of the sacrificial dagger down her arm. As the tip crossed her neck, the girl's eyes grew wide and she held her breath—but the dagger moved on, without cutting any skin.

"…unless a kzaktor actually got hold of him. But somehow, he seemed too smart. For. That."

He enforced those last words with a small cut in the woman's flesh… one across her stomach and one on her left arm. The girl screamed out in both surprise and pain. Blood trickled down her skin all the way to her legs.

Not wanting to run around like a madman after the night he ran into Raylan, Corza had traveled further south to their fallout base. He had to be there to oversee the final preparations anyway; and he could use the time to get some of his strength back after the long march through the White North. The rest was doing him well, but he had to trust incompetent men to track down what he desired most.

"And every single time they're spotted, they let them slip away," Corza complained. He crouched and looked up to meet the girl's panicked eyes. "Did you know my men say a ferocious beast accompanies them? Larger than any man."

Putting his face to her lovely soft thigh, he licked the small, dripping stream of blood from her skin. "It can only mean the egg has hatched. It can be nothing other than a dragon, by what they describe. MY DRAGON!"

238

Another cut, across her thigh, provoked an agonizing scream.

"Please, lord. Please, no more. I'm sorry that I offered myself to you. Please, let me go…"

Corza ripped a piece of cloth from her dress and stuffed it in her mouth. "You misunderstand, woman. You're here just to listen!"

Tears ran down the girl's cheeks as she tried to move away from the blade. Two more cuts, this time on her hand and cheek.

"See, this creature—this *dragon*—was going to be my weapon. Under my command, it would destroy anybody trying to oppose my will."

The point of the dagger slid along her skin to her right breast. Corza straightened the blade, and put pressure on the point, pushing it slowly into her skin. The girl's muffled cries were as delicious as the panic in her eyes.

"Just like High General Wayler. That son of a bitch got what he deserved when I threw him off the cliff." He dragged the point through her breast, making a large cut across her nipple. "Oh, sorry, did I accidentally cut you?" Corza joked as he glared at the woman. "But that dragon will be mine, I'll tell you that."

Another cut.

"With it, I will walk up to the Stone King. No shadow will be able to stop me!"

Another cut, and another.

"And destroy him completely! Or perhaps, just get rid of that devilish arm of his and take a leg or two… I have not decided, yet. But rest assured, once I'm done, none will be my equal!"

The girl barely reacted to the cuts anymore; her body hung limp in her restraints, her breath rasping. Blood flowed. Her head hung low; eyes staring at the ground.

Corza lifted her head and looked her in the eyes. "It seems like you've learned your lesson."

Her eyes focused sluggishly on him, her blank stare slowly turning into hope.

Corza smiled. "Of course, now that I've told you my plans, I could never let you walk free."

As he turned away, the girl started to scream and beg behind her gag. Corza walked over to a chest in the corner of the room and opened it. He took out a scroll and turned back to her.

"Might as well get some use out of your body…" he said as he approached and started the incantations.

"Look at how they flop around," Galirras called out to Raylan, who stood on the cliff.

The dragon shot low across the water toward the rocky island where they had spotted the sea lions. Raylan observed his friend's approach as the animals scurried away in response to an alarm call from one of the females. His stomach tightened as a sudden wind shear pushed Galirras left, but the dragon niftily corrected himself and continued his path.

As they traveled along the cliffs toward the Drowned Man's Fork, Galirras had regularly taken flight below them, playing with the wind currents swirling around the rocky shore. Any animal unable to see the wind would have had trouble navigating the swiftly changing currents of air slamming into stone. Flying too close meant a serious risk of being thrown into the rocks, or being swallowed by sprays of seawater, yet Galirras did not seem bothered at all by this.

The only other animals daring enough to fly near the cliffs were small, arrow-like birds. They appeared to have nests built into the rocks and feasted on small insects living on the forest's edge. The speed and agility of these little creatures allowed them to quickly adjust to any changes in the unpredictable air currents. Their flight patterns were very reactive, filled with sudden movements; unlike Galirras, who was learning to read the wind and to anticipate its changes. Nonetheless, the little creatures were a treat to watch, and Galirras had highly enjoyed trying to imitate and to chase them up till now. Even if it would take a thousand of them to fill his stomach.

Below, Galirras threw himself on a sea lion that was too slow to get to the water. It was a good and swift kill, efficiency likely driven by the hunger Raylan felt overflow from the dragon. This was the third day of traveling along the coast and they had not seen a lot of big prey lately. So, it did not come as a surprise that Galirras had been eager to go after them when Raylan had spotted the animals as they came across a sheltered fjord.

Raylan watched as the others of their squad continued their way along the coast. When he saw Ca'lek turn around, he gestured for them to go on—they would catch up soon enough.

"*They are so helpless on land,*" remarked Galirras internally, as he continued to eat. "*But once they hit the water they are gone in an instant.*"

Raylan watched as the long shadows swiftly circled the rocky island Galirras had claimed as his temporary dinner table. To his surprise several of the more daring animals already climbed back out of the water, to continue sunbathing, completely choosing to ignore the dragon eating one of their own. Perhaps they thought one would be enough for the predator, but Raylan knew better.

And, sure enough, Galirras was already eying those close to him before he swallowed the last piece of his meal.

With a roar he jumped at a small group laying near the edge of the water, but before he could reach them the animals rolled back into the water and darted off. In his enthusiasm, Galirras leaped off the rocks and glided after one of the shadows before throwing himself head-first into the water to grab it.

"Galirras!" Raylan called out. He shot forward only to skid to a halt near the cliff's edge.

Below him, the dragon surfaced in a turmoil of water as Galirras beat his wings and thrashed with his limbs.

"*I cannot get out.*" Galirras' panicked voice sounded loud in Raylan's head.

Every time the dragon tried to extend his wing, the other side of him would submerge as waves washed over him. He twisted his neck around, trying to keep his head from being dragged below the water as he paddled with his front legs.

Raylan threw a look down the coast, but their group had already disappeared from sight. He scanned the cliffs to find a place to descend, but there was none. He could jump, but the strong waves would probably smash him against the cliff before he could reach Galirras. He felt utterly helpless, so he did the only thing he could do—he yelled.

"Your tail! Use your tail!"

He looked around again, hoping he might have missed some other way down, but it was useless. The dragon was slowly pushed toward the dark rocks that rose from the ocean.

"*You have to turn around,*" he screamed, sending the words with his mind. "*Put your wings flat on the water and use your tail to push!*"

Raylan feared Galirras would quickly grow tired, fighting against the water. Perhaps there was a tree he could chop down and let fall off the cliff. But then he saw the struggling dragon slowly turn.

It seemed the biggest panic had subsided as Galirras put all his efforts into swimming and splashing back toward the sea lions' sunbathing spot. After what seemed like an eternity to Raylan—who stood frozen to the spot as he watched his friend from the cliffs—the desperate, water-treading dragon finally reached solid ground beneath his claws.

Exhausted, Galirras pulled himself onto the slippery ground where he slumped awkwardly.

"*I am okay,*" rumbled Galirras' voice inside, in response to Raylan's worried thoughts. "*I just need some rest.*"

It was past midday before the dragon hoisted himself back to his feet and found the strength to jump into the air and fly toward the cliff. As he landed, Raylan flew forward and threw his arms around the long, curved neck.

"You gave me quite a scare there, little one. Do you think you're rested enough to catch up with the others? They'll be wondering what's keeping us."

"I am, but I think… I will walk for a bit, if you do not mind."

"And the next time we come across sea lions, perhaps you can stick to the ones on land?" said Raylan in a soft voice as he scratched his friend above his scaled eye.

A shiver ran across Galirras' back all the way to his tail, as he watched the dark ocean below. They turned south and started to walk, when, after a few steps, the dragon's voice rumbled inside Raylan's mind. "*I think that is a good idea.*"

CHAPTER SEVENTEEN

Rescue

RAYLAN PUT HIS hand in the crack around the corner of the boulder. Pushing off with his feet, he carefully shifted his weight onto his right leg. His fingers cramped. This was always the trickiest part, but he was getting used to the movement he needed to make—which was not all that strange since he had made the climb multiple times per day in the last fortnight.

The first time, it took several attempts to find a suitable route. He had been forced to climb down again a number of times until he finally found the hidden handhold on the blind side of a large overhang.

After Galirras' ocean dive, they had traveled a good few more days along the coastal cliffs, before reaching their current encampment. More than once, the group had been forced to backtrack as their route led to a dead-end. They took it slow, taking every precaution to avoid patrols.

When they finally neared the end of the landmass, they had run into a large rock wall. It blocked them from reaching the most western point, where the Drowned Man's Fork was located. They had decided to move along it toward the south, to see if another path would allow them to continue, but the rock wall never lowered or gave way. It was like someone had knocked the entire western point upward with one giant kick, lifting the ground in one giant mass.

The south cliffs had not offered a better view of the Drowned Man's Fork, which left them with two options: they could place a lookout at both the northern and southern coasts of the landmass to keep an eye on the ocean—putting at least a day's travel between the two points—or they would have find a way to get up there.

They had surveyed the wall for possible climbing routes, which took them another day to map out. After many attempts, Raylan had been the one who managed to finish a climb, successfully, for the very first time. His discovery of the hidden handgrips had allowed them to reach the top of the wall. From there, it was just a relatively short journey to an excellent lookout point that provided a full view of the three mighty pillars and allowed Raylan to see the water of the Great Eastern Divide from a wide angle. No ship would go undetected.

And so it came to be that Raylan made the climb, at least once—but more often multiple times—per day. Their group had established a small hidden campsite, where they could wait for their rescue.

Rotating small scouting parties, they kept an eye out for any enemy patrols; a direct confrontation would be disastrous—there were not a lot of places to run, or hide, if they were discovered. Thankfully, their luck held.

As Raylan pulled himself over the top edge, he heard Galirras approach and land a small way from him.

"*Why did Gavin not want to make camp on this plateau?*" remarked the dragon as Raylan rolled on his back and took a moment to catch his breath.

"Because—" Raylan panted. "Because not everyone will be able to make that climb, and there's not enough prey here to hunt either."

But Raylan understood the dragon's concern. His brother had voiced them as well; every day the chances of being discovered increased. But it could not be helped. If they wanted any chance of getting home by ship, they had to stay here and signal the vessel when it arrived... and Raylan hoped, with all his heart, it would arrive.

"*I know that, but I could hunt for everyone,*" offered the dragon. "*Just like I could fly around the pillars, from time to time, to check out the water for any ships. It would save you a lot of energy by avoiding these climbs.*"

"I'm fine," Raylan said, sitting up. "Besides, a dragon flying around a well-known landmark is bound to draw attention from the wrong people, which we *don't* need. I promise, when we leave these lands behind, there'll be less sneaking. We can go see places, explore. I'll show you the far corners of Aeterra, and Shid'el, of course. I think you'll like it there."

"*Tell me again what it is like,*" said Galirras.

"Well, the kingdom itself is vast. Spanning from sea to sea. There's a few dozen good-sized cities and thousands of smaller settlements, strongholds and villages scattered in between them. The capital, Shid'el—where Gavin and I were born—is built against the face of a large mountain that is part of the Crescent Moon Massif," Raylan began as he got to his feet and they started to head to the lookout. "They call it that because the mountains rise up from the coastal area in the west and run both north and south like the points of a sickle moon, bending off toward the east. The capital is amongst the oldest cities in our kingdom and lays on the southern side of the northern moon point, bathing in as much sunlight as the seasons can give."

Raylan had told the story a dozen times now, but he saw Galirras' eyes swirl excitedly, as if it was the first time he would hear the tale.

"When you stand on the walls of the city, you can look across the tremendous grass plains with patches of forests and yellow farmlands that reach as far as the eye can see. Beyond it, on the far horizon, the mountain peaks of the southern moon point can be seen, but only on a clear day," continued Raylan. "It takes a horse and rider just under a week to reach the southern end of the crescent moon ridges... but I bet you could fly it in a day or two."

"*What else?*" said Galirras.

"The lands that go east are filled with rolling hills. Turn north, and you get to the thick forests of Dahalaes. The cities there are as green as the forests themselves and many famous archers come from there."

"That is where Kevhin and Rohan are from, correct?"

"Right. Dahalaes guards the north, but the northern wilderness held no real threats... nothing more than a few scattered outposts and the occasional hermit—or so we thought, up till now," said Raylan, as he pictured the large Doskovian force that had traveled the northern regions.

"Eventually, those thick forests give way to the impassable mountains of the White North. We had to travel awfully close to that harsh region, with its high-altitude mountains and everlasting ice, in order to get to you, you know? It's completely bare of vegetation with little wildlife worth mentioning."

Galirras shuddered, obviously thinking about the freezing air of those high peaks.

"The opposite is true when you go south. You can follow one of the many valleys to reach the southern borders of the kingdom. You must get around the southern moon point to do so, of course. But beyond it, the valleys are smooth, and wet with many lakes and rivers. It is a place with many different types of birds—thousands—but it makes traveling in a straight line very difficult there. And the lowest parts are all high above sea level, making any journey there a challenge for anyone that is used to living near the coast. One of my father's customers once said the summers were nice but way too short, while the winters were filled with unpredictable weather shifts that bring mist and rain. It's often very wet."

"*What else? What about the people? And those outside of the kingdom?*" said the dragon, as they continued their trek.

"Haven't I told you this many, many times already?" said Raylan.

"*I have no idea what you are talking about?*" answered Galirras, obviously playing ignorant.

Raylan let out a laugh. "Fine," he said, giving in once more with a smile. "Aeterra, and its people, have a tumultuous history. But that was all before my time. The last Great War ended almost a hundred years ago, but Aeterran history is filled with bloody royal family feuds, betrayals, deceits, and all-out wars. In the end, all that was left were three of the larger noble families, each trying to come out on top, and many cities in ruin. The king's family, being one of the final three and ruler of Shid'el, managed to turn things around—against all odds—and put a stop to the fighting. For the first time in many years, people worked together again. Fragile peace treaties turned into more trusted arrangements, like joint marriages, and—ultimately—into the Aeterran Kingdom. But because of its history, the Aeterran people are certainly a mixed bunch. Each region has its different ways and habits."

"*How do you know all this?*"

"I have my dad, and a certain girl's rich family, to thank for that," said Raylan, not making Galirras any wiser.

"*Do many people come to Aeterra?*"

This was a new question for Raylan. One he had to give some thought before answering. "Some? Many? I don't know. There are always those that will look for good fortune somewhere else. I've run into escaped slaves from the southern cities. And you can always find those that are fleeing from whatever warlord is trying to control a piece of the southern wilderness, next. Others are perfectly content with the way they live, like the people of the Water Clans. They're nomads, fishermen, spread out over the islands in front of the southern cities on the eastern coast. But don't be fooled, not all people are friendly. I've even heard of tribes that *eat* people if they're caught trespassing—although the guy that claimed this did have half a bottle of rum in him."

"*You have seen so much of the world already,*" said Galirras; was that jealousy tingeing his voice?

"Really, I haven't. But sailors like to brag, and I know a lot of sailors. There are so many places still to see. Aeterra, the mountains, the plains and rivers, the southern cities, Tal'Kabur, the Arosh'ad Islands. I can keep going and going, and let's not forget the mysterious Tiankong Empire."

"*Xi'Lao said the Tiankong Emperor would like to meet me,*" Galirras said, with some excitement in his voice.

"Exactly. And, I think it will be good to see the lands where you came from, even if you were still an egg. Rumors say the Empire is as big as Aeterra, but the western continent is broken in two. The Tiankonese sailors call it the Broken Tooth, with the Empire laying on the northern half. But I have no idea what it all looks like. The Tiankonese actively ward travelers from their lands. They mostly trade at sea or within the archipelago of the Arosh'ad Islands."

When Raylan started serving on a merchant ship, he had been surprised not more sailors wanted to visit the Tiankonese Empire. But most merchants did not care about setting foot on the western continent, as the goods from there— like silk, spices and gems—were of the finest quality. The fear of offending and losing such a valuable trading partner was enough to hold most back from satisfying their curiosity about the mysterious mainland. That, and the fact that trespassing was said to be punishable by death.

Raylan's mood turned nostalgic as his mind soared on the fond memories of sailing the oceans: manning the sails; learning to use the wind to their advantage; balancing on—and climbing up—the ropes. He had thoroughly enjoyed the physical connection with the ship, while he absorbed the feeling of freedom and took on the challenge of mastering the winds.

Mastering the winds… He looked at Galirras. His winged friend took those words to a whole new level.

"*I think it will be amazing,*" said the dragon. "*The Empire, I mean.*"

"Me too. But first, we have to get there, which means we've got to lay low for a little while longer," said Raylan with a smile. "So, just hold on, okay? And no flying in plain sight. If we're discovered here, there'll be nowhere for us to go… at least not for the ones without wings."

"*I would never abandon you!*" said Galirras, offended.

"I never said you would." Raylan let out a laugh. "But one shouldn't forget to keep other people's limits in mind when planning ahead. We're all in this together."

As they walked the last stretch to the viewing point, Galirras let out a rumbling sigh. "*I guess you are right.*"

A short while later, they reached the lookout point. Raylan had chosen it well. There was a flat stone that always warmed up in the afternoon sun; it made for a comfortable seat. It was even possible to slide down next to it and take a quick nap. The stone's location provided views of all three pillars and most of the north to western part of the ocean. If he wanted to check the southern side of the landmass, he only had to walk three hundred feet, where he would reach a gap in the low shrubbery, allowing him to see miles down the southern coast. There were several inlets down south, some bigger than others; although it was hard to tell, as most of the inner reaches of the inlets remained out of sight behind the high cliffs and forested hills.

After checking the waters, Raylan took his place on the stone slab. "Looks like it'll be another day of waiting."

Galirras took his place next to Raylan, head resting on his own front legs. "*I heard those strange sounds, again, last night when I woke up. They seem to be coming from the south,*" he said.

"Did they wake you?" Raylan asked.

"*No… I was dreaming again.*"

"The song from before?"

"*Just bits and pieces. It always sounds like it's coming from very far away. What do you think it is? The creaking and cracking that is…*"

"I don't know. It's been almost two weeks since we've first heard it, no matter if it's day or night. It doesn't seem to be getting any closer and I don't think it's an animal. At least I hope not, because it sounds big."

They had first heard the noise, in the early morning, when arriving on the landmass. Up until that moment, the terrain must have blocked most of it; or, it was drowned out by the constantly crashing waves against the cliffs. Ca'lek had scouted south, but he did not want to get too far away from the main group. He came back empty-handed, so to speak.

"The sounds have a familiar feel to them. It's almost like the sound of a sailing mast being tested by strong winds," said Raylan.

"*Whatever it is, I do not like it much. It gives me a bad feeling when I listen to it during the night.*"

Raylan took another look across the sea.

"*I wonder if the ship will show up today,*" said Galirras.

"It would be most welcome," said Raylan. "Everyone is getting restless. Staying in one spot for so long does not sit well after constantly being on the move. But everything depends on that one pigeon. If it didn't make it, we're waiting here for nothing. Gavin said, if all went well, the ship should have gotten here days ago. But it's likely they encountered some low wind days, or perhaps got caught in a storm."

"*At least Galen has recuperated well, with all the rest. He looks more relaxed, and Richard told me he seems to be back to his old self, again.*"

"True…"

Raylan let himself sink backward onto the stone. As the sun rose to its highest point, the stone slab got pleasantly warm and he felt himself quietly doze off.

"*Raylan, wake up…*" Galirras' nose poked him, softly, in his side.

He grunted. It felt as though he had just fallen asleep.

"*Raylan, wake up. I think I see a ship.*"

He shot up and looked around. The position of the sun meant it was just past midday. "What? Where?" he said.

"*There…*" said Galirras, using his head to gesture. "*On the horizon, just left of the second pillar.*"

Raylan followed Galirras' gaze and squinted his eyes. The water reflected a lot of the sunlight, making it hard to look that far out. The dragon's eyesight being far better than that of any human; it took some time before the little dot on the horizon was big enough for Raylan to recognize it as a ship.

"You're right, and from the looks of it, it is heading this way! Go down and tell the others. It will give them time to get ready. I'll keep an eye on it and confirm it's one of ours. It should be here by the end of the afternoon, I expect. I'll be down after that."

As Galirras left, Raylan felt wide awake; anticipation coursing through his veins. If this was their ship, they could finally get out of there. No more sleeping with one eye open, no more jumping at the snap of a twig in the forest, and no more of that mysterious southern sound.

As the ship approached his lookout post, he recognized more of its shape. It appeared to be a caravel. Two large towers at the stern castle and one small one up front, near the forecastle, about eighty feet long. They were quick, light ships, able to move into the wind—if necessary—with their triangle sails. Its wide, rounded deck sat high in the water; it was obviously traveling light, for speed. The main deck was narrow but would be enough to hold a dragon.

Two small ballistae could be seen on the port and starboard sides of the ship. Another was on the bow. It looked like the ship was used either for hunting small whales, or to catch and overtake pirate ships. They could harpoon other ships and reel them in while their speed and agility helped them outmaneuver enemy vessels.

The ship was finally close enough for Raylan to spot people on deck, but just barely. It was a busy scene of people running back and forth. Strong winds blowing to the south allowed them to make excellent speed, but also required all hands on deck, especially given the treacherous waters near the cliffs.

The waters round the Drowned Man's Fork were known amongst all serious sailors. Those who tried to sail round the Dark Continent, looking for trade routes and unknown riches, knew to steer clear of the three pillars. Stories of the strong currents swirling around them, the difficult wind directions often blowing toward the deadly waters and underwater rocks much further from land than one would expect, were brought back over time only by the luckiest of men. Any good captain would do well to heed their warning. It seemed this captain was fully aware of the dangers, as they veered off south, well in advance of perilous waters.

The caravel's shallow depth allowed it to move more easily through the maze of hidden rocks. Raylan saw it turn toward the coast and then further south again, as it finally showed the colors it was sailing under. Raylan's heart jumped with joy as he recognized the four familiar symbols on the banner of the Aeterran Kingdom high up in the mast. Three represented the royal families, who together had formed Aeterra more than a hundred years ago.

The bow, for the northern royal family of Dahalaes, who were considered to excel in the art of archery. The sickled moon, which represented the western royal family of Shid'el, who had ruled the region of the Crescent Moon Massif with its endless farmlands. And the ship, for the eastern royal family of Thyraulos, whom had ruled the harbor area of Azurna, their destination, and home to the best sailors in the world. The fourth symbol was a crown, to represent the current ruling king.

The royal symbols were divided by a cross made up from three swords pointing toward the middle, with a fourth sword pointing upward, representing the support of the families for the unified kingdom.

Raylan knew enough. Abandoning his post, he ran back toward the rock wall. He descended as fast as he dared, forcing himself to slow after almost losing his grip on the steep wall.

He jumped the last few feet and found the camp already buzzing with activity.

Gavin came running up to him. "Please, tell me it's good news."

"Aeterran banner… south side," Raylan panted, while nodding. "They should be coming into view by the time we get to the south cliffs."

Gavin turned to the group. "Peadar, pack those herbs… the rest of you, finish up packing. We're going home. South cliffs, it is," he called out. "Let's make sure they don't have to be anchored for long, especially with the enemies still looking for us."

"Where's Galirras?" Raylan asked, as he looked around.

"*I am here,*" said the dragon, in his mind, as he came in low over the trees. He retracted his wings during his approach, moving between a few of the trees and touched down, skidding to a halt. In his jaws, he had the bloody remains of a sea lion.

Gavin turned back at the same time, not knowing Galirras had already replied. "He went to get a final meal. We don't know what the supplies will be

250

on the ship and if they have calculated enough for a hungry, growing dragon," he said. "Galirras, I suggest you eat your fill and give any leftovers to Kevhin, to cut up and pack for us. We'll be leaving soon."

Corza sat, staring at the map in front of him. Outside, the yard was a constant sound of hammering, sawing and shouting.

"Tell me, captain. How is it possible that you've lost track of them once again?"

The man, standing at attention, seemed to know better than to answer; no answer would be satisfactory for the mood the High General was in.

Corza had been planning ways to cast his net across the land to entrap the enemy squad and reacquire his dragon. It would probably be a little bit harder to train now it was hatched; but he was sure he could manage.

But to catch it, you had to find it. His men had spent weeks searching the surroundings of the lake, but it seemed to him, the group had already moved on.

"The key," he said to the captain, "is figuring out what they aim to do. Why travel south? Do they know about the southern mines? About the deep forest farmlands? Or are they acquiring information on the gathering of our forces?"

"Perhaps they plan to fly that dragon back home," joked the captain, in a clear momentary lapse of sanity.

"You find this funny? You've been outwitted by these people. You think it's a joke that they can roam around freely with this much at stake?"

"No, sir… my apologies, sir," said the man. "Perhaps they have a boat hidden somewhere?"

Corza pointed on the map to west of the lake. "I want this entire northern coastline checked by you, personally. They might have doubled back. It wouldn't be the first time. Send out birds to these five forest fortresses. I want people there on this by the end of today. Meet up with each of them and keep me informed."

Corza looked at the map again. "…and send out a ship, north of the trident. I need to know if they have a ship waiting, somewhere."

The captain made a hasty retreat, and the door had barely closed when there was a knock on it.

"You wished to see me, High General Setra?"

"Ah, Colonel Mercar, come on in. How are preparations going?"

"All on schedule, sir. Our ships are being prepped for departure and should be ready to go within two days."

"Good, good. How many ships are currently finished?"

"Eighty-three ships are seaworthy and stocked for the voyage. Another twenty windships are also nearly complete. A few still need to receive their coat of paint, but all the sails have been made dark. None of them will be easily spotted at night if we run without lights. Work will continue, after we leave, on the second wave of ships, of course."

Corza looked over the documents which lay before him. "Excellent. High General Cale and High General Nodak will be leading the other flotillas. Adding to their numbers, we'll have a total of three hundred and fourteen ships departing, accompanied with seventy windships. Each ship will be able to land three platoons of foot men, plus they'll have fifteen ghol'ms in the hold. The windships hold a smaller crew of half a platoon and ten ghol'ms—two in use. That makes roughly forty thousand men and six thousand ghol'ms. That will be sufficient for our first phase. The second run will might not even be needed."

"Yes sir, it seems preparations are going well."

While this was good news, Corza scoffed at this inside. It meant he had little time left, or he would be forced to choose between leading the flotilla and staying behind to figure out what happened to the dragon. "Yes, the Stone King will be pleased to see his plans are right on schedule," he added, coldly.

"Speaking of which, sir… if I may be so frank, I was wondering if Lord Rictor will join us here before we depart?"

"Don't be stupid. The man has other things to do. I'm sure he'll join our ranks when he finds it appropriate," replied Corza. *And the longer he stays away the better.*

There was another knock on the door.

"Go away, we're busy!" Corza yelled, annoyed.

"I'm sorry, sir, but it's urgent," a soldier spoke through the door.

Corza let out a sigh. "Fine, come in."

The soldier quickly opened the door and entered the room.

"What is it?" growled Corza.

"A ship, sir. It approaches… moving south just under the trident's cape. It's not one of ours, sir."

"Are you certain?"

"Positive. All our ships are accounted for. It's also a lighter design than our own. What are your orders?"

Corza looked at the map again. "That's it… the ship is here for them. That's why they've been moving south…"

"Sorry… sir?" said the soldier.

"Colonel Mercar, take the *Firestorm* and get rid of it. No survivors."

The colonel slammed his fist against his chest and hurried outside to prepare for departure.

"You. Go find Captain Sellock. Tell him to send another batch of men down south along the coast. I want to make sure our wandering friends have no place to rest or hide."

Raylan and the others sat below the tree line, following the ship. Galirras pushed himself flat to the ground to stay out of sight as much as possible. One could not just fly a dragon onto the ship. That would be madness. The crew would either fight or flee at first sight of him. They would have to first explain the situation and prepare the captain.

"Is the fire almost ready?" asked Gavin.

"Almost," replied Peadar.

"All right they're about to lay anchor," said Ca'lek.

Raylan peered down over the cliffs edge. "Are you certain about this Gavin?" he said.

"It's either that or track for half a day to find lower ground."

Raylan threw his brother a look.

"It'll be fine. The cliffs are not that high on this side anymore, and the waves run parallel to them, which means there's little chance to be pushed back against the rocks. Besides, you said it yourself, the water looks deep enough and all of us can swim sufficiently."

Raylan looked down again and frowned.

"So, as soon as the rowboat is in range, I'll jump down and meet with the captain," continued Gavin. "He should know me. Once I give the signal, the next four will jump and meet up with the boat. A second trip will pick up the rest and that will give me time to prepare the crew for Galirras' arrival with our packs. He can just fly over. It's the quickest way I can come up with to get out of here."

He looked around to see if anyone had any final objections.

"All right, Peadar... start the fir—"

"Wait! What's that?" Ca'lek called out, as soft as possible.

"What? What do you see?" came the whispers, from multiple people, at the same time.

"There, the second inlet, just behind the tree cover."

Raylan peered toward the trees Ca'lek pointed out. He did not see anything.

"There!" said Ca'lek.

Now, Raylan saw it too. Something slid by, just behind the treetops. He could not believe his eyes as he saw the shape slowly emerge from behind the trees.

"Is that a… ship?" he stammered. "How can it be flying like that?"

CHAPTER EIGHTEEN

Plan

"I DID NOT know ships could fly," remarked Galirras.

"They can't. They shouldn't…" said Raylan.

The ship rose above the trees, turning toward them. It seemed quite a bit longer in size than the caravel. There were small sails to the side of it and one triangle sail at the bow, but few were in use. The main sail had been replaced by a giant bag filled with air, it seemed. It was held in place by netting across the entire length of the ship. It looked like a much bigger version of the market tricks Raylan had seen as a kid. A sack or bladder would be filled with hot air and allowed to freely float off into the sky, where it would come crashing down once the air inside escaped. The curious figure showing his tricks had called them *balloons*. This flying ship seemed to have a very large version of such a balloon. To the side of the massive balloon, cloths waved in the wind. The balloon, being point-shaped, stretched out at the bow and stern, for quite a few feet.

The woodwork was elegant but simplistic. Raylan's experienced eye saw the boat was designed for practical use. No luxury, but the workmanship had been done by skilled hands. The wood had been darkened, being somewhere between deep brown and black. Even the sails were not your normal white, but a gray-black. The bottom of the ship was equal to any seafaring vessel; it even had a rudder, but at the back were two strange wheels, or rather, flattened blades positioned in a circle. They were turning at a very high speed.

"*Those blades push a lot of air,*" said Galirras, "*I can see the spiral of air moving behind it.*"

In a short time, the flying ship was right upon the caravel. They saw the crew on deck, looking at the spectacle, some ran around, the captain shouted orders. Four men took place at the ballistae, two on each. Crossbows were handed out amongst the crew. After all, they were near enemy territory and one could not take any chances.

They now saw people moving on the deck of the flying ship as well. They seemed to ignore the shouting from the caravel crew below and worked their assigned tasks.

As the flying ship approached the anchored caravel from above, Raylan saw multiple hatches open on the side. Small plank gutters were positioned out of the hatches.

Just before the flying ship turned to port, the captain of the caravel gave an order to send a warning salvo. The crew of the caravel released their shots, while large, round-shaped packs were slid out of the hatches. Each the size of a small barrel, they fell toward the caravel below.

The arrows from the Aeterran crew flew upward. A few hit the bottom of the flying ship, others went up toward the balloon. But before they hit, the arrows got tangled up in the waving cloths that were loosely stretched on the sides. Clearly, they were designed and placed for precisely the deterrence of such an onslaught. The caravel's ballistae had been designed to shoot horizontally, so the larger harpoons, which might have pierced the cloths and balloon, were not able to fire high enough to even try.

At the same time, the sacks hit the anchored ship or water close to it. On impact, they split apart, breaking the leathery skin, spraying an oily substance everywhere. The sails turned dark, while the deck instantly became a slippery surface to move on. Oil streaks floated on the water as more sacks rained down. The flying ship dropped a dozen sacks on its run—in one fluent motion.

As the ship in the air turned away from the sea-bound vessel, a final hatch opened on the stern of the flying boat. Raylan recognized the familiar orange color of fire as a large barrel was shoved out of it. It lazily tumbled downward, before hitting the deck.

The caravel crew was in disarray and could not react fast enough to avoid the falling barrel. A massive fireball consumed the entire ship, as it hit and shattered.

The sails burned away instantly, while people were thrown backward by the force of the explosion. Sailors that had been covered in the oil immediately caught fire and several of the crew were blown overboard into the water. It might have brought relief to hit the water, had the entire surrounding sea not also become one great inferno.

Raylan heard the screams of the burning men. The initial explosion had been so bright, they had to divert their eyes, except for Galirras, who had instinctively closed one set of his eyelids and witnessed the entire thing. But he seemed to refrain from commenting on the dreadful image of sailors literally being ripped apart by the force of the fireball.

It was all over in a heartbeat. All of them were holding their breaths as their only chance of escape went up in flames.

"We have to help them," said Galirras, as he readied himself to take off.

"No, wait!" shouted Raylan. "It's too late…"

"But I can still see some of them moving," Galirras pleaded.

"No, Raylan's right. They won't survive those burns, even if we are able to pull some of them out of the sea. And… we can't be discovered," added Gavin. "I'm sorry."

Raylan clenched his fists.

As they watched, they saw the flying ship turn around once more, to do another pass. Another two sacks were dumped overboard toward the burning ship, creating smaller fireballs, ripping the caravel apart. Over the rail, and from the hatches, a number of men leaned out with crossbows and spears, picking off anyone that still moved on the ship or in the water.

It was clear they meant to leave no one alive.

"We need to get out of here," said Xi'Lao, who had quietly moved over to them. "There is nothing we can do here, and we *must* stay out of sight."

As they retreated under the cover of the trees to where they had left the horses, they saw the flying ship turn back in the direction it had come from. Before long, it disappeared into the inlet further south, as if it had never been. The remains of the burning caravel sank shortly after, leaving only debris and corpses.

That night, it was quiet around a small campfire. It had begun raining again, dampening an already dark mood. They had just seen their hope of returning to Aeterra sink to the bottom of the sea. The idea of going back north and finding their way home over land, looked unpleasantly long. It would mean moving back through dangerous territory… territory Gavin was sure the enemy would be watching like a hawk.

"What now?" asked Raylan.

"I don't know," said Gavin.

"Do we go back north? Continue south? Perhaps send out Galirras?"

"I don't know," Gavin repeated.

"What do you mean, you don't know? You're supposed to know! We need to come up with something… we can't stay here, Gavin. We need to keep moving before they come looking for us."

"Don't you think I know that? It's my job to get you all back to safety. I just don't know how," Gavin yelled, pinching the bridge of his nose as he tried to think.

Xi'Lao laid a hand on his shoulder. "It's okay, we're still here. There's still time."

"Look, I'm sorry. There are too many uncertainties right now. I need to think on this. I'll make a decision in the morning."

And with that, Gavin headed for some sleep. It did not take long until the rest, including Raylan, silently followed his example, while Richard took first watch.

Raylan's wake-up call came much too fast when Richard's hand startled him awake. After a moment of disorientation, Raylan got up with a groan to start the midnight watch, together with Galirras.

"*What do you suppose we will do?*" asked Galirras quietly when they sat alone in that late hour of the night.

"Good question. I really don't know, yet. I've always kind of expected Gavin to come up with the plans," he admitted with a sense of shame.

They silently watched the surroundings again until they heard the now familiar cracking sound reach their ears again. It was muffled by the rain, but it was unmistakably the same sound they had heard every day on the landmass. It still sounded far away.

"Galirras?" said Raylan, after he pondered for a while.

"*Yes?*"

"How high would you be able to fly in this weather?"

"*It looks like rough weather. There is a storm is coming. The wind is twisting all around, up there. It is quite beautiful to look at. I am sure I can manage, though,*" responded the dragon. "*Why? Did you have something in mind?*"

"Would you be able to go high enough for people not to notice you?"

"*That should not be too difficult on this dark night. It will be hard for anyone to look up with this falling rain, while I can see everything downward with ease.*"

Raylan fell quiet and thought, long and hard.

Galirras observed him with a curious glint in his eye. Perhaps the dragon felt Raylan's thoughts come together to form a plan. It was clear he did not want to interrupt the process, or push Raylan in any direction. His patience was rewarded, when Raylan looked at him, reaching a conclusion.

"All right, I don't like to put you at risk, but I think you can help us make more sense of the situation…"

"*You want me to scout down south and check where that flying ship came from, right?*"

"Yes, we need to know what we're up against. Fly down there, high enough to be safe, but low enough so you can clearly see things. I want you to see if there are more of those ships. Also, where and how they are docked.

The sound we kept hearing might be tied into things, so check if you can find an explanation for that. We need an estimation of the number of soldiers down south. Is it just one ship or a small harbor? As soon as you've seen enough, come back right away. Use the dark of the night and the rain for your cover and report back as soon as you can. And under no circumstances should you land, until you are back here. If you leave now, you'll have most of the night still available and you'll could be back before Gavin wakes up... I don't know if he, or Xi'Lao, would agree to this."

"*I will be fine. They should not worry, nor should you.*"

"That, my friend, I can't help. Just get back as soon as you can."

With that, Galirras walked out from under the tree, where they had been sitting, and launched himself into the air. Quickly ascending into the night, Raylan saw Galirras was right. It was hard to track the dark shape of the dragon against the raindrops. Within moments, Raylan lost track of him, as the dragon made his way south.

"*I will be back before you know it.*"

After that, he felt the dragon slip from his mind.

As the night carried on, doubt began to nag at Raylan. Galirras had much improved with his flying, but perhaps he should not have put him in danger like that. The wind was picking up more, thunder rumbled in the distance and lightning streaked the sky. But Raylan did not see an easier or safer way to get the information they needed. Traveling that distance by ground would be much too dangerous and would take far too long.

The approach of squishy footsteps on a soaked forest ground announced the next person on watch.

"Time to get some more sleep, kid," said Harwin.

Raylan looked up. "If it's alright with you, I'll stay a bit longer. I'm not sleepy, yet."

"Where's Galirras?" asked Harwin.

"Close, he wanted to do some night hunting."

It was not entirely the truth, but Raylan did not want to inform the others of the risk they were taking, until he knew it was worth it.

"Not afraid he'll get into trouble?"

"Always, but he's likely the biggest predator in these woods, by now. As long as he doesn't bite off more than he can chew, he should be fine. I'll wake you when he's back and we can switch."

"Sure thing. If I learned anything on the battlefield, it's that you should get your sleep when you can, and this body can do with some more."

Raylan returned to his thoughts as Harwin returned to his sleeping mat. The rain was easing. He hoped Galirras would be back soon.

Time is relative as it flows and winds through the day. Spent together, a day can go by in an instant; but waiting for something or someone, even for just a short time, can feel like an eternity. Raylan noticed himself tracing the scar on his right arm. It felt... restless. It did not exactly ache, or burn, but he noticed a certain feeling flow through it that he could not completely put his finger on. His other hand ran along the skin, following the scar as one would trace a river on a map with a fingertip. After a while, he attributed the strange sense to the ongoing storm. His scar had always acted up when a storm came. It was like his skin remembered the night he had received it; but he was not entirely sure... the feeling tonight was slightly different, almost as if it was outside of the skin...

Raylan had no idea how long he spent in his thoughts, but the moon was on its descent when he finally felt Galirras' presence enter his mind again. It had stopped raining a while ago and the cloud cover had started to break up, improving visibility. It would make it more dangerous for Galirras to fly around unnoticed.

"*I am back.*"

"*Where are you? I can't see you yet,*" replied Raylan, in his head.

"*I am coming in on foot. I know you told me not to land until I got back, but the night became too bright, so I decided to walk the final part in case anyone was following my place of descent. There is also a small group of soldiers a few miles east of us. Seems like a small scouting party.*"

Raylan heard movement coming from his right, and Galirras soon came into view. The dragon had this relaxed way of walking, while still showing his alertness as a predator. It was clear he did not want to be surprised, by anything. The dragon looked properly wet and dirty from the walk through the forest, but it did not seem to bother him at all. Raylan found himself, once again, taking in the sight of this majestic beast. The muscles across his neck, going down his shoulders and back, bulged and gleamed in the shadows of the night. His scales took on a dark greenish brown in this light, while his eyes shone like fireflies.

"Any chance they saw you?"

"*Unlikely. Most of them were asleep, and I was up high; but it was the reason I came through the woods, after landing in the opposite direction of our camp and circling around them.*"

Raylan nodded. "That... was very clever of you." Raylan smiled. "Okay, so tell me, what did you find?"

Galirras' eyes twirled, in excitement. "*Something is definitely going on. As I followed the coast south, I came upon the inlet where the flying ship disappeared. The first thing I noticed was the trees... they had all disappeared. The hills had gone barren, almost no trees left standing. You probably could not see it from the ground, but a large part of the forest has been taken down. It was so sad. I was wondering what destructive force could do such a thing to a beautiful forest, when I noticed men taking down the trees. Even in this storm, they were still at it. I saw a large tree go down as the cracking of wood could be heard. That's the sound we have been hearing, all this time.*"

"They're chopping down the trees? What for?"

"*I did not know at first, but I figured it had to be important to them, if they would continue even in this weather. As I saw a tree go down, one of the men did not see the tree falling his way until it was too late. I do not think he made it,*" said Galirras, somewhat perplexed.

"*The other men were shouting warnings, but they were drowned out by the wind and the rolling thunder. The storm created rivers of rainwater, flowing down the land. Mudslides were tearing away at the earth, sweeping away sand as it was not held together by the tree roots, anymore. I saw a group of men, knocked down by the water, disappear below the surface. They did not come up again, either. It was very strange, because it seemed they were tied together with chains around the neck. It looked very impractical to me, to work like that.*"

Raylan shook his head. "Those were slaves. They're forced to work under such dangerous circumstances, not by choice. They probably wouldn't waste the lives of their soldiers on work like this."

"*Oh, you mean Sebastian had to do stuff like that?*"

"Maybe, but I think he was mostly carving out rocks in the mines."

"*Well, I did not see any mines, but I saw piles of small rock later, so maybe they have even more slaves nearby. I did not see any other groups like that though. I followed the trail of destruction, and after two hills, the entire bay came into view. It was amazing! It was filled with ships, at least a hundred...*"

"A hundred?" whispered Raylan, in surprise, "Could you see a lot of people there?"

"*The ships seemed quiet enough, just a few men on deck, for guard duty. However, on land, it was very busy with people walking everywhere. There were structures, buildings—big and small—and a lot of tents. Raylan, there were so many lights! Three hillsides were completely covered in tents, on the east side. People were moving around, even at that time of night... and more were arriving. A long trail of lights poured in from the east. A constant stream of soldiers, and other people, all on their way toward that bay. They were too many to count, going all the way out into the hills."*

Raylan tried to form a mental picture in his mind.

"More than that," said Galirras, who picked up the image.

"More?"

"At least four times more…"

"But that would mean thousands and thousands of soldiers. How can we fight against something like that?"

"They were building more ships, too. They were using the trees to construct more."

"What about the flying ship? Did you spot that?"

"I did. It was anchored in the bay with a dozen or so similar ships. I easily recognized them, because of the balloon and the strange sail placement. They were apart from the normal ships. There were several on the shore still, too. Those piles with rocks I saw were being loaded into the airships."

"Airship?" asked Raylan, his head spinning from all the information.

"The flying ship… a ship in the air. Airship seemed like an appropriate name for it."

Galirras looked at him for a reaction. He even saw a playful swirl of Galirras' three pupils in the dragon's eye.

"Airship… definitely shorter than flying ship. Short and simple, I like it," said Raylan. "But why load up rocks on ships that need to fly? Won't it make them extra heavy?"

"I do not know. I am just telling you what I saw. There were a few smaller airships, too, but they were off to the side of the docks."

Raylan went over the presented information, in his head, for a while. "Okay, I think it's time to wake the others," said Raylan. "Gavin needs to hear this."

"You did what?" exclaimed Gavin.

Raylan looked at his brother, to see if he was serious. It was not the reaction he had expected.

"…I sent Galirras to gather information."

"And you didn't bother to check any of this with me first? I'm your commander for God's sake. I can't have the members of my squad just go out on their own and do whatever they like. Did you even think about how it would look if my own brother does not bother to respect the chain of command? Especially when it possibly involves a mission-endangering decision!"

Gavin let out a cry of frustration.

"Oh, come one Gavin. You know you've got our squad's respect. We've been too far from home for too long to not surpass the strict hierarchy. You're our leader and we listen to you. I just thought it would be good for us to have more information on the situation. We need to know what we're up against."

Gavin was about to go on a rant, when Xi'Lao put a hand on his shoulder and leaned over to him. "Don't let the annoyance of your little brother not listening to you cloud your judgment on the fact that he made the right choice," she whispered softly in his ear.

His brother let out a sigh; his anger seeped away. "What if he'd been seen or followed?"

"I was not, I made sure of that," said Galirras, with confidence. "And, I believe Raylan made the right call to send me. It was the fastest and least dangerous option for gathering information, else I would not have easily agreed to it."

The last of his brother's resistance broke as he finally gave in. "Fine. Let's gather everyone around and hear what you've discovered."

Gavin and the others listened to the information Galirras provided. His brother had to admit, they had not been able to get this kind of information, in such a short time, in any other way.

"We'll never be able to fight that many soldiers," said young Peadar. He was normally the optimistic one, but it was clear on the lad's face that these numbers even made him wonder if they would ever get home alive.

"It's a lot of soldiers," said Raylan, "and I've been trying to figure out why there are so many here. It can't all be for us, can it? Or for Galirras? They've only found out about him a few weeks back. There wouldn't have been enough time to get that many soldiers together. This must have been going on for months already, perhaps years. Something else is going on—something big. The ships. The men. It's like—almost like—"

"—an invasion force," said Gavin.

"As if getting out of here and saving our own lives was not enough," said Harwin. "We now have to worry about a bloody invasion?"

"If that's so, we need to warn the king," Richard put forward.

"But we've got none of our birds left. How do we get such a message back?" said Peadar.

"It will have to come from us. We need to get back home as soon as possible," answered Gavin.

"With the number of soldiers Galirras saw and the provisions being collected and loaded up, it won't be long before they leave," said Xi'Lao. "Staying here only means using up those provisions while waiting. A large force like that needs a constant supply of food, either by food coming to them or them going to the food. They can't stay in one place. It will be hard to stop them once they start moving."

"We need to steal one of the ships," said Raylan.

All of them looked at him in wide-eyed disbelief.

"Steal one of the ships?" said Kevhin. "Were you even listening? What about the thousands of soldiers between you and those ships?"

"He's right, Raylan. We can't just walk in and take one," said Gavin.

"Can't we?" wondered Raylan. "Galirras mentioned there's a small scouting party nearby. I think we could surprise them and use their armor to disguise ourselves. Seb knows the local language well enough for a small number of us to sneak into the enemy camp. With the amount of soldiers pouring in, it shouldn't be too difficult to join the new arrivals. Together we could scout the boats that are anchored in the bay and see which one is right to take."

"How would we get the it out of there?" said Sebastian. "A few of us will not be enough to sail away, even if we were to pick up the others, somewhere close by, along the way."

"Galirras will create a distraction," said Raylan.

"I can fly to the far side of the harbor. I will break something, or at least get myself noticed, and quickly retreat south. It should create enough of a panic. I am sure, if Corza is present, he will jump at the opportunity to get another shot at us. Maybe even send out a force after me," added Galirras.

"After that, he'll circle back and join us on the ship as we depart," continued Raylan. "As the soldiers focus on Galirras, the rest of us will sneak in on the north side of the harbor. We can meet up at the water, take a small dinghy to get on board the ship, and then set sail, right away."

Gavin looked at his little brother. "No, it's much too risky. If anything goes wrong, the enemy force will be able to overwhelm us in a matter of moments. Besides, what about the flying ship… or airship, whatever you call them?"

"You're one to talk about risk. You wanted us to simply jump from a fifty-foot cliff," pressed Raylan.

"That was a calculated risk, you know that. There was simply no other easy way to get down to the caravel," answered his brother.

"Well, I don't see any other way this time, either," said Raylan. "We've got to get back to Aeterra and warn them. We need transportation, which is only available in the hands of the enemy. Land travel would take too long to warn the kingdom, and there's no way Galirras can cross the ocean to relay a message. Not to mention the fact people would probably attack him, or run away screaming, before he could say anything."

"What about patrols?"

Raylan looked at Galirras for the answer.

"There are no walls or gates," said the dragon. "I saw very few guards around. It should not be too difficult to sneak past any patrols, especially if I can create some turmoil on the south end."

"You still haven't mentioned the airships. What about them?" Gavin said to Raylan.

"I might be able to rip the balloon, if any come after us," suggested Galirras. "Without the balloon, it would just be another sailing ship, right?"

"Not good enough," said Gavin, shaking his head. "There are too many uncertainties. Not to mention that a large part of your plan depends on the one thing we're here to protect and return safely to the Emperor of the Tiankong Empire."

"Galirras can take care of himself. He can easily outfly any horse or man, and if he approaches the airship from above, they shouldn't even see him until it's too late. I really don't see any other way to get back home fast enough to beat them there, other than to cross the ocean."

"Are you certain they will go straight to Aeterra?" asked Xi'Lao. "They might have a very different direction in mind."

Gavin gave a small smile. "True, but like you said yourself, such a large force needs to keep moving for provisions not to run out. For the same reason, they wouldn't be able to stay at sea for long periods of time. They would need to go ashore and restock provisions, at least. The mid-continent is the closest landmass to do so. They might not show up at our shores right away, but it's more than likely they'll land on our side of the ocean."

"And if they would go south around the mid-continent to the Empire, for example, they would possibly be stuck fighting on two fronts against both our armies. That seems like an unlikely choice," remarked Richard.

"That's *if* the king would send out soldiers to assist the empire," said Harwin, skeptically.

"Still, could we take that chance? Take the long way around? I don't think so," Ca'lek put in.

"I agree. So, are we going to do this or not?" asked Raylan. "If we want to catch the scouting party for their armor, we'd better get moving."

Raylan watched as Gavin looked around at each of the members in turn. He knew what his brother was seeing, was thinking—all of them had eager looks on their faces. These men did not do well without a purpose. They needed a goal, a task to focus on. The wish to return home was driving their will to forget the high risk involved. It was a dangerous mindset to be in for a soldier, to lose sight of the dangers involved. But it would be more dangerous to wander around aimlessly, waiting for the enemy to find them again. His brother had been unable to come up with any alternative course of action since their rescue pickup was lost, and not doing anything was just not an option.

"...fine," Gavin said, reluctantly. "Everyone, gear up and get ready to leave. It's time for us to get a new set of clothes."

As the group stirred into motion, Raylan saw Xi'Lao put her arms around Gavin's lower back and pull him close. They had become more open, showing their affection in front of the group, which was somehow comforting to see. They were now more than just a group, they were family.

As he walked away, Raylan heard his brother's whisper. "I've got a bad feeling about this."

The remark stung, driving Raylan to prove Gavin wrong. He quickly gathered his stuff and joined his older brother as he loaded up his horse.

"Gavin, I'm sure we'll manage," said Raylan.

Gavin shook his head as he pulled a saddle strap tight. "I don't think you fully grasp the situation, yet."

"I do. Actually, I think for the first time in my life, I finally understand your need to protect. To shield those you love... people... friends from danger. To keep them safe at all costs," said Raylan, "but to do that, you sometimes have to put yourself in harm's way."

Gavin looked at his little brother, in silence, but Raylan noticed his brother's expression change. It was only the slightest of movements from the muscles in Gavin's face as his brother looked him in the eye. At that moment, Raylan was certain his brother saw him in a different light.

Gavin turned to finish up packing the horse. He glanced over his shoulder, before he spoke. "It seems you have indeed grown up... a little. Still, it doesn't change the feeling I have about all this. Just promise me you'll keep on your toes the whole time."

"Don't worry, I will."

CHAPTER NINETEEN

Infiltration

RAYLAN WATCHED the mass of soldiers slush by in the direction of the bay. The road was packed with them. Many had large tattoos on their arms and faces, while every single one of them had at least three different weapons. Axes, swords, spears and morning stars, but also smaller knives, daggers and more exotic-looking weapons. Raylan had just spotted one man with some sort of claw tied to his arm in the shape of three large, spiky blades extending from the back of the soldier's hand. It reminded him of Galirras' claws.

The soldiers looked sweaty, dirty and intimidating. It was not so much a march, more a constant flooding of soldiers in the direction of the harbor. Fights occasionally broke out, quickly creating circles as they shouted and yelled encouragement to the fighters in the ring. This, in turn, would block the flow of soldiers, resulting in more conflicts and pushing. Eventually, one of the more highly-ranked soldiers, often on horseback, broke it all up and got everyone moving again.

Raylan glanced sideways at Sebastian. Acquiring the enemy's armor had posed little difficulty. They had located the scouting party late in the morning. And with the element of surprise—and Galirras' help—they quickly overpowered the small group. Raylan had tried to come up with a way to spare the soldier's lives, but he was overruled by Gavin, who did not want to take any more unnecessary risks. The attack was swift and clean. They ended up with eight full sets of armor, more than enough for the small reconnaissance team Raylan and Sebastian formed. The others would use the armor for their own disguise on their approach from the northern cliffs.

If not for the stench of blood and the fact that it was taken from a dead person, the armor itself was quite comfortable. Still, Raylan had felt an intense resentment when he put it on. It was simple enough armor, covering most of his chest; but expertly made, no sharp edges on the inner metal. Black in color, with patches of leather here and there, the shoulders had less mobility than his own armor. The multiple plates of metal bent over each other, again finished to a polished deep black. Raylan wore an open steel helmet, while Sebastian had one with flaps on the side, to cover the slave mark on his cheek. The boots were a bit of a loose fit, but had sturdy, metal protectors on the shins. Flexible leather pants, with heavy leather patches on the front of the upper legs, completed the armor. It was clear the enemy had put their faith in protection over speed.

Along the road, soldiers constantly moved in and out of the main column. Finding some drinking water, taking a piss, or perhaps, going for a quick hunt, for whatever the reason, they should have no trouble joining the river of soldiers moving west. Still, Raylan saw Sebastian held the same doubts about putting themselves in the middle of the enemy's forces. The plan to infiltrate the harbor, to scout the surroundings, and to find a suitable ship had sounded simple enough, but the implementation took more courage than Raylan expected.

He looked at Sebastian, took a large breath, gave a short nod and began to move. Without looking back, he heard Sebastian follow him down the hill and exit the forest. Making a short hop onto the dirt road, he found an open spot in the constantly moving hoard and adjusted his walking speed to match the soldiers around him.

As he carefully glanced around, none of the surrounding soldiers paid him any attention. His hair was darker than many of those around him but was not uncommon; and although he and Sebastian did not have any tattoos, not all soldiers showed the patterns on their body.

He checked his right and saw Sebastian maneuver closer to him, both were carefully making sure not to lose track of each other.

On their approach that morning, they had tried to choose a spot close to the harbor to join the constantly moving stream of soldiers but ended up hiking around an entire area where they were cutting down trees. Seeing the felling of trees for himself and remembering what Galirras had told him, Raylan thought it likely most of it was used for ship construction. Guards in similar armor had been moving between the slaves, but he did not want to risk looking suspicious.

Because of the detour, he and Sebastian spent half the afternoon walking amongst their enemies, before—finally—the first harbor buildings manifested from between the hills.

By the time they entered the seaside settlement, the sun had begun to set, which suited Raylan just fine. Easier to stay hidden if needed. He observed a few soldiers move away from the main column to drop off bundles of provisions, swords, straw mats and the like. Other soldiers would grab the gear before setting of in the direction of the bay. As the land descended toward the water, he saw ships floating in the bay, from between the different structures. Most of the buildings looked to be quickly-constructed warehouses, meant more for basic protection against the elements than providing any kind of luxury.

Raylan tapped Sebastian on his arm and pointed to some men moving the provisions. They both headed over and each took a load on the shoulder after which they moved in the general direction of the bay.

Galirras had been right. The harbor buzzed with activity. Soldiers were everywhere. Large trees were being dragged to the edge of the settlement where carpenters set to work creating everything from planks to large masts for the ships. A constant mix of hammering and sawing resonated throughout the bay. Further along, livestock were herded by butchers, if the cleavers on their belts were anything to go by. All the activity had the harbor almost resemble a small town.

It surprised Raylan a little that he really saw no everyday civilians. No farmers, hunters nor shop owners. There were the butchers, but they seemed to be soldiers who had taken on the tasks. Normally, such a large force would draw in all kinds of people looking for the opportunity to make a little bit of extra money. But not here.

The only women Raylan saw were transported in a caged wagon, all of them with iron rings around their necks, connecting them to the bars of the cage. He noticed other slaves pushing carts holding barrels and boxes, most of their neck rings were chained together. Several of them carried large pieces of wood toward the water. The slaves were skinny; their hair filthy and full of knots. Their skin was darkened with smears of dirt and sweat from the forced labor. None of them dared to look up, or talk, fearing the whip that already cracked often enough without provocation.

Moving between two buildings, they heard a woman scream behind a door; the laughter of men accompanying it. Rage boiled within Raylan. He threw down his pack and stormed toward the door when Sebastian grabbed his shoulder and softly shook his head. Swallowing hard, he hesitated, before picking up his pack again, cursing and defeated. Sick to his very core.

As they moved off, he noticed a soldier studying them, following their movements. The man had been talking to some of the butchers, who now continued on their way. But this single soldier lingered behind and still watched them with great interest.

Has he seen me go for the door? Seen Sebastian stop me?

He followed Sebastian when he noticed the soldier start after them. Increasing his pace, he pushed Sebastian into a small passageway.

"Move, someone took notice of us," he whispered.

They ducked along the side of the structure, and Raylan thanked his luck when the door he tried swung open. They quickly moved inside, closing it behind them, hopefully unseen.

Raylan rested his back against the door, listening intently for footsteps. Nothing. He heard Sebastian slump to the floor. Both had been marching nonstop since they joined the soldiers; but only now they had arrived, did Raylan feel how tired his legs were.

No torches lit the space, and there were few windows to let in the moonlight. Raylan heard Sebastian breathe out deeply in the dark, the sound of his breath wavering slightly as if taking a moment's rest allowed his friend's nerves to unwind.

"Can you see anything?" Raylan whispered.

"Not yet, just waiting for my eyes to adjust."

While he could barely see himself, Raylan felt the size of the room was very large. Perhaps, it was the way the sound carried, or maybe he subconsciously took note of it when they entered; but it felt like a massive hall with a high roof. He tried to remember how high the roof was when he had looked at the outside of the building, but his attention had been on the woman's screams.

He dropped his pack to the floor, pushed off the door and took a few steps forward.

"Where are you going?" asked Sebastian.

"Just trying to figure out what's in here. That guard might still be outside. We might need to find a different way out."

Inching along, Raylan slid his feet forward, stretching out his hands, trying to prevent himself from walking into anything or knocking something over. He jumped at the touch of something hard and cold in front of him. As it remained immobile after his touch, he carefully ran his hand across the surface. It felt cold and rough. His hands followed the form, slowly developing a picture in his mind of the thing in front of him.

Chest... arms... head and big, taller than me...

The image became painfully clear in his mind, feeding the knot in his stomach as he recognized more and more of the shape. He rested his forehead against the chest of the statue, cursing it silently. With a disappointing groan, he bumped his forehead against the stone chest multiple times.

A ghol'm… a damn ghol'm. Why am I even surprised to see it… of course they would have a ghol'm here.

He heard Sebastian shuffle closer, attracted by the sound, no doubt.

"What is it?" he asked.

"A ghol'm…"

As he stepped back from the roughly carved ghol'm, Raylan noticed his eyes had finally adjusted to the low light. Outside the clouds parted, allowing moonlight to filter into the building. With the darkness slightly lifted, the size of the hall became fully clear. The sight of it took both their breaths away.

"Oh crap, that's not good," said Sebastian.

"How many are there?"

The hall was indeed large—one big space.

"It must be at least three hundred feet long," said Sebastian.

As the moonlight illuminated the dark stone of the ghol'ms, they saw some parts sparkle from the black crystals in the rock. The number of ghol'ms in the hall was sickening.

"There must be hundreds of them," said Sebastian. "I've seen how many the mines produced in those early days. They kept going for all these years… they must have thousands…"

"Thousands? That means thousands of scrolls… thousands of people… children… all those small infants… how can someone do that? Damn them. Damn them all!" Raylan hissed through his teeth, as he kicked the ghol'm in front of him. It did not budge at all.

A loud clank echoed through the hall, as they suddenly saw the light pour in a set of double doors that had been thrown wide open at the other end of the warehouse.

Soldiers streamed in as orders were shouted.

Both Raylan and Sebastian automatically ducked to the floor, forgetting their disguise.

"They can't find us here, even with this armor on," said Sebastian, after he realized what they were wearing.

"What are they shouting?"

"Something about this being the last batch. That they have until sunrise to get everything loaded up."

"Sunrise? Are they that close to setting sail? We've really got no time to waste. Grab your pack—we'll go back through the door."

They quietly opened the door and peaked through a crack to see if anyone was around.

"Empty," said Sebastian.

"Let's go."

They moved into the abandoned passageway, and rapidly continued their way toward the water.

Shifting between the workers, they moved quickly and smoothly, making sure not to be in anyone's way and avoiding those who might ask questions.

As they approached the final buildings before reaching the water, they took position behind a pile of crates next to one of the smaller structures.

The bay was filled with ships, just as Galirras had said. Dozens of large sailing ships were anchored along the coast with smaller ships spread throughout them. Raylan could not see them all, nor did it matter. Where Galirras had seen mostly empty ships and a quiet harbor, the water was now packed with dinghies moving soldiers back and forth to all the ships.

"We're too late… no way we'll be able to take over a fully loaded ship with that many soldiers on it," Raylan spat.

"What about the smaller ships?"

"I don't see an easy way to get to them with that many eyes on the water. We'll be spotted for sure. They could instantly block us in and board us… it'd be suicide."

"There must be something we can do. What about the one on the far end? I don't see any one on deck there yet," Sebastian said.

"Seb? Seb is that you?" whispered a very soft voice, nearby.

Both Raylan and Sebastian froze in the middle of their hushed conversation, looking around for where the voice was coming from.

"Up here," the small voice said, quietly. "I thought I recognized your voice. What are you doing here?"

Sebastian looked up to a small window lined with metal bars. Two of the bars were grabbed by dirty hands, and a face pressed against them, trying to squeeze through as far as possible, to look downward on the two surprised men.

"Marek?! Is that you? I—I thought you were dead," hissed Sebastian.

"Not yet, although sometimes I wish I was," the voice said, half joking. "Listen, you need to get out of here. It's swarming with soldiers."

"We know," said Sebastian, pointing at their armor. "We're here on a mission. We're going home Marek… back to Aeterra."

"Seb!" said Raylan, as he grabbed his arm to shut him up.

"It's okay, Raylan… Marek's a friend. He was on my father's ship, and he always had my back in the mines. No way would he expose us…"

"It's true. I'd never betray Seb… oh, shit!"

272

The skinny face disappeared from the window. A moment later, a guard's voice thundered on the other side of the wall. The clank of a metal gate opening was heard. The window let out more shouting, and Marek's voice protested for a moment before grunting under the sound of something hitting flesh. It was clear that the guards continued to abuse their prisoner until all resistance seeped out of him. Laughter echoed from the open window as the guards walked away and shut the metal door with a loud bang, followed by the cold clank of the lock falling in place.

Unable to look into the windows from the outside, Raylan and Sebastian stood against the wall, staying out of sight as much as possible, and waited. After the silence carried on, Sebastian finally looked up.

"Marek? Marek… you still there?" he whispered, softly.

They heard someone move inside softly, slowly. A hesitant hand grabbed the bars as Marek pulled himself close to the window again with a grunt. His face showed deep bruises and there was a cut on the side of his head. One eye was already swelling up so much it was hard to keep it open.

"I'm… here…" Marek looked at them both. "The soldiers aren't too friendly here. I suggest you guys don't get caught…"

Raylan noticed the iron ring around his neck.

"How long have you been here with that?" asked Sebastian, pointing at his own neck.

"Ever since I was recaptured in the forests…" Marek struggled to keep hold of the bars. "When we broke out from the mines, some of us got split up… I guess I was just one of the ones that didn't get away."

"If I'd known, Marek…" Sebastian let the words linger.

"Then what? You would've gotten yourself killed trying to rescue me? I've never blamed you, Seb, or anyone—and I never will. I'm just glad to see you've made it," said Marek. "But what are you doing here?"

"We're here to get a ship," whispered Raylan.

"How are you going to steal a ship with just the two of you? They've been loading up the ships for days, and this morning they started assigning soldiers to each of them. There must be at least forty on each of those ships…"

"We didn't know until we got here. If only we'd been a day earlier," said Sebastian.

"If not this, what other options would we have? None," said Raylan. "We've got to find a way."

Marek looked behind him, spooked by a sound, but heard no soldiers coming. He turned his attention back to them. "Do you see those weird-looking ships down the waterline? The ones with the large sacks? They're called windships, and they can fly. You might not believe me, but I've seen it myself."

"We saw one, yesterday," said Sebastian. "It was… surreal."

"There are two types in the harbor. The big ones carry a full force of soldiers but the smaller ones run with a much smaller crew. I would think they'd use it for scouting, they're quite fast in the air. Those would be your best bet."

"Best bet on what?" said Sebastian.

"To get out of here, you idiot. I'll be damned if I don't help my friend escape from these damned lands."

"How do you know all this?" asked Raylan.

Marek touched the ring around his neck and grinned. "It's a burden, but it does have its advantages. You'd be surprised what you can pick up just by being close to things."

For someone who was just beaten up and has lived years in slavery, Raylan was surprised at how optimistically Marek's look on the world still was.

"But even if we could take over one of the small airships… or windships, overpower its crew, we'd have no idea how to fly it," Sebastian said.

"I know how," Marek whispered.

"You do?" Sebastian said, surprise in his voice.

"But that means… you'll have to help me first. I want to come with you. Please, can you get me out of here?"

Marek looked from Sebastian to Raylan and back with a hopeful glint in his good eye.

"Are you sure you know how to fly it?" asked Raylan.

"Positive!"

Raylan looked at Sebastian, who read the question on his face. He returned it with a slow nod. It seemed Sebastian was certain Marek could be trusted.

"Okay, how many guards are there inside? If we're going to do this, we need to know as much as possible. Are they large or skinny? Do they have swords? Axes? Where will they likely be in the building? Who carries the keys? With just the two of us, we'll need to use our speed to make this work."

"There's a minimum of three guards at all times, and there are usually two in front of the building near the main entrance. They all have swords, but they leave them near the entrance and handle the prisoners with small iron rods. Those will likely be on their belts. The keys should be on the highest-ranking soldier in the building. It should be the biggest one… I heard the key jingle when he kicked me…"

"How many rooms?"

274

"All the guards should be in the main room. There are ten cells on this row, five each side, but it's another ten on the other side. So, after you enter turn left… mine is the third cell."

Raylan ran over the information in his head, quickly. "All right, we'll try and get you out but you'll have to wait. Stay quiet, rest up and let them ignore you. We'll have to wait until our friend creates a distraction."

"When'll that be?" asked Marek, nervously.

Raylan saw that Marek's face already started to swell even more. "Not for a while, just be ready when we come for you," said Raylan. "We need to go. If we stay here, we'll draw attention to ourselves. Let's keep moving and explore as much as possible."

"We'll be back… I promise," said Sebastian to Marek, who looked doubtfully as his old friend disappeared from the barred window.

As they walked away from the slave cells, Raylan took in as much as he could of the place. Several of the large airships were close by, being loaded up with the stones Galirras had seen from the air. Farther down, they saw the ghol'ms being put on larger transport boats, to be moved to the various ships in the bay. There, they were loaded into the cargo hold by a system of pulleys. Some of them were redirected to the airships, too.

They dumped their packs and grabbed a cart filled with stones, pushing it toward the end of harbor, where the smaller airships were located.

The ships were put on a wooden structure apparently made to fit the form of the ship's hull. The design was similar to the bigger version they had seen attacking the caravel, but only had one of the large bladed wheels behind it to push itself forward. The cabin on deck was less elegant, too, although it did look like the hull had space for quite a bit of cargo.

Moving near similar carts, they walked around the small ship. The balloon hung flat to the side, and Raylan saw the long cloths used to protect the balloon from arrows, spread along the side of it. The poles that held the cloths took up less space while docked. Now that they were so close, Raylan noticed some sort of pipe running upward from the deck. The balloon was at the end of it, tied with a complicated rope construction and metal rings. The side of the ship's hull had a large cargo door, which currently stood open for loading. It did not seem to have any of the small hatches on the side like the other ship, just several smaller view ports.

They moved from spot to spot, avoiding contact as much as possible. If spoken to, Sebastian quickly answered with a general term, using short sentences to limit any chance of people recognizing his possibly foreign accent.

At times, they moved away from the water; other moments, they purposely walked the shore. The night slowly progressed as the moon reached its zenith and then started its descent. Some soldiers began to seek out places to sleep, so they decided to do the same. Sitting against a few crates near the water, they rested and bided their time. Slowly but surely, the moment approached.

Raylan silently contemplated that his disguise gave him a certain safe feeling. From afar, no one would recognize them as any different from the Doskovian soldiers. Of course, the ruse would never hold up against any direct, in-depth questioning. But as they sat there against the crates, looking at all the people go by, their armor felt like the safest place in the world, hiding in plain sight.

Raylan's exhaustion seeped in. His legs were heavy from walking, his eyes fought a losing battle to stay open. The world gently faded to a dark, peaceful place as the harbor's sounds blended into a monotonous noise that guided him to sleep.

Raylan jerked awake. The sharp pain of a metal boot hitting his thigh doing its job. Looking up, five soldiers stared at him and Sebastian, who from the looks of it, received the same gentle wake-up call. No light lit the sky yet, but he was sure it could not be much longer, gauging how the moon moved closer to the ocean waters in the west.

We must have dozed off! Are we too late?

The closest soldier shouted at them. It took a moment for Raylan to remember he was not speaking Terran, as he tried his best to make sense of the jumble of words. Sebastian was already at that point and tried to answer in his best Kovian possible.

Unfortunately, the soldier did not seem satisfied by Sebastian answering for him. The man took a step toward Raylan, asking another question, directed at him more clearly.

Raylan could not understand, let alone answer. His muscles tensed, reacting to the danger. Slowly, his left hand checked for his sword. The soldier noticed, immediately, and put his own hand on his dagger. He shouted another question, or perhaps a command, Raylan had no way of knowing. This was getting ugly fast.

Raylan slid his foot forward, adjusting his body's position to have his side closest to the enemy. The less area to hit, the better. He checked, in the corner of his eye, to see if Sebastian was ready. He knew Sebastian was only a self-trained fighter, the difference between their ability would probably be quite large. He had to try and take down as many as possible as fast as he

276

could and keep the enemy focused on him so Sebastian would be put less on the defense. He would have to be quick…

Raylan shifted his foot to launch his attack, when he felt a familiar tingle enter his head.

"*I am going to get started!*"

As Galirras' dark shadow glided overhead, following the harbor waters to the south, he let out a large deep roar directly above. It was so loud, even Sebastian and Raylan flinched from the surprise, for a second.

"*That was some roar! Have you been holding back all this time?*" replied Raylan, privately. "*Go get them!*"

The five soldiers in front of them completely forgot their inquisition as they stared at the sky in shocked surprise. Galirras' dark shape shimmered in the light of many torches. His wingspan was an impressive forty feet already. He let out another roar, announcing his arrival, before using his front claws to topple over a large pile of crates. As they crashed heavily to the ground, the weapons inside tumbled out, creating even more noise.

Trumpeting in a job well done, Galirras flew on to the south side of the harbor. Picking up crates and slamming them into people and wagons; cutting a rope to the sails of a ship… he left a trail of chaos for the soldiers to follow.

By now, the alarm was going off, following Galirras' movement. The five soldiers in front of Raylan and Sebastian sped off without giving them a second glance. It looked like they were all taking the bait.

"Come on! We need to get Marek, first," said Raylan, as he started to run toward the slave cells.

Corza woke to the sound of thunder. Or at least that was his first thought, as the deep sound rolled across the sky. He lifted his head, groggy from the little sleep he had gotten. The preparations had kept him up most of the night. It was too bad sea travel normally did not treat him well, or he would have skipped the night and slept on one of the ships.

When shouting and yelling followed the sound of thunder, the feeling that something was out of order crept along his skin like a spider. The harbor was never quiet, but this sounded like chaos. He dressed quickly, and was just tugging on the last strap of his armor when a pair of hurried footsteps neared his door.

A loud knock. "Sir? Are you awake?"

"I am. Come in, already. What's with all the ruckus?"

"The dragon… the one we've been hunting. It's here!"

"What do you mean, it's here?"

"I mean, here! In the harbor! It flew into the harbor and started trashing things. It's currently on the south side, attacking one of the ships."

Corza had little time to process it all, as he heard another loud crash, coming from outside. He looked out of his window and across the south part of the bay. The glow of fire rose from behind one of the buildings. Soldiers ran back and forth, some toward the fire, others toward the presumed location of the attacking creature.

Wasting no more time, Corza ran out. He flung open the door and stepped into chaos. Everywhere, people shouted. Soldiers ran with buckets, forming a line from the water to the fire. Guards moved in squads toward the south side of the harbor.

Corza saw a shadow glide across the water. It never stayed still for long, if at all. Suddenly, it turned toward him, growing in size as it drew closer. At the last moment, it adjusted its flight, bending off to the right, releasing a crate which crashed heavily into the roof of one of the buildings across the street from Corza.

For just an instant, Corza saw the dragon in the shimmering of torchlight. He marveled at the sight of it.

Yes! You'll be mine. What a marvelous and destructive creature you are!

"You," said Corza to the soldier who had come to get him. "Go get the netting squads and have them meet me at the southern entrance. Get the crossbows squads up on the roof, but only fire nonlethal shots. You hear me? The person that kills that dragon, I will flog to death myself! I want it captured alive."

The soldier sped off with his orders. Besides the door, two guards waited for their general.

"Follow me and try to keep up," commanded Corza, as he marched off toward the south end of the harbor.

"Captain… Dreck, has Captain Sellock checked in, yet?" said Corza, after looking over his shoulder to see who he was speaking to.

"No, sir. Nothing has come in, yet," answered the captain.

"Well, send out a rider to retrieve his party from the northern coast-line… and send orders to Colonel Mercar to launch the Firestorm. I want this dragon hunted on its own turf, as well as from the ground. Make sure he has some steel nets before taking off."

Corza had ordered the creation of the nets once it became clear the dragon posed a real threat to any soldier trying to attack it head on. They were made of thin steel mesh, specifically designed to weigh down the animal and restrict its movements.

As Corza arrived at the water, he saw the crew of one ship fighting a fire on deck, while another two boats had their ropes cut, trapping the men under a large fold of the heavy mainsail. Corza surveyed the bay. Something was off. He could not pinpoint it yet, but the spectacle seemed… off in a way.

"Where are the soldiers accompanying the dragon? They would not leave such a valuable asset unprotected," he said, to himself.

"Sorry, sir. What?" said the soldier at his side.

Ignoring him, Corza said again, "The enemy soldiers. Where are they? And why isn't it attacking any of the other ships?"

"His attacks appear very random, sir… but surely the beast wouldn't know what it's doing?"

"Don't be an idiot," said Corza, and then muttered to himself, "why not go for the smaller ships, if you're attacking anyway? They're easier to take out. He seems to attack the south end only… something isn't right."

Corza thought it over and decided to play it safe. "Go to the barracks and form a few small-sized patrol squads. Make sure the east and north end of the harbor are kept under watch and have them sound an alarm as soon as they see anything suspicious." He smiled to himself. "In the meantime, I'll go and catch myself a dragon."

CHAPTER TWENTY

Chaos

RAYLAN AND SEBASTIAN quickly approached the slave cells, both halting at the corner. They took a deep breath to ease their panting.

"All right, just like we discussed," Raylan said. "Use nonlethal force, if possible."

Sebastian gave a short nod. "Here goes nothin'."

As they turned the corner, they strode over to the two guards at the door, resisting the urge to run.

"High General Corza requests your presence at the south end," said Sebastian in his most fluent Kovian, hooking his thumb over his shoulder. "We're here to take over."

With a nod, both guards knew better than to second guess a High General's order, and raced away in the direction of all the shouting.

Raylan waited until both were out of sight, then pushed open the door. Two oils lamps in the corner barely pushed back the shadows, as two soldiers looked up from a card game. The third, busy sharpening his sword, ignored them completely.

Raylan's heart skipped a beat and his adrenaline kicked in when he took in the face of that third soldier—it marked as a skull. As if a dark shadow had fallen over the soldier's face and ripped the skin off. But it was the murderous vibe pulsing from the man that jolted Raylan's alertness. Like the two at the stone arch crossing that had set his blood to ice. Back then, he had been lucky enough not to end up face-to-face with them. That would not be the case this time.

Stepping inside, Raylan saw a lot more detail on the soldier's marked face. His white eyes stared out from black rings, and his nose was completely blacked out to match the look of a skull; but his mouth was the eeriest part.

It must have been tattooed. Raylan could not imagine a person being alive, if what he saw was truly the case. From afar, it had seemed the two soldiers at the stone arch had no skin below their nose, showing a row of teeth and muscles on the jaw. Now that he was closer, he saw that it was indeed a tattoo, too real for comfort. The design completely covered the jaw and cheeks of his face. It gave the impression the soldier was always slightly smiling… without lips or skin. The back and top of the head was completely colored black, as if a liquid shadow seeped over his face like tar.

One of the card players spoke, but the question was lost on Raylan. He dared not let the only armed soldier out of his sight, especially one so dangerous. Besides, it was best he did not to react to any foreign language directed at him. Sebastian would answer in his place, and when he did, Raylan intended to close the gap and make the first strike.

Sebastian stuttered some words, and Raylan looked back to see Sebastian's gaze locked on the skull-faced soldier. He saw fear resonate in the former slave's eyes. It disrupted Sebastian's concentration and blatantly revealed any inexperience in the Kovian language. Instead of quelling the guards' suspicion, it instantly raised their alertness.

Raylan cursed inside. If he did not make his move now, he would never make it. He stepped forward, closing the distance to the armed soldier. The others would need to get around them to reach their swords, although he did notice a dagger on the table. But he and Sebastian had swords, they would easily take control of the situation if he managed to cut the skull-head down.

As he reached for his weapon, he heard Sebastian shout after him in the Terran language, shattering any of the ruse that they might have had left.

"Raylan, no. We need to get out. He's one of the Darkened!"

But it was too late to turn back now. Raylan had already begun to draw his sword. Turning his back on the man and fleeing would mean instant death. He just needed to cut down the skulled soldier, after which he could focus on the two lesser threats.

Unfortunately, the sound of his sword being drawn was a well-trained trigger for the Darkened one. With lightning speed, his enemy blocked his incoming horizontal slash. Pushing off to the left, the dark one let his chair tumble backward, away from Raylan. With ease, the soldier rolled across the floor, getting to his feet in one fluid motion. He grabbed another chair, close by, and swung it sideways into Raylan's left flank. The chair shattered from the force, and Raylan felt instantly grateful they had put up with this heavier armor. A sword strike from above, and Raylan parried to his left. Exchanging blows, back and forth, the two danced around the room.

Sebastian engaged the other two soldiers. Inexperienced in combat as he might have been before his capture, he had trained rigorously for many years, though not under any skilled supervision. His fighting style had very little structure, which made it lack focus; but also made it very difficult to interpret. He cut down one of the two soldiers with his third swing; unfortunately, the second knocked away his weapon with a chair. The fight looked more like a bar brawl than two soldiers engaged in combat.

It was a good thing Galirras was doing his best to provide as much chaos as possible. It kept the soldiers outside occupied, and hopefully, drowned out any of the noises their fight created.

Raylan, using two circular upward slashes, drove the Darkened backward a few steps. The Silent Shadow immediately retaliated with a stab, turned backward, and slashed as he struck out with his sword. The reach of the backward turn made Raylan take a step back, but as the slash passed his body, he quickly stepped in and moved past the Darkened, slashing his left thigh on the edge of the armor. The wound was not deep enough to do any real damage, there was still too much armor in the way, but it was a start.

The Darkened lashed out with his left fist, hitting Raylan across the face. The force of the blow ran as a tremor through his skull. Another slash from above with too little time to dodge. Raylan blocked it, locking himself to the Darkened by grabbing his wrist—his enemy mirroring the move. A sharp pain struck his lower back as his kidneys were pushed into one of the higher tables.

Raylan stared into the Darkened's face, barely inches from his own. It was clearly meant to intimidate and terrorize. To his horror, Raylan saw the mouth of his opponent was sewn shut. The tattoo hid most of the thread from view when seen from a distance; facing him head on, the stitches were painfully clear. The Darkened opened his mouth, a crack, stretching the strings between his upper and lower lip, and made a hissing, gurgling threat that sounded inhuman. The smell of his breath was nauseating. Raylan felt like he was staring death in the eyes.

His instinct kicked into overdrive, every fiber in his body wanted to get away from this dark monstrosity. He would almost rather fight a ghol'm… almost. He pushed back with all his might, then suddenly released all tension. Shifting to the side, he used the force of his intimidator's weight to slam the Darkened one's head into the table.

It seemed to have little effect. The Darkened launched another parry of attacks, coming in low to the knee, followed by two slashes that marked a cross on Raylan's torso armor. He dodged a third slash, across the chest, after which he once again moved in to take advantage of the small opening.

As he stepped forward, he felt the soldier's foot impact straight into his stomach. The Darkened had quickly adapted and fully expected Raylan's attack to the other leg. The kick to his stomach sent Raylan crashing against a door, which flew straight open. Tumbling backward, Raylan rolled quickly to his feet. The Darkened was already charging, but instead of a straight thrust, the soldier came at him with a diagonal upward slash to the left. It made it impossible for Raylan to destabilize his opponent's footwork.

Raylan jumped back and glanced down; a stream of blood ran down his fingers from a cut to the back of his hand. Both he and the Darkened were panting heavily, studying each other from a distance.

Behind the Darkened, in the other room, Sebastian exchanged blows with the soldier, using anything he could get his hands on to either throw at, or swing at, the enemy's head. His opponent, having the advantage in size, shrugged of the attacks and used every opportunity he spotted to give a counter blow. Furniture lay everywhere. The Doskovian soldier suddenly grinned and crouched behind a table. Rising swiftly, the enemy guard lunged at Sebastian with the long dagger, who parried the attack with the leg of a broken chair.

It was all Raylan could see, as the Darkened movements forced him to circle. As they did, their new surroundings seeped into Raylan's mind. They had ended up in the row of cells that housed the slaves. From the corner of his eyes, the silhouettes of those locked up were squirreled as far back into the corner as possible.

Flat shadows in a dark cage.

The smell of feces and urine hung thick in the air.

The Darkened stepped sideways, his gaze remaining locked like a hawk. It was studying his movements, learning from every move, exploiting his every mistake. If Raylan did not finish this quickly, he might not survive at all. He had to do something unexpected.

The Darkened one took the initiative. Two slashes Raylan dodged, another stab, he deflected, but his wrist was unexpectedly grabbed—the grip like an iron clasp. Their stance prevented the soldier from performing a direct slash, so the Silent Shadow hit Raylan's arm with the back of his sword, and with such power he was forced to drop his blade. Raylan gave a quick left hook and pushed his opponent away. He glanced at his sword… he would never reach it alive, besides, the soldier was already coming at him again.

The Darkened did not wait for Raylan to recover. He jumped forward, coming at him with a strong downward slash. Raylan leapt forward, closing the distance between them. Passing the blade's path, Raylan grabbed his enemy's shoulders and threw himself backward. Rolling back and pushing off hard with his feet, he threw the Darkened into the steel bars of one of the cells. A loud *clang* resounded like the toll of a church bell. Whimpers and surprised yelps rang from the slaves.

The attack had less effect than Raylan had hoped. The Darkened was back to his feet in a flash, ready to launch his next assault. Sword in hand, the fighter stepped forward, determined to make a more precise and calculated slash. A hand snaked through the bars, grabbing the Darkened sword hand and yanking it back. Two skinny arms clasped around the Darkened's entire arm, tightly, pulling it against the cell. Raylan spotted the dirty, swollen face of Marek behind the bars.

Have they beaten him even more?

"Your sfword! Ge'f your sfword," shouted Marek, his lips so swollen it was hard to understand him.

Raylan dove for his sword as the Darkened turned and grabbed Marek by the back of his head, crushing his face against the steel bars. Marek grunted, whimpered, but used all his strength to keep hold of the enemy's sword hand.

The Darkened released Marek's head and went for the dagger on his belt. Raylan leaped, his sword sinking into the side of the soldier's neck and straight down into the Darkened's chest. Marek stumbled back as he let go of the Darkened, staring at the enemy monstrosity trying to grab the blade grip stuck out of his shoulder. But tension left the soldier's body, and it slumped to the floor. Still. Silent.

* * *

Sebastian barely saw anything between the blood and the sweat pouring down his forehead. He was losing this fight and he knew it. The soldier had more experience and a better weapon. While he fended off the dagger, it cost him several blows to the head, and he was starting to feel numb.

The soldier stabbed again, forcing Sebastian to backpedal. His left foot got stuck on an overturned chair, and he slammed to the ground. The guard was on him in an instant, dagger coming straight at him. Sebastian grabbed the man's hand to block the attack, but the soldier's momentum pinned him to the floor as the man used his weight to push the dagger toward Sebastian's heart. Though Sebastian's arms were strong from traveling through the trees for years, they now quickly grew tired, fighting the full weight of his assailant. The dagger inched closer to his chest, going for the spot just above the edge of his armor. He sucked in short breaths, afraid to relax his muscles. His arms started to sour.

Another inch.

Another.

The blade edged past his armor.

The tip pressed against his flesh.

The sting of broken skin.

First blood.

He roared in his mind, out of breath, no power left to shout for help.

This was it.

He would die on this rotten continent.

After all these years.

Unable to change anything.

Unable to be an influence in the world.

Unable to help.

Raylan! Where are you?

The soldier straightened for one final push, when suddenly the tip of a sword pierced out of the front of the man's neck. The shock on the soldier's face was accompanied by his last blood-gurgling breaths as Raylan put his foot on the dying man's ribs and pushed him to the side. The soldier crashed heavily to the ground, dagger still in hand. Sebastian's hands still clamped around the man's wrists, unwilling and unable to let go.

* * *

Raylan watched his enemy's muscles relax as the light in the soldier's eyes faded away. He crouched next to Sebastian, who lay panting on the floor and took his friend's hands off the dead man's wrist.

"You okay?"

Sebastian's eyes, wide open, met his gaze. "I thought for sure I was a goner. You saved my life, thank you."

"I guess that makes us even now," grinned Raylan. "Come on, we have to keep moving. This already took much longer than I thought it would. We need to hurry."

"What about the Darkened?"

"He's dead," said Raylan, pulling Sebastian to his feet.

"That's incredible… I've never known anyone to survive a Darkened one. They're like death itself."

"Yeah well, I wasn't sure I'd survive, either. Thankfully, I had a little help. Grab some of that soldier's armor, I've got the keys."

They ran back to the slave cells, and Raylan unlocked the door of Marek's cell and threw in the armor.

"Quickly, put this on. We need to move."

Marek began putting on the armor. He was slower than Raylan would have liked, but it was clear his body was hurting from the beating. It did give them a moment to catch their breath, though. Raylan looked to the other slaves in the cells, and carefully observed them.

"Why are you the only one alone in a cell?" asked Raylan.

"I'm no'f, bu'f the guys in my cell had a falling ou'f. The guards came and fook fhem yes'ferday morning… I'vfe no'f seen fhem since." Marek hopped on one leg to put on his final boot. "Ready…"

"All right, follow me," said Sebastian, as he disappeared through the door.

Marek followed him. Raylan started to move but hesitated near the door. When he looked back, the other slaves stared at him from their cells.

He grabbed the keys and headed back. "I don't know if any of you speak Terran and can understand me… there are a lot of things going on outside, but you might be able to make use of this and make your escape. I hope you all make it…"

And with that, he threw the ring of keys into the hands of a young female slave, and then ran out after Sebastian and Marek.

* * *

Galirras surveyed the bay from the air. He felt Raylan out there, but it was hard to pinpoint him in all the turmoil; nor did he have time to focus on his friend in the fray. He darted to the right, moving away from several crossbow soldiers standing on a ship's deck. It was becoming increasingly difficult to move around. At first, he had the element of surprise. He enjoyed not having to keep a low profile, anymore. Moving from one place to another, spreading his wings for all to see, it was his job to attract their attention after all.

After his announcing roar and flight across the shore to draw attention to himself, he had first focused on the piles of resources he could find. He located crates and barrels, picked them up and threw them down at soldiers

286

or buildings or—if that was too complicated—just knocked them over; that often worked fine, too. He flew low to scare livestock brought in for the slaughter. He took the opportunity to frighten some horses in an attempt to break them out, but they were too well secured. He swooped in and picked up a small pig, which he snacked on in the air. It was the first time eating while flying, as well as his first time eating a pig, both of which he very much enjoyed. It took some getting used to, reaching down to take a bite while keeping himself from crashing, but he was skilled enough by now to quickly adjust his wing-beat to compensate.

Unfortunately, part of the pig was just wasted, when he lost his grip as he made evasive maneuvers to avoid a thrown spear. He circled back and darted toward the soldier, roaring so loud the man tripped over backward.

Serves you right. Letting me drop my meal.

He managed to knock over an oil lamp, which spread a pool of flammable oil. The surrounding wooden structures quickly caught fire, and in no time, a couple of small sheds in the south end of the harbor were ablaze.

He shifted his attention back toward the ships, where soldiers had just started coming to deck, woken by all the commotion. He tried to tear at the sails, but it was difficult to get close with all the ropes and masts everywhere. Thankfully, he had excellent vision, not only in the dark but also in the twilight hours. He saw the air flow around the objects, which warned him when he needed to steer clear of obstacles.

Slowly circling, he took a moment to overlook the bay area. He had little time left. From the looks of it, the Doskovian army was getting more organized. Archers were getting to the watch towers and rooftops and they were already putting out the fires he had managed to start.

He saw one of the airships take off. It quickly ascended and then headed toward him. From the looks of it, it was the same ship that had taken out the caravel. He banked away. Things were becoming too dangerous to stay on the offense much longer, and Raylan did warn him not to take any unnecessary risks.

All right, one more pass and I will draw them further south. I hope the others were given enough time.

He set in a low dive, aiming for the large open area in front of the south exit. *A quick windblast to knock over that large pyramid of barrels, and then I am out.*

He dove forward, leaving the airship behind. He saw a few archers shoot off their arrows, but the smoke and darkness of the night made it very difficult to hit him. He only had to evade one of the flying projectiles.

Pulling in the tip of his wings to pass the large structures, he compensated with some upward wind currents. He quickly glided through the lane he had chosen for his approach. Everything was going smoothly, until he suddenly spotted movement on his far right. On a smaller building, two soldiers had been hiding. As he passed, they threw a net toward him, which was now soaring at him, fully spread. He tilted his body to the left but had too little room to maneuver freely between the buildings. It caught on his hind right leg and immediately partially wrapped around it.

Surprised by the weight of the net, he realized it was not constructed of rope but steel. Entering the plaza with the barrel pyramid, and thrown off balance by the net, Galirras came dangerously close to crashing into the ground. He skidded to a halt, limping as he kicked his hind leg to get free of the net. Soldiers poured into the plaza from all sides, spears at the ready. Others carried more nets. The archers and crossbows were the biggest problem. They were quickly becoming too many. Galirras kicked his leg furiously, finally throwing the net off as it unwrapped from the movement. It flew across the square, knocking two unlucky soldiers over. He stretched his neck and gave a full force windblast roar toward those holding crossbows closest to him. The blast lifted the soldiers off their feet and threw them backward. *They must weigh much less than the bear*, he thought, satisfied by the result.

Instead of taking to the air and exposing himself to the archers, Galirras turned and dashed toward the southern exit. Pouncing onto two soldiers, he quickly broke through and made a run for it. His tail whipped from left to right as he ran down the street, knocking over small food stalls and piles of crates. He heard crossbow bolts hit the wood to the side of him as he shifted left and right, finally deciding to take his chances in the air. With a giant leap, he launched himself into the air, pushing the wind upward with all his might, shooting into the sky at lightning speed. Having gained some initial height, he darted quickly—and erratically—back and forth, to throw the archers off target. Retreating south, he heard the shouts of many follow him into the forest. He trumpeted a challenge and wondered if Raylan would praise him on a job well done.

CHAPTER TWENTY-ONE

Alarm

Raylan, Sebastian and Marek moved to the north side of the bay. The streets of the northern harbor were a lot emptier now, but were not completely deserted. They would have to choose their route carefully. Raylan forced himself to move slowly, walking silently and acting like he belonged.

Marek had a similar helmet to Sebastian's, providing cover for his swollen face. It had hurt to put it on but walking around without it was not an option. The ring around Marek's neck was tugged below the slightly over-sized armor he wore—not ideal, but there was no time to try and rig it open. They arrived at the edge of the harbor and moved into the shadow of one of the buildings. Standing below the roof overhang, they stared into the forest. Every eighty yards or so, there was a sentry along the border of the small settlement, and they noticed three guards just leaving the area—moving into the forest to patrol.

They slid along the buildings until they came to the northern-most structure. The small airships waited near the water, and they would not have to cover much ground to get to them; but first, they had to meet up with the others.

"Wait here," said Raylan to Marek, as he and Sebastian took off around the corner.

They checked all sides as they approached the edge of the settlement. The guard to the right of them was facing south, transfixed on the orange glow coming from that other end of the harbor. The fire and smoke gave an eerie feel in the early morning, and they heard the shouts carrying through the night across the water.

"Let's do it now, while the other guard is distracted," whispered Sebastian.

Raylan gave a short nod, and he inched forward; the guard was barely twenty feet from them. The man, standing dutifully with his long spear, never saw the blade coming. Raylan kept a hand over the soldier's mouth, slipping the blade along the throat—the same maneuver Gavin performed the night they raided the enemy camp on that rocky hill so long ago. The night Raylan had first killed a person. It almost felt normal now. He shuddered, nausea swirling at the realization and began dragging the dead soldier from his post. Sebastian grabbed the dead man's spear and retook the dead guard's position, watching the forest. Just shadows, trees and rocks.

An owl called softly into the night. Sebastian returned the call. Two shadows took shape on a rock at the base of a small group of trees. The shapes morphed into figures as they ran silently, passing Sebastian without a word.

Galen and Gavin…

The others followed on the pre-determined signals, crossing the small open area between the edge of the forest and the line of structures. As the last one passed, Sebastian slid back into the cover of the building. Raylan propped the dead guard up on a barrel, making it look like he was asleep… at least from a distance. Sebastian put the spear on the slumped shoulder as a final touch.

"What kept you so long? We've been waiting ever since Galirras launched his diversion. And who's this?" said Gavin, who had just spotted Marek.

"He's our ticket out of here," said Raylan. "He's an old friend of Sebastian's. He'll help us fly out of here with one of the small airships."

"Fly? Are you crazy? We were going for a boat, not going after the airships," hissed Gavin.

"The ships are all loaded up already, with at least fifty soldiers per boat. We'll never survive an open approach over water with that many men waiting for us on deck. Galirras will surely have put them all on high alert. Marek says he knows how to fly one of those airships. Sebastian thinks he can do it."

"We'vfe go'f to movfe quickly fhough. Fhose ships… fhey need some prepara'fion fime before fhey're able fo fake off in'fo fhe air…" added Marek.

"Good God, I can hardly understand you…" Gavin muttered. "What do you mean preparations? How much time?" Gavin shook his head. "You know what, never mind. We can't turn back now, even if we wanted to. Raylan… you lead the way. It was your plan, make it happen."

Raylan threw Gavin a look. Being called out like that once again strengthened his desire to prove himself to his brother. He quickly took the lead and guided the group, unseen, through the smaller passageways, until they came right upon the edge of the airship plaza. The outermost ship's cargo doors were closed, its balloon flattened to one side. Raylan only saw two men on deck, so it was likely the rest had gone off to check out the chaos Galirras was creating.

I hope they have finished loading up provisions.

During the earlier reconnaissance, Raylan had gotten an idea on how to get aboard the small airship without getting noticed. Together with Kevhin and Richard, he moved to the far side of the ships and crawled under the fabric of the balloon. It felt like a rugged kind of leather, fully worked and oiled to be airtight.

Lifting the fabric, the balloon was much heavier than he would have expected. It took all the three of them—and quite some effort—to squeeze themselves under it and start climbing up the side of the ship. For a moment he was completely enshrouded by it, trapped between the wooden planks of the ship and the greasy skin of the balloon. It was so different from the open air and sea he was used to. It pressed him against the ship's hull. As he pushed off another step, he felt like he was suffocating. His breathing increased as cold sweat broke out on his neck. His hand tightened around the wooden ridge, and he felt his head start to pound. He needed to get out of there, *now*. The heavy skin of the balloon seemed to increase in weight with his every breath, as he looked nervously back and forth.

A hand shot out from under the fabric and grasped his left shoulder. "Raylan, you okay?"

It was Richard.

"Yea—yeah," said Raylan, swallowing his panic.

"Let's go then. We're almost there."

Together, the three pushed onward, finally reaching the handrail on the edge of the deck. Slipping over it, they moved into the space between the rail and the balloon, Raylan going one way, Kevhin and Richard the other. Kevhin moved first, approaching one of the guards on the deck with barely a sound. Raylan moved in on the other, fighting to retake control of his breathing and willing his knees to stop shaking. Richard headed for the cabin door, disappearing below deck.

"Excuse me," said Kevhin to the guard's back.

The guard spun, already drawing his sword. Before the man could do anything, Kevhin used the handle of his dagger to hit the soldier on the side of his head. The guard slammed hard into the deck, out cold. The other guard turned, hand on his sword when Raylan hit the man in the back of the head with his sword hilt.

They moved both guards against the handrail and bound them tight. Two dirty cloths functioned as primitive gags. No one would be able to see them from the ground.

A ruckus from below made both Raylan and Kevhin run toward the lower deck entry, but before they reached it, all was quiet again.

Raylan carefully slid along the cabin wall, toward the open door.

"Richard… you there?" he whispered.

No answer. Raylan looked at Kevhin.

"Richard," the archer hissed, more urgently.

Footsteps climbed the stairs behind the door, but it was still too dark to see. Kevhin's knuckles turned white around the handle of his dagger. Raylan raised his own sword and prepared to strike fast.

Richard popped his head out, smiling. "All clear."

"What was all that ruckus?" asked Raylan.

"That? Oh, I tripped over some rope and knocked over a bucket of water or something."

"No soldiers?"

"Just one, sleeping. He woke up, so I put him back to sleep again. Someone help me tie him up, he's quite a big bloke… I already found some rope," said Richard, grinning again.

Kevhin followed Richard below deck while Raylan signaled the others to come aboard. In no time, the full squad was on the ship. Harwin, Galen and Sebastian stripped the guards of their armor and took to the deck, keeping up the pretense of guarding it.

Raylan studied the ship. It was similarly built to the caravel they had seen in the bay, perhaps a little less tall from the deck up, and it appeared to be less wide than the normal seafaring ships. It felt very sleek indeed, and built for speed.

Instead of masts with multiple sails, the ship just had a single metal pipe rising out of the deck near the cabin. It went directly into the bottom of the balloon, where it was clamped with metal and rope, just like he had seen on the ship flying above the bay. The deck contained dozens of ropes which formed a flexible frame around the balloon, all of them carefully laid out, so they would not tangle. The upper deck, above the cabin, contained the steering wheel to the normal rudder. Two smaller sails could be extended to the side of the upper deck with a setup of pulleys and lines. Although the setup looked complex, and was laid out more horizontally, Raylan was pleased he could easily figure out how it functioned, since the principle of normal sails had stayed the same. Two larger sails could be extended on the main deck toward the bow, but together the total surface of the sails did not even come close to that of a normal sailing ship.

The front deck was spacious, and without many obstacles; Galirras would fit perfectly, if he did not thrash around too much. A large bowsprit was sticking out the front, with a rope running back toward the balloon again. It was not the only rope but looking at where the other ones were attached to the rail, Galirras should be able to find a spot where he could still slip through onto the deck. Although, with the speed the dragon grew, Raylan wondered how long he would be comfortable in the available space. *I wonder if he'll outgrow the ship. The words coming as an afterthought.*

Raylan saw Gavin take the two unconscious soldiers below deck. Marek disappeared after them, and Raylan figured the youngster would get the preparations started. He quickly followed their newest member to see if he could learn more about the internal workings of the ship.

Below deck, the layout was made as efficient as possible. The cargo doors were high on the hull, directly opening in the main hold, where the provisions were stored. There were rooms with hammocks for the crew, multiple thick pelts hanging on the walls to act as blankets. A basic galley and common area in the back. There were a few smaller view ports in the back wall. Looking out, Raylan saw the single bladed fan below him.

It must enter the ship directly below the galley.

He moved to the lowest deck and found two unwelcome sights in the main hold. Two dormant ghol'ms were positioned along the wall, next to the cargo doors. In the backroom, under the galley, the large iron bar of the fan outside came in through the wall. It attached, after several ninety-degree corners, into the wall so it could freely turn. It was fortified by a couple of bars, attaching the entire setup to the floor and ceiling of the room. The shape reminded Raylan of one of those hand drills his father had lying around in the workshop. Turning it would turn the wheel of the fan outside, like a reverse windmill.

The rest of the lowest deck was mainly occupied with piles of black stone with green veins in it and some wood. Raylan noticed a few hatches going up into the main hold, which would be used to move cargo to the lowest deck.

He found Marek on the lowest deck, looking at something that resembled a closed-off smith's oven. Only this oven was made of metal plating resting on stone support blocks. A pipe ran up through the ceiling to the main deck; it was the one connected to the balloon.

"Okay, let's see if I can make this work," mumbled Marek.

"What do you mean 'let's see'?" asked Raylan, who had gotten used to Marek's temporary speech impediment. "You said you knew how to fly this thing!"

"Well, I've seen them do it so many times… how hard can it be?"

Marek looked at him with such a blank expression, Raylan did not know what to say, at first. "How hard can it be? Half of these things none of us have ever seen in our lives. Until yesterday, it was common knowledge that ships do not fly! For all we know, it could be magic."

"Everyone knows there's no such thing as magic."

"Like there's no such thing as dragons, right?"

"Dragons?"

"Never mind… let's just figure this out, as fast as possible. What *do* you know?" said Raylan.

"See this? This is an oven used to burn these stones," said Marek, as he grabbed one of the green veined rocks. "I've seen them throw in the stones. As they heat up and burn, it releases a green vapor, forcefully. The vapor wants to go up very much. They catch it in the sack on deck, which lifts the ship when filled enough."

"Okay, so that makes it float, and the bladed fan thing at the back of the ship pushes it forward, helped by the sails on the side?"

"Yes, I've seen them take off lots of times. It should not take long for our balloon to fill, one stone releases a lot of green air," said Marek.

"Leave firing up the oven to me, I've done it hundreds of times for my father's smith's oven. Get me some of that cut wood and keep those stones ready."

Raylan found that the person who had made the oven had been very resourceful. Air intakes sucked in constant air to keep the fire from suffocating, while the hatches were placed in such a way as to quickly and efficiently create a full force furnace. In no time at all, the temperature in the oven reached high enough to start burning the rocks. Everywhere were handles on the oven, used to regulate the amount of heat, wood and stones. It took Marek little time to figure out each of them; though, there was a close call as he almost dumped the entire burning load while trying to figure everything out.

Raylan ran up to the deck to see how things were going. On his way, he noticed the captured soldiers had been secured in one of the hammock rooms where Ca'lek kept watch. He passed Gavin and Xi'Lao, who were discussing provisions, and dived past Peadar, who was setting up their stuff, making sure nothing was in the way—but could be found, if needed. Once up on deck, Raylan noticed the sky losing its darkness in the east. The sun would be up soon.

Raylan still could not feel Galirras. He knew the dragon was supposed to stay away while they prepped the ship; but he wondered if his friend was doing all right. It seemed the chaos on the south side of the harbor had quieted somewhat; but there were still fires burning that needed to be put out. Most of the soldiers would still be too occupied by the mayhem to return to normal duty. At least, that's what Raylan hoped.

The other small airships nearby, all had their balloons hanging over the side. It shielded the group from the guards on those decks, which was the reason Raylan had chosen the farthest ship. He looked at the balloon but it did not seem to have moved at all. He pushed the fabric, nothing. He raced down into the belly of the ship again.

"Marek! Something's not right... the balloon is still as flat as ever," he shouted.

Marek looked at him from behind the metal contraption. A strange moan filled the room.

"What's that?" said Raylan.

"There's too much green air. It's building up in the oven too much. The metal can't handle the pressure."

"Well do something!" shouted Raylan, as another long moan filled the room together with a loud clang.

Marek hobbled round the metal barrel. Checking each entrance, handle, and pipe. He stopped at the main pipe and tapped on it. Another tap, while he held his ear to the pipe.

"Empty..."

"What about this?" said Raylan, "did you flip this already, before?"

Marek looked at the part Raylan pointed to. They had not recognized it as a moving part yet, as it looked different from the other handles. Marek took another look, left and right, finally pushing it upward. It turned the part of the pipe, that was in place, higher, as another shifted in its place. A hiss rushed through the pipe as metal groaning came to a stop.

Marek looked at the pipe and shook his head. "How smart. It's a safety measure that will automatically stop the push of vapor into the balloon, if the pressure in the balloon and thus the pipe becomes too high. See... to protect the balloon from rupturing. There's no way to release vapor from the balloon quickly, but there is in the oven."

"As long as it's working now," said Raylan, relieved. "It's almost dawn... we need to get out of here before we're discovered. Let's get as much stone burning as possible. The sooner that balloon is full the better."

Raylan returned to the upper deck after filling the oven with stones. Marek would keep at it, supported by Rohan. He was pleased to see the balloon already rising as it quickly filled with the green vapors.

Most of their group remained out of sight. Patrols passed but none of them had come close. Now that the balloon increased in size and lifted, they were bound to draw attention.

By now, the balloon was almost completely off the ground. As it started to float, it pulled the ropes that tied it to the ship skyward. The deck became less cluttered as the ropes straightened out, allowing Raylan to take in the full size of the deck. It was a good size ship, indeed thinner than a caravel, but it had plenty of space.

Raylan walked along the handrail, pulling on a couple of the ropes. He was still able to pull the balloon down by hand, but the tension on the ropes increased with every passing moment.

It shouldn't be long now.

Rohan came up to the stairs. He had found a stash of arrows in the hold, which he and Kevhin were now distributing around the deck, for easy access. Harwin was sent down to assist Marek with the oven. Raylan again checked the ropes, and this time he was not able to pull them down.

A shout came from below. At first, he thought it was one of the soldiers who had woken and removed his gag. But another shout allowed him to pinpoint the sound; a small group of armored men headed their way across the plaza to where the small airships were docked.

Raylan jumped down and joined Sebastian on the main deck.

"What's he saying?" asked Raylan.

"He wants to know what we're doing with his ship…"

"He's the captain? It's still too soon, we need more time… stall him!" urged Raylan.

"How? He's gonna see we're not from here as soon as he reaches the mooring point," said Sebastian.

The four soldiers were coming up the scaffold that lead to the gangway.

"Let them come aboard. Tell him we received orders to get his ship ready to leave," whispered Raylan.

He walked to the cabin and quickly hopped down the stairs. Gavin and Xi'Lao were still in the main hold.

"We've got a problem. The captain of the ship is here."

"Do they know it's us?" said Gavin.

"Not yet, but I don't know if we can keep up the pretense."

"How much longer until we can leave?" asked Xi'Lao.

"Impossible to know, but not very much longer."

Gavin frowned in thought. "Okay, so we just need to buy time. Xi'Lao, go to Peadar and prep every crossbow we have. Keep them in the main hold. Before that, tell Marek and Harwin to work as if their lives depend on it, 'cause it probably will. We're going on deck," Gavin said to Raylan with a nod.

As they moved swiftly up the stairs, they heard quite a commotion. The captain shouted at Sebastian in Kovian, barely giving him the opportunity to say anything in return. What he was able to say was clearly unsatisfactory, as he jerked Sebastian's helmet off to see his face.

As soon as the helmet came away, the four men drew their swords at the sight of the slave mark.

The first arrow hit one of the soldier's backs before any of them could attack. The soldier fell dead, his mouth open in shock without a sound coming from it. Another arrow, shot by Rohan from the bow of the ship, hit a second soldier in the shoulder. The man spun from the force, slamming into the deck. He immediately crawled toward the railing to get away.

"Stop them!" shouted Gavin.

But in the time it took Kevhin and Rohan to reload, the captain and the remaining soldier took a swing at Sebastian, forcing him to retreat. Both the attackers made for the edge of the ship. The soldier stormed off the gangway, more tumbling than running, as the captain jumped over the handrail and landed heavily on the scaffold halfway down. Raylan heard the grunt from his impact as he raced toward the side rail. Both fleeing men did not waste any time licking their wounds, but made a run for the nearest cover, shouting and raising the alarm. Two arrows flew, simultaneously, and hit their mark, silencing them both; but the damage was done.

Within moments, a sound of metal clanging carried across the bay, for the second time that night. It was picked up on several other points in the harbor, alerting the entire settlement to a new danger in their midst. The chaos Galirras had created still had part of the armed forced preoccupied, but the entire bay was already on alert.

Retaliation would be swift and fierce.

CHAPTER TWENTY-TWO

Escape

"WE NEED TO go, now!" shouted Raylan.

Not a moment later, the ship shifted under his feet. The balloon was almost able to carry their weight.

"Gavin, do you feel that? The ship is moving… we need to get lighter! We need to dump stuff!"

Gavin rushed to one of the speaking tubes they had discovered while exploring the ship. It allowed a person to shout commands directly to the decks below without having to use the stairs. "Listen up, everyone. We're going to have company. Peadar, get the cargo door open and dump everything we don't need out of the hold. Harwin, Ca'lek, help him. Xi, I need you and your knives on deck."

A small group of soldiers came around the corner. Seeing the dead lying on the ground, they noticed the airship prepping for departure. Letting out a war cry, they rushed in with swords drawn. Both Kevhin and Rohan readied their arrows and took down two before the group got near. Raylan was surprised to see the other soldiers did not even blink or slow. They clearly did not care for their fellow soldiers, even when all of them were picked off one by one.

None made it to the ship.

Below, the cargo doors swung open with a bang. Peadar threw out buckets, armor, weapons and more from the hold. A deep *thump* made Raylan glance over the edge. One of the ghol'ms had been toppled out by Harwin, Ca'lek, Richard, and Galen. There was no way the four of them could have lifted the ghol'm, but it was close enough to the open doors to topple it outside. With a bang, the second ghol'm was toppled but this one landed facedown inside the ship. It proved too heavy to move any further. The woodwork had taken a beating, but the ship shifted again now that one of the statues had been thrown out.

Marek clearly still fed the oven in the lower deck as the tension on the leather balloon continued to increase.

It won't be long now…

As if his thought was a final push, the ship swayed in a familiar fashion, the ropes around the balloon creaking from taking the ship's full weight. It felt like the ship was in the water, bobbing as it slowly gained altitude.

Soldiers came pouring out of passageways, and around corners, from multiple sides now—most of them carrying swords and spears. There were too many for the archers to take down, even with the help of Richard and Peadar, who were now firing crossbows out of the hold through the open cargo doors. A dozen soldiers with shields, now formed a row. Protected from the constant threat of arrows, the enemy soldiers started to move closer.

The gangway fell as the ship slowly lifted skyward; but the scaffold, to which the gangway led, was still high enough for soldiers to jump on board. On the flank of the ship, several enemy soldiers were already climbing the side, much the same way Raylan had done only a short while ago. The only difference being this time the balloon was not in the way.

Gavin spotted the first soldiers as they came over the handrail, and together with Raylan they moved in with a unified roar. Despite their effort, there were too many enemies coming on deck to effectively guard Kevhin and Rohan, and both archers broke off their attacks to mount a defense.

Raylan cut down his first opponent, circled another and kicked the attacker in the back, shoving the soldier in front of Gavin, who struck the man down in one fluid motion. Raylan rushed to the handrail and hit another soldier, just climbing aboard, on the head with his sword hilt. The soldier keeled over backward, slamming to the ground. A hand clamped on the handrail as a new Doskovian brute tried to board. Slashing down, Raylan severed the hand from its owner, and the soldier disappeared with a high-pitched scream.

Kevhin turned to face an enemy running at him and stabbed him in the throat with an arrow before loading it to his bow and taking out another soldier closing in on Rohan from behind. Rohan spun with his dagger, ducking, and stabbing another attacker in the armpit. Both archers resumed loosing arrows on the increasing number of soldiers coming from the plaza, but were constantly interrupted by new attackers. It seemed futile to fire at so many men, like trying to stop water drops from hitting your face while standing under a waterfall.

A shock shuddered through the ship as the lines that anchored it snapped taut. The ship had only risen a few feet, still allowing soldiers to jump aboard from the dock.

"We've got to cut those lines, or we'll be stuck here," Raylan called out to his brother, but Gavin was too preoccupied with his fight against two enemy soldiers to hear. As the soldiers struck from all sides, his brother swung his blade, furiously, trying to block the incoming attacks.

Raylan raced over to the handrail and cut one of the lines holding the ship to the ground. Another shock went through the ship as the tension on the line disappeared and the ship tilted into its new position.

A nearby soldier threw a spear that landed with such power on the lower side of the hull that it stuck firmly into the woodwork. Another soldier ran and jumped, pulling himself up onto the thick spear, before grabbing the hull and climbing upward. Others immediately followed this example. But Xi'Lao was ready to intervene. Here knives blurred left and right, slashing any hands that made it to the rail.

Under them, the cargo doors were under constant attack. Harwin acted as a formidable roadblock for any soldier trying to climb through. He had found a new shield in the hold and was happily using it to slam those soldiers' faces, sending them crashing into the ground below.

Peadar fired off crossbows whenever Harwin gave him an opening, while Ca'lek continued dumping things out of the ship. Galen resurfaced on deck, using a newly-found war axe with so much enthusiasm Raylan wondered if he would clean out the entire deck all by himself.

Raylan ran to the second anchor line and slammed into the back of a soldier attacking Sebastian, who used the opening to cut the soldier down. Raylan did not stop, diving at the second line and slashing it with his sword. It took three swings before it finally broke.

Another jolt surged through the ship. Raylan saw his brother's attackers stumble. Gavin, always sure-footed, kicked one in the chest, sending the man backward and knocking the soldier who stood behind him over the handrail. As the soldier went over the side, he dragged another attacker down with him. Both hit a spear stuck in the hull on the way down. It broke away, spinning their bodies around before they slammed into the ground.

A larger commotion at the end of the small plaza made Raylan look across. Multiple soldiers galloped around the corner. The horses were armored with metal plating on their heads and necks. These were not horses built for speed; they were broad and heavily muscled. These steeds were bred for battle.

Even from this distance, Raylan recognized the person giving orders. *Corza!*

Corza sat on his horse, overlooking his soldiers extinguishing the fires. The dragon had fled to the south, narrowly escaping capture by his men. It was the first time he had encountered it in person, and he had to admit the creature was impressive. Several of his soldiers had to be executed as they had panicked and fled. Corza always regretted the Stone King's indoctrination methods were not one hundred percent successful.

He shook his head. *No matter what we try, how much guidance or structure we give them, you'll always find disappointing ones amongst them.*

The executions were a simple and cost-efficient way of dealing with those that developed the capacity to think freely and used that freedom to not follow orders.

At first, the dragon had been close-by in the air, using crates and barrels as projectiles. But before Corza had rallied his men—as well as his archers—with netting, the clever beast had increased his distance. Starting some fires to create smoke cover, he had focused on the more isolated ships where the soldiers had less knowledge of what was going on and could still be taken by surprise.

But then the beast had come back, straight along the street they had deliberately left vulnerable. And they had been so close. The metal netting proved useful, but still needed improvements. It needed to be larger and his man needed practice… *or perhaps a different method to throw the net.*

When he saw the dragon get stranded, Corza had figured that was it. Spearmen would surround it on the small square where it had crashed. He was already galloping toward it with several horsemen, each of them carrying a heavy set of ropes with hooks. The idea had been to throw the ropes over the beast's back, forcing it to the ground. Securing the dragon with heavy duty chains would be the final step before Corza would have his very own flying pet.

As they had rounded the corner, he saw the dragon level a group of crossbow soldiers and then dart down the street before taking to the air with a gust of wind.

He had sent out a group of three hundred soldiers, of which several dozen on horseback, to immediately give chase. Together with archers and spear men, their orders were simple; track it down and capture it alive. In support, a few hundred soldiers had been ordered to comb through the woods and locate anyone who was not supposed to be there.

He looked up at the sky; the night was drawing to an end. Those not chasing the dragon or putting out fires were ordered to finish up with their preparations. They did not have a lot of time before they were scheduled to depart.

As Corza watched the flames roar, evaporating any water his soldiers threw on it, the clanging metal of the general alarm reached his ears. First distant, but soon other alarm bells joined in the cacophony.

"Captain Dreck!" Corza bellowed. "Make sure this fire is put out as fast as possible. Tear down the neighboring buildings if you have to. Under no circumstances does this fire reach the scrolls, you hear me?" To his subordinate horsemen, he yelled, "Follow me!"

Captain Dreck began shouting orders, while Corza turned his horse and galloped toward the center of the harbor, the thunder of hooves following in his wake.

As they rode up on the harbor command center, a soldier ran forward. "Sir, the alarm came from the scout windships. It looks like someone is trying to steal one."

Corza whipped his gaze to the waterfront in fury. "Prep the other windships! Signal the *Firestorm* to circle back and stop that ship from taking off. I knew it! That beast was a distraction." With a growl, he spurred his mount in the direction of the windships. "And get a couple of ghol'ms to the windship area. And I mean *now*," Corza shouted over his shoulder as their horses thundered across the stones.

It was increasingly busy on the street as they neared the windship plaza. They plowed through the soldiers in the streets, shouting for them to get out of the way, pushing aside those who were not quick enough. As they turned the final corner, the windships came into view.

Corza momentarily took in the scene to decide his course of action. The plaza was crawling with soldiers. One of the smaller windships had a fully inflated air sack and was already hovering above its docking station. It only had the two anchor lines at the stern still connected, making it tilt dangerously toward the back. There was fighting on the deck as his soldiers tried to board. He saw arrows fly from the ship, rarely missing. Most, it seemed, were fired from the cargo hold.

After spotting the nearest ranking soldier, Corza immediately called him over. "Commander Lurik! Why's no one firing back at them? Don't you have arrows?"

"No one dared to risk damaging the balloon, sir! Especially with the invasion starting soon."

Corza chewed his lip in thought. "As they should," he yelled to be heard above all the noise from the fighting.

As he saw the doors in the ship's hull swing closed, Corza took charge of the situation. "Have your men clear a way for our horses. We need to stop that ship from leaving. Then, gather men with additional claw-ropes, and have them secure that ship!"

The commander did not hesitate at all, ordering his men to clear a path for the High General's group.

With the cargo doors now closed, the arrows were flying significantly less, allowing Corza to lead his small group of men to the bow of the windship unchallenged.

Riding across the plaza, they grabbed their clawed ropes that hung from their saddles. Several of them spun their ropes then niftily slung them over the handrail of the windship. Six ropes flew, all of them attached, after which the riders quickly tied the ends to their saddles to secure them. Commanding the horses to move slowly away from the hovering vessel, they began to pull the entire ship back toward the ground. Soldiers, who had been looking for a way onto the ship, jumped at the ropes, increasing the weight and tension on the anchor lines. A couple of them were already on their way up to the deck, climbing along the ropes.

"Go to the far side," ordered Corza to the men who came running with more of the claw-ropes.

Even with the added weight of the soldiers and horses, the initial decrease in height was only short-term. Slowly, the ship started to pull skyward again, as its air sack continued to fill.

Somewhere in the distance, two deep thumps were heard. Corza knew the sound all too well; it meant help was on its way.

"More men… get more men up there. Reinforcements will be here soon!" he roared.

A soldier, falling from the battle taking place above, slammed to the ground, barely missing him. Another screamed as he tumbled, landing on three other soldiers holding a rope. A different group of men fell as the rope gave way. It had been cut from the handrail.

Corza looked up and saw Raylan looking down at him.

"Raylan! We meet again. I—" But the boy had already disappeared.

Corza's blood boiled. *How dare he ignore me!* "I want them brought down! Get those men back onto the ground. Drag them over the edge, if you have to!" Corza screamed furiously at the soldiers around him.

A couple of soldiers broke off and ran to the side of the ship. Several people were fighting along the railing, but they were all wearing Doskovian armor.

"What are you waiting for? Do it!" yelled Corza.

The soldiers slung their ropes over the side of the ship. This time, not aiming for the wood, but fishing for people.

On deck, the hooked claws landed heavily on the planks. Instantly, the soldiers on the ground pulled the rope back in. As the hooks skidded across the deck, friends and enemies alike jumped out of the way to prevent their feet from being caught. One of the Doskovian soldiers moved too late and went face-first into the wooden planks as his leg was pulled from under him. The other ropes hooked into the handrail, allowing more soldiers to pull the ship down, and providing a way to climb toward the deck.

A grunt made one of the soldiers, with a rope still in his hand, look up. He saw one of the fighters pushed against the handrail, another pinning him against it. The pinned fighter had the unmistakably mark of a slave on his cheek. The soldier made use of the situation, straight away. He quickly threw his claw over the rail, saw it hook on the shoulder of the slave, and pulled.

The slave, who had just taken a step forward to fend off his attacker, stumbled back, pulled toward the handrail, hook firmly dug into his shoulder muscle. But the soldier could pull all he wanted, the slave kept a firm grip on the woodwork, lowering his center of gravity in order to not be pulled over… which made him a sitting duck for attackers.

Raylan saw the hooks come over the edge. He had lost sight of Corza when they moved to the end of the ship, but he immediately saw what they were planning to do.

Up till now, they had been able to fend off the stream of soldiers that successfully climbed aboard. By hitting the ones coming over the handrail quickly enough, only very few made it all the way onto the deck to pose an actual fight. The biggest point of entry was the scaffold, which Harwin now blocked, as the cargo doors had been closed and secured. It was enough to keep them all busy though.

Gavin and Galen had made a strong team, taking on any newcomers on the side, running back and forth on the main deck. Kevhin fought at his lover's side as Rohan was attacked by two enemies that had managed to climb the bow of the ship. Xi'Lao provided support.

Apparently, Peadar had joined Marek down below. While Ca'lek and Richard made sure no soldiers made it below deck to attack them. This left Raylan in a position to freelance over the ship.

As he spotted the hooks, he sprinted up against the incline to the front of the ship. The hooks caught wood and the ship leveled out as weight was put on the ropes. Reaching the bow handrail, Raylan kicked a soldier in his face, pushing him back off the rail. To his left, another soldier's head popped up, so he brought his sword down. As the soldier flung his head to the side, to dodge the slash, Raylan's sword cut off his left ear and struck his shoulder armor. The soldier screamed as he, instinctively, grabbed his ear, lost his balance, and fell rearward, crashing into a small group of men. Raylan looked down over the rail and stared directly in Corza's face.

"Raylan! We meet ag—"

Raylan had no intention of listening while his friends were fighting. Besides, he needed to cut those ropes. So he ran to the other side of the bow and cut another two ropes, picking up the hooks that remained stuck in the woodwork.

Running back to the main deck, he put one of the hooks in the back of a soldier's neck as he ran past him. He dove under one of Galen's giant axe slashes and continued his way to the stern to cut the remaining anchor lines.

As he was just about to run up the stairs to the upper deck, he saw a soldier had pinned Sebastian against the railing, sword against sword. Flipping over the second hook in his hand, he took a step toward them and threw the hook on the back of the soldier's head. Dazed, the soldier stumbled, allowing Sebastian to finally shove him off. Sebastian cut the man down and made a quick gesture of thanks for the help.

But Raylan did not even see the gesture, as his attention was drawn to the hook coming in from behind his friend. Flying over Sebastian's shoulder, it dug straight through armor and into flesh as the rope was reeled back in over the rail.

"Sebastian!"

CHAPTER TWENTY-THREE

Freedom

SEBASTIAN LET OUT a scream of pain as he dropped his sword and grabbed the hook in his shoulder. He tripped—pulled backward by the rope—and hit the handrail. With widespread eyes, he let go of the hook and grab the railing, forcing himself down, bracing his back against the wood. He gritted his teeth as the tension on the hook increased and dug into his flesh.

Panic clenched Raylan's gut as he rushed to his friend. Yanking on the hook he found the rope was pulled too tight. He rose and readied his sword to cut the line, but before he could bring down his blade, two other ropes flew up. Cursing, he duck out of the way to dodge them, in fear of being caught himself.

Recovering quickly as the two hooks caught on the railing, he rushed back to Sebastian. He lifted his sword, when suddenly the entire airship tilted sideways. He slammed into the handrail, barely able to stay on his feet. The other people on deck lost their balance. Most slid over the deck toward the rail, though one or two managed to grab hold of something, just in time. Raylan saw an enemy soldier hit the railing and instantly tumble over it. As he followed him with his gaze, the reason for the sudden movement came into view. Two ghol'ms were reeling in several of the ropes, pulling the airship to one side with their strength.

"Oh, no..."

Without warning, Sebastian was pulled over the side by the rope, Raylan had forgotten to cut it. He saw him go over, the scaffold breaking his fall halfway, before tumbling to the ground. A few enemy soldiers were knocked down with him.

"Hold on, Seb!" he shouted as he saw his friend already scrambling to his feet. He jumped over the rail.

"Raylan, what are you doing. Come back here!" he heard his brother shout behind him.

"I *have* to help him!" he called back. He landed onto the scaffold, pushed two soldiers off, slid in between the wooden poles, and swung himself right next to his fallen friend.

"Damn him," cursed Gavin, at his little brother's foolishness. "Archers! Help me cover them. Galen, get those cargo doors open again. I'll go get them. Richard, on me."

As Raylan's feet touched the dirt, he barely had time to counter an incoming strike aimed for Sebastian's head. Diverting the blow, Raylan let out a roar as he dislocated the soldier's elbow with a punch of his armored arm. He cut the attacker down and grabbed his sword.

"Seb, you with me? Grab this. You need to focus," yelled Raylan to his friend, as he shoved the sword to him.

Multiple soldiers were already closing in. Raylan turned his back to Sebastian, ready for the next attack. Next to him, Sebastian shook his head, took the sword in his good hand and turned to face the incoming attackers.

The scaffold was somewhat protecting their backs, but they were far more outnumbered here than they had been on the deck. Raylan had to stand his ground instead of being able to freely move and dodge the incoming attacks. If he left Sebastian's side, it would not end well for either of them.

Two spearmen took a stab at him, simultaneously, which Raylan barely sidestepped. One of them got struck in the neck by an arrow, creating an opening for Raylan to move in and strike the other down.

Sebastian was fighting off an attacker that came in with a spiked club. The short soldier was dangerously fast with the thick club, but Sebastian's range with the sword allowed him to cut the inside of his attacker's arm. The club fell harmlessly to the ground as Sebastian quickly stepped in and stabbed the soldier in his stomach.

Both Raylan and Sebastian repositioned themselves and, again, formed one front. The ring of soldiers closing in on them was suddenly broken. Two soldiers were felled by arrows as Gavin and Richard jumped from the lower part of the scaffold onto the necks of three other soldiers, knocking them onto the ground.

"Quickly, come on!" his older brother shouted.

Richard dragged Sebastian back with him onto the scaffold, but before Raylan or Gavin could make it back up there, they were cut off by four soldiers on a full attack run.

Forced back, Raylan and his brother parried the attackers. As he was fighting, Raylan felt the familiar movements of his brother, more and more. Raylan duck under his brother's arm. Gavin stepped back when Raylan pulled him clear from an incoming slash. They easily circled past each other, blocking incoming strikes from all sides. It did not matter from where the attack came, they felt as one, they fought as one. Their sword practice as kids, their weapon training in the army, their experience during this journey, everything flowed into this one moment where Raylan finally felt his brother's equal—no longer in his shadow, but together facing the world.

Then, the moment ended abruptly, as they both darted in a different direction to dodge a soldier who was wielding two double-bladed axes.

In an instant, they had both been isolated, surrounded by a full circle of soldiers. Raylan was closest to the scaffold, but Gavin was being pushed farther and farther from it.

"Gavin, hold on I'm coming!" yelled Raylan as he furiously attacked the soldiers who were preventing him from reaching his brother.

"Idiot, make your way back to the ship. I'll be right behind you!" shouted his brother, as he cut down two reckless soldiers who had come too close.

But Raylan felt it. Even if they had the upper hand in weapon combat, the odds were not looking good. The sheer number of enemies made it difficult to block all incoming attacks. Raylan felt a cut to the back of his leg. Another stabbed his left arm, as a club knocked off his helmet, leaving his ears ringing from the force of the impact.

He saw his brother not fare any better. A spear scratched his side as it was thrust just below his armpit. Gavin blocked an incoming sword, but another soldier came around with the back end of a spear and hit him directly on his leg.

"Leave him alone!" Raylan yelled.

The soldiers were almost upon them both, when Raylan finally felt the link return.

"Hang on, I'm coming!"

Before Galirras had even finished his private announcement, Raylan heard his roar descend from the heavens. The dragon came in low, wings pushed back as far as possible to increase his speed. The first soldiers were already knocked over by his hanging claws and tail as it whipped around; but the devastation only truly came into its own as Galirras threw himself into the midst of the attacking soldiers surrounding Raylan.

Three enemies were instantly crushed under the dragon's weight as Galirras clawed his way through another group of five soldiers. His tail slashed back and forth, knocking down any soldier that happened to be in the way. The dragon pounced onto the double-bladed axe wielder, ripping off an arm and tossing him to the side.

The ferociousness of Galirras' attacks drove the soldiers apart, freeing up some ground for Raylan.

"*Hurry, get back to the ship. I'll take care of the ropes,*" said Galirras' in Raylan's head.

"*But Gavin...*"

Galirras sent out a windblast, knocking over another five soldiers who had been too close. Gavin used the opening to break free and started to fight his way to the scaffold.

"*Now, go!*" urged the dragon.

Finding renewed bravery, several soldiers ran at Galirras, spears stuck far out in front of them. Galirras spun around and slashed out with his claws, snapping two spears in half. One soldier threw his spear at Galirras' back and, briefly, Raylan was afraid that Galirras would end up pierced. But the spear ricocheted off Galirras' scales and struck down a soldier on the other side of him. Two soldiers with swords ran in to hack away at Galirras' shoulder. But before they could hit anything, Galirras swung his neck sideways and threw both soldiers through the air, knocking over a number of others.

At that moment, another soldier saw an opening and thrust his spear on the inside of the dragon's hind leg. Galirras roared in fury, as the spear stuck out of his lower flank. The soldier, realizing he did not have a weapon anymore, tried to retreat; but he quickly found a furious dragon left little room for getting away. Hooking his claws in the soldier's back, Galirras jumped into the air and darted straight up. The spear was worked out of his leg by the movement, and dropped back onto the ground, as he flew higher into the air. He circled around, as he threw the soldier away in an upward arch and faced the airship. As the wounded soldier plummeted to the unforgiving ground, Galirras boosted himself forward. Flying parallel past the ship, Galirras scraped his claw along the woodwork, cutting every rope attached to the ship. He took the opportunity to snatch up the last two remaining Doskovian soldiers on deck. They had been gripping the railing, so as not to fall when the ghol'ms turned the ship. As he peeled them off the rail, he swung around and threw them down onto the masses on the plaza.

With a jolt, the ship straightened out and started to tilt the other way. Xi'Lao had managed to cut the anchor lines at the stern but a group of soldiers had another rope on the other flank side of the ship. Galirras sent out a windblast, knocking them over. Now that nothing was holding back the ship anymore, it bobbed freely in the air and instantly started to move again.

Richard Sebastian had reached the top of the scaffold during all the commotion. Fending off several attackers, Richard now eagerly waited for the cargo doors to line up with the scaffold. Galen stood in the opening, ready to assist any of them coming aboard.

"Jump!" shouted Richard, as he gave a big shove to Sebastian's back.

Galen easily caught the wounded ex-slave and saw Richard follow, quickly, by jumping aboard. Several enemy soldiers came speeding up the scaffold, trying to do the same; but Galen planted his axe in the chest of the first to jump aboard, and Kevhin and Rohan cleared out the rest with their arrows.

"Raylan, Gavin, hurry up. You don't have much time!" shouted Richard, as the ship began to rise at an increasing speed.

On the ground, Raylan looked over his shoulder to see how far Gavin was behind him. His older brother hacked and slashed feverishly, making his way through the enemy forces. Raylan saw the prolonged fighting begin to take its toll on his brother's endurance. He felt the same for himself, too.

As Raylan put his first foot on the bottom of the scaffold, Galirras threw himself—for a second time—right on top of the soldiers. It was a slaughter, as Galirras refused to stand still for long, preventing any further painful attacks. In no time, he had directly opened up a path for Gavin to escape.

Unfortunately, both ghol'ms had no purpose serving as anchors anymore, as the ropes had now been cut. Galirras saw the dark statues push through the crowd of soldiers, coming straight at them. He fired a windblast, which slammed into the stone men, full force. It had no effect at all; both statues continued at him at high speed, forcing him to take to the air and effectively cutting off Gavin from the scaffold.

Raylan had scrambled up the scaffold as fast as he could. Now on the top, he turned around, expecting to see his brother a small way behind him. Instead, he saw Galirras take off, as a ghol'm rushed in slamming his fists into the ground. His brother was stuck behind two ghol'ms and an increasing number of enemy soldiers.

Raylan looked at his brother, trying to find a way to get back to him. At that moment, he saw Gavin turn around, triggered by a sound he heard. Raylan followed his gaze to find Corza's warhorse running straight at Gavin through the crowd.

The exhaustion kicked in at a disastrous moment for his brother. Too slow to dodge the incoming attack, Corza hit Gavin square across his head with a metal rod. His brother spun around and landed on his knees. Raylan saw his brother slowly rock back and forth on his knees, dazed by the blow.

Corza circled around and calmly dismounted. Slowly walking up to their squad's commander, he unsheathed the dagger that was hanging on his belt, horizontally, behind his back.

He saw how Galirras tried to get close, but one of the ghol'ms was constantly blocking him. The other seemed to shield the general from any incoming projectiles, as it jumped straight into the path of a fired arrow aimed at Corza's neck.

* * *

Galirras trumpeted in frustration as his desperation set in. He needed to save Gavin. For Raylan. He felt Raylan's panic flow into him. A nervous shudder went down his spine, after which he inhaled deeply and give a roar unlike anything ever before. It was not a loud, far carrying roar. Instead of stretching it out and giving it air, his roar seemed to be sucked into place right in front of his widespread mouth. Pushing all air inward, Galirras condensed it in a ball of pressurized air. He did not remember doing anything like it before. He was not even sure how he knew what to do.

As the pressure in the ball increased, he strengthened the shell of spinning air around it. Reaching the point where he could put no more air into it, he pushed it out, instinctively, with a focused burst. A shockwave pulsed from where his windblast hit the ball.

The spinning ball launched forward, straight for the high general's location. Immediately, a ghol'm moved to intercept, crossing both its arms to block the unknown projectile. As the ball hit, the confined air broke through its containment and exploded outward. Several soldiers near the ghol'm were swept away by it, crashing into the ground more than fifty feet from where they began. Shards of stone flew around as part of the ghol'm's arm shattered on impact.

Corza shielded his head behind his arm, moving a few steps to get away from the flying debris but he was shielded from most of it by the ghol'm's large body. Gavin, who had been kneeling more to the side of the ghol'm, immediately got knocked over from the blast. Trying to push himself up again, he could do little else but lay there, exhausted and coughing.

"Wow! Impressive!" Corza shouted up to the dragon, as he slowly clapped his hands. "But you'll have to do better than that. Archers, I have had enough. Please pluck this annoying creature from our skies… alive, barely… preferably!"

Happy to finally have an authorized target to engage, the archers on the plaza loosed their arrows at once, forcing Galirras to hastily retreat to a greater height. He saw Corza move in on Gavin. The general dragged him to his knees again and there was nothing Galirras could do.

"Corzaaaa! You leave my brother alone, you hear me!" shouted Raylan, his panic and anger clearly spiking.

"What's that, boy? Brother you said? I can barely understand you..." said Corza with a smile. "Don't you wish you'd given me the egg, now?"

Spellbound, Raylan watched as Corza walked behind his brother and pulled his head to the left with his hand.

"Raylan, get out of here. You've got to warn the people back home."

It was all his brother could shout, as Corza lifted his Roc'turr and plunged it in the right side of Gavin's chest. Raylan saw Gavin's mouth open, in shock. Corza yanked the blade out and shoved Gavin away.

"NOOOO! Gavin! No! Nonononooo!" Raylan's voice left him as he fell to his knees.

* * *

The world slowed to a crawl as Raylan saw his brother topple forward. Colors and sounds disappeared from the world till nothing but whiteness surrounded them; red blood sprayed from Gavin's chest, forming a beautifully horrifying contrast against it.

Tears ran down Raylan's face, his mouth opened but no sound coming out anymore, his eyes spread wide unable to look away from the scene. As Gavin's body hit the dirt like a bag of flour, his blood mixed with the blood of their slain enemies.

On the airship, Xi'Lao let out a scream and sank to her knees, sobbing. The ship had been bobbing in the air, deciding—by itself—to leave or stay. But without the ropes tying the ship down, the green vapors in the balloon began to win against the pull of gravity. Slowly, the vessel moved skyward, away from the scaffold, increasing in speed with every passing moment.

The remaining members of their group that were on deck had seen Galirras flash by and cut the ropes. Now, they found themselves watching the scene without a word, unwilling to believe they had just lost their leader.

The world came rushing back in as his brother's body remained motionless at Corza's feet. Colors... sounds... voices... Raylan actively tried to push them out, refusing to acknowledge the reality... but there was nothing he could do as they forced their way back into his head. Behind him, Galen, Richard, and even Sebastian, were calling out to him.

"Raylan, get up!"

"You *need* to get up, Raylan!"

"Raylan, hurry. The ship is leaving."

But Raylan refused to hear them. Their voices distorted into monotone sounds, carrying no meaning. The world before him looked wet from his tears, as the silhouettes behind him started to slide away, still calling out to him.

My fault... it's my fault. I wanted to steal a ship... I killed him. The words rambled over and over inside his head.

Somewhere in the distance, Raylan registered the movement of the scaffold, as soldiers ran up it, toward him. The airship drifted off, further and further, making it harder and harder to jump the distance. Kevhin and Rohan shot any person with a rope and any archer they could spot and reach. It seemed that despite this disastrous turn of events, they had no intention of letting up and wasting their one chance to get away.

"Raylan, can you hear me?"

The voice was familiar. He felt he knew this voice... deep inside. Raylan knew he cared about it... cared enough for him to be reached by it.

"Raylan, come back to us. We need you. I need you."

It had helped him once before... in a dark well.

"Raylan, please... I am sorry. There was nothing I could do..."

Why would this voice have to do anything... it's my fault... my fault alone, thought Raylan.

"You need to get up, Raylan. They are going to get you, if you do not get up, right now. GET UUUP!"

Raylan looked up, startled. He felt he was waking up from a dream... or a nightmare. Galirras circled around up high, looking down at him, nervously. He jerked his head around to check the airship. Richard and Galen looked back at him, around the corner of the cargo doors, the ship already too far from the scaffold to make any attempt to jump aboard.

"I can't make that jump, anymore. Do you see another way out?" said Raylan to his eyes-in-the-sky.

"I... I do not know... wait. There! The horse... quickly, the horse on your left side below the scaffold. Hurry! A ghol'm is coming."

Raylan saw it, too. One of the ghol'ms moved his way, even as soldiers were nearly at the top of the scaffold. He heard a horse whinny, but did not see it, yet. He took off to his left, as Galirras had said, and looked down. *There!*

The soldier had been a part of Corza's group of mounted men, assisting in securing the airship. Now that the ropes were cut, he was ordering his steed around amongst the wounded, giving orders on what to do.

Looking behind him, he saw the ghol'm bring back his arm, ready to smash the entire scaffold.

"*Jump!*" howled Galirras, in his head.

And that's what he did. He jumped, not sure if he would land where he had hoped. Behind him, the scaffold shattered, as the ghol'm rushed into the side of it, there was nothing left to stand on. The Doskovian soldiers crashed down to the ground, some of them even tumbling over the ghol'm.

Raylan crashed behind the mounted soldier, hitting the back end of the saddle. The warhorse immediately bucked. Holding tight to saddle and rider, Raylan knocked the rider out of balance and pushed him off, barely able to stay on the horse himself. Somehow, he managed to swing his leg into position as the horse stomped between the wounded soldiers around him.

Archers were already moving in, as well as some soldiers with spears; he needed to get out of there.

"*Which way?*" he called out, in his mind.

"*Left. Your left. Go north, out of the harbor!*"

Raylan finally got a hold of the reins and wasted no time spurring the horse into action. The large steed was incredibly powerful, completely different from Luna who he had gotten to know so well over the last months.

The horse had metal armor on its head and chest. As its hooves thundered across the ground, Raylan steered it north. Any soldier in the way would get to know the full force of an eighteen-hundred-pound warhorse on the move.

As a salvo of arrows took flight, a windblast from above crushed them into the ground. Galirras made nosedives all over the place, attacking any long-range soldiers he could find, completely disregarded his own safety. Suddenly, the dragon called out as two sharp pains hit his side.

No time to check… Raylan heard the dragon's own thoughts trickle into the back of his mind.

Glancing behind him, he saw the airship slowly turning as Sebastian gestured and explained how to pull out the side sails. It seemed they had dragged him onto the main deck, where he was resting against the cabin while shouting what they needed to do.

As Raylan sped off on the horse, Galirras tried to make sure neither he, nor the airship, fell prey to the arrows. The squad quickly lowered the cloths on the side of the airship, which helped stop a number of arrows that Galirras could not reach in time. Following the path the arrows took, Galirras quickly took out the archers, before they could release any more.

The speed of ascension was ever increasing, as the airship moved higher and higher, out of the harbor. Galirras flew close to them, whenever possible, pushing them with his winds as much as he could. By the time they cleared land and drifted off over the ocean waters in the bay, Raylan had reached the edge of the plaza. He rammed past the last of the soldiers blocking him, dodging arrows and swords coming at him from behind.

He had no idea how he was able to pull it off. Had his thoughts been clearer, he might have realized the sheer size of the Doskovian army had worked in his favor—not every soldier knew he was an enemy with the Doskovian armor he still wore.

But Corza had no intention of letting him go. Speeding past the last line of soldiers, Raylan glanced over his shoulder and saw Corza and the remaining riders in hot pursuit, for the second time, in these cursed lands.

With the airship now out of range of the archers and climbing steadily, Galirras tried to get closer to Raylan. But the chase had led them into the forest, where Raylan could do little else but ride as fast as possible, for as long as possible. The path he was on was steadily climbing. He suspected where it would lead, but there was no way to go around it. His horse was breathing heavily, quickly tiring from the steep climb.

"*I'm sorry, little one, there's nowhere for me to go…*" he said to Galirras, as he noticed the dragon's dark form slide across the treetops.

"*No! Do not say that. Keep going.*"

"*They'll catch me eventually, my friend. There's nowhere to hide… nowhere to run.*"

"*It does not matter, just keep climbing! As fast as you can!*"

"*You don't understand, Galirras, it's going to be a dead end… the cliff… it won't have a way off.*"

"*Yes, it will! Just keep going, keep going even if the path does not go on. When I had just hatched, I trusted you with my life… now trust me with yours.*"

Behind him Raylan heard the shouts of his pursuers. It looked like they were planning to run their horses into the ground if that meant catching him.

At moments the climb was so steep his horse almost had to jump to get up higher. The path made several sharp turns, allowing Corza and his men to get dangerously close. Arrows thumped into trees next to Raylan as he ordered the horse to go through the next turn. The animal's hooves skidded and slid on the loose gravel of the path. At one point, the horse's hind leg kicked loose a boulder, starting a small avalanche of tiny stones. The boulder barely missed one of the riders in pursuit as Raylan heard a waterfall of curses follow him up the hill.

Raylan felt the pressure mount inside his ears from ascending the hill at such speed. As he neared the top of the path, the forest opened to rocky ground, announcing the edge of the cliff. He was headed straight for a pointed overhang. On a normal day, the view from such a place would have been amazing; now, it only made it painfully clear it would be the end of his escape as Raylan saw the dark bay water looming… way, way down.

We've must have climbed over a thousand feet, thought Raylan to himself. "*I'm sorry, Galirras, this is it… there's no more road. I've got to stop…*"

"*No! Keep going, even if the ground stops. Keep going. Trust me,*" the dragon said, forcefully.

Raylan saw his friends across the bay, flying the airship toward open water. He smiled. They deserved to make it. He was happy they had made it.

"*Okay… okay, I trust you,*" he said, giving into the inevitable, more than understanding what the dragon meant.

With shouts following him out of the forest, Raylan spurred his horse to its top speed. The warhorse, bred to ignore his own fears in favor of following commands, disregarded his own instincts, sped up and headed straight for the edge of the cliff.

The final few yards suddenly went by at an incredible speed as the warhorse pushed off and left the solid rocky ground of the cliff for good. Corza and his men slid to a halt, trying to keep their mounts from falling over the edge. The stream of curse words sent after him by Corza were lost on Raylan. He was in his own world, and had never so intensely felt the promise of freedom.

CHAPTER TWENTY-FOUR

Aftermath

As RAYLAN AND the horse tumbled forward, Raylan felt himself lift out of the saddle. The horse dropped away from under him, plunging toward the sea. He found himself weightless for just a moment longer as the momentum of the jump continued, but then gravity caught up with him and showed its inevitable influence.

He did not bother to move. He was tired... his mind numb. As he fell, head-first, toward the water, he saw Corza and his riders come out of the forest, just before the edge of the cliff removed them from sight. He closed his eyes, and felt the wind rush through his hair as he silently sped down to the sea.

"I'm sorry, brother... you were right. I'll be able to apologize to you in person soon. I'll see you in a bit..."

But a gust of wind announced a different path.

Galirras moved in, and Raylan felt the push of air next to him. The dark shape of the dragon blocked out the first rays of sunlight coming over the mountains in the east. If Raylan had not known Galirras as a close friend, he might have thought a demon was coming to drag him to the underworld.

As Galirras' dark silhouette engulfed him like a monster from the deep seas, Raylan smiled with sadness more than happiness.

I'm sorry, brother. It seems I'll be a little while longer...

Galirras carefully closed his front claws around him and pulled him close. "*I got you!*"

With a sudden yank, Raylan felt the force of a sharp turn push his guts down to his toes. The tip of Galirras' claws punctured his arms as the dragon's scales scuffed against his skin. Blood seeped from the small wounds on his arm, but Raylan welcomed the pain. It meant he felt something... that he was alive.

The dragon turned away from the cliff, skimming the water close enough for Raylan to feel the wet drops from breaking waves. The warmth of the dragon's skin against his front was a strong contrast to the cold water splashing on his back. It was like hovering between life and death.

Galirras beat his wings strongly to gain altitude again, moving away from the cliff and harbor.

"We got company. The large airship that was following me tonight just entered the bay ahead of us. The other airships are launching, too. The first have already taken to the air."

Raylan did not say anything. He felt light-headed from the flight, and turned his face as far as he could. Peering around Galirras' arm, he spotted the harbor. The wind collected his tears as the morning sun announced itself over the hills, but the lights of torches and lamps still lit across the coast. Everyone was flowing toward the water. Sails were being raised all over the bay. He saw four or five airships leaving their docks and quickly gaining altitude. It seemed like a strange and faraway world, something that could not possibly exist.

He looked up and saw Galirras' neck stretch out in front of him. Raylan felt the muscles move under the scales. The powerful strokes of his wings made the dragon's entire body wave and flow, like a gust of wind playing with leaves.

In the distance, beyond Galirras' head, they closed in on their freshly-liberated airship. He saw shapes on deck, but his tears made it impossible to see who it was.

Raylan would have preferred to stay here… in this in-between. Here, nothing was real; it was just a shelter from everything out there. There, on the ship, the others would bring reality…

As Galirras approached the airship, he came in low. Using his wings and wind power to hover almost completely still, he grasped the railing with his hind claws and put Raylan down as careful as possible in between the ropes on the upper deck… which resulted in Raylan bouncing his behind on the deck a few times until rolling onto his back.

"Raylan!"

It was Peadar, who just arrived on deck, as Galirras approached the rail. Several others followed.

"You all right? That must have been some ride!"

Peadar had been below deck the entire time, obviously unaware of what happened on the battlefield. But as Raylan got to his feet, he did not know what to say. Tears ran across his cheeks again. He stood swaying, as he looked at Xi'Lao behind the others, not saying a word either.

"What's wrong? You okay? Why aren't you saying anything?" said Peadar, as he shook Raylan's shoulder. Peadar looked around, slowly. "…where's Gavin?"

Galirras let himself drop away from the railing again. "He… did not make it," said the dragon, as he disappeared over the edge.

Raylan stumbled to the stern and grabbed the handrail. He wanted to throw up. But when nothing came, he slumped to the deck, back against the wood, putting his hands over his eyes.

"It's my fault. It's all… my… fault. If I hadn't pushed to steal a ship… to expose ourselves like that… my fault," he mumbled, continuously.

A small stream of blood ran from his cuts. The spear wound to his leg felt as numb as his head. He was more tired than he had ever felt in his life.

The others looked at him in silence, but before anyone could say anything, shouts carried on the wind. As they looked to port side, they saw Galirras dive at the larger airship that had been coming their way. Soldiers fired arrows and cross bolts at him in an attempt to take him out of the sky.

"What's he doing?" called out Richard. "He's going to get himself killed!"

* * *

Galirras looked back at the squad, before refocusing on his target. He had tried his best not to give the enemy a chance to hit their mark by planning his attack carefully. To avoid too many archers from targeting him, he had approached the airship from high above. In response, the enemy had immediately sent their archers up on the balloon, but only two made it up the ropes by the time he started his dive. He tried to make another wind ball, but he lacked the energy. And to be honest, he was not sure if he knew precisely how to recreate one. So, he dove forward, claws at the ready. His windblast knocked the two archers off the balloon, sending them falling to a watery grave.

But as they fell, one of them seemed to completely ignore his imminent death as the man took aim and shot one last arrow. If it had hit Galirras on the back, it would probably have bounced off harmlessly; but with his belly exposed, the dragon felt the sharp pain as the arrow struck him in the chest. Galirras roared, in surprise, as he passed the skin of the balloon. He threw out his claws to rip it, only to find the fabric was much thicker than he expected. His attack only left a few small punctures from his claws behind; but as he looked back, he saw green vapor rushing out of every

319

hole. He let out a satisfied rumble. The ship would likely lose altitude soon enough. They would not be able to follow them.

As he got back to their own flying ship, his injuries and fatigue caught up with him. He had spent most of the day's early hours flying, and while the injuries did not look serious, they were very uncomfortable. The amount of time he spent in the air had been much longer than he had ever done before. So, after he crawled aboard as carefully as possible, he could do little else than lay heavily on his side on the front deck... panting. As his eyes swirled, one by one his eye lids closed. He felt like he could sleep for a week.

* * *

The rest of the crew had run to the main deck when Galirras attacked the other ship, while Raylan barely moved at all. Peadar sprinted back up the stairs toward the front to check on Galirras and his injuries.

Raylan seemed oblivious; he sat quietly against the wooden barricade, his own blood slowly dripping on the deck. Footsteps approached and halted before him. He looked up to find Richard staring back at him.

"Raylan... let's get you patched up."

But Raylan could only stare.

"Look, I'm sorry about Gavin... I truly am, but as second-in-command, I've to ask you to pull it together. You're still a soldier, and we still have a mission."

Something about the fall-in-line order struck Raylan like a blow. "The mission? Soldier? I didn't even want to be a soldier!" he shouted. "Gavin was the soldier. He wanted to protect everyone... he tried to protect his stupid little brother... and see where that got him!"

"So, you are just going to stay down and do nothing?" Xi'Lao's voice broke in as she approached the two of them. "Do you think you are the only one hurt by losing him?" she continued, ice in her voice. "That none of us feel his loss?"

Raylan shook his head. "But it's my fault... I pushed him to listen to me. I put him in danger. I made him do that."

"*That* was not your fault!" Xi'Lao snapped. "Do you truly think you could make Gavin do anything? He was not just your brother, he was your superior! He might have made a decision against his better judgment, but it was his decision to make. No... no," she shook her head vehemently. "I will not allow you to feel sorry for yourself. Not while you have someone depending on you so much!" She looked over her shoulder to Galirras.

She turned back to him. "Gavin did not just jump in to save his little brother. He saw you for the important part in all this that you are, without you Galirras would be lost and the entire mission would be in danger. So he decided to put everything he had out there and get you back to this ship…"

"And I hate myself for it!" yelled Raylan. "I failed him! Again!"

"How have you failed him? You are here, are you not? On this ship… with the only dragon alive in the world, as far as we know. A creature you swore to protect. You will not fail him, unless you quit," countered Xi'Lao, but this time her voice sounded slightly warmer.

"She's right," said Richard, "We all heard him shout to you, telling you… *ordering* you to get out of there. He wanted you to be with Galirras, to take care of this creature we've begun to see as one of our own."

Raylan looked at them in silence for a long time. He slowly pushed to his feet and stepped forward. As he walked past them, he whispered, "Thank you, but it *is* my fault."

Raylan crossed the ship to Galirras, his concern growing with each step. Drops of blood followed him across the deck. When he arrived, he saw Peadar yank free the last of the three arrows, sending a shudder through Galirras' body. He quickly put his hand on the dragon's head, as Peadar put pressure on the wound.

"*I'm sorry I wasn't there for you, my friend,*" he said, when Galirras opened one eye in response to his touch.

"*I am sorry I could not protect him for you…*"

"*…it wasn't your job to save him, little one… that was on me. Thank you for trying.*"

Raylan put his forehead against Galirras', as tears ran down his cheeks again. The dragon closed his eyes as they both shared their sorrow.

Part of Raylan did not want to open his eyes again, he felt so tired he could sleep for a week.

"*So could I,*" said Galirras.

Soft footsteps approached from behind. A polite cough announced itself, but Raylan was not yet ready to let the world in again.

"Ahm… Raylan… sorry to interrupt," said Kevhin, after another moment, "but Richard asked me to come and get you…"

"What's wrong?" asked Raylan, after letting out a sigh. It seemed he would not be able to rest just yet.

"Sebastian has lost a lot of blood from the hook, and needs to rest," Kevhin said. "Which means you're the only one that knows anything about sailing. The armada is gaining on us… they'll catch us if we don't figure out how to fly faster."

"I can take them down," said Galirras.

"No, my friend, you need to rest. If you exhaust yourself too much, it could end very badly," said Raylan. "Peadar, how do his injuries look?"

"He's losing some blood, but it's nothing serious. I should be able to stop the bleeding soon. He, however, needs to rest and heal. Flying will only increase his injuries."

"That decides it then, we need to outrun them with this little ship. So, let's see what she can do," said Raylan, grateful for something to occupy his mind. As he got up, Galirras opened his eyes and he turned his head. "Don't worry, I'll be back soon," Raylan said. "You just get some rest."

"*I know you will. I just wanted to say we need to fly higher. The winds… up there… they are blowing west. We need to get to them if we want to outrun them.*"

Raylan looked up. It would never have occurred to him that the changes in altitude could provide different winds. All of a sudden, he was not just sailing on a flat surface, he had a completely new aspect to think about. "*Thanks, I'll tell them. Now go rest.*"

As he limped off to join Richard and the others on the main deck, Galirras rolled over to give Peadar better access to the wounds; then he slumbered again, every now and then, twitching his skin as Peadar cleaned his wounds.

"How bad is it?" asked Raylan, as he reached Richard and the others.

"Look for yourself," said Richard.

As Raylan leaned over the handrail, he felt the cuts and carvings in the wood from all the fighting. Looking behind them, he saw the full armada on the move. A handful of airships were on their tail. They were all still quite low, catching up horizontally, but still had to close a very large vertical gap. Even further below, the entire sea fleet could be seen as they headed for the bay's exit.

"We need to get higher," said Raylan. "Galirras says there's a favorable wind blowing up there for us. It will be our best chance to get away. I had a chance to look around the ship as we prepared to take off, so I know what to do; but first, Marek needs to get us higher."

Richard gave the commands, through the tubes, and right away they felt the ship rising.

"We also need to get the air blade—the fan behind the ship—moving, but it's heavy," added Raylan.

"Galen, you're the strongest," said Richard. "See what you can do. Rohan, Kevhin, go give him a hand. What else?"

"The rest should help me with the sails. If we can set them up correctly, we should be able to outrun them before they can reach the same altitude and wind speed," Raylan said before limping to the closest sail.

"Don't you need to take care of that leg first?" Richard called after him, but Raylan waved him off.

Below, the air blade slowly came to life as Galen and the two archers put everything they had left into turning the gears.

"*You need to get a little bit higher still. You're almost there,*" said Galirras' sleepy voice in his head.

Raylan had just secured the sailing line, when the wind fully caught hold of it, and their ship jolted into high speed. He half hopscotched to the port side to check on the sails, until everything was optimally set.

He joined Richard and Xi'Lao on the upper deck. Xi'Lao stared, silently, at the receding harbor as Richard kept a careful eye on the increasing distance between them and their pursuers.

As their airship exited the bay, and Raylan felt the wind pick up even more, the full view of the Doskovian coastline could be seen. "It looks so peaceful from up here."

Ca'lek came walking up the stairs with powerful strides. "Richard, the captured soldiers are coming around," he said.

Richard turned to him. "Good, let's get some answers. The more information we can bring home, the better." He put a hand on Raylan's shoulder. "I won't let Gavin's sacrifice go to waste."

As Raylan looked at him, he had trouble accepting Richard as their new commander… it meant accepting Gavin was gone.

"Now have Peadar, or Xi'Lao, take a look at that leg of yours and get some rest."

As the words were spoken, something beyond Richard, far off in the distance, caught Raylan's eye. He walked past Richard, staring off toward the south. "No… it can't be… why does it only get worse?"

"What is it?" said Xi'Lao, as she joined him at the railing.

"The problem just got bigger. I fear you'd better start asking those questions, Richard, because we're going to need all the information we can get," said Raylan.

As the other two joined them, Raylan pointed toward the south. There, miles down the coast, the small silhouettes of hundreds of ships spread out from one of the bays, like tiny ants. Beyond that, the morning sky turned dark again, from the number of airships heading off toward the west... too many to count.

As their own airship sped away on the wind, Stephen's last words to Raylan crept back into his mind.

The crumbling darkness is coming... we're all going to die...

- To be continued -

Please consider leaving a review or rating in the online store and on Goodreads if you enjoyed the story. There's no greater gift you can give to me as a writer and it really helps other people find their way to the world of Aeterra and the oncoming battles against the armies of the Stone King. Thank you for your support.

About the Author

Author A.J. Norfield lives with his loving family on land, but below sea level. He tries not to worry too much about climate change and the melting of the polar ice caps. His wife, and two rascals of children, keep him engaged and grounded in life while he pursues goals of publishing a story that has been stuck in his head for years.

As a longtime forest and mountain enthusiast, he often wonders about his flat surroundings and how to escape them. In his free time, if available at all, he enjoys a wide variety of gaming, reading/writing, drawing and socializing. His interest in (dragon-fantasy) novels has followed him throughout his life, ever since he was young enough to read. It was this interest—with a number of broken nights thanks to his daughter's sleeping schedule—that eventually lead to his current undertaking to write his own dragon-fantasy series 'The Stone War Chronicles' and put it out into the world.

Inspired by established names like Anne McCaffrey, Terry Goodkind and Naomi Novik—to name only a few of many—he is ready to find his own path among the genre's greatest writers.

Follow The Stone War Chronicles online:
Website: http://www.ajnorfield.com
Facebook: http://www.facebook.com/ajnorfield
Twitter: @AJNorfield
Goodreads: AJNorfield
Bookbub: https://www.bookbub.com/profile/a-j-norfield

Be sure to follow A.J. Norfield on Bookbub and Amazon to stay informed on any upcoming releases!

Printed in Great Britain
by Amazon